MURDER IN STATE

Other novels by E. Howard Hunt:

The Berlin Ending
The Hargrave Deception
The Gaza Intercept
Cozumel
The Kremlin Conspiracy
Guadalajara

As P.S. Donoghue:

The Dublin Affair
The Sankov Confession

MURDER
IN
STATE

E. Howard Hunt

St. Martins Press
New York

Library of Congress Cataloging-in-Publication Data

Hunt, E. Howard (Everette Howard).
    Murder in State.
        p. cm.
    "A Thomas Dunne book."
    ISBN 0-312-04353-8
    I. Title.
    PS3515.U5425M87   1990   813'.54—dc20   89-77672

First Edition
10 9 8 7 6 5 4 3 2 1

In memory of Allen Welsh Dulles.
Wise leader, constant friend.

Perhaps the most tragic thing about the human situation is that a man may try . . . to falsify his life.

José Ortega y Gasset

CHAPTER 1

Alan Stuart's law office was on the top floor of a sprawling modern building near the intersection of M Street and Wisconsin Avenue in Georgetown. The building's street level incorporated a warren of arcades, their shops and boutiques set closely together, and his office windows overlooked the Key Bridge and the Virginia side of the Potomac River. His secretary's reception area opened onto Stuart's larger office, which was paneled on two sides, the third mounted with shelves holding law books.

Framed prints from the Corcoran Gallery hung chastely against one walnut paneling. The furnishings were eighteenth-century American antiques, collected by his former wife on forays into remote Virginia towns not yet pillaged by dealers. Stuart was grateful for Sandy's efforts, which had occupied her during the final year of their unsuccessful marriage, while he was finishing night law school at George Washington and working days at the Department of State.

Thirty-two and six feet tall, Stuart kept his muscular body at one-eighty by prudent dining and periodic workouts at the University Club, where he religiously played squash twice a week. On weekends, weather permitting, he sculled on the Potomac between the Key and Memorial bridges, having pulled number three oar on the Princeton eight during his undergraduate years.

Alan Stuart's law practice was limited to a number of elderly clients, some friends of his late parents. Their estates, taxes, and investment affairs he managed with meticulous care. His face was oblong and masculine, his brown eyes a shade darker than his hair. Sandy had once remarked that his eyes were ambiguous, kindly, and sensitive one moment, cold and remote the next, but Stuart had replied that they were simply the ones he was born with and served him well. His wife's more serious complaints, though they seldom crossed his mind, added up to a dissatisfaction with a life-style centered around cultural events at Kennedy Center— music, ballet, and theatrical performances. Sandy, it emerged, had anticipated the role of Georgetown Hostess, whereas Alan thoroughly disliked entertaining government officials, diplomats, and social lionesses—the usual mix at Georgetown parties.

That Friday afternoon Stuart was reading correspondence dictated earlier in the day, when Mrs. Appleby buzzed. Stuart signed the letters, got up, and opened the door on Blake Selwyn, a senior Foreign Service officer he had known slightly at State.

Selwyn, tall, lean, and handsome at forty-odd years old, was dressed in State's gray-flannel uniform, white button-down collar, and subdued paisley tie. They shook hands. "Alan, I appreciate your seeing me on short notice," Selwyn said. "Hope I'm not delaying your weekend getaway." He sat down and faced Stuart across the desk.

"Not at all," Stuart said. "I'm not leaving town, just having dinner tonight with my sister and her husband. No other plans."

Selwyn sat back and half closed his eyes. "That'd be— um—Larry Brigham, right? I've met him around town. And your sister . . ."

"Patricia," Stuart supplied.

"Of course. Diana sees her occasionally at Bennington

alumnae gatherings." He seemed tense, preoccupied, as though reluctant to reveal why he had come. "Your brother-in-law's name comes up in every big land-development deal around town.

"He's very good at what he does," Stuart acknowledged. "So, what can I do for you, Blake?"

"First I want to establish confidentiality, Alan—a lawyer-client relationship."

"Easily done."

Selwyn got out a checkbook, dated a blank check, and looked up expectantly. "Oh," Stuart said, "make it out for a hundred dollars."

After Selwyn had handed it across, Stuart said, "Relationship established, Blake. But understand, I have a very limited prac-tice—estates, probate, taxation."

"I know that," Selwyn replied, "but I've come to you for two reasons. One, you know the inner workings at State—how long were you there?"

"Not quite five years."

"The second reason is that I value your integrity, feel I can trust you. You're not a stranger to whom I couldn't unburden myself, and that's what this involves." He looked around the office anxiously. "I take it your secretary doesn't eavesdrop?"

"I'd fire her if she did."

Selwyn shook out a cigarette. Inhaling, he began, "The last year and a half I've been working in the Bureau of Disarmament Affairs, been to Vienna and Geneva several times with the U.S. delegation as one of the working party. One never expects negotiating with the Russians to go easily, particularly where balance of forces is concerned, but to find them apparently aware of our positions and intentions is damn disconcerting."

"They break our codes from time to time and there's always a lag between when they start reading our traffic and when we realize it."

"I'm well aware of that," Selwyn said testily, "and so is the department. That's why communications between Geneva and the secretary are handled by courier—diplomatic pouch. Radio traffic is limited to personnel and support matters." He dropped the ash from his cigarette. "To avoid the possibility of compromising our working papers in Geneva, we type them ourselves, so it's not as though some infatuated secretary were passing copies to her KGB lover." He sat forward abruptly. "Look, Alan, I'm not dumb or paranoid, and I've worried about this for months. My conclusion is there's a high-level leak in the department."

After a few moments Stuart said, "State security looking into it?"

He shook his head dejectedly. "What have I got but suspicions? I can't take suspicion to Tom Scudder and ask his office to investigate. Anyway, an investigator would have to be part of the give-and-take of negotiating before he could begin pinpointing a leaker. He'd have to *feel* the situation as I have. Those gumshoes specialize in unlocked safes, marital infidelity—you know what they're like, what they do."

"Isn't an FBI agent assigned to the delegation?"

"Sure, always. But that's cop mentality. And the secretary and Scudder have made it clear they don't want the FBI invading our turf and internal security." Sitting back, Selwyn stared up at the ceiling. "You're the only lawyer I know who's had experience at the department, Alan."

"But I'm not an investigator, Blake, never was. What is it you want me to do?"

Selwyn shook his head slowly. "It's not easy to put into words. No, I don't want you to mount an active investigation—not for now, anyway. But I'm pretty sure my phones are tapped—home and office—and I've sensed being tailed from time to time."

"Here or Geneva?"

"Both."

"If you haven't mentioned your suspicions to anyone, why would you be a surveillance target?"

"I didn't say I'd never voiced my concern. In Geneva I'd blow up when the Soviets clearly anticipated our moves, and I've done the same at the bureau. Then, after I was convinced I was under some sort of surveillance, I shut up." He leaned back and exhaled. "State's a closed, incestuous body—you know that—and probably the most gossipy department in existence. When anyone expresses dissatisfaction, word gets around quickly. The backbiters are vicious, particularly the ones with an eye on your job."

"And that's the case?"

"I have to assume so—everyone's constantly looking for advancement, and the Bureau of Disarmament Affairs has become key. After six months I made class one. Next foreign post I'll be a counselor of embassy, maybe minister-counselor, and most Foreign Service officers never make that grade."

"Very few," Stuart agreed. He found himself glancing at the old pendulum wall clock mounted by the doorway.

"Nor boring you, am I, Alan?" asked Selwyn somewhat stiffly.

"Of course not. It's that I don't have any idea how I can be of use."

Selwyn smiled thinly. "Get to the point, eh? I don't like prolonged meetings either, so here's what I have in mind—and I'm not paranoid or undergoing any mental crisis, Alan. In case the circumstances of my death should appear at all unusual, I want you to have them thoroughly investigated."

Stuart twirled a pencil and looked over at his new client. "Expecting to die?"

"Not of natural causes."

Stuart grunted. "In Georgetown alone, half a dozen people die every day. If the cause of death is suspicious, the police always investigate. I can't compete with homicide investigators, Blake; I wouldn't even try. If you feel threatened, talk to the Seventh Precinct. And you can hire electronic specialists to check your telephones for tapping—*The Yellow Pages* are full of their ads—apparently it's big business in Washington."

Selwyn said grimly, "I've thought of those things, too."

"Have you told any of this to your wife?"

He sighed. "Diana would want me to see a shrink. But I tell

you there *is* a top-level leak to the Soviets; I have been followed and I'm sure my phones have been tapped."

Stuart decided to humor him. "Mail opened?"

"How would I know?" Selwyn said wearily. "Those things are done cleverly."

"Then to validate your suspicions you ought to keep some kind of journal—a diary, say. Review it after a month. You'll probably find that some incidents have reasonable explanations, others not. Bring whatever's left of substance to me and we'll go over it together. I might be able to suggest a course of action then. Right now that's all the counsel I can come up with." He picked up the retainer check. "Blake, I can't take this, I haven't done anything."

Slowly Selwyn rose. "You've listened. And you can do one final thing, Alan: write up a summary of our conversation and put it in a safe place; you know, memo-for-the-record format. The check can pay for that."

Stuart nodded. "All right, Blake, if that's what you want." As he got up, Selwyn said, "Meanwhile, not a word of this to anyone, right?"

"If I violated your confidence I could be disbarred—you know that."

Selwyn laughed shortly, bitterly. "If I'm still alive to charge you." He stubbed out his cigarette and took a deep breath. "You were wise to leave State when you did, Alan. Not much future there for a fellow who calls things as he sees 'em."

"So I surmised."

They shook hands, and in the reception room Stuart had his secretary make out a receipt for Selwyn's check. Pocketing it, Selwyn managed a smile. "I feel better, Alan—glad I came."

"Good to see you." He watched the State Department officer leave, then told Mrs. Appleby he'd see her Monday.

Alone in his office, he typed up a summary of his conversation with Selwyn, dated, initialed, and sealed it, and placed the envelope in his office safe.

* * *

After turning off the lights and locking his office door, Stuart walked down the wide staircase and turned onto M Street. It was a fine May evening, cool and pleasant, with no hint of summer's inevitable humidity. As he walked east he noticed the ethnic food joints attracting early crowds of shabbily dressed customers. Outbound traffic fought curb to curb, spewing exhaust fumes across the sidewalks, and Stuart found himself wondering how the administration could reduce pollution nationwide when it couldn't even control the nation's capital.

Walking on, he mused that with Washington becoming Murder City, USA, Blake Selwyn's fears might be realized sooner than even he expected. Yet, much as he would have liked to, he couldn't dismiss Selwyn's suspicions as paranoia. The man had put together a number of discrete incidents and drawn conclusions from their sum.

In a month, Stuart told himself, we'll go over his journal, talk things out. But my guess is he won't come back. He'll get a firmer grip on himself and I'll never see Blake Selwyn again.

At Thirty-first Street Stuart crossed M and walked the four-block rise to his house on Q Street. Set back from the street, his house was similar to others on the block: two-story detached dwelling, façade shorn of Victorian gingerbread, its clean lines painted clamshell white. He'd added only a few pieces to the furnishings Sandy had agreed to leave, keeping the interior uncluttered and comfortable to live in. In the pantry he poured Black Label over ice, showered, shaved, and dressed for dinner with the Brighams.

Driving over to their home on Foxhall Road, Stuart found himself hoping Pat hadn't arranged for a female dinner companion. His sister was an incorrigible matchmaker, and he smiled as he thought how stubbornly she resisted the idea that her younger brother was by no means eager to reexperience the hemmed-in feeling and general dissatisfaction of married life.

CHAPTER 2

S creened from Foxhall Road by a tall hedge, the three-story, antiqued brick Brigham home was near Nelson and Happy Rockefeller's one-time residence. Stuart's nephew and niece—Greg, ten, and Prudy, eight—were on the top floor being read to sleep by their nanny, a feisty Scottish widow named Erskine who was more than a match for her wily charges. Their mother had already kissed them goodnight and was now sitting with her drink between Stuart and her husband in the library. Larry had switched off the giant TV screen, asked the Honduran servant for drinks, and stretched back comfortably on his leather Barcalounger, velvet opera slippers level with his balding head. He was wearing a smoking jacket, a white ruffled shirt, and a black bolo tie that suggested his Texas background. Son of a Fort Worth oil million-aire, Larry had been sent east to Exeter and MIT, then taken an M.B.A. at Tuck before doing battle with some of the District's shrewdest land speculators. He owned four large shopping malls within a twenty-mile radius of Washington and an office building off Farragut Square, and he had turned an entire street of decayed houses into desirable yuppy dwellings. He and Pat owned summer residences at Plum Point and Mount Desert Isle and winter quarters in Antigua and Hobe Sound, and they frequently traveled abroad.

Pat was describing an upcoming cruise through the Caribbean and down the eastern coast of South America as far as Rio. "It's only for a month, Alan, and if you can find the time, why don't you come with us?"

Stuart sipped his Scotch. "I might get away for a week, but a month's out of the question. Thanks anyway."

"Your trouble," Larry pointed out, "is that you work alone and can't delegate responsibility like me. You've become a slave to your clients. Why work so hard? You don't need the money." He sat up to take a drink.

"I like what I do," Stuart replied. "In fact, I'm quite satisfied with things the way they are."

"But you never *go* anywhere," Pat objected. "And you could have your pick of any number of attractive young women if—"

"Oh, I go out two or three nights a week—Kennedy Center, National Theater. I'm hardly going to seed."

"My man," his brother-in-law declared, "you're getting stodgy. You need some excitement in that dull life."

"What kind of excitement?"

"Any kind—love affair, politics, travel—singly or combined."

Stuart smiled. "Suppose I were to tell you I'm deeply involved in a romantic affair with a lady who must remain nameless?"

"I wouldn't believe you," Larry snorted.

"Nor would I," said Pat. "You're too . . . too disgustingly *proper*." She rattled the ice in her glass for emphasis. "Really, Alan, with all you have to offer the world—Washington in particular—you're a hermit hiding your light under a bushel basket. Surely you've gotten over Sandy by now."

Stuart took another sip. "Nary a tear at parting," he said truthfully, "and civilly we went our separate ways. Case of different temperaments, simple as that." Then, to change the subject he said, "An old acquaintance at State came in today, became a sort of client. Pat, you know his wife from Bennington associations—Diana Selwyn?"

"I do indeed," she nodded. "Bright, active, and much closer to your age than mine." Her eyes half closed. "After Diana graduated I seem to remember her family giving a dorm to the old school."

"Gratitude for letting her graduate?" Stuart suggested.

"No, in fact it was because she'd done very well at the Big B. Her family's name is . . . Stuyvesant? No, Sturdevant. From some horsey place in New Jersey . . . Bernardsville. I take it you've never met?"

Stuart shook his head. "I barely know Blake. He's, oh, forty-plus, I'd say."

"Then he's a good ten years older than his wife," Pat said. "What'd Blake consult you about? Divorce in the air?"

"A confidential matter, Sis, but divorce was never mentioned. Anyway, that's not something I could help him with."

Larry nodded. "You're too young to specialize, Alan. Since you're a workaholic I could throw a lot of business your way. Of course, you'd have to cram real estate law for a couple of months, but it'd be worth it in the end."

"Sure—triple bypass. No thanks, Larry." As he finished his drink, his brother-in-law pressed a concealed call button. Presently the Honduran came in—María de los Angeles, she called herself—and Larry joked that it was because she'd made the trip when the route to Los Angeles was safer and easier. Her limited English was better than the Brighams' Spanish, and she worked long hours six days a week without complaint. The cook was a thin, brown man from Sri Lanka, and there was also a bedmaking, ironing, day maid from Washington's East Side. Probably, Stuart figured, the only legal servant in the house.

María made fresh drinks and announced that dinner could be served whenever the señora desired. "Give us ten minutes," ordered the lord of the manor, holding up both hands, fingers spread apart. "*Diez minutos mas.*" After she went away Larry said,

"I've forgotten most of the Spanish I learned playing with Mex kids around Dad's ranch. But I knew it once, I knew it." He drank deeply. "Didn't help me at Exeter, though. German, French, and Arabic were the "in" languages. I want Greg to learn Japanese—so he can deal with our financial masters on their own terms."

"And Prudy?" Pat asked irritably. "You're satisfied to see her master needlepoint and violin?"

"Nothing of the kind. It's German for her, so start looking up Swiss boarding schools." Reaching over, he patted his wife's hand. "Our children are going to have to hang onto their inheritance in a world where the dollar is just another currency, not the standard it used to be."

"That's a dismal thought," Pat remarked, "but I guess it's all too true. Alan, you agree?"

"I've put several of my clients into German and Japanese securities and they've done very well."

"Only one thing better," Larry drawled, "and that's D.C. real estate."

"Until the bomb drops," Pat swirled the ice in her drink. "Then everything goes, of course. Which is why"—she said with a glance at her husband—"I support public-spirited people and organizations that work for peace."

Larry shrugged. "Your money. Waste it as you choose. The Kremlin pays no attention to those kooks anyway—except the groups they subsidize. You'll notice, Pat, that they don't allow peace demonstrations in Russia—that's for over here. Useful idiots," he reflected. "Lenin was so right."

"Well, I believe in giving peace a chance. Alan?"

"I've never met anyone who wanted war. Anyway, what happened to your ecology enthusiasms?"

"Oh, the problems are just too monstrous even to try to resolve. But peace—that's within our grasp if we work for it. Did you happen to know Edward Beamish at State?"

"Beamish?" Stuart squinted at the blank TV screen. "Not personally, but the name . . . I connect him with International

Organizations—very senior in the department. I think he was our ambassador to UNESCO, then retired."

Larry grunted. "Ed didn't exactly retire, Alan—we pulled out of UNESCO, you recall, leaving no job for dear Ed."

Pat said, "He's been very active since then promoting world peace. You've heard of Passage?"

"Vaguely," Stuart replied.

"Larry's upset because I'm sponsoring a reception at the Sulgrave before Edward's lecture next week. Perhaps you'd like to come.?"

"Not my sort of thing," Stuart declined with finality.

Larry said, "Don't be too sure, Alan. Your clients will be there in force—half the old ladies from the F Street Club. You ought to go and protect them when the hat's passed, they'll give away the store." He sucked noisily at his drink. "Beamish is very glib, very plausible. Pat and her friends think he's the Second Coming."

"And you, Larry?"

"A snake oil peddler who's made a damn good thing out of preaching peace." He looked at his wife. "'Passage'—what's *that* supposed to mean?"

Tightly she said, "It refers to free passage across frontiers, the abolishment of national boundaries. Is that so reprehensible?"

Larry grinned. "Tell you what, sweetheart, I'll sign up when Ed gets the Russkies to tear down the Berlin Wall."

"Well," she pouted, "that's what we're all working toward. Until all missiles are abolished, our children will live under the threat of nuclear war."

"Since Hiroshima, the whole world's lived with that possibility, dear, and managed to adjust to it. Greg and Prudy will too." He got up from his recliner and took his wife's hand. "Dinnertime. Let's find out what Rama Singh's prepared for our delight."

A thin fish soup prefaced the main course, which turned out to be curried lobster with steamed rice. For dessert, pistachio mousse, and black, syrupy coffee, Turkish-style.

Larry took his demitasse to his computer terminal off the library and linked up with an associate in Honolulu, explaining that it was still daylight in Hawaii and he wanted a report on some Maui ocean frontage that both he and Tokyo interests were bidding for.

Seated again in the library, Pat sighed, "I'd complain about Larry's devotion to business, except that when he's not buying or selling he's cross as a wounded bear. It's not the money, Alan—with Larry it's a game, like Monopoly. He needs the excitement, the challenge of matching wits."

"Does he ever lose?"

"Occasionally, but he shrugs it off and goes on to another project. At least"—she smiled slowly—"it keeps him away from bars and women. And I arrange these trips of ours because they're the only relaxation Larry ever gets. I'd prefer not being a young widow."

"It's an enviable marriage," Stuart said.

"Compared to others I know of, definitely yes. Cognac?"

He shook his head. "I'm going to scull in the morning, so I think I'll run along."

"Hard week?"

"Enjoyable—and profitable. The only problem I couldn't solve was Blake Selwyn's, and I have a feeling that'll just go away."

"Could I interest you in staying here while we're off cruising?"

"I'd rather not, but I'll look in from time to time."

"Nanny will contact you if there's a problem." She put down her cup and saucer and leaned forward. "When we get back I want you to meet Sally Barnes—lovely girl, Philadelphia background. Dobbs and Sarah Lawrence. Her husband died about a year ago, so it's time she began getting around. Sally's a year or so younger than you and very enthusiastic about Passage. When I arrange dinner I won't have you turn me down. Understood?"

"Understood." Stuart kissed his sister good night and looked in on Larry to wave good-bye. Back at Q Street, he watched a late news program until he began yawning, and he went to bed.

* * *

Saturday morning Stuart sculled on the Potomac. In the afternoon he played squash at the University Club and had dinner at the Jockey Club with a lawyer he had met at Bragg when they were earning their berets.

Sunday morning he sculled again, lunched near Leesburg at the Laurel Brigade Inn, and attended an evening concert at Kennedy Center, Mehta conducting.

Monday morning's paper brought him the news.

visiting his mistress in rural Virginia. On the way back to Annapolis the governor's car had broken down, and the Virginia State Police, who disliked his high-handedness and arrogance, had leaked the story to the press. That publicized incident of moral turpitude threw other suspicions that ballooned into indictments and convictions for graft and misuse of office. After serving time in prison the governor died of a heart attack—like Blake Selwyn, Stuart reflected, though he doubted that Selwyn had ever engaged in any criminal enterprise. He wasn't the type at all; had probably never even pinched any office paper clips.

Finding the day's calendar flexible, he asked his secretary to arrange appointments with the Montgomery County medical examiner and the chief of State's medical services.

"In what connection, sir?"

"As attorney for the late Blake Selwyn."

"Yes, sir. Bill the estate?"

Stuart thought it over. "No, it's prepaid." A prepaid death, he reflected as he sat back in his chair—like buying your burial plot in advance. You retain a lawyer to examine the circumstances of your demise, make sure everything's kosher. Not a bad idea, but one likely to be resisted by heirs and beneficiaries.

The telephone book gave Blake's address on upper Connecticut Avenue, an affluent section near the Taft Bridge. Stuart noted the address and phone number. Actually, he mused, there was no reason whatever to get in touch with Selwyn's widow. If he represented himself as Blake's lawyer she'd want to know why her husband had retained him—and the death of his client did not relieve Stuart of the burden of confidentiality. Nor did Stuart particularly want to reveal Blake's concerns—to anyone. He'd come off as a latter-day McCarthyite rumormonger.

Mrs. Appleby came in to say that the medical examiner could see him in his Rockville office at two o'clock. The State appointment was set for next morning at ten. Twenty-four hours away, Stuart noted, and applied himself to pending work.

* * *

After lunching at the nearby Bistro Français, Stuart rode the
Metrorail to Rockville and located the medical examiner in the old
county building, its front lawn dominated by a memorial statue of
the Confederacy. The high-ceilinged office showed its age. Worn
flooring, uneven plaster walls, and flaking paint that revealed old
coats of white, brown, and green. The wood furniture was scarred
but utilitarian. Half a dozen file cabinets stood undusted against
the far wall.

Short, plump and balding, Dr. Blenkinsopp sported a bristly
gray mustache and wire-rimmed glasses. His hands were bleached,
his fingernails almost invisible. He eyed Stuart across his desk and
said, "When I mentioned you to Mrs. Selwyn she said she'd never
heard of you."

"Not surprising, Doctor. Blake retained me only last Friday
afternoon."

"You were friends?"

"Acquaintances at State—I worked there before I went into
law. That's why Blake consulted me."

The medical examiner sat forward. "May I ask what he
consulted you about?"

"The matter was confidential and remains so." Stuart placed
his card on the desk.

Glancing at it, the medical examiner dropped it into a desk
drawer. "Well, I won't press the point," he said, "and I'll accept
your representation. What can I tell you, Mr. Stuart?"

"I'd like a copy of the death certificate, to begin with."

"Thought you might." He handed across a form. "Next?"

"I'd like to know just where Blake's car was found and which
way it was headed."

On a wall map of the county Dr. Blenkinsopp traced Route
112. "About a mile south of Darnestown," he said, "and though the
police report doesn't say so, from personal observation at the scene
I can tell you that the deceased's vehicle was on the shoulder on

the east side of the road, pointing north toward Darnestown. During the night a trooper noticed the car and stopped to offer assistance; the road is lightly traveled. The trooper found the body slumped over the steering wheel. He checked for a pulse and called an ambulance."

"That was about what time?"

"Three-fifteen. Internal body temperature indicated death some three to four hours earlier."

"You autopsied?"

"I did—and it kept me from church yesterday morning." He sighed. "People pass away at inconvenient times, I've found."

"According to the newspaper, death was due to heart failure."

"That was my finding. Nothing organically wrong with Mr. Selwyn's heart—it simply stopped beating."

"I'm checking his medical history at State tomorrow."

"I can save you the trouble, sir. The deceased had a record of malaria and a bout of amoebas, but his last departmental physical exam—four months ago—evinced no cardiac problem."

"Then how do you account for sudden heart failure? Smoking?"

The doctor shook his head. "It happens. The man's time had come—that's all I can say."

"I take it the car doors weren't locked."

"That's so. The trooper opened the driver's door." His eyes narrowed. "If you suspect suicide, forget it. And there was no evidence of a recent passenger."

"Such as?"

"Lipstick-stained cigarette stubs in the ashtrays, Kleenexes, liquor . . . apparently Selwyn was alone."

Stuart hesitated. "Did his widow say where he was going, or why?"

"In a criminal case, of course, it would be appropriate to ask, but if Mrs. Selwyn knows anything, she hasn't revealed it. Nor is she required to." His hands fidgeted and he looked expectantly at Stuart. "If there's nothing more . . ."

"Can't think of anything. But for the record, you found nothing abnormal, unusual, out of the ordinary, about Blake's death?"

"Nothing whatever. If I had there would be a criminal investigation underway, and there is none."

"You gave Mrs. Selwyn a copy of the death certificate?"

"I did. And the cadaver is scheduled for release to Lawler's sometime today, Mrs. Selwyn having made formal identification."

As Stuart rose he asked, "And Blake's Chrysler?"

"It's been taken to the pound behind the courthouse. Mrs. Selwyn said she'd claim it later. Want to see it?"

"No reason to." He extended his hand across the desk, which Dr. Blenkinsopp shook briefly, and said, "Thanks for your time, Doctor. I appreciate it."

"Part of my duties," Blenkinsopp said rather tightly. "Good day, sir."

Stuart walked back to the Metro station, satisfied that he had complied fully with Selwyn's request. It was too bad that the widow had learned of his interest in Blake's death, and he hoped she wouldn't inquire. If so he'd have to stonewall, which might get unpleasant.

Still, he thought as he fed coins into the ticket machine, for the next week or so she'd be occupied with the funeral, burial, and memorial arrangements. After that, Blake's will, probate, and so on. By the time she remembered his visit to the medical examiner it would be too unimportant to bother with.

But Alan Stuart was quite wrong. A message from Diana Selwyn was on his desk when he returned.

When she came on the line her voice was choked, less with grief than fury, Stuart thought, as she cried, "Who *are* you, anyway, you cheap ambulance chaser? What the hell are you doing snooping around my husband's death? Now hear me, *Mister* Stuart, there's no money in this for you, understand? Nothing. You stay out of my affairs and Blake's or I'll have you disbarred!"

For a few moments Stuart said nothing. Then he spoke calmly, "There's a perfectly reasonable explanation, Mrs. Selwyn, and I'll be glad to discuss it when you're less distraught. Call for an appointment any time."

"Oh? Wait, don't hang up—what are you telling me?"

"Blake retained me last Friday."

"He *did*? Can you prove it?"

"I have his check."

"I want to see it." She paused. "If I'm wrong about you I'm sorry. I'll get back to you when I can. We must clear this up."

The line went dead and Stuart looked at the receiver in his hand. With a shrug he replaced it and buzzed Mrs. Appleby. "That check of Selwyn's," he said, "don't deposit it. And call State to cancel my ten o'clock tomorrow. It's no longer necessary."

"Yes, sir." In a few moments she brought Selwyn's check to him and Stuart placed it in a desk drawer. Mrs. Selwyn sounded bitter and imperious, a woman accustomed to having her way regardless of whose toes she trod on. He felt an impulse to phone his sister for an estimate of Diana Selwyn but decided against it. Pat, full of good deeds waiting to happen, might intervene with the widow and arouse additional wrath. So let it go, he thought, let it go.

He considered the sealed envelope containing his summarized conversation with Blake Selwyn. Was his widow entitled to it? There was an ethical question, and he might have to consult the bar section concerned with such niceties. He could destroy the memorandum, but it would always be on his conscience. No, better leave that decision to the future. And hope Mrs. Selwyn never followed through. Stuart left early for the University Club, worked out, enjoyed a sauna and massage, and dined sparingly in the dining room. Even after two Black Labels he felt inwardly shaken by Mrs. Selwyn's onslaught. He wasn't accustomed to the unbridled rage of arrogant young women; his female clients tended to be elderly gentlewomen of few words.

Some of her bad behavior he could attribute to shock, some to grief, and the rest to honest outrage at an unknown prying into private concerns. But as he stirred sweetener into black coffee, Stuart wondered whether the widow's violent reaction could have been brought on by fear that a stranger would uncover secrets of her life—or Blake's.

Last Friday, he mused, had been an evil day. He wished fervently that Blake Selwyn had never confided his fantasies to him. He might now be involved in things alien and menacing— espionage and sudden death—if Selwyn's suspicions ever proved to be true.

Stuart walked in the cool night air to the National Theater, taking his seat in time for the curtain of a new Neil Simon play's pre-Broadway tryout. But he was too preoccupied with the day's events to concentrate, and when he left the theater he realized that he had hardly any grasp of what the play had been about.

Automatically he accepted a leaflet thrust into his hand as he waited for a taxi. On the way home he read it and found that the public was invited to attend a meeting at the University of Maryland auditorium. It was sponsored by an area ecumenical council and a coalition of faculty members and students from the University of Maryland and George Washington, Georgetown, and Catholic Universities. The evening speaker would be Ambassador Edward Beamish; his subject: Are Frontiers Necessary?

Stuart folded the leaflet and slipped it into a pocket. His sister's pet organization, Passage, was coming to town.

CHAPTER 4

On Wednesday Stuart rode the Metroliner to New York for an investment conference at Chase Manhattan, after which he reviewed and adjusted the holdings of two clients accordingly. He stayed overnight at the Westbury, returning in time for Blake Selwyn's afternoon burial in Georgetown's huge, ancient Oak Hill Cemetery. Stuart stayed on the mourners' fringe to avoid possible confrontation with Selwyn's widow. He identified her by a heavy black veil, proximity to the grave, and her placing a red rose on the casket. Her features were not visible, but Stuart expected to see them soon enough.

Stuart recognized a number of State Department acquaintances, who acknowledged one another's presence with solemn nods.

From the cemetery Stuart walked down to his office, stopping along the way for a bracing Scotch at an M Street tavern.

Leaving the tavern, Stuart noticed a man lingering on the opposite side of the street, someone he had noticed among the mourners. The man was wearing a dark two-piece suit with a black tie, and when he caught Stuart's gaze he turned and strode off in the opposite direction. After a moment Stuart strolled on.

A detective? Mrs. Selwyn could afford private investigators to look into Stuart's affairs, but it would be a waste of money. He thought he had damped her suspicions of him, but maybe not. Well, one private eye didn't make a major incident, and since Stuart wasn't sure what the man was actually up to, he dismissed the encounter.

After consulting his New York notes Stuart dictated letters of notification to the clients involved, made an appointment with an IRS auditor on behalf of another client, and was preparing to leave for the day when Mrs. Appleby buzzed to say that Mrs. Blake Selwyn was on the line.

"Alan Stuart," he responded, and heard a cool, steady voice say, "Acting on your suggestion I'd like to meet with you as soon as convenient. Could you possibly see me at home?"

"I don't usually make house calls," Stuart told her, "except for the aged and infirm." He glanced at his desk calendar. "Set a time tomorrow and I'll be glad to see you in my office."

"Very well, then." She paused. "Ten o'clock?"

"I'll expect you." He made a note on his pad. "I was pleased to see so many of Blake's friends at the cemetery."

"Oh—you were there? Why didn't you make yourself known to me?"

"Seemed like a poor time," Stuart said.

"I'm in better shape now," she said. "Until tomorrow, then."

He hung up, saw the hold button blinking, and heard his sister's voice. "Alan, could you possibly come to the Sulgrave with me this evening? Larry had to fly out to Honolulu and I detest receiving guests alone. It's the Passage affair I told you about. I've tried reaching you since yesterday but you were in New York."

"Got back earlier today," he told his sister, "for Blake Selwyn's funeral. His widow's coming in tomorrow."

"Diana? Please give her my condolences."

"I will. But as for tonight I have to disappoint you—too late to change plans," he lied. "Anyway, I see that Ambassador Beamish has been busy gathering converts from the flock."

"Yes, he had very successful exposure last night. More than a hundred new members signed up. Alan, I *do* wish you could meet Edward. He's a serious, important man, and if you were to hear him out I think you might change your mind about what he's trying to accomplish."

"Since you're sponsoring him, inevitably we'll meet. Until then I'll keep an open mind."

"Please do. I know you don't care about political things, but Passage is something universal, something everyone should care about."

"Well, I'm sure you'll have a gala evening without me. When are you leaving on that cruise?"

"Saturday. We fly to San Juan and board the *Queen Elizabeth II.*"

"Sorry about tonight, Sis."

"Love you anyway," she said and hung up.

Regretting the white lie, Stuart consoled himself with the knowledge that he would have been acutely uncomfortable at the fund-raising reception for Passage and its chairman, former ambassador Beamish. Stuart had no difficulty defining the general character of Beamish's constituency: pacifist priests, activist academics, and bored socialites, among whom Stuart reluctantly had to include his sister. So with that justification he put the Sulgrave affair out of his mind and looked forward to a good dinner at the George Towne Club and a comfortable evening at home watching TV.

When Diana Selwyn arrived for her appointment she was wearing a subdued gray dress and a black silk scarf placed loosely around her neck. She wore a platinum wedding band and a large diamond engagement ring; her brown hair was short and layered, complementing an oval face with clear, almost translucent skin. Even subtly applied makeup could not conceal the fatigue that registered around her large eyes, but Stuart found her to be an extremely attractive young woman. Legs modestly crossed, she looked at Stuart across his desk, and said, "First, do you have Blake's check?"

Wordlessly he handed it over. She glanced at the signature and handed it back. "Next," she said, "what did Blake consult you about?"

"Because of lawyer-client confidentiality I can't go into that, Mrs. Selwyn."

"I see." She bit her lower lip, seemingly at a loss. Presently she went on, "Did Blake leave any papers with you? Any kind of documents?"

"No. That much I can tell you."

"Can you tell me if Blake was considering divorce?"

Stuart weighed the question. After a few moments he said, "If he was it formed no part of our conversation. Would you care for coffee?"

"Tea, if you have it, please."

Via intercom he asked for two cups of tea, and when he looked back at his visitor she seemed more relaxed. To his surprise she asked, "Are you satisfied that Blake's death was . . . normal?"

"I have no reason to suppose it wasn't. You've read the death certificate, and the medical examiner had nothing to add beyond suggesting that heart failure in an apparently well man is not unusual."

"Do you know what Blake was doing on that road so late at night?"

"No idea. Frankly, I thought you might."

She looked away. "In confidence, Mr. Stuart, we didn't communicate well. We had dinner together that evening and Blake told me he had to go out and said not to wait up. I assumed he was going back to the department.

"But he didn't say?"

She shook her head. "I went to bed and slept until the police called me at dawn." Taking a deep breath she said, "Since then it's been a nightmare—and when I heard you were looking into Blake's death I blew up. Nervous reaction, I guess."

"Understandable," he said as Mrs. Appleby brought in the salver with their teacups, cream, and sugar.

When they were alone again Diana Selwyn said, "It was good of you to attend the funeral. With so many friends there I realized how well thought of Blake was in the department, which helped steady me."

Taking a sip from his cup Stuart mentioned, "I think you may know my sister, Pat Brigham—she was at Bennington some years ahead of you."

"Pat? Of course—but I had no idea you were her brother." She shook her head slowly. "That does bring you into focus . . . I'm terribly sorry for everything I said when I called." She gazed at him, eyes large. "Please forgive me. I had no idea . . ." Her voice trailed off.

"There was a misunderstanding, so there's nothing to forgive, Mrs. Selwyn."

A small handkerchief dabbed briefly at her eyes before she said, "That's kind of you—Alan. Having Pat in common I'd be more comfortable with first names."

"So would I. Now, I assume you have an estate attorney who's handling things for you, but if there's anything I can do, officially or unofficially, I hope you'll let me know."

Her head tilted slightly. "What sort of practice do you have? I mean, do you specialize in a particular kind of law?"

"Generally my practice involves estate matters—probate, investment management . . ." He shrugged. "My brother-in-law, Larry, calls it stodgy and I guess he's right—but I'm satisfied."

"And I have the feeling you do it successfully." She drank the last of her tea and set aside the cup. "Would you consider having me as a client?"

Stuart looked upward for a few moments while he thought it over. "There could conceivably be a conflict of interest because Blake retained me. But I feel I've fulfilled my obligations to him, and if you'll agree not to press me regarding them, I'll be delighted to represent you in any way I can."

"Then it's settled," she said in a firm voice. "I knew I was going to need an attorney to sort things out, and finding you is providential. All our papers are at the house, I'm afraid, so if it's not asking too much I hope you'll be willing to go over them there."

"That's agreeable. The will comes first. Do you have a copy?"

"Somewhere. But the original is in Blake's safe deposit box." She gestured. "At Riggs, across the street."

"I'll need power of attorney from you to open it, and I'll have to notify the IRS to have a revenue agent present."

"May I be there?"

"If you choose. Insurance policies?"

"Filed at home. And Blake's office is boxing his personal papers and effects for me. How do you prefer to bill me?"

"I'll take a thousand-dollar retainer and bill the estate monthly, if that's okay."

She nodded and got out a checkbook. While she was making out the check Stuart asked Mrs. Appleby to draw up a general power of attorney, which Diana signed and Mrs. Appleby notarized.

"It might be a day or so before I can arrange to have the safe deposit box opened," he explained, "depending on agent availability. Meanwhile, I can read your copy of the will and prepare it for probate court. Did you have joint or separate bank accounts?"

"Separate," she said, "and both at Riggs."

"Blake's will be frozen for a time, then transferred to you." He held up Blake's retainer check. "This, for instance, would not be honored at the bank."

"I can give you another."

"No, it can be negotiated later on. Is Blake's car still in Rockville?"

"Yes, and I don't know what to do about it."

"Unless you need it for transportation, I'd suggest selling it."

"Very well. I never want to see that car again."

"I'll arrange to have it brought to the District and garaged pending its sale."

She sighed. "I'm just beginning to realize how many things have to be done. So I'm particularly grateful you'll be handling everything. You have an air of competence about you, Alan—and I don't find you stodgy at all. How soon can you begin sorting through Blake's papers?"

Stuart glanced at his calendar. "I could come out this afternoon, say around three. Is that convenient?"

"Quite. I'll be expecting you." Rising, she gave him her hand. "I'm tremendously relieved it's worked out like this." She smiled tentatively. "Must be fate."

"Could be," he agreed, "and I am a believer. We can dip an oar into the current, but generally I feel we're sort of swept along toward whatever destiny fate has in store for us."

"My feelings too," she said, gathered up her handbag, and left the office.

The Selwyn residence was out on Connecticut Avenue between Kalorama and Ashmeade, just short of Taft Bridge. An imposing gray stone building of neo-Gothic lines, it was set back from the street in a section favored by old money and long-established families. In contrast, Stuart thought, to the glitzy high-rises that had erupted near the Department of State and catered to affluent lobbyists and politicians.

It was three o'clock when a uniformed maid admitted Stuart and showed him to a sunny drawing room where Diana, wearing casual slacks and shirt, was speaking on a cordless telephone. At his appearance, she terminated the conversation and smiled up at him. "I took a two-hour nap I badly needed, and now I'm ready to be of help. Follow me."

She led him into a book-lined study that contained a small fireplace, a broad desk and several leather-covered chairs. There was a four-drawer file cabinet in one corner, to which she pointed, saying, "Everything's there, I think. Whatever you need, just tell me."

"My secretary may call me; otherwise I'm not expecting any interruptions."

"When you want coffee, tea, or a drink, just buzz here for the maid—and thank you for coming." When she'd left the office, Stuart laid his briefcase on the desk and got out a pad of lined yellow sheets—a lawyer's most useful tool. He opened the top file drawer, and while he was writing down the file captions Diana came in and laid a photocopied will beside his briefcase. Stuart unfolded it, checked the date—it had been drawn and witnessed a year earlier—and scanned it long enough to determine that Diana was executrix and principal beneficiary, with enough capital set aside to maintain Blake's mother in her Arizona nursing home.

"A dear lady," Diana remarked, "But incompetent for more than a year. Alzheimer's, I suspect, but Blake never told me."

"Any reason not to?"

She shrugged. "It was his way. He held some things very close inside. My husband was—I suppose 'a private person' puts it as well as anything. Secrecy was part of his work and I suppose it flowed over into other things."

"The Washington psyche. Half the city is busy keeping secrets while the other half tries to uncover them."

"I suppose so. Did you do classified work at State?"

"Some—everyone does."

The phone rang. Diana answered, spoke a few words, and then left the room, saying, "I'll leave you undisturbed, Alan."

Taking each file in turn, Stuart listed each significant document he would have to work with, flagging those of particular importance. He worked methodically through the drawers, grateful that Selwyn's files were in good order. In one folder he found Blake's membership card for Passage—a discovery that surprised him, but he supposed Selwyn had wanted to keep informed on what the unilateral disarmers were doing.

The door opened and Diana came in with a tray holding glasses and a crystal ice bucket. "Cocktail time," she announced. "What's your choice?"

Startled, he glanced at his wristwatch—six o'clock. "Had no idea it was so late," he said, stretching his back and arms.

"You're a steady worker, I'll give you that. Well?"

"Scotch and a little ice, no water."

"A man's drink." She went out and returned with a bottle of Pinch in one hand, vodka in the other. She was wearing a dress again, one that displayed slim legs to advantage, and as she handed Stuart his glass she touched hers to it and smiled. "First today but not the last tonight."

"One good drink deserves another."

She sat beside the desk and looked across the neat pile of folders. "This must be very tedious."

"It's what I'm paid for. All of Blake's records seem in good order," Stuart replied.

"Any surprises?"

"Not really. But I noticed that Blake belonged to Passage. My sister's involved with them."

"Yes, I received an invitation to Pat's Sulgrave soiree, but under the circumstances I couldn't attend." She sipped her iced vodka. "Did you happen to know Beamish before he retired?"

Stuart smiled. "He was way, way above my level—as was Blake."

"And where did it get him?" she said tightly. "Dying alone on a dark road." Her lips quivered and she raised her glass quickly.

"That night," he said gently, "—what time did Blake leave here?"

She looked away. "I'm afraid I didn't pay much attention. After dinner he came in here and closed the door. I made some phone calls for a hospital committee I'm on, and when I finished he was . . . gone."

"Did he make any calls?"

"We only have the one line."

"Any idea what he was doing in here before he left?"

"Working, I suppose. I heard the file drawers opening—they squeak, as you probably noticed."

"Did you hear him close them?"

She shook her head. "Why all the questions, Alan? Is there some mystery?"

"Just the original mystery—where Blake was going that night, and why."

"He went to his office—isn't that so?"

"After hours there's a register for anyone entering or leaving. Blake didn't go to the department. If you know where he went, I think you ought to tell me. I won't reveal your confidence—in fact, I couldn't even if I wanted to."

Her eyes narrowed. "What makes you think I'm withholding anything? Haven't I told you what little I know?"

"I hope so." Stuart left the desk and walked over to the brick-lined fireplace. Kneeling, he reached into the rear of the grate and brought out fragments of black ash and a small triangle of unburned paper. "Been burning things?"

She sat forward, face rigid. "Certainly not."

Stuart stood up and brushed his hands. "Someone has. How often is the grate cleaned?"

"In winter quite often . . . but now . . ." She shrugged. "There's not been a wood fire since early March . . . that sudden cold spell." She sat back in her chair. "You're suggesting that Blake burned papers before leaving that night?"

"Is there another explanation?"

"I can't think of any," she admitted, "but quite frankly, I don't appreciate being interrogated. If Blake burned a few things there, so what? Maybe they were old love letters, I really don't care. And if he had a romantic secret of some kind, well, many men have. He's dead, and I don't want the past raked up"—her lips trembled again—"the way you pawed through those ashes."

Stuart drank deeply and took a seat beside his client. "Suppose your husband—late husband—was burning classified papers. Wouldn't you want to know?"

"No," she snapped. "Even if he were, I'm sure he was authorized to have classified material in his possession—and to destroy it if he chose to. Like other officers, he often brought home documents from the department and took them back in the morning."

Stuart looked down at his glass, then met her gaze. "Always?"

"I can't swear to it—and I don't have to. I *assume* so. And for God's sake, let's change the subject! What's Pat up to? I haven't seen her lately."

Resignedly, Stuart went back to the desk and began fitting yellow pages into his briefcase. "She and Larry are leaving for a month's cruise. She thinks her husband works too hard and I agree. I also think there are other things in life worth more than money."

She looked up at him. "Such as?"

"Contentment, comfort, personal satisfaction."

"Some men—women too—can achieve those things only by making big deals, winning in the marketplace. Blake wasn't that way, thank heaven. His priorities were his career and our marriage."

She watched Stuart close the briefcase zipper and finish his drink. "Are you married? I don't know even that much about you."

"For two years," he said. "Sandy wanted one thing, I wanted another. We agreed to disagree–permanently. She remarried a few months ago—Seattle." He walked toward Diana and then halted. "I'm sorry I upset you, but I felt obligated to ask those questions."

Rising, she placed a hand on his arm. "Let me explain something that should avoid a recurrence. Blake and I were married almost five years. He'd been married before, briefly. I told you his priorities were his career and our marriage, and that's true—but his career was at the top of the list and our marriage way down at the bottom. We stayed married because it was mutually convenient, but I don't suppose we'd been . . . intimate for at least two years. I entertained to advance his career, and Blake did very well. But we had separate rooms. Now do you understand why I paid no attention to his departure that last night?"

Stuart swallowed. "I do," he said huskily, "and I appreciate your setting me straight. The subject won't come up again."

She walked beside him to the doorway. Before he opened it she said, "With that out of the way, how's your work progressing?"

"Smoothly," he said. "Blake was an organized man—his files show it and it makes my job much easier."

She smiled. "We can be friends now, can't we?"

"I hope so," he said, "and before I return I'll give advance notice. Oh, one thing—can't get into the safe deposit box until next week. We have a tentative appointment for Tuesday morning. I'll call to confirm."

With that, Stuart went out and closed the door. He walked to his car thinking that Diana Selwyn, in addition to beauty and breeding, possessed a core of steel.

He was in bed when the telephone wakened him. Sleepily he heard Diana Selwyn, sounding as though she'd been drinking. "Alan? Something I should have told you today but didn't . . . you there?"

"I'm listening."

"Good. Relia- reliable man," she slurred. "Like you. Want you to know something im- important, but it's very . . . very personal—understand?"

"How personal?"

"Intimate."

Stuart blinked his eyes open, ran a hand through his tousled hair. "Go ahead."

"I want you to know," she repeated, and for a time the line was silent. When she resumed she said, "I told you about the separate beds, didn't I? Alan?"

"You did."

She coughed. "Didn't love each other—not after the first year—maybe after the first month. But in all that time I was never unfaithful to my husband . . . never broke my marriage vows." Another long silence. Then, "Believe me?"

"I do."

"What do you think of it?"

"Commendable," he said. "You want congratulations?"

"Not necessary. Just want you to know I can keep a vow."

"I never doubted it," he told her. He heard a prolonged yawn, then silence. Finally he heard the receiver replaced, then slight metallic sounds which brought him fully awake—two barely audible clicks, then nothing but current hum. Diana Selwyn's phone, he realized, was being tapped.

Or was his?

CHAPTER 5

*A*t his office the next morning Stuart decided his assumption was absurd. Diana had had too much to drink, and in replacing the receiver her hand must have jiggled the cut-off contacts, causing the clicks. Diana wasn't involved in illegal activities and he certainly wasn't, so why would any government unit—the FBI or State Security—eavesdrop on either phone?

It was possible, of course, that Blake Selwyn had been the target of a government tap, but Blake had proclaimed concern over possible leakage of vital information, so it was hardly likely that he'd have come under security suspicion. Besides, the government wouldn't continue to tap a dead man's phone; no judge would permit it.

But, logic aside, if there *was* an eavesdropper the tap had to be unauthorized and illegal, Stuart mused, the project of some foreign power.

Better than having his and Diana's phones checked would be maintaining telephone discipline, letting a tapper hear nothing of interest. Then tapping would end.

Yet Stuart was disturbed by the ash he'd found in Blake's

fireplace grate. What had Selwyn been burning before his death? Perhaps Blake really had been conducting a clandestine love affair. But why burn love letters at that particular time, unless Blake had reason to fear death that night. Few men know in advance when their time has come.

It troubled Stuart that no one knew where Blake had been going on that out-of-the-way road that led nowhere. Still, the circumstances were unusual but not suspicious. Stuart had gone as far as he could, and he wished he could get the whole thing out of his mind.

But why had Diana called him last night? Why had she wanted her new lawyer to know of her uncommon fidelity? It was a strange and intimate revelation, one she would scarcely have made fully sober. *One good drink deserves another*, she had remarked that evening, and clearly, she'd followed through.

Stuart could understand that a recent widow was entitled to dull her grief as best she could. But he couldn't understand what lay behind her call. Was Diana indirectly letting him know that a woman who had been celibate yet faithful for two years was not sexually available? Conversely, was she telling him that should they become lovers, he could count on her fidelity? The workings of the female mind baffled Stuart.

Well, enough speculation concerning the Selwyns, he thought, and turned to papers from Blake's files. Using the photo-copied will, he prepared probate documents, though he couldn't present them to the court without the original attested will. That was unavailable until next week—presuming that it lay in Blake's safe deposit box. Blake's four insurance policies totaled $250,000, and for each he needed a certified death certificate. Mrs. Appleby volunteered to obtain them from the Rockville office of the medical examiner and to bring back Selwyn's Chrysler. Within a week or two, Stuart reflected, Diana would have a quarter of a million untaxable dollars at her disposal—prudently invested, a sum that would bring a reasonable income. Not that the widow needed money. The magnificence of her home and her family background suggested substantial affluence. Diana's net worth was at least on a par with that of other of his female clients; she just happened to be the youngest by a good many years.

Shortly after Mrs. Appleby's departure Stuart took delivery of an air-expressed communication from a lawyer in Springfield, Illinois—Harvey W. Scott, Esquire.

As Stuart opened the inner envelope a cashier's check fluttered onto his desk. It was made out to bearer in the sum of ten thousand dollars. A good introduction, Stuart thought, and turned to the letter with escalating interest:

> Dear Mr. Stuart:
>
> This communication to you complies with instructions from my late client, Blake F. Selwyn.
>
> The check is to facilitate any investigation you may care to conduct concerning the circumstances of Blake's death.
>
> The enclosed sealed envelope was entrusted to me by my late client, from whom I received verbal instructions to convey it to you in the event of his death. Its contents are unknown to me.
>
> As you may know, Blake was a native of this area. I was family attorney for many years and his untimely death is for me a matter of great sorrow.
>
> Sincerely,
> Harvey W. Scott

Stuart picked up the thick, letter-size envelope on which his name was printed. The other side was sealed with tape and dark red wax. He held it in his hand, anticipating an unwelcome message from the grave.

Mrs. Appleby had not yet returned from her Rockville mission, so he was alone in the office. Reluctantly, Stuart opened the envelope and spread out six handwritten, numbered pages. The first page began: "To Whom It May Concern."

As Stuart began reading, he remembered Diana's query as to whether Blake had left any papers or documents with him. Had she known of these pages, or was her question general? Had Diana been aware of Blake's unusual arrangements?

Blake had dated one communication beside his signature on the final page—five weeks before his death. Obviously, the man had long felt in personal danger.

The first two pages covered most of what Blake had told Stuart in the office. Page three cited instances in Geneva and Washington when Blake Selwyn believed U.S. disarmament positions compromised.

Either the Soviets are incredibly prescient or else they've acquired advance intelligence. I've voiced my concerns on numerous occasions, though until now I've never named the officer on whom my suspicions unavoidably fall. Imprudently I shared my suspicions with this officer before becoming convinced that he is the one responsible for revealing our secret positions to the Soviets, who use that information to drive harder bargains and extract greater concessions from our negotiating team.

Stuart turned to page three, where Selwyn continued:

The reader will understand, I trust, that I have been unwilling to take my findings to the security office or the FBI because I lack one "smoking gun." Circumstances over the past two years, however, point to my chief, Assistant Secretary Rolf Kingman, as the sole officer with access to the complete range of our office's classified memoranda and position papers. Moreover, Kingman's official status, his access to our working papers, and his wide contacts with members of the Soviet delegation in Geneva and their Washington embassy's second secretary, Yuri Bendikov, combine to point directly to him.

On numerous occasions at Washington social gatherings I've noticed Kingman and Bendikov talking privately. By itself this would be unremarkable, except that FBI information identifies Bendikov as major or lieutenant colonel with the KGB.

Anyone familiar with inner workings at State will realize that to come forward with unsubstantiated charges reflecting on the loyalty of a superior would be to commit career suicide. It may be that in the future I will be able to obtain proof, in which case I will take the information to investigative authorities and this blind narrative will become superfluous—*caput mortuum.*

I must note further that Rolf Kingman maintains cordial relations with former ambassador Edward Beamish, who is employing his U.S. strategic disarmament policy experience to propagandize public opinion in favor of U.S. unilateral disarmament. Department records will show that Kingman was a favored protégé of Beamish while the latter occupied what is now Kingman's position. I have personal knowledge of the fact that Kingman has attended several Passage meetings at which Beamish was the speaker. As the officer in charge of key matters regarding our staged disarmament policy, Kingman might well be thought to be keeping informed on our domestic opposition. But the degree of cordiality—even intimacy—between Kingman and Beamish is something I find highly suspect. The relationship gives off an odor of treason on Kingman's part.

I must include two related matters that have come to my attention, although I am without proof. I believe my office and home telephones have been tapped. And for some weeks I have felt myself under sporadic surveillance, and so have concluded that a hostile organization is looking for opportunity to still my voice.

This narrative, then, is directed to someone, not yet chosen by me, to examine closely the circumstances of my death and, in any event, to press the proper authorities to make Rolf Kingman the target of a thorough security investigation.

Stuart put down the pages, noticing that his hands were clammy. He left the desk and walked to the window overlooking the Potomac. He felt as though Selwyn's hand had gripped him from the grave. But what Blake wrote was no spirit message, it was as real as the cars and trucks rumbling over Key Bridge, the tall office buildings rising from Rosslyn. High above them a plane banked toward National Airport. Stuart turned back to his desk, picked up the check, and fingered it briefly. A decision was being forced on him, but he wanted more information first.

He dialed the Springfield lawyer's office, gave his name, and said he was calling from Washington. Presently a deep, tired-sounding voice said, "I'm Harvey Scott, Mr. Stuart. How can I help you?"

"I'm not sure, sir, but I feel I should talk with you."

"Concerning my communication, I assume."

"That's right."

"I know you Washington lawyers charge a lot, but if the fee is not sufficient—"

"Oh, it's satisfactory," Stuart broke in, "and that's not an issue. Before I undertake our client's request I need information regarding the circumstances behind it."

"I'm afraid I can't help you there. I have no knowledge of what may have been asked of you. My function was merely to serve as a conduit, you understand."

"Still, you may have some collateral information, and I'd very much appreciate it if you'd see me."

"I'm afraid I haven't the time or strength to travel to Washington," Scott said, "so you'd have to come out here—even though I doubt I could add anything to what you may already know. Can't we confer by phone?"

"I don't feel that's a good idea under the circumstances,"

Stuart told him, "and since I've been paid in advance I feel obliged to follow through. Also, the client's widow has retained me to represent the estate, so my obligation is dual."

"In that case, I'll certainly see you. When were you thinking of coming?"

"Will tomorrow be okay?"

"It will be. Now, I'm not familiar with aircraft schedules in and out of our little city, but I believe there are connecting flights from both St. Louis and Chicago. So if you'll give me your itinerary I'll have you met. Or you may come directly to my office"—he paused—"less than a block from where Lincoln practiced law."

"Thank you, sir. See you tomorrow."

Opening his door Stuart saw that his secretary had not yet returned. He went back to his desk, folded the holographic sheets, and returned them to their envelope, which he placed in the safe. The check and Scott's transmittal letter he left on his desk.

His travel agency was on the building's ground level. One of the amiable young women fed his proposed itinerary into her desk computer and in a few moments told Stuart he could leave National at 11:00, change planes in St. Louis, and arrive in Springfield at 3:15. "Will that be satisfactory?" she asked.

"Fine. How about returning tomorrow evening?"

Consulting the computer again, she said he could either leave Springfield at 6:00 and return by way of Chicago, or depart at 8:00 via St. Louis. He asked her to confirm the earlier flight, put him on standby for the later one, and phone his office when the tickets were ready.

Mrs. Appleby was now at her desk, taking copies of Selwyn's death certificate from an envelope. Looking up, she said, "The car is in that parking garage on Pennsylvania just beyond the Parkway Bridge. I put five gallons in the tank."

Stuart thanked her and asked her to begin processing the four life insurance claims, a procedure she was familiar with. Rather than bother Diana with such lugubrious details, he'd sign the claims as her attorney.

Next he gave Mrs. Appleby the cashier's check for deposit and handed her Scott's letter, saying he would be flying to Springfield and could be reached through Scott, if necessary.

"Will you be away long, Mr. Stuart?"

"Back tomorrow night."

The telephone rang, and Stuart took the call in his office. It was Diana, saying, "I'd hoped you might come out today, Alan. Last night I made an utter fool of myself and I wanted to apologize in person."

"I was so sleepy that I don't remember what you said," he lied, "so there's nothing to talk about. But I do need to go over a few things with you—I'm leaving town tomorrow—so if you're free I'll stop by before five."

"I'll expect you—and I'm grateful for your courteous and convenient amnesia."

The hold button was blinking as he hung up. Harvey Scott's secretary wanted to know if their meeting could be postponed until Monday. A glance at his calendar told Stuart that by advancing one appointment he could accommodate Scott's request, so he asked his secretary to change his flight schedule accordingly. That gave him the rest of the weekend to himself, to resume his normal pursuits. Sunday afternoon he might take Prudy and Greg to the National Zoo, giving their nanny a few hours off.

Physically he had safeguarded Selwyn's confidences, but what was he going to do about their substance? Because Selwyn hadn't confided in his wife about the Springfield lawyer, Stuart felt no obligation to do so yet. Besides, Harvey Scott might be able to throw enough light on the whole matter to guide him.

On impulse he dialed Diana Selwyn. "If it's not inappropriate, would you consider having dinner with me? I know several places out your way where we could dine quietly and unobtrusively, if you'd care to."

"I'd like that very much," she said. "Hypocritically playing the grief-prostrated widow isn't at all what I have in mind. So we'll have drinks here and go on to dinner. Thank you, Alan."

As he locked up, Stuart reflected that only a week ago Blake Selwyn had left his home for the final time and driven off to a waiting fate. Now his files were organized and current, and his wife was adjusting remarkably to widowhood.

Stuart walked home and looked up the phone number of Cortland Barnes, an older friend who had been involved in arms control during a previous administration. "Corty, I've got a couple of quick questions for you if you've got a moment."

"Sure, but we're on our way out. How can I help you?"

"Were you with State's Bureau of Disarmament Affairs?"

"No, I was at the Arms Control and Disarmament Agency, an independent body, but personnel flowed back and forth between us and State."

"You knew Blake Selwyn?"

"From meetings and conferences. You know how it goes."

"Rolf Kingman?"

"The same. Are you thinking of getting into that racket?"

"Not exactly. You must have known Ambassador Beamish?"

"Ed? Yes, he was in on everything, and I mean everything. Very jealous of State's turf. Did all he could to lobby against our agency's existence. Now that he's outside he's continuing his crusade. I suppose you've heard of Passage?"

"My sister, Pat Brigham, told me about it. She's an enthusiast, but before joining I thought I'd sniff around."

"Lot of prominent people involved," Barnes commented, "but two years of trying to outmaneuver the Russians taught me there are no easy solutions, least of all unilaterally disarming."

"That's pretty much my opinion," Stuart agreed, "and I won't keep you any longer. Many thanks, Corty."

Hanging up, he made a mental note that Barnes was a potential source on the principal players in Blake Selwyn's drama. Or was it all a charade?

He shaved, changed, and drove his Audi to the Selwyn home.

* * *

Diana had ice and glasses ready in the sun-room. She was wearing a gunmetal-gray silk dress, pearls, and her diamond engagement ring. Her wedding ring, Stuart noticed, was absent.

After preparing their drinks, Stuart retrieved Selwyn's insurance policies from the file, explaining to Diana that they were needed to process her claim as beneficiary. "I won't be leaving town until Monday, so I'll have to postpone our Tuesday bank appointment to another time."

"Will you be gone long?"

"Just overnight."

"Does your work bring much travel?"

"Rarely," he said. "Has State sent over Blake's personal papers?"

"Someone phoned to say I could expect them next week." She sipped from her glass. "Something there you need?"

"No, just curious."

She smiled. "That's rather a characteristic of yours, Alan—curiosity. Of course, the way I've been pouring out my heart to you sort of eliminates your need to ask questions."

"Then I'll ask one now: what are your immediate plans?"

"You mean . . . after dinner?"

"No—next week, the week after. Will you stay here or go away?"

"I've been wondering about that. Considering a cruise, for one thing. But I should visit my father soon. Since mother died he's been spending most of his time in Jamaica—we have a bungalow on the north side of the island. He didn't attend Blake's funeral because his arthritis is getting worse and a synthetic hip joint isn't working out as expected. He's lonely and I know he misses me."

"Then you should certainly go. And if you'll have your maid let me in occasionally, I can finish up while you're away."

"Nothing more for me to sign?"

"Your power of attorney covers everything."

She sighed. "You've relieved me of so much that I was concerned about. I'm glad you're my lawyer and I'm grateful for everything you're doing."

"Wait'll you get the bill."

"Whatever you charge, it's worth it."

He sat down across from her. "I haven't had time to go over Blake's investment portfolio, and I don't know that you want me to. Are you satisfied with your financial advisor?"

"Blake always dealt with him. Why, something wrong?"

"No reason to think so," he said, "but while you're away something important might happen—a market plunge, for instance—so you ought to have confidence in whatever protective moves he makes."

"You're so right." She sipped more of her drink. "What do you recommend?"

"Nothing, until I can compare your portfolio's performance with a market standard."

"Then I'd like you to, Alan."

The cordless phone rang. Presently she said, "No, Edward, I'm dining with a friend . . . Monday evening?" She covered the mouthpiece and said to Stuart, "You'll be away?" He nodded and she told her caller that Monday dinner would be fine. "Doing pretty well, considering. I don't believe in suttee." She replaced the phone and shrugged. "Ambassador Beamish, an old friend of Blake. Perhaps you know him."

"I don't, but Pat does."

"Of course—the Sulgrave affair. I suppose Edward believes strongly in his cause or he wouldn't have organized Passage. And it makes him feel he's still part of the national affairs scene. Rolf Kingman succeeded him at State, you know."

Stuart nodded. "Were Blake and Kingman on friendly terms?"

"As far as I know. Rolf came to the funeral, and he's making arrangements for Monday's memorial at the cathedral. I can't say they were close, but then Blake seldom commented on office matters to me." She smiled briefly. "My husband was as secretive as you are curious—I'll have to get used to the change."

They dined at Chez Tante Marie, a small restaurant near the Maryland line owned and managed by a middle-aged French couple. The menu and wine list bore no prices, effectively discouraging budget diners. The couple's daughter and son-in-law waited tables with calm efficiency, and there was no overly friendly "Enjoy your meal" when dinner was served.

Afterward, at her door, Diana invited Stuart to share a nightcap. "It's early and the servants are off until Monday."

Stuart hesitated before taking her key and unlocking the door.

While he was pouring Hine cognac into two small snifters, Diana put on a Debussy record and came over to sit beside him on the sofa. "I'm really grateful for your company, Alan. This is a big house, and even while Blake was alive I was often lonely. Now, even more so." She touched her glass to his and sipped thoughtfully, then asked if he and Pat had other siblings.

"Just the two of us," he said, "and we've been lifelong friends."

"My younger brother, Peter, was a wonderful boy. Three years ago he was killed hang gliding near Big Sur. Within the year my mother died—now Blake." She faced Stuart. "It's been one tragedy after another. In a way I've gotten used to death, but not to the loneliness that follows. I'm thirty now, Alan, and I need happiness to fill the void." Her hand touched his and her head moved to his shoulder. He kissed her forehead, and her face lifted until their lips met. At first hers were cool, then they warmed and her mouth opened on his. As his tongue felt the velvety touch of hers, her torso turned and one hand pressed the back of his head.

"I suppose you know what you're doing to me?" Stuart said.

"You're so ethical," she murmured, "I knew I'd have to make the first move. I need you, Alan, and I'd like you to stay tonight."

"I've wanted you," he said tightly, "since the first time I saw your face."

"I've thought of you, too—often. Wondering if my lawyer could be my lover."

"If no one knows."

"Trust me," she whispered, "as I trust you." Then she led him up the broad staircase to a thoroughly feminine room. She lighted a candle and undressed beside it while Alan, a lump in his throat, shed his clothing beside the wide bed.

Then she was in his arms, her small nipples hard against his chest, breathing fast as her body trembled. Without breaking their embrace Stuart lifted her to the bed. He saw the candlelight reflecting in her eyes. Diana moaned, her arms tightened around him, and her thighs went slack. He made love to her tenderly and completely, bringing her to climax after shuddering climax in shared ecstasy. Utterly relaxed they fell asleep in each other's arms.

During the night he was vaguely aware that she left for a while, then returned and pillowed her head on his shoulder. Fresh perfume, the soft scent of lilacs, reminded him of the garden in his boyhood home. Before sleep returned, Stuart realized he could easily fall in love with this intelligent, passionate woman.

Diana made a late breakfast for them in the empty kitchen: ham-and-cheese omelet, biscuits and honey, and aromatic Venezuelan coffee. Before getting out of bed they had made love again, and both were as avid for food as they had been for each other just an hour before.

When he told her his plans to take his niece and nephew to the zoo that afternoon Diana offered to come too. She needed the air, to be out in the bright world among people instead of being cloistered in a silent house. He admitted that he'd hoped she'd come and said he would pick her up at two. Driving back to Georgetown, Stuart reflected on the unexpected, marvelous night, and wondered how far their new understanding would lead.

After unlocking his front door, Stuart crossed through the living room and stopped in shock at the library door.

Books pulled from their shelves lay heaped on the carpeting. File folders had been raped, their contents scattered. His mouth went dry.

CHAPTER 6

Stuart went from room to room checking the silver, paintings, and other valuables, but none had been taken by the burglars. Not even the liquor cabinet had been tampered with, nor the VCR or the CD player. Bedrooms and baths were untouched, except that a night table drawer was partly open, revealing his Browning 9-mm pistol. Strange thieves, he reflected.

He went downstairs and through the kitchen to the rear door, where crowbar marks on the wood jamb showed how entry had been gained. He reached for the wall phone to call the Seventh Precinct, then figured that it would be a waste of time. He could report nothing stolen or damaged. The police would write it off as vandalism, tell him he was lucky; in Georgetown there were half a dozen incidents every night.

Instead he called Diana, who offered to come over immediately.

"I was hoping you'd lend a hand," he said gratefully, "—and you didn't even wait to be asked. Love that volunteer spirit."

"Only natural—after all, we've become close friends, haven't we?"

"Closest possible," he agreed. "I think we can get things straightened up and still give the children a good afternoon."

"I'm on my way."

She was there in twenty minutes, and together they replaced books on their shelves in order to get at the masses of scattered papers. Stuart laid empty file folders on every flat surface, then he and Diana began restoring order.

As she knelt beside him she asked, "Any idea what the thieves were looking for?"

"Not the faintest," he lied. "Unless they thought they might find cash or negotiable bonds, maybe a cache of gold coins. In Georgetown everything goes and is seldom seen again, so I feel lucky. Not even my pistol was stolen."

"How odd," she murmured. "Unless they were frightened away."

"Could be, but we'll never know."

"I suppose it happened last night while—we were together. Now, if you'd been here instead, you might have been attacked and injured."

"I've thought of that," he admitted. "It's incredible the way good things come to pass. Convinces me that last night was intended to be."

"And you'll never berate me for—seducing you?"

He laughed and kissed the side of her face. "Lovely word, proper and erotic. No, my dear, ignition was spontaneous."

She sat back, crossed her legs and rubbed her knees. "I like your home," she said, "—except for this mess you're not responsible for. Do you have someone to keep things tidy?"

"Every few days a woman comes in to clean up, change the bed, do laundry and ironing."

"Alan, this is the first time I've been in a bachelor's place since I was married—quite a long time ago. It's a strange, almost illicit feeling. Even my toes are tingling."

"Even though you slept with me last night?"

"That was *my* place." She touched his nose. "Familiar and

safe. You arrived as my invited guest, left as my invited lover." She kissed his lips lingeringly. "I'll never forget. Never."

"Nor will I. And I cherish the memory." He took her hand but she withdrew it. "To work, to work, or we'll never get finished."

Another hour and it was done. While coffee filtered Stuart showed her through the house. "I'd offer lunch but I really recommend the zoo's hot dogs, and so do Pat's children. They'll eat at least two apiece, plus Cokes and candy."

"I'll try to restrain myself, but my new feeling of becoming my own person again may make me irresponsible. As my lawyer, please help me avoid excesses."

"I promise."

After calling the children's nanny to say they'd be there in half an hour, Stuart tilted a chair under the kitchen door knob though he realized that a determined thief would have no trouble getting in.

Back in the living room, Diana was scanning the photos and paintings on the walls. "Such a determinedly masculine atmosphere—it's as though no female has ever been here."

"A few," he admitted, "but very few, and very transient. So, if what you've been hinting at is do I have a current 'relationship,' the answer is no."

"Am I that transparent, dear?"

"'Fraid so. But may it always be thus."

They took both cars, and after making introductions to the nanny and the children—Diana was "a friend of Mother's"—they drove out to the zoo. Prudy rode in Diana's sleek little Mercedes roadster, while Gregory was snugly buckled into the Audi. Before reaching the zoo, Greg asked. "Uncle Alan, are you going to marry that lady?"

"The subject hasn't come up. Think I should?"

"She's very beautiful and I like her voice. Besides, she and

Mom know each other, and you could come to the house more often."

"Would you like that?"

"I always like it when you come. Dad's away so much that—" The boy stopped, but Stuart could see that his face was troubled, so he said, "Your father works very hard to make a good life for all of you."

"I know," Greg said after a while. "Mom tells me that, but I wish he didn't have to work *so* hard—then I could see him more." His face looked up at his uncle. "Did you see Grandpa Stuart all the time when you were a boy?"

"A lot," Stuart replied. "He was a surgeon but he didn't have all the different responsibilities your father has. Anyway, that was, oh, twenty years ago, and the world didn't move so fast then. Things seemed simpler," he reflected, "and families saw more of one another."

Greg nodded. "Mom says that too. Uncle Alan, if you and that lady get married and have children they'd be my cousins, wouldn't they?"

"Prudy's, too," he nodded. "But I've only known Mrs. Selwyn a week."

"How long does it take?"

He looked over at his nephew and laughed at the shrewdness of the young. "Good question, and I don't know the answer."

As always, the zoo's panda quarters attracted the largest crowd, but the children liked the miniature horses too, and the monkey cage. Prudy cringed from the reptiles while Greg made ugly faces at them and stuck out his tongue.

Stuart was glad of Diana's company. She had an easy, natural manner with the children, and as they strolled the grounds Stuart felt that they made a handsome-looking family. At the snack bar they bought foot-long hot dogs estimated by Stuart at no more than nine inches, slathered then with ketchup, relish, and mustard.

"Delicious," Diana declared. "I don't know why I don't eat here all the time."

"Because it closes at dark," Prudy instructed, "and you'd never get any dinner."

"Or breakfast," Greg added. "On one meal a day you'd get skinny and die. You're too young to die."

"Why, thank you," she said with a small curtsy. "I agree."

Stuart patted his nephew's shoulder. "You're getting pretty opinionated for your age," he remarked, "—and very personal."

"But he was complimenting me," Diana objected, "and I like compliments from a handsome young man." Bending over, she planted a kiss on his forehead. "Thank you, Greg. Your uncle is very tight with compliments. He could learn from you."

"And will," Stuart vowed. "Okay, use your napkins, kids, get all that goop off your chops, and we'll move on."

"Cokes," Prudy demanded.

"Next stop. Surely you don't think I'd forget?"

After returning Greg and Prudy to their nanny, Diana said, "If there's anything to eat at your place I'll make dinner. Otherwise, let's buy out Joe's Delicatessen and picnic at home."

"Not much in my freezer, I'm afraid."

From the deli they carried off a tub of potato salad, rye and black bread, sliced turkey, ham, tongue, and spiced beef. Diana set the table and Stuart poured chilled rosé. After taking a sip she said, "It was a wonderful afternoon, Alan, and I needed it, I really did. Pat's children are absolute charmers, and I thoroughly enjoyed them—made me feel young again."

"Young? You're barely out of pigtails."

"That's nice of you to say. And you're only—what?—two years older. But you've done so much with your life, in contrast to mine."

"There's a lot ahead of you," he reassured her. "And as for investing my years wisely, I've often wished I hadn't stayed so long at State."

"Why?"

"No feeling of accomplishment—but I guess all big bureaucracies are like that. In the army at least I was learning things every day. State was just a dead end." He crunched down on a thick combination sandwich. "To be successful you have to like your work—as Blake did. I could never whip up any enthusiasm over foreign affairs. Just wasn't my bag."

"And your—wife?"

"She adored the social side of State, but I found it pretty dull."

"So did I. But that was part of an unspoken contract with my husband, so I tried to do all the right things." She looked away. "Blake said it helped with promotions and I suppose it did, but there was nothing in it for me. Alan,"—she stretched out her hand to touch his fingers—"after last night and today I realize I've been emotionally dead for years. You wakened me, and I'm grateful. I don't know how things will turn out between us, but I don't want to monopolize your life just now. We both need space, time . . . do you understand?"

"I do," he said, "and without monopolizing you I want to see a lot of you—after office hours."

She spent the night with him, sharing the bed he had only rarely shared with others, and to Stuart their lovemaking was even more thrilling than the night before. Soon after dawn she dressed, touched up her makeup, and called softly from the doorway, "I'll miss you while you're gone. Call me when you return?"

"You know I will." They kissed and she was gone, the soft whisper of her feet on the stairs lingering in his mind.

By nine he was at the office, bringing along a small overnight bag for his Springfield trip. When Mrs. Appleby brought the airline tickets to his desk he asked her to get a *Blue Book* appraisal for Selwyn's Chrysler and to advertise it for sale. Before leaving Georgetown, Stuart crossed over to the Riggs branch and left

Selwyn's communication in his safe deposit box, having concluded that it—or something similar—was what his house had been searched for. The implication was that either his office phone was tapped or a watcher had seen Scott's express mail envelope delivered to him. Maybe both.

He took a taxi to National Airport and read a paperback and dozed on the flight to St. Louis. From there he took a short hop to Springfield on a Britt Air commuter plane.

No one met him, so Stuart taxied to Scott's office on Adams, facing Capitol Plaza. He went up a flight of worn wooden stairs to the numbered door on the second floor.

HARVEY W. SCOTT, ATTORNEY-AT-LAW read the chipped gilt legend. Below it a cardboard sign was lettered CLOSED, and centered on the oaken door was a black crepe bow.

His pulse raced as his flesh grew cold.

He knocked on the door, heard the sounds echo within, and looked around. The adjacent office was open, so he asked the receptionist there if she knew why Scott's office was closed.

"Unfortunately, Mr. Scott was killed in an automobile accident last night," she said. "It was horrible . . . horrible. And he was *such* a nice man, too." Swallowing, she looked at Stuart. "You're a friend of his?"

"I wanted to be," he replied tightly, "but I never had a chance." Picking up his bag he walked down the staircase into the bright afternoon sun. The air was warm but his skin felt clammy. Fear began to sink tentacles into his mind as he realized that at every step, Blake's apprehensions were proving valid. There *was* a conspiracy, and now he, Alan Stuart, was lethally involved.

CHAPTER 7

*T*he story was front page news in the Springfield paper, the *State Journal-Register*. Stuart read it in The Feed Store, a handsome soup-and-sandwich restaurant facing the old capitol building, a few steps from Lincoln and Herndon's law offices on Sixth. Scott's photograph showed a gray-haired man with an open, rectangular face, wire-rimmed glasses, and a bow tie.

The story, headed "Road Accident Claims Life of Prominent Attorney," read:

Harvey Winston Scott, a prominent citizen, onetime mayor, and lifelong resident of Springfield, was killed last night when his automobile veered off Interstate 55 near Jerome and crashed into an abutment. Preliminary indications are that the attorney, 74, may have suffered a heart attack, causing the fatal accident. Scott, a graduate of the University of Illinois, received his law degree from the University of Chicago in 1939. During World War II, Mr. Scott was a member of the army's Judge Advocate General Corps, serving at Fort Sill, Oklahoma, and with the Third

Army in Europe. He was discharged with the rank of lieutenant colonel.

Returning to Springfield in 1946, Scott engaged in the practice of civil law, representing, among other well-known clients, the late Governor Adlai Stevenson. Active in civic and in Republican party affairs, Mr. Scott entered politics as a Springfield city councilman and three years later was elected mayor of Springfield for a two-year term. His only son, Winston, was killed during the Vietnam conflict, and his wife, the former Mary Emma Bates of Peoria, died in 1982. There are thought to be no other living relatives. Services will be announced later by the Jorgenson Funeral Home.

Paying for his coffee, Stuart asked directions to police headquarters. Carrying his bag and the folded newspaper, he walked there, entered the courthouse by the marked entrance, and found himself in a stone-floored reception room. There were benches, a wooden railing, and a desk with several telephones. Behind it sat a uniformed policeman wearing sergeant's stripes. Stuart gave him his card and asked to speak with whoever had investigated Scott's accident.

The sergeant eyed the card. "You come all the way from Washington to investigate? You with an insurance company or something?"

"We shared a client," Stuart explained, "and there was an estate matter to discuss."

"Nice man, Mr. Scott. The governor offered him a judgeship but he wouldn't take it."

"Wonder why not?"

"Said he was too old, the bench needed younger men. Anyway, after his son was MIA Mr. Scott sort of lost heart. I guess living alone, no wife or nothing, takes it out of a man."

"I'm sure it does. So—is the accident investigator around?"

"Should be. Lieutenant Parmisano." He punched a phone button, spoke inaudibly, and said to Stuart, "The Loo says you can go back—second door on the left." He handed back Stuart's card.

Stuart entered a neat, recently painted office, gave his name to the man seated behind the butt-burned desk, and shook his hand briefly. After examining Stuart's card Parmisano asked, "You handling the insurance?"

"No. I came here on behalf of a client we had in common, went to Scott's office, and saw the black bow." He tapped his newspaper. "Were you the first on the scene?"

"The ambulance and paramedics were already there. No skid marks on the highway—car just went off the road and slammed into a big concrete abutment. Car was totaled." He sighed and rubbed the stubble on his chin. "If Mr. Scott wasn't dead before he hit, the crash woulda done it. Chest all caved in, skull bashed pretty good."

Stuart considered the gruesome information. "Was he wearing a seat belt?"

Parmisano rubbed his chin again. "Sounds like an insurance-type question, Mr.—Stuart," he said, glancing again at the card. "Sure you're not investigating his death?"

"No, Lieutenant. I'm curious because I came here on a fruitless mission and I'm irritated because Mr. Scott's secretary didn't bother to phone me to cancel. I've got time to kill before my return flight to Washington, and as long as I'm here I'm anticipating questions our—now my—client will probably ask."

"Sorry," Parmisano said, and reached for the telephone, asking for the paramedic's office. "Parmisano here—that you, Mike? Okay, answer me this: when you found Mr. Scott's car, was he wearing a seat belt? Umm . . . I see. Well, thanks."

Shaking his head he replaced the receiver. "Seems he wasn't, Mr. Stuart, not that he'd have survived if he had. But I have to wonder why a man as old and careful as Mr. Scott wouldn't give himself that edge."

"No one expects death," Stuart remarked. "I suppose his secretary is pretty broken up, but before I leave Springfield I'd like a few words with her—about files and such."

Parmisano nodded. "That'd be Milly Richardson—been long years with her boss, even when he was mayor. Old and crotchety, but take it easy with her and you'll get what you want." He opened a phone book, traced the columns with a finger, and wrote down an address and phone number. "She's out East Lawrence—lives alone. I suggest you call first. It's a dollar ride by taxi."

After thanking the lieutenant, Stuart walked out to a pay phone and dialed the secretary's number. When an uncertain voice answered, Stuart identified himself and extended his condolences.

After a moment Milly spoke up. "I clear forgot to phone you, Mr. Stuart, and I'm real sorry you had to make the trip for nothing. But I was just beside myself with grief—still am. Mr. Scott . . ."—her voice quavered—"was such a fine man, and a thoughtful employer as well."

"If it's not asking too much, could you spare me a few minutes before I leave town?"

"I . . . I guess so, but I don't know what you want to talk about. And my home is a mess—haven't turned a hand to anything since . . . I heard." She sniffled.

"I'll be there shortly," Stuart said. "And thank you."

"It's the least I can do to make up for your inconvenience."

Milly lived on the second floor of an old house converted into two apartments. Stuart walked up the outside staircase and was admitted by a white-haired lady whose reddened eyes peered from behind thick, gold-rimmed lenses. She wore a long, flowered housecoat and bedroom slippers. "Would you like a cup of tea?"

"Thanks, but I don't want to trouble you, I want to make this as brief as possible."

"Then what can I tell you? I suppose Mr. Jared Wilson will be taking over our files and clients, few though they were."

"Is there a file for Blake Selwyn?"

She shook her head. "There was an old file, long retired, but it concerned his mother and father. The son was never a real client.

Last month or so he wrote Mr. Scott and phoned two or three times, but that was all."

Stuart cleared his throat. "Our appointment was postponed until today. Do you have any idea why?"

She looked down at her gnarled, blue-veined hands and fidgeted with them. "All I know is that Mr. Scott told me something had come up and he'd have to take care of it—whatever it was—before he saw you. So I called your office to arrange the appointment for today. Please forgive me for not canceling."

"Do you know what it was that made Mr. Scott postpone A phone call? A visitor?"

"It was after a phone call, yes. I was changing a typewriter ribbon and Mr. Scott picked up the phone himself."

"You heard the conversation?"

"No. He was in his office, and I just saw that he'd answered. I don't know who the caller was or what it was about. Then a few minutes later he told me to get in touch with your office and set up another convenient time."

"Was he upset, agitated?"

"Not as I recall—but then he spoke by intercom, so I couldn't see his face." Her voice quavered, her shoulders hunched forward, and she began to sob. In a few moments she dried her eyes, saying, "And I'll never see his face again."

"I wish I'd had a chance to know him." Stuart said soothingly. "From all accounts he was a fine man and an outstanding member of the bar."

"That he was. And he admired Mr. Lincoln as much as I do."

"I suppose he was a careful driver, too. I mean, he always wore a seat belt, didn't he?"

"Oh, he insisted on it—wouldn't even start the engine until I was buckled in like he was. Always said, Mr. Scott did, that seat belts would save more lives if only people would use them. I'm sure he was wearing his when he . . . ."

"I'm afraid he wasn't. Do you happen to know what he was

doing driving on the interstate? Visiting someone? Seeing a client? Attending a meeting?"

"Well, most Saturday nights Mr. Scott just stayed home and watched TV. He was gradually getting out of legal work, if you know what I mean. What he did for Mr. Selwyn was just an accommodation because of his family. He wasn't taking on new clients"—she blotted her eyes again—"almost as though he was preparing himself to meet Mary Emma and Winston again, now that I think of it."

"Was he in good health?"

"Oh, he suffered arthritic hands—we all do at our age—but if you mean his heart, why it was strong as Bull Durham's." She leaned forward, hands knotted together. "Which is why I have to wonder about a heart attack."

"What else could it have been?"

"Why a stroke—cerebral spasm. Could have struck him blind, paralyzed him, and he just let go the wheel." She drew in a deep breath. "I'd rather think he died before his car hit instead of getting all smashed and torn up . . . hurting . . ." She began to sob again.

Stuart got up. "It was good of you to see me, Miss Richardson, and if you ever find out just why Mr. Scott changed our appointment or where he was driving that night, I'd appreciate your calling me."

She looked up with blank, hopeless eyes. "I will—if anything comes to mind. But the—"

"Someone might phone you or drop by—you never know."

"He'll be missed," she said to the room. "Missed by everyone, especially me." Her angular Adam's apple bobbed. "I loved Harvey—but he never knew."

Stuart patted the old woman's shoulder and left the way he had come, reflecting moodily on the similarities between Scott's death and Selwyn's.

Had Scott been killed in some manner, with the killer

neglecting to replace the seat belt? In Europe seat belts were not compulsory. In Russian-built cars were they even available?

At the airport he had time to phone Diana. "I'm out in the Midwest and I'll be back tonight."

"Well, that's good news."

"I thought—just in case your dinner date . . . ah . . . canceled or something, we might—"

"It's very much on, Alan, and I'm sure you wouldn't ask me to break it."

"Well, no," he said awkwardly. "Shall I phone you later?"

After a few moments' silence she said, "I don't think that's a good idea. It's been an exhausting day—the cathedral memorial service, you know—and seeing Blake's friends, making forced conversation . . . after dining with Edward I'm just going to go to bed."

"Okay," said Stuart. "I wasn't asking you to stand up Beamish."

"Since it's surfaced, Alan, I think we should understand each other. What's happened between us is wonderful, and I care for you a great deal. But I need to manage my freedom carefully . . . I'm not ready for a commitment—not yet. Please understand."

"I do," he said, an edge to his voice, "and I'll be sure you have the space you need. Call me when you want to see the zoo again."

He hung up, embarrassed at having misjudged their relationship so badly. He'd thought Diana would welcome him after spending hours with that windbag, Beamish. On the plus side, he wouldn't have to tell Diana about Scott's death and its parallels to Blake's—or what Blake had sent him via the Springfield lawyer. That eased his mind, and by the time he boarded the feeder flight to O'Hare he was resolved to give Diana Selwyn all the space and time she might want.

At his office the next morning Stuart was surprised to find a message from one Evan Powell, administrative assistant to Senator

Frank D. Chase. Stuart looked up Chase in the *Congressional Directory* and learned he had begun his government career as a foreign service officer, had been elected to Congress from Kentucky and served two terms, and had been appointed to the Senate fourteen years ago to fill a death-caused vacancy. Chase then had been reelected twice. He was a senior member of the Foreign Relations Committee and chairman of a subcommittee on NATO affairs.

Mrs. Appleby placed the call, and when Evan Powell came on the line he thanked Stuart for calling and asked, "Wonder if you'd find time to come by and see the senator today? He'd appreciate it."

"Can you give me an idea what he wants to discuss or does he just want to see what I look like?"

"Hardly that, sir, but the senator will doubtless unburden himself in private. Would three o'clock suit you?"

"Four would be better." Stuart's afternoon calendar showed no appointments but he didn't want to appear too available.

"Four it is," Powell said, "barring vote calls. And the senator thanks you in advance. Dirksen Building."

Stuart asked Mrs. Appleby to pull Mrs. Rumbolt's file. Her sister in Oregon had decided to contest the will of their recently deceased sister of Palm Beach, and Mrs. Rumbolt had requested Stuart's advice. He welcomed the diversion. He did have other clients, and until he could make another IRS appointment to open Blake's safe deposit box, he had no plans to see Diana Selwyn.

Never fuck a client was a law school maxim rooted in historical experience. Having violated it once, he wouldn't make the same mistake again.

Evan Powell was a rotund, pink-faced man in his late forties. His office was hung with diplomas, certificates of congressional appreciation, civic tributes, and photographs of himself—leaner and younger—shaking hands with the last four presidents and with famed congressional leaders. He was, Stuart thought, a stereotype of the outlander who had carved himself a Washington career by serving succeeding masters with devotion and protective concern.

Powell's blubbery lips enunciated carefully, "So, I read you're out of Princeton and GWU law. By way of State."

"That's right." Stuart looked at his wristwatch—4:00. "If the senator's tied up much longer we'll have to set another time."

"Roll call," said Powell blandly. "Another five minutes should do it. How long at State?"

"Close to five misspent years."

"Didn't like our wine-and-cheese brethren?"

"I felt there were more useful things I could be doing. How did the senator come across my name?"

Powell shrugged. "He'll probably tell you—don't know myself. You have any foreign clients? Represent any foreign countries or firms?"

"If I did you'd find me on the Foreign Agents Registration List, right?"

He shrugged again. "Asking's easier than checking the list. Married?"

"Are *you?*"

"One of my functions is to save the senator time. I ask questions he won't have to. The senator is incredibly busy these days—NATO is occupying much more of his time than he expected." He pursed his lips. "The Germans, you know—all set to cleanse their landscape of nuclear weapons and commence a never-ending love feast with the USSR. The ripple effect on other NATO countries—well, you can imagine."

"I don't follow foreign affairs."

"Hmm. Why not?"

"For years I tried to detect a consistent U.S. foreign policy. Finally I decided there is none. Not only are we a reactive country, any little Fourth World country that kicks Uncle Sam's ass can do it with impunity. Never any reprisals from the 'leader of the free world.'"

"Oh—" Powell started to object, but then the hall door opened and a large, gray-haired man strode in. "Stuart? Alan Stuart?" He thrust out a strong hand. "Forgive my tardiness. Come in and let's get to the point." He opened a polished mahogany door. "Please." To Powell he ordered, "Hold all calls."

Inside, the door closed on Powell, Senator Chase indicated a sofa to Stuart and then seated himself on the opposite side of the coffee table in a red leather chair. "Good of you to come," he said. "And because we're both busy, I'll get right to the point. In less than a week I have to be in Paris and Brussels to review the U.S. position vis-á-vis NATO and deal with our legislative counterparts in the alliance countries. Last weekend my legal counsel, Boyd Saunders, was hospitalized for an abdominal operation and can't accompany my subcommittee to Europe. I'd like you to go in his place." He glanced at a large wall calendar. "You'd be gone a week or ten days."

"Before I decide, Senator, how did you happen to settle on me?"

"Well, a computer search at State indicated you'd left to go into law. Your personnel file shows you speak French and some German, and because you were a State employee, updating your clearances quickly wouldn't be a problem." He got out a pipe and tobacco pouch, filled the bowl, and lighted it. Then he looked expectantly at Stuart, who said, "No personal recommendation?"

"It so happens," conceded Chase genially, exhaling blue smoke toward the air conditioner, "that a mutual friend mentioned your name to me not long before he died. I refer to Blake Selwyn. He and I had a cordial working relationship during his disarmament assignments. Further, we established a confidential relationship—if you grasp what I'm alluding to."

"I may," Stuart said. "But in what connection did Blake bring up my name?"

"I'd mentioned to him that Boyd was facing surgery and I might need a replacement on short notice. Blake told me he was thinking of retaining you in a highly confidential matter. I'm assuming that he did. "

"I'm representing his estate. "

"Beyond that?"

"Anything beyond that remains shielded by the lawyer-client relationship. "

"Just so," the senator said with an understanding nod. "Blake told me he had total confidence in your discretion and loyalty—two qualities essential in our committee work. Then he died unexpectedly—indeed prematurely—a victim of overwork, I presume. "

"So it appears," Stuart said, weighing the senator's proposal. A trip to Europe would be a welcome change from the usual routine, with the added advantage of placing him far from Diana. "How soon do you need an answer?"

"Now, if possible. Any trials set for next week?"

"I rarely appear in court," Stuart told him, "so that's not a factor. I'll have to consider client commitments and get back to you. "

"I'd appreciate your decision in the next few hours. If positive I need to start the clearance wheels in motion. Contrariwise, I'll need to engage other counsel. We'll fly from Andrews next Saturday or Sunday. If you come, I'll load you with committee material beforehand. Powell can tell you the pay arrangements, though Blake said you were pretty well fixed." He stood up. "I'll hear from you? The way bills are moving on the floor I doubt we'll adjourn short of midnight. "

"I'm flattered by your consideration, Senator," Stuart said. They shook hands and he left. As Stuart passed Powell's desk, the assistant looked at him expectantly. "Good night," Stuart said and left the senate office building.

Thin rain slicked the street as Stuart's taxi inched down Pennsylvania Avenue packed with homebound cars. A typical

Washington spring evening, Stuart reflected, mistily ambiguous. Would the rain become a torrent or would the clouds clear away and expose a radiant moon over the Federal City? An umbrella in his office would shield him on the walk home, but he hoped he wouldn't need it.

In Georgetown, traffic thickened, so Stuart got out short of Wisconsin Avenue and jogged to his office. No light showed—Mrs. Appleby had left for the day, taking advantage of his absence. He didn't blame her for that; it was customary to close early when there was rain.

He unlocked the door, pushed it open, and was reaching for the light switch when his ears registered a *whoosh!*. Something struck the side of his head, pain exploded through his skull, and his last sensation was that of falling into darkness.

CHAPTER 8

*E*ven when he opened his eyes darkness prevailed, bringing to Stuart's mind the black crepe bow on the Springfield lawyer's door. Where was he? Disoriented, he started to get up, but a bolt of pain lanced his head and he lay flat on the floor again.

Objects slowly took shape—Mrs. Appleby's desk, the sofa, a painting—but they seemed photographed through a dark filter. Indistinct.

He had been attacked, knocked out—but by whom? Where was he now? Listening, he heard only the usual sounds of M Street traffic. He couldn't lie there forever; he had to get up and do—what? He had some faint recollection of a senator . . . a trip somewhere . . .

Swallowing, Stuart eased himself up, his head aching abominably. For a while he let his system adjust to the altered flow of blood, and when the throbbing diminished somewhat, he gripped the edge of the desk and steadied himself to his feet with a grunt of pain. Nausea.

He turned on the overhead light, his eyes aching from the challenge. Closing them, he sat in the nearest chair, carefully touched the side of his head, felt swelling and the roughness of dried blood. He forced his breathing to regularize as he collected his thoughts.

Reaching for his secretary's appointment book, he looked at the pages without comprehension until he realized that he should be checking next week's appointments. One each on Monday, Wednesday, and Thursday, but these could be postponed. He seldom canceled, so he doubted that the three clients would mind.

Had he decided to accept the senator's commission? Senator . . . Chase, that was it. From Kentucky. NATO . . . German problem. Paris, Brussels . . . a week away. Why not?

For the first time he wished he kept liquor in the office. He walked slowly to the water cooler and drank thirstily. His lips were parched, throat dry. How much blood had he lost? The carpet showed a few drops, and he poured cold water on them.

If the file cabinet had been searched, as his library had been, this burglar was much tidier. The electronic typewriter hadn't been stolen, and his inner office looked just as it had when he left for the senate building. He eased himself into his chair and opened each desk drawer. As far as he could tell, nothing was missing.

Returning to the file cabinet, Stuart checked the Selwyn folder. Everything pertained to the estate and the widow-executrix, and everything was there.

Blake's handwritten letter was in Stuart's safe deposit box.

He returned the folder, closed the file drawer, and sipped more water. Was there a connection between his appointment with the senator and the burglary? Ridiculous; anyone wanting to get in without hindrance had only to watch him leave to go sculling on the weekends. But his trip to Springfield might have triggered this weekday break-in.

On his secretary's desk was a phone message timed 4:27 "Please call Mrs. Selwyn."

He crumpled the paper square, and dropped it into the wastebasket.

To hell with her. She needed space? So did he.

Walking slowly, unsteadily, Stuart went down to the street and got a taxi. The rain had stopped but the pavement was still slippery. The streetlights went on before the taxi let him out at the emergency entrance to George Washington Hospital. After filling out forms and presenting a credit card Stuart was led into a curtained examination room, where he waited for twenty minutes.

Finally a female physician came in, examined his contusion under an intense light, and pronounced that no stitches were needed. With antiseptic she cleaned away the matted blood and applied some antibiotic powder and a small bandage. When Stuart winced she asked, "How do you feel? Dizzy?"

"Weak," he answered, and she gave him two painkiller capsules. "What you need is rest. Keep your head elevated and tomorrow you'll feel a good deal better."

"Thanks, doctor." He swallowed one capsule before he left the hospital. Not up to walking the dozen blocks home he took a cab.

After turning on the living room lights Stuart made himself a drink, then checked the library. No repeat ransacking; today was his office's turn. Even though he felt it a futile gesture, Stuart phoned the Seventh Precinct and reported the break-in, without mentioning the assault.

"Anything stolen, sir?"

"Fortunately not. Mainly the office was ransacked."

"Kids, probably. Well, if nothing was taken . . ."

"Right. Just wanted to report for the record, help the crime statistics."

"That kind of help, sir, we just don't need. But thanks for calling."

Saying he'd been knocked out, injured, would have brought cops and questions, Stuart mused. Questions neither he nor the police could answer. His head ached. Hell of a thing.

The telephone rang. Automatically he reached for the receiver, then drew back. Whoever it was, he was in no shape to listen to client problems, especially if that client was Diana Selwyn. The phone rang eight times before subsiding into silence.

He put on a compact disc—Mahler's Eighth, London Symphony—and noticed that it was seven o'clock. Seated in a comfortable chair, he listened for a while before dialing Senator Chase's office.

When Evan Powell answered, Stuart gave his name and asked for the senator.

"He's on the floor," Powell said. "I'll give him any message."

"I'd rather talk with him," Stuart said, and gave Powell his phone number. Hanging up, he noticed a Kennedy Center ticket on his calendar pad. Tamara Gerasimova was dancing *Giselle*, but tonight he was too weak to attend. Besides, he'd seen the ballet a dozen times and Gerasimova was a second-rate danseuse. Bed was far preferable.

He made a second drink and carried it to his bedroom. He was getting into pajamas when the telephone rang again. It was Senator Chase. "Come to a decision?"

"I'll go with you, Senator."

"Excellent! Now, tomorrow evening at six I'm hosting—the subcommittee, that is, is hosting a reception here for some of the major players, and I'd like you to meet them before we converge in Brussels. There'll be people from State and the Disarmament Agency, some interested outsiders, and my colleagues. Will you be able to come?"

"I'll be there."

"Bring a lady if you want. There'll be drinks and a pretty fair buffet. Out by eight, if you have later plans."

Stuart said he'd be coming alone, hung up, and got into bed. Sleep came slowly, and toward midnight the pain returned. Stuart swallowed the second painkiller and slept restlessly the rest of the night.

In the morning a Senate messenger brought background reading material to Stuart's office and waited while he filled out an application for a diplomatic passport.

Through the intercom Mrs. Appleby said that Mrs. Selwyn was on the line. Reluctantly Stuart answered. "Are you avoiding me, Alan? I've called several times."

"I have other clients," he said rather stiffly, "and I was going to get to you when I could. What can I do for you?"

"For one thing, you can drop the hostility, however much you feel I deserve it. After that you can tell me if and when Blake's safe deposit box will be opened."

"I assure you," he said without changing his tone, "that when the IRS sets a time, I'll inform you. I'm anxious to have Blake's will for probate. Your insurance claims have been submitted and I imagine you'll receive checks this week. The Chrysler is being advertised for sale. Anything else?"

"Nothing . . . except to say that I'd hoped we could continue being friends."

"So had I," he said, "but that's not how things worked out. Incidentally, I'll be away for a week, but it shouldn't interfere with closing out Blake's estate."

"You won't relent, will you? Because I've injured your male pride. Well, I thought it was presumptuous of you to assume that I'd stand up Edward Beamish, even though I only accepted his invitation because you said you'd be away Monday night."

"I only called to determine if your date was still on." He paused. "And I had the distinct feeling that you welcomed the opportunity to distance yourself from me. Well, so be it."

"My, but you're thin-skinned. Get over it, Alan. Life's too short for childish games." The connection broke, and Stuart was left holding a humming receiver. He replaced it irritably, regretting having taken her call. Mentally, he closed the door on Diana Selwyn.

Turning to the Senate file, Stuart was dismayed to find its documents classified confidential or secret, although he had long been aware of such congressional casualness. At day's end he'd return the file to the senator's office, where regulation three-way combination safes would protect it overnight.

Early memoranda dated back to the time of Edward Beamish, transitioned into Rolf Kingman's incumbency, and contained material by Blake Selwyn. As Stuart read, he realized that Blake

had been wrong about one thing: others besides Rolf Kingman—
including Senators and their aides—had had easy access to these
papers.

Stuart recalled Senator Chase's veiled allusion to a "confidential relationship" with Selwyn, and decided to probe tactfully
when the opportunity arose.

Diana. Damn her, anyway. Throwing herself at him, then
pulling back. It was female privilege, of course, but he should have
been perceptive enough to anticipate her game. She, not he, was
the "childish" one.

Mrs. Ellery Throckmorton, a stooped old lady in dark crepe
de chine, a silver-headed cane clutched in her gnarled fingers,
arrived for her eleven o'clock appointment. A grandson had
displeased her by dropping out of Putney Academy, and Mrs. T.
wanted him eliminated from her will. As she sat, fingers clasping
and unclasping the polished rosewood cane, Stuart examined her
current will. The file was thick with codicils and amendments
reflecting Mrs. Throckmorton's vacillating attitudes toward relatives and descendants. Stuart said, "I thought you always held Tad
in high regard."

"I did, I did, I always did," she said tapping the cane
nervously, "but he's a wild one, Alan, and the Lord knows what
he'd do with all that money when he reaches eighteen. I've seen it
happen in other families. Let the lad make his way on his own."

Stuart sighed. No Throckmorton in the past four generations
had had to make it "on his own." "Perhaps Tad will straighten up
to your satisfaction—he's only fifteen, after all, and boys are often
wild, so—"

"Were *you* wild, Alan?" She peered at him intently.

He laughed. "I was far from saintly at that age, and that's the
point I'm making. One term at St. Mark's I was close to expulsion.
My father came up for a tough talk with me and I got religion." He
paused. "Tad doesn't have a father, Mrs. Throckmorton."

"No," she agreed in a distant voice, "that's true. My son never
returned from Vietnam—still missing in action."

"It's hard on a boy," Stuart pointed out, "—hard if he's sensitive and away from home. May I make a suggestion? Landon and St. Alban's are fine local schools. Tad could attend either while living at home. That way he'd have emotional support from his mother and you."

A tear made its way down her wrinkled cheek. She dabbed at it with a tiny embroidered handkerchief and looked away. "Would you arrange it, Alan? I'll talk to his mother, who I'm sure will agree." She swallowed. "Tad's a good boy, really. I shouldn't have gotten so upset, but . . . it's a failing of age, I'm afraid." She pried herself up with the cane. "Thank you, Alan. I'll have his mother get in touch with you very soon."

He closed the Throckmorton file. "I'll look forward to seeing her—and Tad."

In the outer office her chauffeur took over. When she was outside the office, Stuart turned to his secretary. "Funny—I counsel forgiveness, but don't seem to exercise it myself."

Mrs. Appleby glanced at the closed door, then at her employer. "How's your head today, sir?"

Stuart had explained that the bandage was due to the removal of a small sebaceous cyst. "Much better. Bandage comes off this evening." She hadn't asked him about the carpet stains, which she'd removed that morning.

Satisfied that he'd done a good deed, Stuart turned to the affairs of other clients, lunched at Le Bistro, and was back at his desk by two.

At 6:00, changed, shaved, and determined to stay no longer than an hour, Stuart arrived at Senator Chase's reception, held in a large, blue-carpeted room with cream-colored walls, lighted by crystal chandeliers. The senator greeted him warmly. "Glad you could make it—may I call you Alan?"

"Please do."

"You know Evan." He motioned at his administrative assistant, who was standing at the fringe of a gathering crowd.

"Yes. Incidentally, I returned the file to your office for overnight safekeeping."

"Glad you're security conscious—but then you used to work at State." He paused. "That was one of Blake Selwyn's concerns, you know—almost an obsession with him."

"Security?"

"Thought he might have mentioned it to you. He had a hunch that our stuff was being passed around, getting to the other side. Oh, there's Senator Jamieson, minority. Jamie, here's the young man I spoke to you about. Alan Stuart, Senator Jamieson." They shook hands and Jamieson boomed, "Taking over for Boyd, I understand."

"Temporarily," Stuart said.

"Big boots to fill," Jamieson said, "but with Frank Chase behind you I reckon you'll manage. Anyway, this trip is more of a junket, you know. Europe, I like. Africa? Count me out." He laughed heartily, and Senator Chase drew Stuart away, beckoning to a small, pot-bellied man who was taking a drink from a passing tray.

"Sandy," Chase said, "Alan Stuart here is our temporary subcommittee counsel. Senator Sandifer."

Stuart repeated the ritual handshaking, said he was pleased to meet the senator—who, he remembered, had recently been charged with using campaign funds to play the market, employing inside knowledge of defense contracts to buy low and sell high. "What's your party, young man?" Sandifer asked, wiping droplets from his lips.

"Unregistered," Stuart informed him.

"Good, good. Don't want Frank loading the staff with oppositionists. See you on the plane." Clutching his glass, Sandifer elbowed his way toward the long buffet table.

Chase introduced Stuart to Senators Prideman and Vane, then released him to get a drink, saying, "That's the lot, Alan. Oh, perhaps you know Assistant Secretary Kingman—Rolf Kingman."

At the sound of his name a tall, reedy man wearing heavy horn-rimmed glasses and a bow tie turned around. "Senator," he said, "am I being paged?"

"Alan Stuart here is taking over for Boyd for a while. He'll be with us in Europe."

As they shook hands Kingman said, "I've heard your name recently—some other connection."

"I'm representing Blake Selwyn's estate."

"Of course, that's it. Diana told me. You spent some time at State."

"Years ago."

"That Diana, she's something else. Blake barely cold in his grave, and mourning abandoned." His thin lips twisted in disapproval. "She's over there, I think, with the high panjandrum of unilateral disarmament, my predecessor, the honorable Edward Beamish."

Turning, Stuart saw Diana Selwyn in a dark maroon dress, a strand of pearls around her neck. "If you haven't met the ambassador, permit me." Kingman made his way toward a tall, heavy-set man with thick, gray-white hair and a well-rounded face. "Ambassador!" Kingman said loudly, "let me present the subcommittee's new counsel—Alan Stuart. Alan—of course you know Mrs. Selwyn."

Stuart nodded briefly at Diana and shook Beamish's meaty hand. Diana said, "Hello, Alan, you do surprise. Edward, Alan is Pat Brigham's brother."

"Then you come well recommended indeed. Two charming ladies—plus the endorsement of Rolf and Frank. I hope you're as open-minded as Pat."

"That remains to be seen," Stuart replied.

Beamish gave him an avuncular smile and patted Diana's hand. "I'll be in Brussels, too, so we'll probably run into each other again."

Stuart nodded wordlessly, glanced at Diana, whose features

were set in a bland mask, and made his way to the buffet. The Beamish persona, he reflected, was that of a small-college president elected for his bluff manner and fund-raising abilities. Stuart was helping himself to oysters on the half shell when Evan Powell's voice intruded. "I see you've met the principals. Sorry you signed on?"

"Should I be?" Stuart asked without turning. He slid a succulent oyster from the shell into his gullet and reached for another. "As rumored, the Senate dines exceedingly well."

"And this is only a spur-of-the-moment gathering," Powell laughed. "When the full committee lays on a reception, it's Lucullan." His voice held a trace of bitterness. "Remember Frank Harris's description of the Lord Mayor's banquet? Nauseating. Not that our senators gourmandize so grossly, but that's only for fear the press would hear of their behavior." He edged in beside Stuart and swallowed an oyster. "Delicious! Wish I were going on this junket, but someone has to stay home and mind the store."

"I'm sure the senator's affairs will be well managed," Stuart remarked, and took a glass of white wine from a waiter's tray.

Diana Selwyn came forward and touched her glass to his. "Bon voyage," she murmured. "Couldn't you have told me you were going abroad?"

"For all I know it's classified information. I said I'd be away for a while. Does destination matter?" He sipped from his glass.

"God, you can be infuriating! Alan, can't that dull mind of yours realize you upset me because I care for you?"

"Oh, so that's it. I wondered if there could possibly be a reasonable explanation for your about-face. Now I know."

"Damn it, if we were alone I'd punch you!" Her voice lowered. "I do want to continue seeing you, be with you—when it's mutually convenient. You frighten me, did you ever consider that?"

"Frighten you? How, for God's sake?"

"Because you're so damned attractive, so right for me in *every* way, it seems unreal. I got scared you'd see me as just another easy conquest, treat me as just another girlfriend, available when you called, shut out the rest of the time."

"Are you serious?"

She laughed thinly. "I pull out my heart for him and the man—" She shook her head. "Alan, I need to go slowly because I'm afraid I'll lose you if we don't." She met his eyes. "Can you possibly understand my feelings, cope with them?"

Rather than answer directly, he said, "My absence will give us both a chance to think things over, to lower our temperatures."

"Perhaps," she sighed. "You already sound like an arms negotiator, though . . . See you . . . sometime." She moved away with practiced ease. Gazing after her Stuart rebuked himself for his lack of grace. But her rejection still rankled.

An elbow jabbed him. Evan Powell was saying, "Over there—with Beamish."

Stuart looked among the crowd and saw a well-dressed, sturdily built man with thick black hair and Slavic features. "What about him?"

"Yuri Bendikov, Soviet Embassy. He concentrates on the Washington end of disarmament matters, and there's reason to believe he's in intelligence. KGB."

"Looks harmless," Stuart remarked.

"One hopes so, but he attaches himself to our people like a limpet. Now he's working on Beamish, a more receptive audience by all accounts."

"Who invited Bendikov?"

"The senator—reciprocal courtesy. Bendikov sees that our team is invited to his embassy when their Soviet opposites are in Washington. And on the eve of our NATO confab, Bendikov naturally wants to take soundings." He spread some paté over a triangle of toast and swallowed it whole. "The tall fellow joining them is Assistant Secretary Kingman. Now *there*'s an odd trio for you."

"I just met Kingman. Wasn't he Blake Selwyn's boss?"

Powell nodded. "They didn't get along. Kingman likes his job, felt Blake was pushing for it."

"So there was rivalry. Was Blake in line to succeed Kingman?"

"He was a strong candidate, but my money was on another foreign post—a minister-counselor at a large embassy or an ambassador at a small one. State," he said with asperity, "buries its own dead."

Stuart turned to face him. "Referring to Blake's sudden death?"

"Just a general observation," Powell said diffidently. When Stuart glanced back at the Russian, he saw that Diana was laughing and smiling with all three men, more like a debutante than recent widow.

God knows, she's unpredictable, Stuart told himself, and looked at his watch. A quarter of seven. "Anyone else I should meet?" he asked Powell.

"Well, there's General Winkowski, acting head of the Arms Control and Disarmament Agency." He gestured at a tall, straight-backed man of fifty or so, wearing civilian clothing. "A real hard-liner and Russian-hater, but brilliant. Lectures at the Johns Hopkins School of Advanced International Studies and brings top students into his agency—which upsets a lot of people at State." He shrugged. "The senator does his best to impose peace between the general and Rolf Kingman, but as he often says, it ain't easy."

"I imagine not." Stuart walked with Powell toward Winkowski, who was talking with Senator Vane of Massachusetts. Nearing them, Stuart heard Winkowski say, ". . . realize they're mad dogs slavering for our blood, Senator. No ruse, trick, or hypocrisy is beneath them."

"But surely, General, you can't imagine they're devoid of all human feelings? Surely they want peace as much as we do?"

Winkowski's smile was contemptuous. Senator Vane, young and earnest, swallowed Winkowski's silent rebuke. His face was plump and sallow; Stuart recalled him as a leading antiwar activist of a decade earlier. To Powell, Winkowski said, "In case you didn't catch it, Evan, the senator here would persuade me to a milder view of the Russians.

"I've just met the senator," Stuart spoke up, "and I've looked forward to meeting you, General." They shook hands firmly.

"So you'll be watch-dogging the subcommittee? Don't let them give the store away," Winkowski said.

Stuart smiled. "I'll do my best, General, though I'm a novice in disarmament affairs."

"Aren't we all, sir?" He nudged Vane. "Even you, Senator."

"I suppose we are," Vane conceded slowly, "given our notable failure to achieve more significant reductions in conventional and nuclear arms."

"Which," Winkowski said, "I attribute to Soviet strategy and you ascribe to my agency's intransigence. Do you have an opinion, Mr. Stuart?"

"I haven't been aboard long enough to form one," Stuart replied mildly, "but before we reach Brussels I plan to be better informed."

"There's one over there." Winkowski gestured in the direction of Bendikov. "A snotty little Soviet spy, spreading his poison to Kingman and sopping up every word that bastard Beamish has to say. Soul mates," he finished gruffly. "Treason everywhere."

Vane shuffled uneasily until Winkowski placed a large hand on Stuart's shoulder. "Soviets slaughtered my father and brother in Katyn Forest—so you'll understand my antipathy for the *tovar-ichki*. Glad to make your acquaintance before Brussels. Senator—excuse me." As he strode away Powell exclaimed, "Whew! How's that for a short course in U.S.-Russian relations?"

"He's like an old Victrola record—keeps playing the same tune, no matter how inharmonious." Vane moved off and attached himself to an attractive young woman whom Powell identified as a subcommittee secretary, thought by some to be one of Vane's current mistresses. "So don't let Senator Vane see you paying courtesies to the lady—he can hold a real big grudge."

Stuart finished his wine and, using the excuse of a fresh glass, left Powell's side. As he neared a waiter he saw Rolf Kingman beckoning him over. "Stuart," Kingman said, "you should meet Yuri Bendikov—Soviet Embassy, second secretary. Yuri, the subcommittee's new counsel, Alan Stuart."

Showing china-white teeth, Bendikov seized Stuart's hand and pumped it vigorously. "Indeed we should meet. Delighted, Mr. Stuart. It is my privilege to know Boyd Saunders. We never had serious disputes. I hope we will get along just as well."

"It's not my place to challenge representatives of foreign powers," Stuart said equably. "Besides, I expect to be too busy during my ten days with Senator Chase to develop personal opinions on anything."

"Well said," Beamish remarked. "You are a lawyer, so?" asked Bendikov. "What kind of law, please?"

"Civil."

Diana said, "Alan also happens to be my lawyer, Yuri. He and Blake knew each other at State."

"So, you have professional foreign relations background. Senator Chase is commendable on his choice." He rocked back and forth, heel to toe, smiling broadly.

"I agree," said Diana, "having learned one thing about Alan: he's totally single-minded. And having made up his mind, he never backs down." She gazed at Stuart with large, innocent eyes.

"That's a characterization I have to agree with. In the same spirit as issued." Stuart glanced at his watch and took a half step back. "Ambassador, Rolf, Yuri, Mrs. Selwyn—good night. Good to have been with you." Taking leave of Senator Chase, he asked Powell to send back the classified file in the morning.

Powell nodded. "Since you're leaving early, why not take the senator's car? He won't need it for at least an hour."

Grateful for the suggestion, Stuart rode the elevator down to the Dirksen garage. At Powell's signal, a black limousine with USS plates drove up. Powell opened the rear door. "Have a good evening," he said as Stuart got in. "See you soon."

Stuart gave the driver the Brighams' address on Foxhall Road. As the limousine pulled up and out of the garage Stuart saw a couple descending the building's side staircase. Ambassador Edward Beamish, Diana Selwyn on his arm.

Stuart shook his head in disgust, sat back, and speculated on the relationship among Bendikov, Beamish, and Kingman until the driver pulled up at the Brigham gate.

Greg and Prudy had had their dinner, and they played around their Uncle Alan while he ate with their nanny. Missing their parents, they were happy at Stuart's presence. While he was taking coffee, Mrs. Erskine got them into their pajamas and ready for bed.

Lounging at their bedside, Stuart read them two stories from *Dr. Dolittle's Caravan*, then the inevitable *Little Engine That Could*, which, from prior readings, he'd almost memorized. They squealed with delight as he huffed and puffed, and pulled on his coatsleeve, urging the little engine on. The story finished, they begged for another until their nanny said, "No more, children," Stuart kissed them good night, said he'd see them soon, and went down to the library for a cognac and Cable Network News.

One segment showed the West German foreign minister, Dr. Rudolf Henschel, addressing the European union. English subtitles gave the substance of his remarks, which welcomed the lowering of tensions between Germany and the USSR and said that West Germany stood ready to meet concession with concession on the road to world peace. NATO, he charged, had outlived its usefulness; indeed, its existence was not only an embarrassment to member-allies but an impediment to fruitful understanding with the USSR. As the audience cheered enthusiastically, Stuart switched to another channel.

Holding NATO together was an increasingly uphill struggle, he reflected, and he could understand the allies' weariness over maintaining standing armies and grumbling over the continuing tax burden. The Soviets seemed so reasonable these days; why prolong the cold war into infinity?

That mindset, he mused, reflected the excessive euphoria

permeating most of the Warsaw Pact nations. A sense of freedom, of outreach to the rest of the world, was replacing the sullen despair that had for half a century characterized all Eastern Europe. Revolutionary changes, he conceded, were indeed taking place behind the once-impenetrable Iron Curtain, as long-captive peoples attempted to abandon orthodox Communism and define and construct some usable form of economic democracy.

Stuart sympathized with the yearnings of the Eastern Europeans but he felt that the pace of realization was crucial. Too fast, too far, and the institutions of state control, the armies, the secret police, would reassert themselves. Those stone Communists had the most to lose from change, from any surge toward freedom. Overnight the minefields, barbed wire, attack dogs, and searchlight towers could be reimposed. Tanks would roll crushing opposition as in that Prague Spring so long ago, so nearly forgotten.

Within the Kremlin itself the perestroikans remained locked in dubious battle with the True Believers. Let the Red Army prevail in that power struggle, and a mighty fist would pound all Eastern Europe into submission.

As matters stood, he knew from his classified reading, neither the United States or the NATO allies had been able to formulate policies adequate to meet developing contingencies. Did the West want a reunited Germany? Did the Kremlin? If not, how could it be prevented short of war? There were twenty, fifty such questions to be resolved, and all that seemed clear was that NATO inevitably would become a less military, more political alliance. If it lasted another five years.

And what was the role of Passage? Beamish's oratory had a twofold thrust: invective at the West for its alleged misdeeds, while urging Eastern Europe to act ever more audaciously, and in Stuart's opinion dangerously. It was almost as if Beamish *wanted* to banish the glimmerings of freedom from the East. Whatever his underlying motivation, the former ambassador had achieved the charlatan's dream of two discrete audiences, neither of which could challenge him.

So, thought Stuart, when Beamish's utterances become more reasonable, and the Berlin Wall is no higher than a traffic bump, I'll consider joining his organization. Meanwhile . . .

It irritated him that Diana was a Passage enthusiast—or was it the charisma exuded by the former ambassador? At minimum they were close friends, and as Stuart drained the last of his cognac he wondered how far that closeness would go.

He called for a taxi, went home, and got into bed, eager to be away from Washington and the annoyance of Diana.

CHAPTER 9

On Friday morning, Stuart joined the IRS agent in the bank's vault. After waiting ten minutes for Diana Selwyn, a bank vice president opened Blake's safe deposit box. They were taking inventory of the box's contents when Diana appeared, shot Stuart a sharp glance, and took a chair, visibly irritated that her tardiness had not been indulged.

Stuart set aside Selwyn's original will and watched the agent list Blake's birth certificate, a gold watch and chain—his father's, Diana identified—and Blake's commission in the foreign service, signed by Lyndon B. Johnson.

Nothing more.

"All yours, ma'am," the agent pronounced. Signing the inventory, he asked Stuart and the bank officer to witness. The bank officer offered to make copies of the inventory, and went off with it. When the agent also departed, Stuart opened the folded will. After scanning it he said, "It's the same as the copy you had."

"Did you think it wouldn't be?" Diana asked coldly.

"I have known cases in which one vengeful spouse showed the other a purported will when the valid one was quite different."

She shifted in her chair. "And you thought Blake might have done that?"

"I merely answered your question. Now we can proceed with probate. By the time I'm back from Europe the will should be cleared, Blake's bank account will be available to you, and I can have the house title transferred to your name." From his briefcase he got out an envelope and passed it to her. "Proceeds of the Chrysler sale. Eleven thousand two hundred dollars."

"Thank you. You're very efficient." She rose and began putting the box's contents into her shoulder bag. "Not much, is there? And don't ask if I was expecting a trove of gold coins—I wasn't."

"What were you expecting?"

"Mainly the will. Also, I felt obligated to be here—sort of a last service to my late husband."

The bank officer came back with copies of the inventory and gave them to Diana and Stuart. "There's a charge for this special opening, Mrs. Selwyn, you understand. Shall I have it deducted from your account?"

"By all means." She endorsed the Chrysler check and handed it over. "Please deposit this for me."

"Glad to. You'll continue being a customer, I trust?"

"I have no plans to change anything." She smiled and gave him her hand. At the doorway of the bank Diana turned to Stuart and said, "Well, have a good flight, Alan, and a successful mission. Bon voyage."

"Thank you." He watched her walk around toward the parking area, a lump in his throat. On impulse he followed, but then he stopped when he caught sight of her standing between two cars, talking with a neatly dressed man. Thirty, thirty-five Stuart registered. Diana shook her head and shrugged. The man nodded and walked to a nearby car. Obviously, the man had been waiting for Diana, and she informed him that the box held nothing of interest.

It chilled Stuart to acknowledge Diana's special interest in what her husband's box contained. She might have known about Blake's handwritten accusations and planned to intercept them. Whatever game she was involved in—and it was not a "childish" one—Diana was keeping it secret from her lawyer. Now, in retrospect, her first question to him took on added meaning? *Did Blake leave any papers with you? Any kind of documents?*

She *knew* they existed! Only her lawyer knew where they were.

Next morning at 6:30 an air force car drove Stuart to Andrews Air Force Base. Airmen stowed his suitcase in the belly of the four-engine Boeing. Stuart showed his new diplomatic passport to a captain checking arrivals at the foot of the ramp, climbed up the mobile staircase, and found himself in a spacious cabin decorated in air force blue and silver. No first class aircraft he had ever been aboard could compare with the plane's luxurious leather lounges, banquettes, and coffee tables. It was now half past eight, and Senator Sandifer was seated, glass in hand, swirling ice cubes and smacking his lips. He waved Stuart toward him, saying, "Five-hour flight, so I'm starting now. Don't like flying. How about you?"

Stuart sat down, and almost at once a jacketed airman-steward was at his side. "Care for a drink, sir? Breakfast?"

"Orange juice will be fine," Stuart told him, "and I'll have breakfast when we're airborne."

Sandifer said, "Guess this is your first official-type junket, eh?"

"It is." Stuart watched other members of the party arrive, including three wives and four female secretaries.

"Then I'll give you the lowdown—Stuart? That it?"

"Alan Stuart." He took the glass of chilled orange juice from the steward.

"First off, we like traveling in style, and the services make us comfortable because we vote their appropriations. We have the usual escort officers from each service—they're useful mostly to take the ladies shopping." He drank lengthily. "Also, they take care of out-of-pocket expenses, although in Paris we'll help ourselves to whatever funny money we need."

"Funny money?"

"Counterpart francs accumulated from Marshall Plan days. We're supposed to spend them in France, but hell, we can buy dollars with them, Swiss francs, Belgian money, whatever we need." As he emptied the glass, the alert steward took it from his upraised hand. Sandifer wiped his lips on the back of his hand and continued. "In Congress, the salary ain't much but the perks are terrific."

Stuart saw Senator Chase approaching and got up, glad to be rescued. Chase led him to the ladies group and introduced him to his wife, Mrs. Jamieson, and Mrs. Vane, a thin woman who wore a passive expression and an extravagant amount of jewelry. The secretaries—Jan, Alice, Maggie, and Jennifer—dressed in what Stuart took as their Sunday best, had already chosen a banquette. Seasoned junketeers, they ordered Bloody Marys with breakfast and chatted quietly among themselves, while ranking members of the party chose comfortable seating. Chase glanced at his wristwatch and shook his head. "Waiting for the FBI liaison," he muttered. "In J. Edgar's day they'd have been here ahead of us. 'Course, everything's different now. Oh, here's Kingman. High time, too. And the general."

He introduced Stuart to their wives, greeted the husbands, and was taking his seat when a perspiring young man entered the cabin. Spotting Senator Chase, he went over to him and said, "O'Rourke, Senator. Pat O'Rourke." Turning to Stuart the senator said, "Alan, meet our FBI watchdog, Pat O'Rourke. We're all here, let's get a move on."

O'Rourke went forward and spoke through the open compartment door to the pilot, closed the door, and took a seat well to the rear of others. Stuart followed him aft and sat nearby in reach of a desk where he planned to review background papers.

The cabin door closed, the jets began their monotonous

whine, and presently the big plane trundled forward. "Seat belts, everyone," came the pilot's command, and Stuart buckled in, recalling Harvey Scott's demise.

As the plane soared out over the Atlantic, Stuart ordered sausage, eggs, Danish, and coffee. O'Rourke also ordered breakfast, and when their plates arrived, O'Rourke edged a little closer. "Haven't seen you on one of these before. Recent addition?"

"Taking Boyd Saunders's place while he's hospitalized. After that I disappear."

"Wish I could," O'Rourke sighed. "A lot of guys envy me this gravy detail, but they can have it." He forked pancake into his mouth. "I sober 'em up, keep 'em out of jail—and try to keep the secretaries out of Russian beds."

"Is that a problem?"

"Always. Before we get to Paris I'll give 'em my standard talk—don't get intimate with foreigners—but I might as well save my breath. The Senate wives are too busy keeping track of their husbands to be a problem. I'm glad to see Mrs. Vane's along. When he's solo, watch out; Vane'll screw anything room temperature that'll hold still."

"Sandifer?"

"He's trash," O'Rourke said, "but at least he'll stick to his Brussels girlfriend. Last time we ran traces on her she showed no Soviet involvement—but that was last year and things can change." He drank noisily from his cup. "No breakfast at home. Wife's sick, had to feed the kids and drive them to day care. That's why I got here late."

For a while they ate in silence, then Stuart asked. "Do you know Tom Scudder?"

"Sure—State security. Tom stays away from these outings. See no evil, hear no evil, that's Tom. Friend of yours?"

"More of a name," Stuart said. "I worked at State until I passed my bars."

"Wish I had the ticket," O'Rourke said wistfully, "but I'm

basically an accountant. Naturally, I'm assigned to internal security—that's government for you."

"Did you know Blake Selwyn?"

O'Rourke's face turned toward Stuart thoughtfully. "Somewhat," he replied. "The guy's dead, you know."

Stuart nodded. "I'm handling his estate—and representing his widow. I wondered if Blake ever voiced any concerns to you."

"Such as?"

"Information leakage."

O'Rourke shrugged. "Not to me—but if he had that kind of burr under his saddle he should have talked with Scudder. Mind if I ask why you ask?"

"Well, I was an acquaintance of Blake at State. Before he died he asked me to vet the circumstances of his death."

"And?"

Stuart shrugged. "Heart failure. Not unusual, the medical examiner said."

O'Rourke grunted. "Those guys don't get everything—they look for what they expect to find and close the case." He pushed aside his empty plate. "There are poisons that never leave a trace. Even if you *know* a guy was poisoned, there may be nothing to prove it. The Chinese have poisoned some of their own leaders, and the Soviets have their own array of chemical killers." He sipped from his coffee cup. "Last year we were waiting for a defector to come out of the UN building. A man jabbed an umbrella tip in his butt and our guy died on the UN steps. We *saw* the poison injected, but whatever it was the forensics couldn't detect it. Verdict: heart attack. The moral," he said with a grim smile, "is to avoid umbrellas."

"I'll remember." Stuart got out his reading file and adjusted the desk. O'Rourke turned away, made himself comfortable on the lounge, and closed his eyes. Stuart looked at Rolf Kingman talking to two aides, who listened respectfully.

One of them could be me, Stuart reflected, if I hadn't made the change when I did. He remembered State in those days. Even without today's antiterrorist barriers and augmented security force, the place had always seemed inhospitable. A gray building for gray people; functional and impersonal, he reflected, glad he hadn't lingered to become one of State's anonymous drones. Rolf Kingman was one who'd managed to distinguish himself. Next would come an ambassadorship, then a retirement sinecure at some Washington think tank that turned out recondite studies read by few. Or a tenured professorship in international affairs . . . the Carnegie Foundation . . .

Unless, he thought, Blake's suspicion of Rolf could be proved.

Two hours into the flight Senator Chase sat down beside Stuart. "In a few minutes Rolf Kingman is going to give us a special briefing. We'll hold it toward the rear behind drawn curtains."

Presently, Senators Vane, Prideman, Sandifer, and Chase walked past Stuart. General Winkowski, Kingman, and two aides followed. Stuart fell in and found a seat, and an aide drew the heavy blue privacy curtain, isolating them from crew, the women, and O'Rourke, who was asleep.

Senator Chase began, "Some of you have asked why we're stopping in Paris when the meeting is being held in Brussels. Assistant Secretary Kingman and I agreed to withhold that information until we were airborne, to limit the possibility of leaks."

"Meaning we're not trusted to keep a secret?" Senator Sandifer said grouchily.

"Interpret it as you choose, Sandy. We all know our subcommittee hasn't been airtight on certain past occasions, so this seemed the best way around that particular problem. Rolf?"

Kingman stood up. "A couple of weeks ago Senator Chase and I came up with an idea that I'll be putting into effect tomorrow night in Paris. The secretary of state concurred, as has General Winkowski. Now, as you may or may not know, the principal organization opposed to our policy of gradual, step-by-step arms reduction has been Passage, organized and headed by former ambassador Edward Beamish. He wants nothing less than immediate unilateral disarmament by the U.S. and our NATO allies, feeling that under its present new-wave leadership the Soviet Union will follow the West's example."

Senator Prideman said, "Pardon the interruption, Rolf, but why should they?"

"Beamish cites two reasons. One is the Soviet desire to eliminate the heavy budgetary burden of conventional and nuclear armaments. The second is the force of international opinion."

Sandifer made an unpleasant sound with his lips.

Ignoring it, Kingman continued. "Past Soviet behavior provides little precedent for believing that budgetary constraints influence Soviet foreign policy. And as for public opinion—well, it wasn't public opinion that forced Khrushchev to pull his missiles out of Cuba, it was our naval blockade. Nor did the Soviets withdraw from ten years of Afghanistan because of international opinion. A million casualties made the war unpopular at home, and the leadership finally concluded that they were engaged in an unwinnable war—as we had been in Vietnam. So I find Beamish's arguments at best theoretical, without substantial basis."

"Hear, hear," Winkowski interjected.

"Nevertheless," said Kingman, "his positions have drawn support and adherents from numerous groups in Western Europe— the West German 'Greens,' for example, and related activist coalitions in Italy, England, and Scandinavia. Tomorrow night, at the Pompidou Center, Beamish will be urging delegations from NATO countries to cement their ties with Passage. An audience of around a thousand is expected, and Beamish will have it all his own way unless—and here's the crux of it—his positions are challenged by a spokesman for current NATO policy. That spokesman will be myself. The media will be there either to record my presentation or to witness Beamish's refusal to give me the podium." He smiled, "For our purposes, one's almost as good as another."

Senator Prideman said, "Right into the lion's den, eh?"

"What better way?" Kingman responded. "So that's why we're heading for Paris, gentlemen. The following day we'll be in Brussels, as scheduled, with whatever impetus my appearance at Beamish's conclave may have provided."

General Winkowski spoke up. "Sounded crazy to me at first, but on reflection I endorsed the idea. Something has to be done about Passage before NATO's resolve is totally destroyed. We've been too passive about our opponents, too gentlemanly to challenge their actions. Rolf is going to change that tradition and expose the utter fallacy of unilateralist arguments."

Senator Vane said, "If it's a closed meeting, Rolf, how are you going to get in?"

"The FBI acquired a ticket for me."

He looked around for further questions but only Senator Chase spoke. "That's the story, gentlemen, and as Rolf put it, we have a no-lose situation. Either he's permitted to rebut Beamish's talk, or he'll be ejected from the meeting. It's a gutsy move, and I'm backing it completely." He looked around at his colleagues. "Any leakage of Rolf's plans will nullify them, so I urge you to maintain silence—not even your wives, please. It's that important." He drew back the heavy curtain and the delegation dispersed back to their seats.

Stuart returned slowly to his, startled by Kingman's proposal. A man who leaked classified information to the Soviets would hardly stand before a hostile, pro-Soviet audience and challenge its spokesman. Or would he? If it were leaked, Kingman would be barred from the hall, but he'd still be credited with conceiving a bold maneuver and having the balls to see it through.

O'Rourke stirred and blinked. "Where are we?"

"Couple of hours from Paris."

An air force major stopped beside them. "Everything okay, gentlemen?"

"Fine," Stuart said, and O'Rourke nodded.

"I'll take your passports so that everyone can be cleared as a group. You'll all be staying at the Hotel Crillon, by the embassy, and you'll find your bags in your rooms. Any questions?"

"What time we getting in?" O'Rourke asked.

"Local time will be about 1730 hours. The reception's at eight and transportation will be provided."

"Reception?" Stuart asked.

"At the Quai d'Orsay—the French foreign ministry. Weren't you informed?"

He shook his head. "Me, neither," said O'Rourke. "Maybe we're not supposed to go." He handed his official passport to the escort officer along with Stuart's diplomatic passport. The major consulted the itinerary and shook his head. "You're both on the list—some foul-up, sorry. Cars will leave the hotel at 1945 hours—street dress, gentlemen." The major left.

O'Rourke yawned. "Think I'll skip it. Jet lag hits me hard."

Stuart nodded. "I'm not much on receptions. I'll try for dinner and bed. I'm just temporary help anyway. I don't think the senator will mind."

But a few minutes later Chase stopped by and told Stuart he was counting on his presence. "The foreign minister will be there and the president may stop by."

"France isn't a full NATO member," Stuart observed.

"True, but they keep their options open. Anyway, this is a sort of interparliamentary get-together. I'm unhappy that the French government is letting Passage use the Pompidou Center, but it's typical of a socialist regime. Just another way to needle Uncle Sam, their principal benefactor and protector. In any case, by accepting French hospitality we have an obligation of sorts. After Kingman delivers his thunderbolts, the French may well regret the whole thing."

"I imagine they will." Stuart smiled. "It's a great conspiracy."

The senator patted Stuart's shoulder avuncularly and returned to his wife and the other women. This was the kind of high-level travel his former wife, Sandy, would have adored, Stuart observed. Senators, diplomats, glittering foreign settings, attentive aides, socially prominent wives—this sort of thing had been her unspoken goal, her hidden agenda, as the current phrase went. But it was never his. He wondered how Seattle was working out for her, realized he really didn't care.

Senator Sandifer slept nearby, mouth open, nostrils emitting an occasional barking snore, and Stuart reflected on the governmental system that allowed the likes of Sandifer access to its innermost secrets.

He studied the file until the plane crossed the coast of France and began its prolonged descent. Then he summoned an escort officer and asked where the classified file would be secure until they flew to Brussels.

"Aboard the plane, sir. There's a three-way combination safe in the command compartment, and the ship is always guarded." He accepted the file and went forward to secure it.

At Charles De Gaulle Airport they were welcomed by the president of France's National Assembly in a brief ceremony featuring a military honor guard. Senator Chase, as ranking member of the U.S. delegation, replied in English, his words of appreciation interpreted by one of Kingman's aides. Then, in four limousines, the party was driven into the heart of Paris.

CHAPTER 10

W hile baggage was being sorted out in the Crillon lobby and the party registered, Stuart went outside the hotel to the arcade that ran along the Rue de Rivoli, stretched his arms and breathed deeply. The familiar scents of Paris were there—gasoline fumes overlaid by the mouth-watering aroma of roasting meat; the mixed fragrance of a perfume shop; the delicate, sweet aroma wafting from a bakery; the oily odor of the Seine. Underfoot, the sidewalk vibrated from a passing Métro train, a traffic gendarme whistled repeatedly as he tried to prevent a gridlock developing among cars pouring across the bridge into the Place de la Concorde.

Yes, this was the Paris he knew and remembered. Flower-stalls by the Madeleine. Paris, where every corner, every sidewalk table could bring chance romance. Building façades had been cleansed of long-accumulated grime—the Obelisk of Luxor in the center of the Place was now as pink as when it was taken from the granite quarries of Egypt three millennia ago. Everything seemed to sparkle under the sun, and Stuart thought that Paris deserved to have its lovely face scrubbed more often than every two hundred years. For, like many foreigners, he had come to love the City of Light and regarded it as a second home.

His room was large, comfortable and ornate without ostentation. The ceiling was at least twelve feet high, Stuart estimated; tall balcony windows overlooked the Place de la Concorde and the slow-moving Seine beyond, the imposing building of the National Assembly—once a Bourbon palace—on the far bank of the Seine.

Room furnishings were Louis XIV or XV, he thought, covered like the walls with patterned damask in soothing colors. Large walk-in closets, and a tiled bathroom huge by U.S. standards; shower-tub, bidet, and warming racks for thick, oversize towels.

Stuart wondered what the Crillon had looked like when Ben Franklin signed France's recognition treaty with the infant United States in one of its handsome salons. High SS officers and Wehrmacht generals had lodged in the Crillon, then Eisenhower at war's end. And the hotel's atmosphere of sedate luxury continued attracting the notables of the world.

Travel with senators, he'd been told, and it's first class all the way. The special aircraft and now the Crillon confirmed those words.

As he dried himself with a sumptuous warm towel he scanned the site where Dr. Guillotine's invention had efficiently decapitated so much of the French nobility and, eventually, the instigators of the revolution themselves. There was a basket of wine and fruit in his room, compliments of the hotel, and Stuart munched a pear as he finished dressing. The wine he'd sample later.

He was glad to be in Paris and away from the crosscurrents of Washington. He'd spent the summer of his junior year at the Sorbonne, taking classes in conversational French and comparative political institutions. De Gaulle had been president then, and the war in Algeria had been coming to its inevitable close. He remembered the shock that swept France when De Gaulle, elected on a vow to suppress the Algerian rebellion, reversed course and gave Algeria sovereignty, in effect declaring victory and marching away. The colonels and the *pieds noires* had rebelled, and this time the general prevailed, exterminating *l'armée secrète* and executing its leaders, some of whom had been his most devoted followers in World War II. But had the history of France ever been less than turbulent? Stuart adjusted his tie and went down to the lobby, where his fellow travelers gathered like sheep herded by their escorts.

He would have preferred to walk the short distance across the river to the Quai d'Orsay, but he rather liked the idea of reaching the foreign ministry's illuminated façade in an embassy car. The American ambassador shared his limousine with the Chases and arrived ahead of the others. Stuart rode with Rolf Kingman, who seemed immersed in thought; his aides followed in the last car with the three service escorts.

The entrance hall was impressively lined with plumed *gardes republicaines*, their unsheathed swords and cuirasses glinting under the sparkling chandeliers. White-gloved butlers formed a double file, leading guests into a magnificent ballroom whose opulence recalled the imperial extravagance of France's golden age. Senator Chase introduced Stuart to the ambassador and his wife, then Stuart found himself serving as Chase's ad hoc interpreter as they went through a receiving line of deputies and foreign ministry officials.

There were buffet tables along both sides of the ballroom but no American-style bar. Servants passed silver trays of champagne in fluted glasses, and as Senator Chase took one he murmured, "Beats our little Wednesday night gathering, doesn't it, Alan?"

Nodding, Stuart observed, "This is a multipurpose affair—I've counted about twenty foreign ambassadors, and there's a bunch of Soviets over there—distinguishable by their wide lapels and safety shoes."

"You *are* observant," Chase noted admiringly. "So we're sort of additions to the guest list. Absolutely no reason to have Russkies here, in my opinion. Ah—Alexi Kondratsev"—his eyes narrowed—"met him in Geneva. The big fellow with a head like a block of cement. Tough cookie."

"Aren't they all?" Stuart remarked, and made his way toward the nearest buffet, having eaten nothing since his airborne breakfast but the pear.

There were roasts, poached fish, smoked salmon, prawns, oysters, and clawless channel lobster—*langouste*—and an impressive assortment of salads and cold dishes. Dessert and coffee tables were separate. Remembering the standard admonition to eat lightly after a long flight, Stuart took a thin slice of rare roast beef with endive salad and moved toward the rear of the immense ballroom, where he found a chair. With his plate on his lap, he was beginning to cut into the beef when through the crowd he noticed a tall, gray-haired man leaving the reception line: Edward Beamish.

Now, what the hell is *he* doing here? Stuart asked himself. Then, fork in midair, he glimpsed Diana Selwyn moving ahead of the former ambassador. And, what the hell is *she* doing here? he wondered. Apparently his client had become Beamish's constant companion. Free of the receiving line, they accepted champagne from a butler, and Stuart saw them genially greeted by Assistant Secretary Kingman. Beamish was old enough to be Diana's father, he reflected irritably, but he did offer her a glamorous change of pace, one she was thoroughly enjoying.

Angrily he bit into his meat, determined not to be upset by her unexpected appearance. Tomorrow night, though, she would see her escort publicly eviscerated by Rolf Kingman. The prospect cheered Stuart.

Stuart ate a bite of crisp salad and reflected. If Selwyn's charges were true, what better cover for Kingman than taking on Beamish's organization and thus endearing himself to State? In the end, he knew, there was too much momentum in America and Europe to block Passage's influence. Whatever Kingman accomplished would be no more than a tactical setback for Beamish and his colleagues at home and abroad. Contributions would pour in—from people like his own sister, he thought bitterly, people who needed a cause to justify both their existence and their wealth.

As Senators Prideman and Vane and their wives left the buffet they nodded at Stuart, who nodded back. He saw Senator Sandifer walk unsteadily to a chair and sit down, spilling champagne onto the parquet floor.

From an alcove a string orchestra began a Berlioz melody barely audible over the buzz of conversation. By now, Stuart thought, there must be two hundred people in the ballroom, all talking at once. The reception line remained intact, although no guests were passing through it. Abruptly the strings broke off and began playing *La Marseillaise* and the crowd turned expectantly toward the doorway. The red-sashed president of France, followed by his honor guard, entered to mounting applause. He greeted his hosts graciously, accepted a glass of champagne, and moved toward the other buffet table, escorted by the foreign minister and the president of the National Assembly.

Spying Ambassador Beamish, the president altered his course and shook Beamish's hand warmly. Stuart could see Beamish presenting Diana to the president, who bent to kiss her hand and then continued on to the buffet, where he was surrounded by an eager throng. The moment would have been a lifetime high for Sandy, he thought; even Pat would have been pretty impressed, although his sister was no stranger to White House dinners, receptions, and teas.

The Soviet entourage, he observed, followed the president closely—among them, to his surprise, was Yuri Bendikov at Kondratsev's elbow. Ambassador Beamish lingered nearby, but Diana was lost in the crowd.

So, he thought, all of Blake's heavies are present and accounted for: Kingman, Beamish . . . and Bendikov. On returning to Washington, he decided, his obligation was to give Blake's message to the FBI. Let them take it from there. He wasn't in the counterspy business, never had been, and he'd be relieved when Blake's accusations were in the hands of professionals.

As he finished eating he wondered why O'Rourke had introduced the subject of poisons during their breakfast conversation. Was it an effort by the FBI liaison to impress Stuart with his knowledge of arcane matters? Or had O'Rourke mentioned un-traceable poisons in connection with Selwyn's death?

As he considered the possibilities, he regretted having eaten the pear in his room. So far no ill effects, he conceded—and nobody had brandished an umbrella in his vicinity. Was he getting paranoid? Of course, because the burglars who ransacked his library and office had inflicted only a painful and unsightly bruise.

Then he remembered Diana's parking lot meeting just after the opening of Blake's safe deposit box. Considering Blake's custom of bringing classified papers home to work on, Diana would have had the opportunity to read them or even photograph them. Had she been with Blake in Geneva during those disarmament conferences? Blake hadn't said.

If Diana had been ordered by some controller to retrieve Blake's letter or protect Rolf Kingman, seducing Blake's lawyer would be a smart move. And having determined that Stuart was unproductive, she'd broken off their affair. Assuming that Diana *was* being controlled by the Soviets, her closeness to Beamish became understandable. She was there to influence the former ambassador and report his every move.

Stuart rebuked himself for not having explored these possi-bilities before; having done so, he now viewed his client in an entirely different light. The alienation between Diana and her husband could have been due to Blake's suspicions of his wife, suspicions he'd kept to himself, because exposing her would ruin his career.

If Stuart were to let bygones be bygones, perhaps Diana would unwittingly drop more clues and confirm his suspicions. He'd be an interested observer from now on.

Almost as though she possessed ESP, Diana emerged from a nearby group and came toward him. Stuart set aside his empty plate and rose to greet her.

"April in Paris," she quipped. "Seen any blossoming chest-nuts?"

"Not yet, but I'll keep looking. Anyway, the acacias are in bud. Nice to see you, Diana."

"Thank you." She looked around. "What do you think of all this splendor?"

"*Un peu fort,*" he said. "Didn't expect you'd be in Paris."

"You didn't ask—to echo your phrase. Edward Beamish invited me along for his convocation—you know about it?"

"It was mentioned on the flight today." He took two glasses of champagne from a passing waiter and gave her one. "*A là votre.*"

"*A là votre, aussi.*"

They drank and Stuart said, "Staying long?"

"In Paris? Long enough to splurge at Hermès. Too cold for the Riviera so I'm considering a week's sun on Ibiza. I'm not anxious to get back to Washington—it's a rotten time of year." She glanced around but Beamish was invisible. "What I'd really like is a long, restorative cruise like the one Pat's taking. The children are well?"

"And in good hands," he nodded.

"Mrs. Erskine is a jewel. My brother—late brother—and I had an Irish nanny, full of scary old country tales and cottage superstitions. Shall we sit down? I imagine it'll be a while before Edward remembers me."

"I doubt that," he said as they took chairs. "*I* can't forget you and I'm not even your date."

"So you *do* have a human side, Alan. I'd begun to think of you as a cold, flinty-eyed lawyer, even a misanthrope."

Stuart forced a laugh. "I'll have to change that," he said cheerfully. "Thin-skinned, maybe; misanthropic, no."

"Then we *can* be friends again?"

"Right." Their glasses touched. "I haven't enjoyed the unpleasantness between us, Alan," Diana said.

"Neither have I. Can we put it behind us?"

"By all means." She crossed her legs, smoothed her skirt. Her diamond engagement ring was on the third finger, complementing an inch-wide diamond bracelet. "From Paris I believe you go to Brussels?"

He nodded. "So far I haven't done a lick of work. It's just as well that I'm a short-timer; I could get to love the sybaritic life."

"Oh no you couldn't." She made a moue. "Not Mr. Work Ethic himself. When you're back in Washington, hard at work, think of me basking in Balearic sun."

He couldn't resist asking, "Alone?"

"I assume so. If you're thinking of Edward, he's going on to Vienna, North Africa, maybe Saudi Arabia, not places I care to go." Her voice lowered. "Could I interest you in joining me after Brussels?"

"I'm interested," he replied, "interested as hell, but I put off clients for just the time I'd be away with the delegation. I don't want to lose them."

"Well, think about it," she said. "If I get to Ibiza I'll stay at the Fenix."

"The Fenix," he repeated. "I'll remember."

"If you could manage even a day, it would be wonderful."

"So I was thinking." Seeing Ambassador Beamish approach, he got up to observe formalities and was rewarded with a perfunctory handshake. To Diana, Beamish said, "Glad you found a friend while I was tied up with dignitaries. Alan, good to see you. Can you tell me if General Winkowski is here?"

"Now that I think of it, he didn't leave the Crillon with us."

"Probably cutting the affair, knowing there'd be Russians here." He smiled condescendingly. "No way to build rapport, eh? Diana, if you're ready to leave, I am."

As she rose she said to Stuart, "With Edward it's one party after another. See you in Washington—if not before."

"Why," said Beamish, "we'll all be together in Brussels, won't we? Day after tomorrow."

"That's the schedule," Stuart nodded. "See you there. Good night, Diana, Ambassador."

He watched them leave and congratulated himself on his acting abilities. Beamish was the "useful idiot" and Diana his KGB watcher. He wouldn't be caught dead with her at Ibiza or anyplace else. And after he got back to Washington she'd learn that there were penalties involved in playing the Soviets' game.

With that thought in mind, Stuart excused himself to Senator Chase and walked back along the softly lighted quai toward the Concorde bridge and his hotel. A large *bateau mouche* moved quietly along the Seine, music from its glassed-in dance floor filtering across the dark waters. Were Diana what she appeared to be he would be there with her, anticipating the floodlit grandeur of Notre Dame, a spectacular sight for lovers.

As he mounted the steps to the bridge walk, Stuart found himself thinking of General Winkowski. Why hadn't the tough old general attended the reception? Where, in fact, was he? Maybe O'Rourke would know.

Stuart paused to look back at the Eiffel Tower, its massive outline lighted in celebration of its centennial. Bridge traffic was sparse now that the rush hour jam was past, so between cars he was able to hear footsteps scrape behind him. Suddenly alert, he halted. The footsteps stopped a beat later. He bent over as though to tighten a shoelace, listened, and glanced around. A man with his elbows on the railing was looking down at the Seine. Slowly Stuart stood up, and as he resumed walking he noticed another man moving along the far side of the bridge. In the silence between cars Stuart heard the footsteps behind him again, keeping pace with his own. The second man glanced briefly in his direction. Whoever his tailers were, they were professionals, boxing him from both sides.

What was their purpose? There was too much light to throw him off the bridge, he told himself, but if they shoved him in front of a moving car—the perfect crime. Or did an umbrella jab in the rear lie in store? Gradually his pace quickened. He stayed close to the railing so he could grab it if need be. The curb represented danger.

At the end of the bridge he began jogging toward the lighted obelisk, quickened into a run, and sprinted between honking cars as he angled toward the Crillon. Passing the Brest statue at full speed, Stuart recalled briefly that it marked where the guillotine once stood and resolved that his blood would not be spilled there tonight.

Looking back he saw both men racing after him, one almost hitting a car as he plunged ahead. Stuart was grateful for his own good physical condition, for he was outdistancing his pursuers. One of them tripped and fell headlong. Tires screeched and a car swerved to a stop, the outraged driver shaking his fist at the slowly rising man.

A white-gloved traffic *gendarme* yelled at Stuart as he dodged between cars to reach the hotel sidewalk.

Slowing to a walk, Stuart passed the grandly uniformed doorman and entered the lobby, nearly bumping into O'Rourke. The FBI liaison said, "Steady, man, steady. You okay?"

Swallowing, Stuart said, "Almost got knocked down by a car out there—walked back from the reception." He drew in a deep breath, pulse still pounding.

O'Rourke patted his shoulder. "Crazy drivers—ought to be jailed."

Stuart looked around, decided his pursuers had peeled off, and for lack of anything better to say asked O'Rourke if he knew where General Winkowski was.

"Still at the embassy, I guess. Likes to keep in touch with his Washington office."

"At this hour?"

O'Rourke grunted. "He may be retired, but he runs his shop twenty-four hours a day. Like the bureau; far as my supervisors are concerned, it's always high noon." He took his key from the concierge. "See you tomorrow."

"Goodnight." Stuart collected his room key, then rode the lift to his floor and opened the heavy door. Turning on the light he was shocked to see that the fruit basket had been overturned and scattered and the wine bottles smashed, drenching the rug and chair. Across the chair's satin backing, red letters screamed "Yankee go home." Stepping around the debris, Stuart picked up the telephone and dialed O'Rourke.

CHAPTER 11

Crude stuff," commented O'Rourke over breakfast in the Crillon Grill. "Inside job." He chewed a flaky croissant and ladled strawberry jam onto another. "Some anti-American Commie nut the hotel ought to weed out and fire. Not worried, are you?"

Alan shrugged. After being chased across the bridge to his hotel he thought he had reason to be. "A little," he admitted. "Why me?"

"Opportunity. The creep saw you leave and trashed your room." He grunted. "Pig's blood on the dean's files, students 'arresting' CIA recruiters—same sick syndrome. Forget it, Alan. You got another room, the hotel took it in stride."

"But 'Yankee go home'? That slogan's older than I am."

O'Rourke sipped his black coffee, put down his cup. "Probably the only English the creep knew. It was all over Europe's walls long enough, God knows." He grinned. "Like the first English some kids in the U.S. hear is 'Attention, K-Mart shoppers.' Forget it."

General and Mrs. Winkowski were seated at a window table

on the Boissy d'Anglas side. They took menus from the maître and nodded at Stuart and O'Rourke.

The FBI liaison said, "Y'know, it's a federal crime to attack a federal officer, and I guess that includes your present status. I don't recommend you press things with the Paris police. Anyway, you weren't physically attacked—not even your possessions, right? The beef is the Crillon's."

But if those thugs had caught up with me last night, Stuart mused, it would be different.

After switching rooms, Stuart had slept restlessly and risen early. While shaving he had tried to make sense out of the two incidents. If his pursuers were planning to kill or kidnap him, why trash his room? The incidents occurred independently, and Stuart thought he knew who was behind each.

It would be like Beamish to have some wild-eyed peace activist warn Stuart to flee Paris so that Beamish could monopolize Diana Selwyn. The two pursuers were probably working on orders from Bendikov or his Paris counterpart, assuming that Kingman considered Stuart an adversary.

"Anyway," O'Rourke remarked, "you can take care of yourself. You did army time, got your SF beret."

"You know that?"

"Who you think handles clearances?" He poured coffee into their cups. "Sir, I know things about you you've probably forgotten—your parents' and grandparents' background, your school and college grades, your fitness reports at State . . . and more about your former wife than she ever told you."

"Nevertheless," Stuart remarked, "I held top secret clearances. I suppose everyone on the subcommittee got a similar going over before they were granted access to our classified stuff?"

O'Rourke hesitated. "Everyone?"

"I had Senator Sandifer in mind, Pat. Does the bureau consider him discreet and secure despite his alcoholism and possibly unethical conduct? And what about Jeremy Vane, who blew up that Ann Arbor lab to protest something about Cambodia?"

"He wasn't convicted," O'Rourke objected grumpily. "Or tried."

"No, because he hid out in Canada until the statute of limitations expired, came back under Carter's amnesty, and ran for Congress."

"Listen, the bureau just assembles facts, we don't grant clearances. In the subcommittee's case, that's Senator Chase's job."

"Who clears him?"

"The Senate majority leader." He pushed aside his plate. "What's your point?"

"I wouldn't trust Sandifer to bring me change for a five-dollar bill. And I wouldn't trust Vane alone with his grandmother. Jesus, Pat, the standards are completely arbitrary!"

"That's politics," the FBI liaison said indifferently. "I can't change the system."

"I'd just like background investigations to mean something beyond a pro forma check. Blake Selwyn thought there was high-level information leakage from some of these people, and I think he was probably right."

"Did he try to stop the leaks?"

"I don't know. I do know he's dead."

O'Rourke looked at his watch, beckoned a waiter for his bill, and signed it. "Fifteen percent enough?"

Stuart nodded, O'Rourke added it to the bill and got up. "Have to check in with the embassy legal attaché. Have a good day." He left by the side exit and Stuart finished breakfast alone.

Why bother to clear anyone? he wondered as he headed back to the lobby. Near the doorway the maître overtook him and said, "Phone call for you, sir—in the cabinet there."

Stuart closed the door and picked up the receiver. "Alan Stuart."

"And this is Diana Selwyn. 'Morning, Alan, how are you?"

"Usual jet lag stupor."

"After our talk last night I thought I might be hearing from you."

"I don't even know where you're staying."

"The Hilton—alone, if you're wondering. Got plans for the day?"

"Matter of fact I have," he lied. "I signed up for an escorted tour of Versailles, Fontainebleau, and the Louvre. Senator Chase was pretty insistent. *Faute de mieux* I've become his interpreter."

"What a shame. I was rather hoping we could spend time together—stroll the quais, lunch on the Left Bank."

"Sorry," he said, "but we'll make up for it in Brussels, okay?"

"If that's how it has to be," she said reluctantly. "Enjoy your day."

He mumbled something and the line went dead. He had no particular plans, although many delegation members were taking the tour he'd described. It was years since he'd visited the quai bookstalls, where hidden gems could still be found, and over on the Rue de Nevers was a favorite seafood restaurant he'd first dined in with his parents twenty years ago. It was five years since he'd been there and today he'd go back—alone. He didn't want to share old memories with Diana Selwyn, because he intended to return to Paris unencumbered by memories of her intrusion into his life.

Stuart was walking toward the lift when he saw General Winkowski handing his room key to the concierge. The general came over to Stuart. "I'm going for my morning walk, and if you care to join me I'd enjoy your company."

"Fine idea."

After crossing Avenue Gabriel in front of the embassy they took the Cours de la Reine bridle path toward Rond Point and the Arc de Triomphe. The general was no mere stroller but adopted a brisk military stride. Seeing that Stuart had no difficulty keeping up with him, the general smiled. "I used to run this route every morning, to the Arc de Triomphe and back." He gestured at the embassy. "When I was military attaché. Of course arthritis hadn't set in then. You look in pretty good shape."

"I try," Stuart said, "and you've motivated me to keep it up."
Traffic whizzed past them heading up the Champs Élysées.

As they passed the Pompidou statue Winkowski said, "Heard
you had a little trouble last night. Anything stolen?"

"Just vandalism."

"Any idea why you should be the victim?"

"O'Rourke suggested I was a target of opportunity. The trasher
saw me leave, gained access, and wrecked the room. Strange,
though, because a pair of footpads came after me while I was
walking back from the Quai d'Orsay. Chased me right into the
hotel."

"Get a look at them?"

"I was too busy putting distance between us."

They passed the Marigny Theatre set in the wooded grove.
Nodding at it, Winkowski said, "Used to bring my wife here a good
deal. Summer evenings—very pleasant—lots of good memories.
You've lived here?"

"One student summer."

"Then you know the Rive Gauche better than this side."

"Much better."

"How well did you know Blake Selwyn?"

"Hardly at all. At State we were nodding acquaintances."

"But he retained you as his lawyer."

"A minor matter—but it led to his widow's retaining me to
handle his estate."

"Routine work, I imagine."

Stuart nodded. "During the Geneva conferences did you have
contact with Selwyn?"

"Some. He was one of many lads from State. Why?"

"The last time I saw Blake he expressed private concern over
what he called high-level information leakage to the Soviets—
advance knowledge of our negotiating positions. Was that paranoia?

"Hard to say," Winkowski admitted. "The Russian bastards
are always well informed, but they can pick up a lot of dope just by

reading the *Post* and *Times*. Of course, there was a long period when they were cracking our codes, thanks to several moles, but these days we limit radio traffic." He turned to Stuart. "You have some ideas?"

"No, just trying to get Blake into focus."

"His widow could be helpful."

"She seems to be in Beamish's orbit—and he's too comfortable with the Russians for my taste."

"Comfortable is putting it mildly," Winkowski agreed. "If he had his way, Ed would undo every small success we've had in nuclear negotiations since Hiroshima. He's part of that old crowd of intellectuals who supped with Kennedy, Nixon, and Carter, and now sup with the Devil—you know who I mean."

"Yeah, the ones always publishing books and magazine articles saying how wrong they were to advocate deterrent armaments."

"That's it in a nutshell." He grinned wolfishly. "Making my job and Kingman's that much harder. They feed their defeatist shit to the press and become media heroes. By contrast I'm seen as the bloodthirsty old warmonger—in case you hadn't noticed."

Two riders cantered by, and Stuart and Winkowski stepped aside to avoid the trail of dust. Winkowski polished his glasses and replaced them. "Well, there's Rond Point; we'll turn back."

Stuart got in step beside the older man. "What are we supposed to accomplish in Brussels, General?"

For a few moments Winkowski didn't respond. Stuart was about to repeat his question when the arms control agency head spoke up. "The stakes are very high, Alan. The NATO alliance is getting very loose, the old concept of a united force against Soviet incursion is no longer the binder it used to be. West Germany's the key, and if we lose forward-basing of our tactical missiles there's nothing to keep those ten thousand Warsaw Pact tanks from rolling west along the autobahns. Of course, Beamish and his crowd say that'll never happen, but how can they be sure? Old Joe Stalin wouldn't believe hard intelligence predictions that Hitler was going to attack because of his great 'personal relationship' with Adolf. Holding NATO together as a credible counterforce is our goal in Brussels, but I think the wind's blowing against us." His face was bleak. "I fought in three wars, Alan, and I don't want another one, least of all one we can't win. Sometimes I feel that if Europe wants to lie down and roll over for the Kremlin, let 'em do it. They have to do their fair share to stay free, and that means conscription, updating conventional arms, and big defense budgets. Like ours. The dollar's going to hell, and one of the main reasons is our defense outlays. Our people are getting tired of taxes and are all ears for the siren songs of Beamish and his apostate crew."

For a time they walked on in silence. Then Winkowski said, "In confidence, I've wondered at times where Kingman's sympathies lie. But if he brings off that caper tonight I'll kiss his hands and beg forgiveness."

"We can only wish him well."

"Right. So I hope it turns out that his antipathy to my agency is just part of our ongoing turf struggle with State. You'd think that within the world's longest-running democracy, people would cooperate for the common good." He pulled a twig off a branch and snapped it. "Ain't always so."

When they reached the end of the park Winkowski said, "Thanks for walking with me. I'll be in the embassy while my wife takes in the azalea festival over in the Bois de Boulogne. Annual affair. She loved it when we were stationed here." His gaze drifted upward. "We have good memories of our life together. Not every couple can say that. Wasn't just luck—took work, compromise, and accommodation." He smiled, "Like foreign affairs."

Stuart watched the general's erect figure stride across Avenue Gabriel to the embassy entrance, where he showed a pass to the smartly uniformed marine guard and went inside. General Winkowski was a remarkable man, and the administration was lucky to have his resolute and patriotic services.

Stuart crossed to the Crillon, where delegation members and

their wives were getting into assorted cars and limousines for the grand tour. To avoid being seen, Stuart went in the side entrance and consulted the concierge for the address and phone number of a Princeton classmate, Blaise de Chaumont Percival. They'd celebrated together at last year's tenth reunion and Percy had invited Stuart to get in touch on his next trip to Paris. The family was minor French nobility, though his classmate had enough common sense not to tout his title around Princeton, New Jersey. Too slight for crew or football, Percy had nevertheless been a soccer all-American, a distinction of which he was enduringly proud.

To the concierge, Stuart said, "M'sieu Percival is an *avocat*, but I don't know if he's practicing law." The concierge accepted Stuart's input with a nod and presently wrote down an address and telephone numbers.

In his room—undisturbed—Stuart phoned Percival's Champs Élysées office, identified himself to the secretary, and in a few moments heard his friend's cheery voice. "Alan! How glad I am you finally made it. We must see each other promptly, *ça va sans dire*."

"Have lunch with me."

"No, you with me, I insist."

"We'll flip for it, okay? I was thinking of Prunier's."

"Or the Cercle Interalliée? Choose."

"Prunier's is less formal. Meet you there—what time?"

"Noon, if that's agreeable. I'll reserve a table where we can drink and get disorderly—like the Nassau Tavern."

"That's my man. Noon," Stuart agreed, and hung up.

He looked forward to seeing his college friend, who had gone from Princeton to studying law at the University of Paris. "Why should I learn Anglo-Saxon law in America," Percy had asked rhetorically, "when France is ruled by the Code Napoleon?" Stuart turned on the TV set, watched a symposium on modernist painting, and fell asleep.

* * *

When Stuart arrived, Blaise Percival was already at Prunier's *bar de dégustation*, slurping down icy pink *moules*—mussels. Percival's thick, curly black hair, white teeth, and light olive skin were the result of a strain of Corsican blood from a Bonapartist by-blow, he claimed only partly in jest.

After warm greetings and mutual assurances that neither had changed, the two men stood at the ice-mounded raw seafood bar consuming mussels, oysters, and white wine until the maître announced that M'sieu le Comte's corner table was at his disposal.

Seated, Stuart inquired after Percy's wife, Blanche, whose family had a chateau in the south of France.

"She's well," Percy said, "but busy as always with our three children."

"Three?"

"A second daughter born six months ago. Things are a bit strained between us—Blanche has not quite forgiven me a brief fling with a Lido showgirl while she was pregnant. Did you remarry?"

"No, and no prospects." Diana's face flashed through his mind, but he quickly banished it.

"So, you're here with the high American delegation. I always thought you'd make something of yourself, despite what others said."

Stuart smiled. "And what did others say?"

"That you were a born roué, *cher ami*, destined to become a dissolute *boulevardier* and bottom-pincher."

"Sounds more like someone else I know."

"You echo Blanche," Percy sighed, "but it's not so. Just after the reunion my father died and I left private practice to handle family affairs. In addition, I've been drawn into my in-laws' wine business—they're *négociants*—and that takes more time than I'd like." He scanned his menu and ordered sauteed sole and a salad. Stuart said he'd have the same and asked Percy to select the wine.

That done, they talked of mutual friends, the special joys of college, women they had known. When lunch was over they finished with oily, sweet Turkish coffee.

"I have a proposition for you, Alan," Percy said. "I need a correspondent attorney in Washington. Will you accommodate me?"

"I don't know enough about international trade or finance on the level you'd require. Anyway, I'm busy enough. I'd have no time for myself, and free time is important to me."

"Me, too, having very little of it. *Dieu*! How complicated one's life becomes, eh? Why don't they tell us these things beforehand?"

Stuart laughed. "If we found out, we'd become dissolute wastrels, never turning a hand to honest work."

"Well, I don't know about *honest*—that just complicates affairs. Incidentally, Blanche's brother, Julien, has been made *juge d'instruction* for the Luxembourg Quarter. That's the magistrate who weighs evidence and decides if some clown is to be prosecuted or set free. A one-man grand jury, you might say."

"And said very well. So he left the wine business for public service, and you're taking his place."

"Julien says he'll only stay two or three years, but I think he's a better judge than he was lawyer." Percy shrugged. "To each his own, eh?"

"Exactly. And as soon as this Brussels conference is over, back to Georgetown for me."

The Frenchman nodded thoughtfully. "I suppose it's sort of a last chance at saving NATO. Most French are indifferent, you know—legacy of Le Grand Charles, who left us without friends or allies in a hostile world. Do what you can for freedom, *mon vieux*. Don't let the Soviets take our verdant vineyards, our casks of amber cognac," he whimpered and made a dreadful face, reminding Stuart of Percy's turn as an impudent vagabond in a Triangle production.

Laughing, Stuart said, "You should have been a stand-up comedian, Percy. Before me I see theatrical talent tragically wasted."

"And ignored. Blanche, like most Frenchwomen, lacks a sense of humor, particularly if there's anything risqué involved. Well, maybe my children will appreciate me."

"One must hope for the future."

"Ah, *oui*—but what about your future? No wife, no children, not even an *amie*. Come back after Brussels, Alan. I have in mind a fine young woman, just out of the university and distantly related to Blanche."

"These formally educated females . . ." Stuart shook his head. "I'd prefer a sculptress, painter, poetess—creative, not too heavy a thinker."

"Gotcha. Rosy-cheeked, brown-eyed peasant girl with broad hips, tiny ankles, and huge jugs. Adequate description?"

"Put it this way: whatever would have appealed to Louis XIV is fine with me."

They tossed a twenty-franc coin and Stuart won the privilege of paying the bill. As they left the renowned old restaurant Percy said, "Seriously, Alan, I hope you'll come back, spend time in Paris. We're still in the Avenue Foch apartment, won't move to the Rambouillet house until June—plenty of room there, always." They shook hands. "By the way, Blanche rather liked Sandy—said she was crazy not to hang on to you tooth and nail."

Stuart shrugged. "One of those things. Tell Blanche hello and good-bye and say I'll try to get back this summer, when Georgetown becomes a furnace."

"Hope you will."

They shook hands again and went their separate ways, Stuart toward the Louvre. He entered by Pei's crystal pyramid—which he considered an abomination—paid the twenty-franc admission, and paused at the entrance staircase to admire the *Victory of Samothrace* before strolling down the Pavillon de Flore and viewing Donatello's *Virgin and Child*, Canova's *Psyche Revived*, Pilon's *Three Graces*, and the *Slaves* of Michelangelo.

On the second floor a visual feast was served up by Watteau, Ingres, Delacroix, Giotto, and Fra Angelico, in addition to Da

Vinci's dominating *Mona Lisa*. As seldom before he had time to linger before each offering. Then came canvases by Tintoretto, Veronese, Caravaggio, El Greco, Murillo, Rubens, Hals, Rembrandt, and many others. Moving on to the Cour Carrée, Stuart viewed the English School, represented by Reynolds, Turner, Constable, Gainsborough, and other painters of lesser influence. Surfeited, he agreed that the Louvre's artistic treasures were unparalleled. If his NATO trip accomplished nothing else it provided him with an overdue occasion to renew his acquaintance with the resplendent galleries of the largest palace in the world.

Exiting onto the Rue de Rivoli, Stuart walked down the arcaded sidewalk to the Crillon. He was drawing a hot tub when someone pounded on his door and he heard Pat O'Rourke's strained voice calling his name.

Stuart wrapped a towel around himself and opened the door. The FBI liaison bolted in and blurted, "Where have you been?"

"Lunch, the Louvre. What's the problem?"

"Have you seen Rolf Kingman?"

"Not since last night. Why?"

"He's missing, that's why. No trace since noon, and his wife's hysterical. He's due at that Passage conference in an hour."

CHAPTER 12

*H*ell," Stuart said, "Rolf probably got lost over on the Left Bank."

"Yeah? Then why hasn't he taxied back here? *Shit!* Listen, if you see him, or if he calls you, for God's sake tell him to haul ass, and let me know. I'm checking everyone." Stuart locked the door behind O'Rourke and got back into the bathtub.

O'Rourke was not easily upset, he thought, but he seemed frantic. Was it possible that Kingman had been snatched to keep him from appearing on the podium? Kingman was no irresponsible flake. That left *force majeure*. How had the plan been leaked?

Sandifer?—loose morals, loose lips? Vane, talking to impress his alienated wife? Surely not Senator Chase, who seemed discretion personified. One of the air crew, overhearing by chance or design?

There was still plenty of time remaining, and Stuart wondered if anyone had looked for Kingman at the embassy. He got out of the tub and used the wall phone to call the embassy duty officer. No, Assistant Secretary Kingman had not been there since morning. The unthinkable, Stuart thought soberly as he replaced the phone, was Kingman's defection. Only Stuart knew of Blake Selwyn's suspicions; if Rolf didn't appear, Blake's indictment would be confirmed.

As he dried off, Stuart blamed himself for not having taken Blake's letter to the FBI. Now it might be too late. Would they next see Kingman at a Moscow press conference deriding the West and embracing his longtime masters? But then, why paint so disastrous a picture? For reasons of his own, Kingman could be closeted somewhere, rehearsing the most important declamation of his career. That was the most likely possibility, Stuart reflected; he'd done it himself when preparing for public speaking.

He put on a bathrobe, picked up the room service menu, and telephoned for a club sandwich and a half bottle of Montrachet.

Then he wrote a brief note to his niece and nephew on engraved hotel stationery. As he addressed the envelope, Stuart recalled their sunny afternoon at the zoo with Diana, but knowing he'd take the children alone next time. The National Air and Space Museum would be a better bet, unless the children already knew every exhibit by heart.

Dinner arrived, brought in by a frock-coated waiter who opened the wheeled table and uncorked the wine. Stuart signed the bill, tipped the waiter, and turned on the TV, changing channels until he found the station covering events at the Passage conclave. A reporter was describing Passage's background, noting that many antinuclear groups had aligned themselves with its goals. As notables arrived, the reporter identified an American writer and priest whose sensational novels had brought him wealth along with Vatican censure, the turbaned chairman of the Indian peace movement, an English writer of anti-Western books, and an Australian journalist whose fondness for guerrilla movements had gained him a Lenin Prize.

The camera showed Edward Beamish's smiling face as he waved at the television audience, and Stuart glimpsed Diana in the background. Then the camera cut to former minister of culture

Regis Debray, whom Stuart remembered as a survivor of Ché Guevara's ill-fated guerrilla venture in Bolivia.

As he ate, Stuart saw the screen cut to the hall's interior, the crescent-shaped podium where principals were arranging themselves. In vain he searched for Kingman's face among the crowd.

Abruptly the camera cut to the entrance, where a small crowd was gathering. A gate-crasher? Kingman being turned away? An altercation was developing. *Gendarmes* pried people away; arms flailed.

The camera focused closely now, and Stuart saw a tall figure at the center of the melee furiously trying to force his way past the entrance. With a gasp of surprise, Stuart recognized General Winkowski. *Gendarmes* grasped his arms, forcing the general toward a waiting car. The general's face was red and he was shouting, but either the microphone was too distant for his angry protests to be heard or the cameraman had turned down the audio.

Stuart put down his sandwich. Winkowski must have been trying to take Kingman's place, meaning that Kingman's whereabouts were still unknown. He sipped some wine to ease the tightness in his throat. Regis Debray was at the podium, his introductory remarks filled with sugary praise of the international peace movement. Debray cited Passage and its founder, Beamish, as leaders of the antinuclear struggle, and when he yielded the microphone to a smiling Beamish, the crowd roared enthusiastic approval.

Stuart flicked off the TV. He had seen enough.

He walked slowly over to open the balcony doors, and a fresh breeze stirred the curtains. Somewhere in Paris, he thought, Rolf Kingman existed. Had he taken refuge in the Soviet Embassy? Or had he gone to ground in some miserable, roach-infested tenement, fearful for his life? Where did his loyalties lie?

When the telephone rang, Stuart answered quickly, thinking it might be General Winkowski, arrested and needing legal aid. Instead he heard the dry voice of Pat O'Rourke. "Been watching TV?"

"Just turned it off. General Winkowski—"

"Yeah, too bad, but I didn't call about him—it's Kingman."

Stuart clenched the receiver. "Alive?"

"He was found wandering in the Bois de Boulogne, disoriented, babbling nursery rhymes. Doesn't even know his own names. Jesus, what a—"

"Where is he?"

"American Hospital. I'm heading over there, and I think you'd better come along. Meet me in the lobby in five minutes?"

Stuart, heart pounding, muttered agreement and replaced the receiver. He drained his wine glass and stared through the open doorway at the Place de la Concorde. The dark pavement was shiny slick, mist-haloed lamps and lightoliers giving a surreal look to the twin file that outlined the bridge.

The breeze fluttered the curtains and a few droplets struck his hands. Even in the City of Light it had to rain.

CHAPTER 13

An embassy car had taken them out the Champs Élysées and around the Arc de Triomphe, driver honking noisily to clear a lane through the rain-slowed traffic, past the Congress Palace, and into Neuilly, where the American Hospital faced Boulevard Victor Hugo. The five-mile trip had taken more than twenty minutes.

Now they were in a quiet hospital room, looking down at a figure strapped onto a bed. A plastic oxygen mask covered the face and mouth; above it, eyes blinked and rolled wildly. From an inverted bottle, a transparent tube fed clear liquid into an immobilized arm. Thin wires led from the man's body into a bank of cathode monitors. Stuart could see that the heart action was strong but irregular, like the respiration.

Turning away from the monitors, a doctor asked, "You're friends of Mr. Kingman? Members of the delegation?"

"That's right," O'Rourke confirmed. "Is he going to live?"

"I expect so—but in what condition it is far too early to form an opinion."

"What—" Stuart began. "The patient either took or was

administered some species or hallucinogen," the doctor interrupted. "Analysis of bodily fluids is under way, but I don't expect
the results for some hours. His symptoms, though, strongly
resemble the action of PCP, so-called Angel Dust. Our immediate
task is to attempt to oxidize whatever remains in his blood and
brain, while keeping him alive."

On the heart monitor a peak jumped vertically, then sloped
into a jagged plateau. Stuart could hear Kingman's breathing
quicken into harsh gasps, like those of a fish out of water. "Does
Mrs. Kingman know?" he asked.

"She's in a waiting room. Her husband didn't recognize
her—it shattered her composure."

O'Rourke looked around the dimly lighted room. "I want this
place sealed off, access restricted. No bulletins on Kingman's
condition. Nothing."

The doctor's lips pursed. "Well, I'm not sure. Hospital
policy . . ."

Belligerently, O'Rourke ordered, "Hospital policy is whatever
the embassy says it is, and I'm speaking for the embassy. In fact,
Kingman's admission is to be kept secret. Understand, Doctor? Not
a word." Turning to Stuart he spoke in a lower voice. "Whoever did
this to Kingman isn't entitled to know he's alive. Could bring a
second try."

Stuart nodded. To the doctor he asked, "What's the danger of
death?"

"Depending on the nature of the substance, brain centers
could be destroyed, lungs paralyzed."

"Permanently?"

The doctor nodded.

O'Rourke said, "Meaning life on a respirator?"

Again the doctor nodded. Kingman's entire body bucked
against the canvas restraints. As the intravenous bottle jiggled on
its stand, a nurse hastened to steady it. Turning back the doctor
said, "Think of the patient's body as a vehicle being driven by a
maniac. He has no control over his actions or power of speech."

As though cued, Kingman began chanting through the oxygen mask: "See how they run, three blind mice, three blind mice, Santa Claus is coming to town, to town to town to town to town . . ." The words trailed off, his eyes closed, and the monitor showed normal breathing again.

The door opened and Senator Chase strode in. "I've just spoken with Rolf's wife. It's terrible, this thing. Awful." He wrung his hands. "Who could have done it? Why?"

"To keep Kingman off the Passage platform, Senator," O'Rourke pointed out. "Whoever leaked the plan is responsible." His hand swept across the end of the bed.

O'Rourke told Chase the orders he'd given to the hospital and the senator nodded in agreement. "So what do we do now?" asked Chase.

"Either he'll pull through or he won't. That's out of our hands. I'm going to start questioning everyone to try to get a lead on where Kingman was today, who had access to him, and so on—try to establish a minute-by-minute log." He faced the senator. "If I don't finish by departure time tomorrow, I'll continue during the flight and in Brussels."

"Then, who—"

"The legal attaché's office here will follow up, Senator, and take responsibility for protecting Kingman." He turned to the doctor again. "I assume you have a ward for violent patients? I want Mr. Kingman taken there as soon as possible, sealed off from the rest of the hospital population."

"I'll see to it." After a few words with the nurse, the doctor left the room.

"Well," said Chase, "What do you make of it, Alan? Think someone in the delegation talked out of turn?"

"Not necessarily," Stuart said with a glance at O'Rourke. "That's the obvious source, but with the plan being handed around State for concurrences here and there, then to the secretary's office and the White House, any number of personnel could be candidates, starting with typists."

Senator Chase shook his head. "It's just impossible to keep secrets."

O'Rouke said, "Alan's right, Senator. I'll have to initiate an investigation at the Washington end. State won't like it, but Kingman's a federal officer and this is a federal offense, so it's bureau jurisdiction all the way."

"Glad you concur," Chase said as Kingman's body began to tremble violently, jarring the bed on its casters. "God, what a frightful thing to happen to a man. Inhuman. Did the doctor offer any hope?"

"Some," Stuart replied. "A lot depends on identifying the drug that went into his system."

Through the oxygen mask Kingman's muffled voice began chanting, "Frère Jacques, Frère Jacques, dormez-vous, dormez-vous sur le Pont d'Avignon? Little Bo-Peep lost her sheep and don't know where to find them . . ."

The eerie voice chilled them all. O'Rourke muttered, "He's lost more than sheep—he's lost his fucking mind."

The doctor returned. "We'll move him now, Mr. O'Rourke. I suggest that you supervise, to make sure the arrangements are satisfactory."

Attendants began wheeling out the bed and the array of monitors, moving slowly and carefully, while the nurse handed the intravenous hookup. Kingman was raving again, his eldritch keening diminishing down the hall.

That left Stuart and Senator Chase in the empty room. "Christ, what a blow!" Chase said bitterly. "Not only did we lose a rare chance to shaft Passage, we won't have Kingman in Brussels. State'll have to wing out a replacement, and fast." He put his arm around Stuart's shoulders. "I want you to go to the embassy and get off a priority message in my name, summarizing the situation and requesting a replacement in Brussels ASAP."

Stuart nodded.

Chase continued, "My place is with Mrs. Kingman for the next few hours, and O'Rourke will be tied up for a while. Take your

car and driver, Alan, and if it's not asking too much, call me here
to verify that the message has been sent."

"Of course. Anything's better than waiting around."

"*L'Ambassade*," he told the driver and settled back as the
engine started. The car turned around and moved down Avenue
Victor Hugo. When the car swung down Avenue Charles De
Gaulle, Stuart noticed how poorly lighted the avenue was. The rain
had slackened somewhat, but his driver kept a moderate speed on
the wet pavement. The wipers slashed back and forth monoto-
nously.

Still shocked by Kingman's condition, Stuart found himself
questioning Blake Selwyn's charges. Kingman was either a traitor
or a victim of another's treachery; he couldn't be both. If a Soviet
servant, he was too well placed to be destroyed for the sake of a
successful Passage gathering. But for all practical purposes
Kingman's life—his career, at least—had been destroyed. Well, it
was in O'Rourke's hands now, and with a bureau investigation
about to begin, Stuart gratefully felt his own role diminish.

Headlights flashed in the rearview mirror, a car overtaking at
high speed. Stuart sat forward to caution the driver, but the driver
nodded and veered toward the shoulder to allow ample passing
space.

But the vehicle didn't take advantage of the driver's courtesy.
Instead Stuart saw the headlights grow blindingly large and then
felt the sudden shock of a rear-end collision. The driver swore and
accelerated.

A second rear-end smash pushed Stuart's car into a fishtail
skid. Coming alongside, the aggressor collided with a screech of
grating metal. The impact shook Stuart, who buckled his seatbelt
fast and yelled at the driver to brake.

The other car, larger and heavier, Stuart saw, slammed into
them again, at an acute angle. His driver struggled to gain control,
but the rear wheels were forced aside until the front end yawed
across the highway. Abruptly the other car dropped back, but
Stuart's continued on, slewing uncontrollably.

The headlights illuminated a low barrier, a ditch, and a row of trees beyond. With a scream the driver released the wheel and covered his face with his arms. The car parted the steel barrier as though it were a tinfoil ribbon, hit the far side of the ditch, bounced up, and slammed into the trees. The driver's body shot up and back, ricocheting from the roof and smashing the windshield as the car's front end felled one tree, lifted sideway, and rolled over.

The impact drove the seatbelt into Stuart's thorax with the force of a maul. His last conscious awareness was of warm blood spilling from the driver's head across his face and hands.

CHAPTER 14

*L*ight filtered through his eyelids and into his brain. His mouth was sand dry, tongue thick and leathery. From his hips upward pain registered, pulsed, throbbed. The smashed radiator expelled steam in a high-pitched scream—or was that his own voice?

He remembered his fear of fire. Oh, God, how he feared the gasoline blast, skin crisping, peeling down to bones . . . but his nostrils were not filled with gas fumes, it was an antiseptic smell.

Better. He was in a hospital, then. His fingers moved, then his toes. Not paralyzed. Horizontal.

Santa Claus is coming to town . . . Where was the old lyric coming from? The hospital, he answered himself. Neuilly. Rolf's bed. Tube dripping sucrose into veins, fending off shock.

Not Rolf. *Me.*

Opening eyelids was harder than pulling up a wedged garage door. Light dim, walls green. Hands unbandaged. Eyes too heavy to keep open.

No sounds. No *hospital* sounds. Silence.

His mouth opened, dry lips cracking like old parchment as he yawned.

Try to think. *Try.*

Too wearying. Too heavy a burden. A drift in warm, smooth-flowing stream. Warm stream. Blood.

His flesh cringed.

Driver—no seat belt. He'd buckled his.

Lawyer without a seatbelt. Springfield. Darnestown road. Death on the road.

Where now?

Fingers touched his chest bandage. Tightly bound. Ribs broken? Lungs pierced? Heart?

He shivered, starting more pain.

Embassy message. Chase told? Nonarrival . . . smashed up.

Headlights filling rearview mirror. Danger. Bumping, smashing, skittering across the road like a wayward toboggan.

Cold, alone, badly injured, barely alive. Hope doctor good. Why couldn't he think? Form conclusions?

Ah . . . sedated for pain. Don't move. Need more sedation.

Pried eyelids open. Door countersunk in green-painted, insulated wall. No sound in, none out. Crazy ward. Rolf.

Get to embassy. Now.

Elbows down, chest up . . . Kee-*rist!* Pain overwhelmed.

He lay back panting from exertion. His mouth, tongue, mucous membranes, body cells craved water.

No water when guts pierced—that it? Or thirst-causing drugs?

What time? Wristwatch gone. Toes bare. No clothing.

Water needed for life. *Give me.*

General battling constabulary. Yelling but no sound.

Like here. Soundless. Good for sleep. Time to sleep.

He slept.

A tube between his lips wakened him. The tube led into a water glass held by a heavy-faced woman, who said something unintelligible. Stuart sucked frantically until the woman drew the tube away. He begged for more, but she shook her head and left.

His half-opened eyes saw her key in the lock. The door closed, and he heard the slight metallic sound of locking from outside.

The water revived him incredibly. The pain became manageable.

The only thing in the room was his bed—no visitor's chair, nothing—and the roving eye of a video camera mounted high in a corner. Surveillance? Normal hospital procedure. Nurses had monitors at the nursing station.

What language had the woman spoken? Not French, but not everyone in Paris spoke French. Algerians spoke Arabic, Iranians Farsi, Indians Hindustani . . .

The tight strapping around his chest wouldn't let him draw a deep breath. What he could suck in he expended in a shout: "*J'ai soif!*"—I'm thirsty. He needed water to dilute his drugged blood, restore sluggish cells, irrigate his brain. He didn't have to urinate because a catheter tapped his bladder.

His bed was unlike Rolf's—dark metal, low, thin mattress, rigid. The block-faced woman had had to bend over to bring the glass to his level.

Three blind mice with Santa Claus on the Pont d'Avignon. Mary contrary ate a spider and peeped for her lost sheep. The clock ticked thrice and the old man died with the mice. Thrice Lord Mayor of London Town. Dick Whitt . . . his thoughts came from crazy angles, like carnival bumper cars steered by children. No continuity. Had the woman fed him more than water?

The inside of his left arm showed red dots that looked like spider bites. Needle marks. How many? How long? But he had to drink, even if drugged.

A big bumper car had crashed into them, hurtled them into the woods . . . he felt the need to vomit but suppressed the reflex. Was he in this cell-like room to be protected, healed, or . . . "*Where am I?*" he yelled with all his strength.

The camera eye moved indifferently. He shook his fist at it. The effort drained his strength and he closed his eyes.

Again the glass tube for sucking water. Stolid woman built like a Mongolian shithouse. Of course, she was Mongolian. No wonder he couldn't understand her slurring grunts. "Fuck you," he said pleasantly. Nodding blankly, she took away the half-filled glass.

"All of it, god-dam-it!" he yelled at her back. "Full ration, you ugly bitch!"

Mechanically she closed the door with her key, bearing off the treasured liquid.

"Until tomorrow, *hein? A demain*, that it? You ugly bitch."

Tears gathered in his eyes and welled over. His tongue tasted the saltiness. He wept, sobbing uncontrollably. Exhausted, he slept.

A dark-skinned man wearing thick lenses and street clothes was taking his pulse, counting seconds on his wristwatch. Slavic cheekbones, slanty eyes. Mongolians like the brickhouse bitch? Stuart wondered.

"How long have I been here?" No response. He tried French, then German. Same nonresponse. The man dropped his wrist. "I'm dehydrated," Stuart pleaded. "Give me water. I need water or I'll die." The man removed the catheter, turned and walked toward the guilted door.

"*Vodka!*" Stuart yelled and saw the man's stride alter almost imperceptibly. "*Na stroviya*, asshole," he shouted, but without visible reaction the man went out, the key turned.

Locked in for the night. Well, he'd learned something. The man had understood *vodka*. But that didn't mean he was Russian; the word was standard in many languages.

He'd trade his Audi for a glass of vodka. But the Audi was far away. Georgetown. He was in Paris. Some nut farm, a clinic? Did they think he was indigent, a poverty case?

The red dots on his arm were healing, vanishing. Apparently, the drug injections had ended. Were they antibiotics? Someone, for God's sake, was in charge of his case. Why the lack of information?

Imperturbably the camera moved, rotated, and swept back slowly, ever-focused on his bed. Who watched its cathode images? Where?

The overhead light went out. Nighttime? Stuart didn't care. During darkness he had begun to sit up, dangling his legs over the edge of the bed and pressing his soles against the cold concrete floor.

What food he was given came in a plastic bowl—some kind of animal fat flavoring a room-temperature cabbage-beet soup. He'd lost five pounds, maybe ten, but the liquid was restoring his strength.

The pain in his chest was tolerable. He stood up, crouching, swaying, touching the bed for support, and then moved toward the wall. His knees came close to buckling, but he made it. For a while he stood against the cold wall sucking in deep breaths, then slid down slowly and sat on the floor. Better than prone on the bed.

What had they been doing to him? And why? He remembered the pursuit across the Concorde bridge, remembered Rolf Kingman's tense, deranged face on the white hospital pillow. The overtaking, killer car.

Why was he still alive? What did his captors want?

Because his treatment in no way resembled conventional hospital treatment by ethical physicians and nurses, Stuart had concluded that he was a prisoner being given minimal care, enough to keep him alive, able to talk.

About what? He didn't have to think long about that one. What "they" wanted was cached in his safe deposit box. Riggs Bank, Georgetown branch.

But why would they want it now? Rolf Kingman was close to braindead, unable to articulate coherent thoughts and beyond incrimination by Selwyn's letter. Kingman's controllers must feel themselves safe from exposure and the letter valueless.

Unless they weren't sure of what Selwyn had written.

That had to be it, and their ignorance of the letter's true contents gave him leverage. They had to have it.

Meanwhile, they wouldn't kill him, because after his death the safe deposit box would have to be opened in the presence of witnesses. Then Selwyn's letter would be inventoried and read. Routine procedure, just as he'd witnessed the postmortem opening of Selwyn's box.

He could use the letter as a bargaining chip; for now it would save his life.

So thinking, Stuart told himself he had to organize his thoughts, regain mental health, and evaluate his situation.

Judging by his shrunken stomach, the semidehydration, the healing of damaged ribs, and the loss of muscle tone, Stuart calculated that the crash had occurred at least a week ago, more like ten days. He had been unconscious for at least the first five days, whether from a concussion or sedatives. But five days were more than enough to smuggle him out of France. To Moscow? Leningrad?

Soviet-style, he had been subjected to sensory deprivation. The choice of Mongolians to attend him was deliberate, eliminating the least chance of communicating. Isolation and dehydration were standard Soviet techniques. The average person craves human contact, shrivels without it. Thus the one-track Mongolian robots.

Somewhere, perhaps within this very building, was the controlling force. Inevitably they would confront him, make their demands. It was only a question of time, that time being when they considered him in a receptive state. The interval was his to use to plan his response.

He knew, as though written in fiery letters across the wall, that once he was no longer useful, he would be liquidated. He rubbed his back against the wall, relieving a patch that itched under the tight bandage, and went back to bed.

What they might not know, he mused, was that he had taken the interrogation resistance course, beginning at Bragg and culminating in the fetid Panamanian jungles along the Chucunaque River. He had been starved, brutalized, run beyond the point of exhaustion, hung by his feet, deprived of water, denied the rest, and interrogated.

Remembering it made his forehead clammy.

None of that agony had been of the slightest use. Until now. Plus point two.

He must dredge his memory to recapture the psychological points of interrogation: good cop/bad cop; false flag; sympathy; shame; vulnerability; dependence; surrogate authority; identification.

Not knowing one's fate was what broke so many, but he was ahead of them there. He knew they would not kill him as long as he was useful. And he resolved to hold on to that time as long as he could.

The overhead light flashed on. Instantly Stuart feigned sleep.

He thought of himself at point A now—point Z was the eventual disposal point. He would prolong each stage until physical pain defeated him.

If they were in a hurry—and he calculated that ten days had now elapsed—they would introduce hypnotic drugs to speed the process and bring point Z closer. Even the Bragg and Southern Command psychologists acknowledged the overwhelming power of drugs to elicit obedience and information. *God, no drugs*, he pleaded as he heard his cell door whispering open. Don't let them make me a babbling idiot like Rolf.

In guttural English a loud voice called; "Wake up, Mr. Stuart. Mr. Alan Stuart, wake up! Welcome to the Union of Soviet Socialist Republics!"

At those stark words Stuart felt his resolution begin to dissolve.

CHAPTER 15

"*Water.*" The word came out like a frog's croak, the bleat of a sheep, a raven's caw.

"Water?"

Stuart slowly opened his eyes. Shielding them from the light with one hand, he stared up at the man who'd spoken: tall, well built, clean-shaven, black hair slicked across a large, sloping skull. Ruddy skin, reddish-purple capillaries webbing a blunt nose. Peasant features contrasting with a nattily tailored three-piece gray suit.

"Water," Stuart repeated and closed his eyes.

"You don't get water here? They don't give you even water?"

"Enough to sustain life. Not enough to piss." He got off the bed, lurched to the wall. "Hell of a welcome to the USSR."

"Water is available, as much as you want. Does that please you, Mr. Stuart?"

"When I see it, can drink it." His tongue curled over his dry lips. He sat down.

"Well, my damaged friend, you shall see water—soon."

"Now."

"I said soon."

Stuart turned his body away from the man so that he sat parallel with the wall. "Get lost."

"You were hurt, you are being cured. You should appreciate our care and concern."

"What are you? Doctor? Shrink? Head jailer?" The words slurred, as he had intended.

"You are rude. I don't respond to rudeness."

"Neither do I," Stuart said. "Bear it in mind."

"So, since we think alike, we should be friends."

"Aside from being in the workers' paradise, where am I? Specifically?"

"What difference does it make? You are here as a guest until you are cured."

"And that could take some time, right? Ten or twenty years?"

"You are thinking negatively. Think positively."

"I'm hungry."

"You eat what everyone eats."

"Bullshit. I want what *you* eat. I'm not working class, neither are you. Treat me accordingly." Stuart drew his feet close to his buttocks for warmth.

"Why don't you open your eyes?"

"I don't like what I see. Go away, leave me alone."

"First we must talk."

"First we must have water. Then we must have food."

"So stubborn, so accustomed to giving orders, Mr. Alan Stuart. Are all American lawyers like you?"

"Just those with pride and dignity. I'm tired, I need rest." He pried himself off the floor and moved to the bed. Lying back, he yawned exaggeratedly. "When you leave, turn off the light." Covertly he opened an eyelid just enough to see the man's face, which showed uncertainty. Good.

"But we must talk about your future, Mr. Stuart."

"Future? I can't think beyond my next drink. Is it feeding time for the animals?"

"Animals? You think you are in a zoo? You don't get treated like an animal."

"By my standards I'm treated worse. Go away."

Leather soles scraped toward him. Nearer now, the voice said, "We treat you as friend; you must re- re-cip-ro-cate."

"Who says so? Who are you? You haven't answered my question."

"I am Sergei. I am your friend."

"Listen, let's drop this 'friend' business. It doesn't fly."

"Fly? I don't understand."

"Work on it." Stuart turned over and lay face down, despite the pressure on his ribs.

The leather soles scraped away; softly the door closed. The light remained on. Stuart could hear the soft whirr of the camera eye as it moved back and forth. So much for the initial encounter.

He was on his back when Mrs. Outer Mongolia woke him. This time she brought a plastic pitcher holding at least a liter of water. Stuart plunged his face into it, gulping thirstily. When he'd swallowed half of it he looked up, panting, and grinned foolishly at the woman. "Bath time," he said, got off the bed, dropped his pajama pants, and used the remaining water to cleanse his crotch, armpits, face, and hands. The final drops he licked from the rim of the pitcher and handed it back to the woman, who received it expressionlessly and went away.

He felt better, revived, almost euphoric—like the effect of the late-night Dexedrines he taken while studying for law exams.

His fingers scratched the stubble on his face. They wouldn't let him have a razor, of course, and in Russia electric shavers were reserved for the *nomenklatura*. Well, maybe he'd grow a beard.

By now, he thought, the Brussels meeting was history and the air force plane was back at Andrews, ready for the next group of congressional junketeers. He hadn't intended to let Senator Chase down, and he wondered what kind of a search was underway for him. The crashed embassy car and its dead driver would tell Chase and others that he either had been snatched or was an amnesiac wandering the French countryside, another Rolf Kingman.

Pat and Larry, thousands of miles away aboard the *Queen Elizabeth II*, were probably unaware of his disappearance. He hoped so. As for Diana Selwyn, she was doubtlessly sunning her beautiful body on the beaches of Ibiza. Well, he wouldn't be joining her there this season. Besides, if she were any kind of daughter, she'd be visiting her ailing father in Jamaica. But Diana was too self-centered, too able to rise above the sufferings of others. Poor Blake, singlemindedly focusing on his career while his home life went to hell.

As the moisture dried from his body it cooled his skin agreeably—except for the bandaged part. Eventually that tight tape would come off, and he'd be whole again.

He sat on the bed, facing away from the camera, and analyzed his options. One was to strike a deal with Sergei and leave with his life. The other was to escape. From Leningrad he might be able to get over to Finland. From Moscow he'd have to hijack an Aeroflot plane to the nearest non-Communist airstrip.

Wherever he was, escape would mean killing. He'd been trained to kill with his hands, and he wouldn't hesitate if and when it became necessary. The murders of Selwyn, Scott, and the driver were three scores to even.

First he'd try to deal—that was what they would want. And if it didn't work? Then he'd have to get out of this prison-hospital, whatever it was. Killing the woman and leaving in her clothing was one possibility. Under normal circumstances he could take Sergei, he was confident, but as the mouse said to the elephant, "I've been ill."

Stuart laughed aloud. The spasm shot through his ribs, making him gasp. Turning to the camera, he thumbed his nose at it. "Kiss mine," he said, hoping the audio recorder was on.

He got off the bed and measured his cell. Seven paces one

way, five the other. Seventy-foot perimeter. Divided into a mile: fifty-two circuits. He started walking.

His muscles complained, but Stuart managed eight circuits before he sat on the bed, legs trembling, breath shallow and gasping, dizzy from the exertion.

Eight circuits today, he told himself, ten tomorrow. He had to take it in slow, measured increments, for if his diet lacked potassium, his heart muscles would be weakened—the club trainer had told him that.

Prisoners who gave up hope were the first to go. Curled up in the fetal position, they refused food and water and died like caged animals. He'd rather die fighting, taking some of them with him by way of escort to Valhalla.

Sergei's erect bearing and personal neatness hinted a military background. Of course, the KGB, like the SS, was a military organization, and Sergei was probably an officer specializing in interrogation. Rank? Stuart guessed lieutenant colonel, estimating Sergei's age at forty-four or thereabouts. His physical condition appeared good—no pot belly, at least—except for the burst facial capillaries, which revealed heavy drinking. Next time he'd check Sergei's eyes for the yellow of liver damage—the man had stayed too far away before, and Stuart had had other things to concentrate on.

By now, Stuart figured, General Winkowski would be pounding the president's desk, demanding an all-out effort to get back Alan Stuart. State was hopeless, of course, couldn't retrieve a yo-yo on a string, and Winkowski knew it. It helped to think that *someone* in Washington was doing something in his behalf, but Stuart hoped the task wouldn't fall to the CIA. A rescue party would screw it up, and they'd all end up dead. No thanks, he murmured, I'll take my chances alone.

The ceiling light went out.

Stuart lay on his back, gripped the bed rails, lifted his legs forty-five degrees, and held them there until his thigh and back muscles screamed. He rested, then did it again until he wanted to shout out in pain.

Tomorrow he'd repeat the exercise. Until then he'd blank his mind and sleep.

Someone nudged him. Opening his eyes, Stuart saw Mrs. Mongolia holding a plate of food. She fished in her apron pocket and produced a plastic fork.

Rice and meat. No meal at Tante Marie had ever looked more succulent. "Knife," he said with a sawing gesture, but her face remained blank. "C'mon, Momma," he whispered, "when I'm ready to kill you it won't be with a plastic knife," and smiled agreeably before wolfing down the rice.

It had been cooked in some kind of animal broth, adding flavor and making it doubly nourishing. The thin meat slab was about three by three inches, and tough as leather, so he bit off small portions. Delicious!

He took his time. The woman stood at his bedside, hands folded before her apron. She was in no hurry, and Stuart wondered if she was prisoner too. Well, Russia itself was the world's largest prison, and as in any prison system, some prisoners had more privileges than others.

"I'd rather be a Yankee pauper than a Russian commissar," he chanted, winking at the camera. Then he licked the remaining grease off the plate, belched, and handed it back. "Go away, go away, but come and play another day," he sang in a loud voice, patted his flat stomach, and decided to walk off the heavy meal.

Nine circuits were all he could manage before feeling nauseated. He broke off, not wanting to vomit, and sat on the bed to steady himself.

The door opened and Sergei came in. Locking the door, he strode over with a smile. "Better food, yes? You like it?"

"Passable," Stuart commented. "Cook it yourself?"

"*Nyet*—no, no, it is prepared in the hospital kitchen. Special diet for special patients. Now you will soon get strong again."

"I'm looking forward to that," Stuart said. "Coffee tomorrow, or furshlugginer tea? Whichever, plenty of sugar, eh? And when do I see a doctor?"

"Slow, slowly. Your speaking comes too fast. Doctor? Ah, he is busy with sick patients, gravely sick. You, however, Mr. Stuart, are on the mend—is that the expression?"

"Well said, Sergei, but I need care. I want chest X-rays, full blood work-up, urinalysis, and some pills for pain. I mean, not just aspirin, Sergei, something with impact, okay?"

The rush of words left Sergei behind. Stuart wanted to overload the Russian's synapses, keep him confused about minor things. Then, when they got to the nitty-gritty there might be an echo effect. "Okay, don't answer. But treating me well means medical attention, right? Send in the Mongolian doc. Let him take blood samples and I'll piss in his jar. X-rays can wait."

"You are serious, no?" His face looked puzzled.

"I'm serious, yes. How do we know I haven't got kidney damage? That was a hell of a crash I survived—barely." He shook his head. "Crude. The driver, poor bastard, was working class, not an exploiter, but your people killed him."

Sergei's face tightened. "I am not responsible for the way you were brought here. Be grateful for life, Mr. Alan Stuart. You are young, with many years ahead of you. If"—he paused significantly—"you cooperate."

"I'm ready to cooperate," Stuart replied, "assuming I'm given medical attention." He paused, as Sergei had done. "After that, anything is possible."

Sergei's features relaxed. "You promise?"

Stuart nodded. "Also, I need clean pajamas and bedclothes. Everything stinks."

Sergei scratched the point of his chin. "I will see what I can do."

"Hell, you can do anything you want here. You're the big

enchilada, right? Your word is their command. I know it, you know
it, so don't fuck around. No bullshit, eh? Action."

Sergei nodded. "Later," he said, and went away.

Much later, the putative doctor arrived with syringes and a
urine jar. Sergei stood by while the doctor drew blood from Stuart's
arm, and he watched Stuart's dark-yellow urine fill the jar.

After the men left, Mrs. Mongolia brought fresh bed linen and
pajamas. Silently she changed the bed, gathered up the soiled
linen, and left. She returned with a liter of water, which she left
with Stuart. "*Dankeschön*, he said, and immediately began to
drink.

He felt the loss of blood—as much as 200 ml had been
taken—so he was lying on the bed when Sergei came back. "You
are satisfied? Pleased with your care?" he asked, rubbing his
hands together. "See—even water you have."

"Things are improving," Stuart conceded. "Now, what can I
do for you?"

Sergei gave him a surprised glance. Recovering his composure, he said slowly, "You do for *me*?" then burst into laughter.

"What's so funny?" Stuart demanded irritably.

"Oh, that you—*you*, Mr. Alan Stuart, in your, uh, ambiguous
situation, inquire what *you* can do for *me*." He used a pocket
handkerchief to wipe his eyes. "Unusual in my experience.
Unique."

"Well, I'm glad you've had your laugh for the day, Sergei. I try
to cooperate and you laugh it off. Fuck it. Forget it."

"No, I am ready for dialogue."

"Another time," Stuart snapped. "When you're in a serious
mood."

"But I am serious, believe me, and ready to listen. It is that
you are, uh—what is the word? Unpredictable."

Stuart said nothing, apparently considering. After a while he
said, "I was snatched, kept alive, and brought to your country.

Why? You people do nothing without a reason, a valid reason. You took big chances—the crash that killed my driver easily could have killed me. You wanted me dead or alive—preferably alive—right?"

Sergei, face serious again, nodded. "Alive. In good health."

"Well, at least I'm alive. For how long?"

"That depends."

Stuart expelled a sigh. "Talk about ambiguity. I just want to know what's ahead for me."

"Ah, but who can read the future, Mr. Stuart? Not even I."

"This is bullshit," Stuart said sourly, "so let's"—borrowing a phrase from Diana—"stop the childish games. We'll start over. Now, what would you say if I asked for Soviet citizenship?"

Bewildered, Sergei met Stuart's gaze, then looked away. "You mean . . . to become a citizen of the Soviet Union?"

"Right. Moscow or Leningrad branch. Surrender my passport at the embassy and renounce the imperialist U.S.A. Could I be granted citizenship?"

Sergei hesitated. Inwardly, Stuart smiled. Finally Sergei admitted, "I . . . I do not know. I would have to find out, ask others, you understand? And much would depend on your cooperation."

"I said I was ready to cooperate, and you found humor in it."

"One moment—tell me, why would you want to become a Soviet citizen?"

"Okay, I'll tell you. I've led a boring life. Now I find I'm a man who wants change. I have no dependents, no family, nothing to hold me to the United States. From what I know of your legal system, I think you need good lawyers over here. And I'm a good lawyer. So how about it?"

"I—I will have to inquire. It may take time. Here things are not done as fast as in your country. So—there is your temporary answer: I will inquire."

Stuart's misdirection was working. He'd thrown Sergei a

Rosetta stone that would take time to decipher. And since Stuart's words were being recorded, Sergei's chief, whoever he was, also would be distracted by Stuart's interest in becoming a Soviet citizen.

Sergei took a deep breath, then expelled it. "So—we will move on to positive things, yes? Such as—what you can do for me."

"Spit it out," Stuart said. "I'm waiting for an answer."

Sergei acted like a speaker who'd lost his notes. To regain his composure, he jammed his hands in his coat pockets and gave Stuart a hard stare. "How well did you know Blake Selwyn?"

"Hardly at all. We both worked at State, years ago. I was a glorified clerk and he was a high-ranking officer. I hadn't seen Blake Selwyn in four years until he came to my office and asked me to represent him."

"In what way?"

"He wanted to divorce his wife and eliminate her from a new will. I was to draw up that will."

"Did you?"

"That was a Friday. By Monday he was dead. I don't work weekends."

"And that was the only occasion you saw him?"

"The only one. Blake was nervous, upset, because the divorce—his second—would work against his promotion. At State they're very puritanical."

"Then his widow—Diana Selwyn—inherited everything?"

Stuart nodded. "Plus a quarter of a million in insurance, the house, the car"—he spread his hands—"the whole schmier. And here's the irony: because of Blake's surprise visit, the widow hired me to represent her and Blake's estate." He chuckled. "How's *that* for luck? A god-damn gold mine."

"What else did Selwyn ask you to do?"

Stuart remembered his trip to Rockville. "I had to make sure his death was natural. The county medical examiner swore it was. He provided the copies of the death certificate I needed to collect Selwyn's insurance."

"What did the death certificate say?"

"Heart failure—natural causes." He sat forward and stared up at the Russian. "Wasn't it?"

Sergei ignored the question. "You flew to Springfield, capital of Illinois. For what reason?"

"To see the Selwyn family lawyer, a man named Scott. Diana thought Scott might have some of Blake's stocks, bonds, whatever. She wasn't specific and I never found out, because Mr. Scott died before I got to Springfield. A useless trip, but I was paid for my time and expenses."

He was quite sure that Sergei knew he was telling the truth on minor points, lying about the big ones. But Sergei would expect that. Interrogations followed a pattern; first lies, then truths. Each simultaneously probed the extent of the other's knowledge. Stuart folded his arms. "Anything else?"

"For now we leave it as it stands. But before I come again, I urge you to search your memory for anything left unsaid." His hands came out of his pockets. "It will be good for you when you apply for Soviet citizenship."

"Hold on—I didn't say I was *going* to apply, I just asked your opinion of it. I'd have to have guarantees, Sergei—housing, job, salary, dacha, car . . . the perks I'm accustomed to in the States."

"I see . . . that could be difficult."

"Then forget it. Now, if my lab tests are okay, I'll be ready to leave the hospital in a week." He touched his bandaged ribs lightly. "A week, Sergei. I want to be strong enough to enjoy a Bolshoi opera or a Kirov ballet."

Sergei smiled tolerantly. "We should conclude our conversation in less than a week."

"And I can go back home?"

The smile vanished. "We will see."

The door closed, locked, and Stuart scored the first encounter:

Visitor   1
KGB   0

But in the normal sequence of events, the KGB would score the next round—and perhaps all the others. What Stuart was working toward was a tie.

CHAPTER 16

*T*hree rice-meat meals later, Sergei returned.

In the interval, Stuart was walking fifteen room circuits easily and pointing for twenty. He could slant his legs rigidly for five minutes at a stretch, and his thigh and abdominal muscles were gaining tone. Trying to exercise his arms and shoulders brought on too much pain, but he wasn't planning to walk out of prison on his arms.

Without any preliminaries Sergei shouted, "You lied to me, Stuart! You think you can lie and I don't know? Now you will tell me the truth. *All* the truth!"

Stuart, expecting the onslaught, looked embarrassed. "It's true. But how did you find out we were lovers?"

"Lov—? What bullshit are you telling me?"

"I didn't think it gentlemanly to admit that Diana Selwyn and I are in love. Besides, she has nothing to do with this."

"*Nothing?*" Sergei roared.

"Well . . . Blake found out we were sleeping together, confronted me with it, and said he'd divorce Diana—I could have her." He swallowed, looked away. "It was a bad scene—but I didn't kill Blake."

"So why did you go to Springfield?"

"Diana feared that her husband had left something incriminating about her and me with his lawyer. She wanted me to destroy it."

"Did you?"

"Scott's secretary said there was nothing of Blake's in the Selwyn family file, and I took her word for it."

"So, you plan to marry Selwyn's widow?"

"We've planned it for over a year. Too bad Blake found out . . . I think he killed himself."

"And why would he do that?"

"Rejection. His wife hadn't been balling him for years. When he found out she was, uh, sleeping with me, a younger man, he . . . well, put yourself in his place."

"I would never kill myself over a woman, Stuart."

"Well, you Russians are made of stronger stuff. Blake—if you knew him—was the sensitive type. Career oriented, not brilliant in bed." Stuart brightened. "Anyway, Diana didn't shed many tears over him. Nor did I, if you want the truth of it."

Sergei considered Stuart's "confession," one he clearly hadn't expected. Regaining the pace, he said ominously, "And that was your only lie?"

Nodding, Stuart said, "Lie? Omission! Any gentleman would have done the same. It's what we call a 'white lie.' And now you've dug it up; I hope you're satisfied."

"No. Because there are other lies. You *did* receive a message from Selwyn's lawyer."

"Did I forget to mention it? He wanted to go over divorce details with me—he was going to represent Blake." The chronology was wrong; let Sergei straighten it out.

"So that was why you went to Springfield."

"And for what Diana wanted me to do." He looked around uncomfortably. "Look, let's change the subject. I'm not proud of deceiving Blake and I don't want to discuss it any more." He paused. "I'm getting tired of fried leather, Sergei, how about lamb chops next time? With noodles and gravy? Maybe a green salad? Kool-Aid would be good, and hold the cyanide."

Sergei grunted. "You think you can deceive me, exhaust me with foolish talk?"

"No," Stuart replied, "I don't expect to deceive you about anything, I just want better food. When can I get out of here? What are my lab results?"

"First things first," Sergei said roughly. "Blake Selwyn gave you secret papers before he was—before he died. Political papers of great importance."

This was the moment Stuart had been waiting for. "Who told you?"

"That does not concern you. Where are those papers?"

"Where are my lab reports? I want to know if there's blood in my urine. When can I leave here?"

"Tell the truth."

Stuart lay sideways on the bed and drew his knees up into the fetal position. "I'm tired. You're unpleasant. You don't tell me anything, so why should I talk with you?"

"Because I demand it."

Ah, Stuart thought, the sword is slipping from its sheath. He closed his eyes.

"Talk, Alan Stuart. We have ways—"

"Ve haf vays," Stuart mimicked. "Too many Nazi movies, Sergei. Vot vays you haf? Hot irons? Ball-pinchers? Acid? Drugs? You haf *dreck*—which means 'shit' in two languages. Come back when you're in a better mood. And don't forget: lab reports and food."

"You talk to me now. You tell everything!"

"I don't talk with barbarians," Stuart sneered. *"Ne kulturniy."*

"Talk!"

"Take it easy. One word from me and ten choppers filled with CIA killers will be all over this place."

"So? And how will you contact the CIA?"

"Easy. I have this little transmitter implant just behind my ear—maybe I shouldn't tell you that. I press it, see, and the signal goes out. It keeps beeping so the troops can locate me."

The Russian sneered. "That is absurd."

"I heard it was a Russian invention. Anyway, CIA assassins come and you're all dead. *Todt. Kaput. Fini.* So watch your ass, Sergei. Lamb chops, Kool-Aid, and a green salad will square you. Then we'll talk again. But not about adultery or Blake Selwyn."

"I choose the subject."

"*Ja, das ist gut.* Dealer's choice."

"Dealer's . . . what is that?"

"When you come back I'll explain. Very complicated, take long time, *mucho, muy* long. Now let me sleep." He yawned and waved a careless dismissal.

Disconcerted, Sergei stood staring down at Stuart. A few moments later Stuart heard him walking away. Key in lock, turn, open, close, key in lock, silence.

Stuart opened one eye and looked at the closed-circuit camera. He tapped his right ear and closed his eyes.

Cumulative score:

Visitor 2

KGB 0

Exhausted, Stuart felt sleep roll over him in a great irresistible wave. He surrendered to it gladly.

Two meals later—his only chronological reference—a new interrogator arrived.

Number two was a stocky man of about fifty, his bald head rising from broad, powerful shoulders. He wore a badly fitted suit of a shoddy brown material, red tie, and blunt-toed workman's shoes. His eyes were small, round, and set deep in a rectangular face. The fingers that extended from his coat sleeves resembled stubby cigars. He looked like an overaged weight lifter, and enough like Nikita Khrushchev to be his brother. Overall, he projected dominance and power.

One hand held a plastic plate on which Stuart saw two lamb chops and a leaf of lettuce. He stopped five feet from the bed and snapped, "Up. On your feet, Stuart. Show respect."

Stuart got off the bed and faced him.

The man said, "You wanted lamb chops? Here are your lamb chops!" He slammed them on the floor, and with hardly a pause opened his fly and urinated on them. When the flow ended he closed his fly and said, "Get the idea? Things have changed around here. You played Sergei for a fool, but I have no time for games."

"I respect a man who knows what he wants," Stuart said.

"Then you and I will get along." He shook his head disgustedly. "Sergei underestimated you. I warned him you were very clever, to be careful." He shrugged, the coat fabric rippling around his neck. "He wanted to try, so I gave him his chance. Now you will deal with me."

Advancing on Stuart, he suddenly jabbed two fingers into Stuart's ribs. Stuart screamed and doubled over, gasping.

The Russian looked at him, contempt on his porcine face. "See how simple it is to introduce reality? We will deal, you and I, in realities, not the absurd fantasies you wove around Sergei. If you should be so foolish as to lie to me, Stuart, I will punish you. The pain you feel is but a small sample of what you may expect." He stood, legs apart, like a man facing an elephant's charge, solid as granite.

"My name," he said in a controlled voice, "is Ilya Brakov. I represent the Committee for State Security—the KGB—and I hold the rank of colonel. I expect to be addressed by my rank. Is that understood?"

"Yes, sir."

"Yes, *Colonel*."

"Yes, Colonel," Stuart repeated. "Now that you've pissed on my meal, what do you want from me?"

"You don't have to ask, Stuart, because I am going to tell you." He pulled a package of cigarettes from his pocket, shook one out, lighted it, and dropped the match in the puddle of urine. While he was doing that, Stuart estimated the distance between them. Groin kick? Neck chop? If he missed, Brakov would smash his leg or his neck. The man looked as if he could take a dozen bullets without breaking stride.

"What I want to know," said Colonel Brakov, "is the present location of the message or letter sent you by your client, Blake Selwyn."

"I destroyed it, Colonel."

"You destroyed it. Why?"

"It made no sense. It wasn't something I wanted his widow to see. It would have depressed her."

"That is your reply?"

"It is, Colonel."

From Brakov's lips came a sucking sound. "Out," he ordered, thumb toward the open door.

Obediently Stuart walked out. As soon as he cleared the doorway, his arms were gripped on both sides. Two men hurried him along the hall and dragged him, stumbling, down a flight of stairs.

A door opened into a dirt-floored passageway. In the dim light Stuart could make out two iron doors with Judas windows. One thug unlocked the first door and together they shoved Stuart into the dark cell. He fell onto the pack-earth floor and lay there while the door was locked.

The Judas window grated open and Brakov's voice snapped, "Think it over, Stuart. Here you stay until you tell the truth."

Stuart sat up slowly. "One thing, Colonel—I've decided I don't want to be a Soviet citizen."

Brakov grunted. "Why did you change your mind?"

"On reflection I realized that communism is a historical aberration, irrelevant to the twentieth century."

The aperture slammed shut.

The room was dank and cold. Stuart shivered and drew his bare feet off the floor to preserve as much body warmth as he could. He was glad of the time he'd been allowed to play around with Sergei. His ribs were pretty well healed, his muscles had regained some tone, and a normal fluid balance had been established. For now. The average body could exist without fluid intake for about three days, so if water was to be withheld he would have to confess before then—sooner if tortured or drugged.

Getting up, Stuart moved around the cell. The walls were cement blocks, rough to the touch. A grilled window, high above his reach, allowed a little light to penetrate through the flaked paint. He paced the cell's dimensions—six by nine feet—and kept walking to stimulate circulation. The door was sheeted with iron; the only break in its smooth surface was the aperture, which opened from outside.

He wondered how many prisoners the cell had held, and how many had left alive. There was no excrement bucket, no urine hole. At least he was spared that stench, he thought as he kept walking. He remembered the contaminated lamb chops. Brakov knew what he was doing, no question of that. A career interrogator, Stuart thought, applying proven Chekist methods for fast results.

But this wasn't the Lubyanka or its annexes. There the cells were painted and floored with concrete, and the guards were uniformed. These thugs wore street clothing. Stuart could hear the faint sound of distant traffic. If he were in a metropolitan zone, passing trucks would vibrate the packed earth floor, and so far that had not occurred. So he must be on the outskirts of a city— probably Moscow or Leningrad. Well, either way, if he got out he was still unclothed and shoeless and ten thousand miles from home.

It encouraged him that neither Brakov nor his uglies wore

sidearms. When the time came to make his break, it would be man against man. He counted on his desperation to prevail.

Brakov's rib jab had nearly panicked him, more from surprise than pain, though the soreness lingered just over his heart. The heavy bandaging was retaining body heat far better than the thin pajama fabric, so the bandage was a double plus.

Brakov's brutal dominance erased Stuart's small victories over Sergei. His feet were getting cold. He sat down and massaged them, rubbing the soles and his stiffening toes. He lay back and elevated his feet, the torso bandage partially insulating his back from the earth's penetrating cold. His eyes searched the ceiling. No beams to hang from, no video camera surveilling. Another plus. But *how to get out?* He could hit the first guard who came in, block the door with his body, then use the door as a shield to enter the passageway.

That was a last resort, though; his strategy had always been to bargain using Selwyn's letter. Why was it so important to the Russians? Even if Kingman *were* exposed as their agent, he was useless now to either side. Still, perceptions counted, and until Brakov read the letter he couldn't know exactly what it contained.

Gradually light dwindled from the small overhead window and the cell became totally dark.

Stuart moved around blindly to stimulate circulation. Then he would rest, then walk some more and rest. Finally, despite the cold and his stiffening muscles, he fell asleep.

The scrape of feet in the passageway woke him, and as the footsteps approached, he lay on his side, legs drawn up in the fetal position.

The Judas window creaked aside and a flashlight beam played over his body. Brakov's voice barked. "Sit up, Stuart, I'm coming in."

CHAPTER 17

*P*ainfully, stiffly, with exaggerated slowness, Stuart sat erect, heels and buttocks on the cold dirt, arms hugging his legs. He kept his gaze on his feet.

"Not so good here, eh? Not like the guest room," Brakov sneered.

"It's different," Stuart said, "—Colonel."

"How long can you survive this cold?"

"Hadn't thought about it, Colonel. Maybe a week. How long do most prisoners last?"

"Not that long, Stuart. No food or water—less than a week."

"If you're going to kill me, get it over with."

"Colonel."

"Colonel," Stuart echoed obediently.

"But that is the point, Stuart—you are not to be killed. Taken near death, if you insist, but not killed, understand?"

"If you say so, Colonel."

"You are a foolish young man to deny me what I will have. Why be obstinate? Why persist?"

"I have a moral obligation," Stuart replied, "—Colonel."

"I can cripple you, destroy your body so life will not be worth living. Is that worth your 'moral obligation'?"

"I'm weighing it," Stuart replied dully, "thinking it over."

"Excellent. Now, what did Selwyn's letter say that is more important than your life?"

"Put that way, Colonel, I have to say I don't know. Blake must have written it under stress. He made—charges against certain people, reputable men."

"Who? What kind of charges?"

"General Winkowski was one he named. Senator Sandifer's another. And"—he hesitated—"Assistant Secretary Kingman. Selwyn claimed they were security risks, accused them of giving secrets to the Soviet disarmament negotiators. I—I don't remember the rest, Colonel."

"And you did nothing with that information?"

"I'm a lawyer. I looked for evidence, substantiation. There was none." He looked up at Brakov's scowling face. "In America we don't denounce people for no reason. There has to be reasonable cause, something tangible. I had only a letter written by a dead man."

"I see. And so you destroyed it."

Stuart considered his reply carefully. "I destroyed it."

Brakov's shoe connected hard with his thigh. Stuart yelped and hugged the bruised muscle. He tried to skitter sideways to avoid the next painful kick. His reactive impulse was to grab Brakov's foot, twist him to the floor, and crush the Russian's throat, but Stuart suppressed it. Instead he whimpered.

"You talk of moral obligation," Brakov snarled. "Your obligation was to denounce the traitors. Didn't Selwyn pay you for that? You took the money and stayed silent. How moral was that?"

Stuart coughed, swallowed, coughed again. "You make a point," he said tightly, "but how could that have benefited your side?"

"That's not your concern," Brakov snapped. "What else did the letter say?"

Stuart breathed heavily as he massaged his thigh. "Named their controller."

"*Who?*"

"Yuri . . . Yuri . . . Ben—wait, don't hurt me—Bendikov. I . . . I met him later. Looked harmless to me. Seemed rather stupid—Colonel." He had given Brakov four names, of which two were valid.

"Still," Brakov pointed out, "you did nothing."

"That's FBI business. If Bendikov was running them, the FBI should have known. I—I didn't want to get involved, maybe have to testify. It would have ruined my law practice. Everyone would have thought I was a spy too." He lowered his forehead on his knees. "Damn Selwyn for getting me into this! Ten thousand lawyers in Washington and he picks me!"

"You were his friend. He *thought* he could trust you."

He should have gone to the FBI himself," Stuart said resentfully. "But no, his career came first. Damn him!"

"And you persist in your lie."

Stuart was silent. Another kick made him howl and roll away. Furiously, Brakov said, "You kept the letter—you have it. Admit it, Stuart. Lawyers don't destroy things, they keep everything. *Where is it?*"

When Stuart remained silent, Brakov moved back to the doorway, and whistled twice. In a few moments the doctor came in, syringe in hand.

"Oh, God," Stuart babbled, "not that. I can't take more drugs, I'll die." He moved into the corner of the cell and looked up pleadingly.

"You exhaust my patience, Stuart." Brakov turned to the doctor, who stood obediently, syringe in hand. "You will suffer less if you tell me now. *Where is Selwyn's letter?*"

"In—in Washington," Stuart choked.

"Good. You admit you lied."

"Yes, I lied."

"Progress. Where in Washington, Stuart? *Where?*"

"My bank—my safe deposit box. I—I didn't know what to do with it, so I kept it there."

"Which bank?"

"Riggs, across from my office." He shivered.

"Then you will sign a letter to the bank allowing someone to open that box."

"That won't work. I have a key, the bank has a key. I have to open it myself."

Brakov thought it over, then snapped an order in Russian. The doctor lowered the syringe and left the cell.

"I can confirm the procedure," Brakov said. "So—"

"Go ahead, Colonel. You'll find that I'm right."

Brakov's lips made that odd sucking sound Stuart had heard before. "Supposing your presence *is* necessary, Stuart, how can I be sure you will give the letter to me?"

"Send someone with me, Colonel. Let your man bring it back."

"What tricks have you in mind?"

"None. All I want is to get out of this. You get the letter, I get freedom and my life. Selwyn didn't tell me what he was getting me into. I'm sick of the whole thing."

Brakov nodded thoughtfully. "Very well," he agreed at last. "We will do that. And to make sure you keep your end of the bargain, I have something to show you."

When Stuart didn't move, Brakov said sharply, "Get up, follow me."

Stuart limped into the passageway. Brakov spoke to his thugs, and one of them opened the door of the adjoining cell. The other shoved Stuart inside. He stumbled forward, striking the far wall, sensed movement, and peered into dimness. A figure was roped hand and foot to shackles in the wall. Wordless sounds came from the gagged mouth.

Disbelievingly, Stuart moved toward the prisoner and frantically began untying the cords and the thick gag.

Behind him the Judas window slid open. Brakov's voice spoke.

"To ensure compliance, Stuart." As the aperture closed, a sobbing Diana Selwyn collapsed in Stuart's arms.

CHAPTER 18

"Oh, God," Diana gasped, "I'm so glad you're alive—I thought you'd been killed too." She kissed his cheeks and forehead repeatedly.

"We have to talk—*quietly*." Stuart kissed her lips. "How did they get you?"

She tried to wipe the tears from her wet cheeks. "Last night—was it only last night?—I was in a restaurant. The waiter said there was a call for me. I went to the telephone and two men were waiting. One had a gun. He told me to come quietly." She stared at him bleakly. "What else could I do?"

"And they flew you here?"

"*Flew*? I don't understand. They drove me, blindfolded. Alan, where do you think we are?"

"Somewhere in Russia?"

Her hands framed his face. "They drugged you, didn't they? So you couldn't know—we're somewhere outside Paris."

"*Paris*? Shit! I'd have tried to get away." He'd fallen for the charade, damn them!

"Oh, Alan—" Her hand touched his cheek. "What's happening? Why did they bring us here?"

"I have something they want. I've been resisting, putting them off to let my ribs heal."

She looked down, noticing the bandaging for the first time. "How are you now?"

"Better. Not a hundred percent, but functional. Yes, they drugged me, kept me unconscious for days. The drugs"—he wet his lips—"I thought I was going crazy." He kissed her forehead.

"You should have gone to Ibiza."

"How could you think that? I stayed in Paris, hoping, praying for word of you."

"And Kingman? Rolf Kingman?"

"I don't know anything about him." Stuart remembered O'Rourke's blackout orders. She squeezed his hand. "At least we're together. I wanted us to be together, but not like this." For a while they said nothing, then Diana asked, "What is it they want from you?"

"It's better you not know."

"Whatever it is, *please* give it to them." She looked around and shuddered. "Being here is so terrifying."

"I will let them have it," Stuart told her, "but I have to make sure they'll let us go—alive. It's all I have to bargain with, and I'm glad I held out until now." He put his arm around her shoulder, drew her close, held her until his ribs ached.

"I saw the car—the wreck," she said quietly. "That poor man . . . I was so glad it wasn't you."

"Where do people think I am?"

"They think you were found, taken to someone's home . . . that you'd lost your memory."

"I damn near did." He told her about his car having been followed, then forced off the road; regaining consciousness in the soundproof room, Sergei's ineptness, and his replacement by Ilya Brakov. "*Colonel* Brakov," Stuart emphasized. "He's got a thing about rank, so humor him." His eyes had adjusted to the darkness and he could see her face clearly now. God, she was beautiful, and now she was involved because of him. No, because of her husband. Let's keep that straight, he told himself. Brakov was clever, all right, factoring in Diana for leverage against him. What could he do but obey?

"I think they'll let me go to Washington," he said, "to retrieve what they want. But I'll need to know you're free first." He thought for a few moments. "When I call I'll ask about Paris weather. If you're okay, say it's fine. If not, say it's worse than Washington."

Her voice choked. "And what if it's 'worse than Washington'? What then, Alan?"

"Leave that to me," he said with a confidence he didn't feel. "Don't worry. They're not going to torture you or anything like that. You don't know anything, and they understand that. You're a hostage, nothing more." He kissed her warm, pliant lips, recalling their first embrace, their first lovemaking. So much had happened since that night, it seemed years ago. They had become strangers, at cross-purposes with each other.

"I want to tell you about Edward Beamish," she said softly. "You deserve to know, Alan."

But he pressed his fingers to her lips. "Not now. We may not have much time, so listen carefully. I have an old friend I can trust, Blaise de Chaumont Percival. Percy and I were classmates. He's a lawyer, office on the Champs Élysées, apartment on Avenue Foch, summer place in Rambouillet. He'll do anything we need done. His brother-in-law, Julien, is a judge in the Fourteenth Arrondissement." He paused to collect his thoughts. "God knows what he thinks happened to me since we were at Prunier's that last day, but he'll know you're speaking for me if you remind him that I paid for lunch."

She repeated Percy's name slowly. "Prunier's—you paid."

"Flipped a twenty-franc coin. If that doesn't bring him to action alert, something's happened to a very sharp mind."

She looked away. "You were drugged—how awful. Why? What's behind it?"

He turned her face to his. "After we opened Blake's box you met a man behind the bank. Who was he?"

"You were following me?"

"Never mind. Who was the man? Why did you meet him?"

"No big secret—State security asked me to check the contents of the box for any classified papers."

"Meaning they thought Blake might have squirreled some away?"

"Not at all. The security officer said it was routine verification, that's all." She pressed her cheek against his. "And you thought—"

"Well, he was young and good-looking. Unlike Ed Beamish."

"You *are* jealous of Ed!"

"I have reason to be. He's Mister Everything, squires you here and there . . ."

"Alan. My interest in him is *not* romantic—far from it. I—"

The door opened and Colonel Brakov barked, "On your feet, both of you."

When they were standing, backs to the wall, arms around each other's waists, Brakov said, "Stuart, I have decided to give you a chance to get out of this once and for all. Follow instructions to the letter and you won't be troubled again. Fail to, and you will die as certain others have, and so will Mrs. Selwyn."

"This is an exchange," Stuart said. "The item you want for our lives, correct?"

"Correct. Now, I could say I don't enjoy killing, but that is no longer true. Two years ago I was in Afghanistan. I saw what the mountain bandits did to my soldiers and I began killing to avenge my men. Then I killed for satisfaction. So don't think I'm reluctant to kill to gain my ends. I'm accustomed to it."

At Diana's little cry, Brakov smiled unpleasantly. "If Mr. Stuart plays his part correctly you have nothing to fear, Mrs. Selwyn. Merely a few days' inconvenience."

"She's to be freed when I turn over the—the item you want," Stuart stated firmly.

"I have a procedure that guarantees to satisfy us both." He gestured at them. "We will now return to the room where you were cured of your injuries, Mr. Stuart. In your absence, Mrs. Selwyn will be my guest there." Turning, he went out, followed by Stuart and Diana. The two thugs fell in behind. All five went up the stairs and into the soundproof room. There was fresh linen on the bed. A chair and table had been added, and there was a china wash basin and a water pitcher on the table. "Not the luxury you are accustomed to, Mrs. Selwyn, but better than below," Brakov pointed out. "Stuart, say good-bye and come with me. You have a long way to go, and time is short."

"Mrs. Selwyn should know the arrangements, Colonel, so there is no mistake."

"I agree. Stuart, you will go to your bank, accompanied by one of my men. With the item in hand you will go to your office and telephone a number, which you will be given. My man will speak with me, and you will then speak with Mrs. Selwyn."

"Not good enough," Stuart said. "She has to be on neutral territory when she takes my call."

"Why would I keep her? I have no interest in her other than as a guarantee of your conduct."

"I don't know that," said Stuart. "I understand very little about any of this."

Brakov considered. "What would you call neutral territory?"

"The apartment of a lawyer in Paris."

"Who?"

"Mrs. Selwyn will tell you."

"I see you want to keep the advantage."

"Your man will have the item in question, Colonel. He'll tell you so. If he doesn't, you have Mrs. Selwyn. And I don't doubt that the KGB could finish me off with its customary efficiency."

"What would prevent me from killing you both?"

"Moral responsibility, Colonel, besides having nothing to gain from it."

"I hope you will do nothing to provoke violence," he shrugged. "You have one minute alone." He left the room.

Stuart gathered Diana in his arms. "Blaise Percival," he whispered, "and the weather code. Two things to remember. Then I'll come back and take you where they'll never find us."

Her body began to tremble. "I'm afraid, Alan, terribly afraid. For you, me, both of us."

"Don't be." He kissed her lips. "Count on me."

She hugged him painfully tight. "Give them whatever they want," she whispered in his ear. "You must."

"Enough!" Brakov snapped. "Time to go, Stuart."

Reluctantly Stuart left, turned at the doorway, and gave the thumbs-up sign. Brakov locked the door and led Stuart down the corridor to another room. "Your clothing was too badly damaged to wear again—blood, tears, oil stains. These things will do for your return."

The clothing was draped over the back of a chair. Stuart put on a too-large shirt, a reasonably well-fitting charcoal gray suit, and his own shoes and socks. Brakov handed Stuart his billfold and passport. "No tie?" Stuart asked.

Brakov went to the closet and pulled out a red tie. "Sergei's," Stuart noted, putting it on.

"Yes. He will not need it for a while. Come here." Brakov opened a medicine cabinet on the wall, and Stuart could see through a one-way mirror into the adjoining room. From the center of it rose a thick pole supporting a crossbar. A man's wrists were tied to the T-bar. The heavyset Mongolian woman was lashing the man with a wooden-handled whip made up of a dozen or so leather thongs, which she slashed across his red, bleeding buttocks. As the man turned his face in a silent howl, Stuart recognized Sergei.

Each time the woman struck Sergei, her heavy breasts reverberated like water-filled balloons. Her lips were drawn back in a fiercely sensual grimace.

"Punishment," Brakov commented in a hard voice, "but pleasure for her. An odd one, that woman, but who can account for tastes?" He closed the cabinet door. "Be thankful it's not you. Now we leave." They headed down a different flight of stairs to a door, where Brakov waited with Stuart while one of his thugs unlocked it.

The waiting limousine was long and black, with CD plates. It was only ten or twelve feet away, but in that interval Stuart sucked in his first fresh air in at least two weeks. The moon's elevation told Stuart that the time was after midnight. The moon was waning; clouds made it look as ragged as he felt. Brakov got into the front seat beside the driver, Stuart settled in the rear between Brakov's thugs, and the limousine moved off through the night.

Looking back, Stuart saw that he had been held in a large country house surmounting a low hill. Around it lay fields of young grain and a small vineyard. The car turned, cutting off his view. One of the thugs blindfolded him with a handkerchief.

"A precaution." Brakov said nothing more for the next hour.

Stuart could hear the sound of aircraft growing nearer, until the thunder of turbofan engines vibrated the car windows. Finally the blindfold was removed. Blinking, Stuart saw airfield lights. It was Orly, south of Paris.

Looking back, Brakov said, "A special flight, Stuart. Your escort is already on board. His English is fluent. Mikhail is armed and knows how to kill silently—I picked him from a *spetznaz* team in my former command. Mikhail knows that if he loses you he will suffer for it, so he will be with you until our transaction is completed. Do you understand?"

"Yes, Colonel."

"What time does your bank open?"

"Nine o'clock, Washington time. Stays open until two. The safe deposit box key is in my home. Also, I recommend that we use my home phone rather than my office."

"Why?"

"My secretary. She would ask too many questions, waste time. It's better that she not see me until afterward."

The diplomatic-plated vehicle pulled through a guarded VIP entrance, paused while an airfield guard checked the driver's pass, then moved on toward a lighted aircraft on the tarmac. Stuart read the Cyrillic inscription along the fuselage: Aeroflot. He didn't know if it was an Antonov or an Ilyushin, but it was smaller than the Russian version of the supersonic Concorde, so he could look forward to a five-hour flight to the United States. Home.

Then what? he wondered, but not for long, because the limousine stopped near the boarding stairway and Stuart was nudged out. Colonel Brakov preceded him up the long flight of steps, the two thugs behind.

The cabin was dimly lighted, a brown curtain separating the forward section from the aft seats—the Soviet way of insulating Communist aristocracy from the peasants.

As Brakov walked down the aisle a man rose from one of the rear seats and greeted him in Russian. They spoke for a few moments, Brakov gesturing at Stuart, before saying, "Meet Mikhail, your escort."

Dutifully Stuart joined them, and Brakov said, "I have explained the procedure to him, Stuart. If you vary from it in any way, he will kill you." He paused. "And I will dispose of Mrs. Selwyn. Think of that while you fly west."

Stuart looked Mikhail over. He was ruggedly built, perhaps an inch shorter than Stuart, with black hair, a prominent jaw line, a slightly crooked nose, and heavy, muscular hands. Stuart noticed a bulge around his left armpit under his well-tailored gray suit.

Mikhail said, "I don't want any trouble with you. Do what you are supposed to and you will have no trouble from me. Understand?"

Stuart nodded.

"Then," concluded Brakov, "I will leave you together. It will be night when you land outside Washington and I think you should go home, collect your key, and sleep a few hours. At nine Mikhail will escort you to the bank. Telephone calls will be exchanged, and you and Mrs. Selwyn will be free to do as you choose."

"That moment can't come soon enough." Stuart got into the window seat indicated by Mikhail, who took the aisle one.

Brakov surveyed Stuart for a few moments, turned abruptly, and walked forward, followed by his thugs. As soon as they left the cabin a steward emerged from behind the curtain and began closing the door. The hum of its hydraulic mechanism merged with the starting whine of the aircraft's jet engines, lights flickered, and the plane began moving ponderously forward.

Within ten minutes they were airborne, the plane banking as it gained altitude, giving Stuart a magic-lantern view of the Paris lights—the spidery boulevards, the Eiffel Tower, and the Arc de Triomphe. Majestic, Stuart thought, and beautiful. Ever-welcoming Paris, the traveler's sentimental home. Well, it hadn't been all that great for him this time, nor for Rolf Kingman or Diana. He remembered the flagellation of Sergei and wondered if Brakov had shown him that scene to suggest subliminally that Diana could be the next such victim.

"Mikhail," he asked, "anything to drink on this skybird?"

His guard shrugged. "Tea? Vodka?"

"Both. How about food?"

"You'll be home soon. Can't you wait?"

"I haven't eaten in a day."

Mikhail pushed the overhead call button, and after a while the steward strolled back. Mikhail ordered in Russian. The steward said *da* and sauntered forward, disappearing behind the curtain.

Where was the soft, soothing music? Stuart asked himself. And the movie screen? Even a rerun of *Alexander Nevsky*, or any current SovFilm offering, for that matter, would divert his mind from what lay ahead.

In ten or twelve minutes—Stuart still had no watch—the steward returned with a tray bearing two glasses of tea, two smaller glasses of vodka, and a plate of pickled beets, onions, and slices of black bread.

Stuart kicked back the vodka and followed with a tea chaser. Then he made a sandwich of the bread and vegetables and ate it, though his stomach rebelled. Mikhail watched him indifferently, adjusted his seat, and leaned back. After a while he closed his eyes. Mikhail had drunk his tea but the vodka glass was untouched. Stuart drank it in two swallows and leaned back against the corner of the window. The plane's running lights were blinking. There was cloud layer below, and mist began to gather in the cabin from the imperfectly operating air circulator. Stuart hoped the mist would purge the dust that had erupted through the cabin during takeoff.

After a while the air grew cold. Stuart got up and began stepping across Mikhail's legs when he felt his belt grabbed and pulled. "Relax," he said to an angry Mikhail, "I just want a blanket, maybe a pillow. Is that allowed?"

"I will get it myself." He stood up, rummaged through the overhead compartment, and tossed Stuart a blanket and a pillow whose case should have been washed several flights ago. Both items bore the Aeroflot logo, probably to reduce theft. As he gathered the blanket around his neck, Stuart belched sour onion fumes, waved them away, and closed his eyes. Before he slept, he scripted a scenario for tomorrow. Then he developed a second one for emergency deployment. "Even when you're well dug in," the Fort Benning platoon sergeant had lectured, "always have a way out. *Capisce?*"

Dear Sergeant Marcantonio, Stuart thought, how I wish you were with me now. The thought purged his mind and he drifted off to sleep.

Mikhail woke him during the plane's long descent. "Less than an hour," he said, rang for the steward, and ordered more tea.

Cabin pressure was dropping and Stuart felt his eardrums react. He yawned, held his nostrils, and blew against them. Mikhail watched with interest, then did the same. Pleased, he asked, "Where you learn that?"

"Scuba diving," Stuart lied, not wanting him to know that it was an early part of parachute indoctrination.

"I would like to learn scuba," Mikhail remarked, "but in my country water is very cold."

Like the people, Stuart thought. He looked down and saw the lights of a ship far below, then glanced at Mikhail's watch, still on Paris time: 5:25. So it was after midnight in Washington. A good hour for a black flight to arrive.

Scattered lights marked the coastline—a broad patch could have been Wilmington, he told himself, or Philadelphia, not knowing the corridor allotted to Aeroflot. They wouldn't be landing at National, he knew; very little night traffic was allowed, and no international arrival facilities. So his guess was Dulles International in Virginia. It was half an hour from there to Georgetown in thin traffic, where Stuart would be on home turf, oriented and mobile.

Surprisingly soon, the plane settled into its glide pattern, and before it touched down, Stuart saw Dulles's distinctive silhouette. After the plane braked and began trundling off onto a bypass lane, Mikhail pointed at the lighted terminal and commented, "Named after your intelligence chief."

Stuart shook his head. "That was *Allen* Dulles," he corrected. "The airport is named in honor of his brother, John Foster, a secretary of state. Both good men."

"Bad men," Mikhail intoned. "Worse, your President Bush was intelligence chief."

"So was Yuri Andropov," Stuart reminded him, "and he got to the top. Big deal."

"Big deal?"

"Means don't get upset about it." He glanced through the window and saw that the aircraft was moving not toward the terminal but toward a dark area beyond a group of maintenance hangars. He wondered if U.S. Customs and Immigration would make an appearance. Not if the flight was supposed to be diplomatic.

The best thing that could happen to me would be to get picked up for questioning, he reflected, but that wasn't going to happen. Besides, unless the deal with Brakov went through, Diana and he would pay the price.

After the plane came to a stop, Stuart could see vehicle lights on the tarmac and men with colored flashlights moving around. Finally he heard the bumping junction of mobile stairway and fuselage, and the cabin door ground open.

"Wait," Mikhail ordered motioning him to stay in his seat. The brown curtain parted and a passenger Stuart hadn't seen before came out, turned abruptly, and went out the doorway.

Stuart's face stayed expressionless as he heard a car approach the stairway to take on the plane's single VIP passenger: Yuri Bendikov, Second Secretary of the Soviet Embassy. The man Blake Selwyn said had handled Rolf Kingman for the KGB.

CHAPTER 19

It was good to breathe stateside air again, but Stuart warned himself not to become euphoric. Alignment was taking place, nothing more; the chess pieces were being placed on the board, but action was hours away.

Bendikov's embassy limousine had already driven off before a black Ford with diplomatic plates pulled up at the foot of the stairway. Mikhail got in first, then Stuart, then another man, an obvious guard with a boxer's broken face and a brush cut that made his blond hair almost invisible in the near darkness. Stuart assumed they were driving to Georgetown, although Mikhail hadn't asked for his street address.

The uniformed driver was alone in the front seat. He drove directly to a VIP exit and was on the Airport Access Road heading east for Washington in less than five minutes. Neither Mikhail nor the brush-cut guard spoke to him or to each other. Good. He could concentrate.

Fifteen minutes later the driver took the south exit onto I-495—the Beltway—and followed it to the I-66 intersection. The car turned east again through the bedroom communities of Falls

Church, Ballston, and Clarendon, until Stuart could see the tall buildings and lights of Rosslyn ahead. Over the Potomac on the Key Bridge, a right turn by the car barn, and onto Georgetown's M Street. The driver braked at Wisconsin for a traffic light, then continued on to Thirty-first, where he turned left and took the incline up to Q. Left again, and presently Stuart was looking up at the dark face of his house.

The car stopped. "You have a key?" Mikhail asked.

"One's in Paris but there's another." He followed Mikhail out of the car and said, "Let's go."

Mikhail's handgun was now in the pocket of his coat, Stuart noticed, probably to lend confidence in a strange environment. They went up the short walk together and mounted the steps. Stuart stepped around a wooden support column and reached up to push aside a section of moulding.

The key was there.

He offered it to Mikhail, who shook his head. "You." Apparently Mikhail was afraid of a bobby-trapped door. Good, Stuart thought, his nerves are on edge. He fitted the key into the lock and the door opened.

"You first," Mikhail said, and Stuart stepped inside.

"Lights?" Mikhail asked.

"As few as possible. This house has been dark for a long time. Why make neighbors—or the police—curious?"

Mikhail nodded and Stuart led the way upstairs. There he turned on a low-wattage table lamp and went into the bathroom to relieve his distended bladder. He left the door open and saw Mikhail looking around. After flushing, Stuart said, "I'm going to take a shower and get into bed. That's my bedroom, yours is next to it." He gestured at an open door.

"No," said Mikhail, "I stay in your room."

"Then use the chair or the floor. You *spetznaz* guys are supposed to be accustomed to hardship."

Peeling off his borrowed clothing, he turned on the bathroom light, then the shower.

The mirror reflected a drawn face, white where not covered with dark stubble. Automatically, he started to lay out shaving gear, then changed his mind. It would be harder to grow another than to shave and some premonition told Stuart that disguise might in some way prove useful. Instead, he took scissors and cut away the torso bandaging. The flesh looked white and macerated, showing the bandage impressions as well as areas of fading discoloration. I was lucky, he told himself, as he stepped under the shower's hot needlepoints. God, how lucky I was!

He covered his body with thick lather, reveling in the cleanliness. Through clouds of steam he could glimpse Mikhail beside the open doorway, hand in pocket, holding his gun. And as Stuart turned away, he realized how eager he was to drop the cowed, submissive pose that had become second nature since his capture. Only a few hours more, he told himself, checking his impatience, after a good night's sleep in my own bed.

He rinsed in tepid water, dried himself off with a thick towel, and brushed his teeth meticulously. It was amazing how soap, shower, and toothbrush could make a new man of you, he thought.

Towel draped around his hips, Stuart entered his bedroom and took clean pajamas from a drawer. While he was getting into them, Mikhail searched all the bureau drawers looking for a weapon. Finding none, Mikhail looked around for a place to settle down. Stuart pulled back the bed covers. "Get a pillow and blanket from the other room," Stuart suggested. "Make yourself comfortable."

As Mikhail left the room, Stuart leaned over, ostensibly to look at the digital clock on the night table: 2:15. Dawn in Paris. Quietly he slid open the night table drawer and pushed his 9 mm Browning pistol to the rear. After Mikhail returned with a pillow, dragging a blanket on the floor, Stuart left the bed and got some handkerchiefs from a bureau drawer. He blew his nose loudly with one, dropped the others in the night table drawer, and adjusted himself under the covers.

Mikhail doubled the blanket and spread it in front of the closed bedroom door, then lay back, head on the pillow.

Stuart hoped his unwanted guest wouldn't snore.

A little after dawn Stuart woke and took a moment to orient himself.

No, it wasn't a dream. The Russian lay on his side, still sleeping. Stuart tiptoed to the bureau, got out his stud box, and palmed the safe deposit box key. He put on a spare watch and was getting into boxer shorts and stockings when Mikhail moaned and turned over on his back, eyes still closed.

We're like scorpions in a bottle, Stuart thought, neither daring to strike. Yet.

He laced up his black oxfords and pulled on a blue button-down shirt. He selected a gray flannel suit and dark-blue tie. He was tying it in front of the bureau mirror when Mikhail sat up, blinking. He pulled himself off the floor, opened the door, and went into the bathroom. Stuart heard the toilet flush and the basin water running, then Mikhail appeared at the doorway.

"Better shave," Stuart said, "we've plenty of time."

Mikhail touched his overnight stubble. "Why?"

"The bank likes clean-shaven customers."

"But you don't shave."

"Obviously, I'm letting my beard grow." He finished his tie knot and got into his coat. "While you're shaving I'll make breakfast."

"No."

"Look," Stuart pointed out, "if I wanted to cause trouble I could have done it any time during the night, or just now, while you were sleeping. I'm hungry." He kicked aside Mikhail's blanket and pillow and went downstairs. Plugging in the coffee maker, Stuart opened the refrigerator and got out eggs. There was bacon and a loaf of sliced bread in the freezer compartment for Sunday emergencies, and he took them out along with a container of frozen orange juice.

When he heard tap water running upstairs, Stuart went quickly to the library phone and disabled it by switching the setting from tone to pulse. While bacon was frying, he made a pitcher of orange juice and dropped the frozen bread slices into the toaster. He set the dinette table with butter and boysenberry jam, sugar, cream, and vitamins, swallowing four of the latter.

He heard Mikhail clump down the staircase, and without looking around said, "Eggs. Scrambled or sunny-side up?"

"What's that?"

Stuart beckoned him to the range, broke an egg in the hot bacon grease and showed him. Presently Mikhail said, "Over, please." Inwardly Stuart smiled. Between captor and prisoner the equation was subtly changing: Mikhail was no longer in full control.

Stuart laid the bacon strips on absorbent paper and fried three more eggs, two sunny-side up and two over hard. He poured two glasses of orange juice, filled the coffee cups, and placed toast on a plate between them. They attacked the breakfast hungrily. Swallowing a few bites, Mikhail said, "Good."

"Better than Afghanistan, eh?"

"Much better. Sometimes there we nearly starve."

Thanks to our Stinger missiles, Stuart thought, and I wish all of you bloody bastards had starved.

His efforts at calm and congeniality were paying off in Mikhail's increased tension. The Russian looked at the kitchen clock from time to time, then at his wristwatch, a cheap model with a stainless steel case. Probably army issue, Stuart figured. He began eating more deliberately as he noticed the speed with which Mikhail cleaned his plate. "More?" he asked.

Mikhail shook his head. "Just coffee."

After Mikhail had refilled their cups, Stuart said, "While you're up, rinse your plate and put it in the dishwasher, Mikhail."

The Russian looked around. "Where is it?"

Stuart leaned over, opened the door, pulled out the wire racks. Mikhail stared at it. "To wash dishes," he said in near disbelief.

"Glasses, silver, pots, and pans." Stuart turned from it and continued eating. He ignored Mikhail, who rinsed his plate and laid it horizontally on the rack. "Vertical," Stuart corrected. "I guess you've never seen a dishwasher before."

"No," admitted Mikhail and smiled tensely. "We have women for that."

Stuart chuckled. "Great idea." He refilled his coffee cup and stretched luxuriously in his chair. "I don't smoke, but go ahead if you want to."

With a pained expression Mikhail said, "I was shot through one lung. I can never smoke again."

"Tough luck, but at least you're alive." Stuart sipped from his cup. "I imagine you lost a lot of friends over there."

Mikhail nodded solemnly. "Many," he agreed. "Too many. And for what? " He sat down facing Stuart. "Like America in Vietnam, right?"

"You should have learned from that. Never start a war you can't win."

"But we did not lose," Mikhail objected. "We withdrew according to plan."

"Sure," Stuart nodded. "The Red Army regrouped to the rear—all the way back to Moscow." Like McDowell at Manassas, he thought. Civil War engagements would be lost on the Russian.

As he dawdled over his coffee, Stuart thought of Diana and wondered what kind of treatment she'd gotten since his departure. Knowing he was going to follow Brakov's orders, she probably wouldn't give way to despair. So far Stuart had no reason to revise his estimate of her basic toughness. True, she'd done some sobbing in that isolation cell, but who could blame her? Hardened as Brakov was to human suffering, he would prefer a tranquil prisoner to a screaming, hysterical one.

"The time is eight o'clock," Mikhail noted.

"So we've got an hour's wait."

"How far is the bank?"

"A ten minute drive. In my car."

"But—"

"*My* car," Stuart repeated. "It's a small bank. If they see those uglies of yours, they'll hit the burglar alarm and we'll all be in deep shit."

Once Mikhail was off his hands he'd need to talk with Senator Chase himself—not with the androgynous Evan Powell. Then Pat O'Rourke. Together they could work out a cover story to explain his absence, then let Pat follow through.

As he looked at Mikhail, the Russian's face seemed to dissolve into Blake Selwyn's, Harvey Scott's, and the embassy driver's. He would never forget the blood gushing from the driver's smashed head, the horror of that night. But for Diana, he'd have killed Mikhail by now.

His sister and Larry were probably still on their cruise. It'd be a week or so before they returned. He had lost track of chronological time, he knew, and it seemed unimportant compared to the next few hours.

Bendikov's presence on the flight had surprised him, and Stuart wondered to what extend the KGB officer was involved. His post was Washington, but the timing of his return had to be more than coincidental. Was Mikhail under Bendikov's orders now? A local controller coordinating with Brakov made sense. Well, what happened to the letter in Soviet hands was immaterial to Stuart.

He got up and set his dishes in the dishwasher. Then he turned on the counter TV and found an old western on Nickelodeon.

Mikhail's face brightened. "John Wayne!" he exclaimed. "I like John Wayne."

"Me too." Methodically Stuart returned the unused bacon, eggs, and juice to the refrigerator. "Excuse me. Morning nature call."

"Eh? What's that?"

"Toilet," Stuart explained. "I prefer privacy."

Mikhail shrugged and continued watching his cowboy hero, now drawing a bead on a warpainted Indian.

Stuart took out the Browning and covered it with handkerchiefs to muffle sound. He drew back the breech and jacked in a ready shell. Then he replaced it, leaving the drawer partly open so that only handkerchiefs were visible. From there he went to the bathroom, washed and dried his hands, and flushed the toilet.

Back in the kitchen again he said, "Your turn, Mikhail."

"I go later," Mikhail said, still transfixed by the movie, "when we come back."

So they *were* coming back to place the call to Brakov. Welcome news. So far everything was according to plan.

Just before nine they got into Stuart's Audi and backed out of the garage in the alley. Stuart noticed that Mikhail didn't buckle the seat belt. "This your first trip to America?"

"Yes."

He turned south and drove down to M Street, braking for the light. "Hard to believe," Stuart said, "your English is so good." Then he laughed shortly. "Probably learned it in one of those special villages: Hometown America, right? Maybe you trained at the one outside Lytkarino?"

"No, at—" He gave Stuart a sharp glance. "Never mind. I was student only at Foreign Language Institute."

Either way, Stuart said to himself, you're KGB, *boychik*, with a graduate degree in killing.

He turned right, and at Wisconsin Avenue drove into the bank's parking lot—where he had seen Diana and the man from State security. Before entering the bank Stuart said, "You'll have to wait for me outside the vault; I'll be a few minutes." Leaving his escort, Stuart signed the access card and entered the vault with the attendant. Together they opened his box and Stuart took it in a cubicle, where he removed Selwyn's letter. Using the copy machine located nearby for customer convenience, Stuart made copies of each page unseen by Mikhail. In his cubicle he placed the copies in his box and returned it to his numbered slot. After the attendant had double-locked the box Stuart asked her for an envelope, inserted Selwyn's original letter, and placed it in his inner coat pocket. As he left the vault he wondered which way the action would move. He had his own plan, but he had no idea what Mikhail might do once Mikhail had the letter. That was supposed to satisfy Brakov, but would it?

Outside the vault he rejoined Mikhail, who was visibly nervous.

Stuart led Mikhail from the bank and around to where his car was parked. As he unlocked the car door Mikhail said, "The letter, please."

"Not yet," Stuart said, getting behind the wheel, "certain formalities remain. You call Brakov and we'll both speak to him."

In silence they drove back. Stuart left the car in his small garage, and they entered the house through the connecting door. Once inside, Mikhail picked up the phone in the library and consulted a card from his pocket. He punched some numbers, listened, and turned to Stuart. "Something wrong—doesn't work."

Stuart shrugged. "That's a sick phone," he said, "been ailing a long time. We'll use the bedroom phone." He went up the stairs, followed by Mikhail, who picked up the receiver. Stuart moved close to the night table.

"Show me the letter," Mikhail ordered. Stuart got out the envelope, unfolded the pages, and waved them at the Russian, who ordered, "Give it to me."

"Make your call."

Mikhail sat on the far side of the bed, and while he was punching the call sequence Stuart surreptitiously opened the night table drawer a little more. When Mikhail looked around, Stuart took a handkerchief from the drawer and blew his nose. Satisfied, Mikhail concentrated on the call.

An answering voice was audible. It must be Brakov, Stuart

assumed, because Mikhail stood erect, as though in the presence of his superior, and began to speak in Russian. Then he passed the phone across the bed to Stuart.

Brakov said, "Mikhail says you have the letter."

"And you have Mrs. Selwyn. Take her to the lawyer's place and let her phone me. When I'm satisfied, Mikhail gets the letter."

"You can speak with her now if you want to."

"We'll follow procedure," Stuart said. "I'll expect to hear from her in about an hour."

"No tricks, Stuart," Brakov warned.

"And none from you, Colonel," Stuart replied, ending the call. Handing the receiver over to Mikhail, he said, "We've got time to kill. Maybe you can find another TV movie."

"I have no time for movies," Mikhail retorted. "Now you will give me the letter."

Stuart edged a little closer to the night table. "So Brakov told you to kill me."

"I follow orders," Mikhail said curtly. "The letter. Now." His left hand reached out as his right hand began moving toward the gun holster under his coat. Stuart pulled out the envelope and tossed it beyond the bed. Reflexively, Mikhail grabbed at it, and in that moment Stuart went for his pistol, his hand curling around the grip as Mikhail jerked out his revolver.

Stuart was dropping to his knees when Mikhail fired. The shot went over his head, and before Mikhail could fire again, Stuart squeezed the Browning's trigger. The bullet struck Mikhail's chest, forcing him to stagger back against the wall. The Russian lifted his revolver as Stuart was sighting on his heart. When the revolver steadied, Stuart pulled the trigger again.

Mikhail's features froze in an expression of disbelief. Spun around by the impact, he sank to the floor. Stuart heard the revolver strike the floor. He vaulted over the bed, kicked the revolver away, and saw blood staining Mikhail's shirt and jacket. He felt for the carotid, and his fingers pressed the neck artery, the pulse ceased and Mikhail's eyes rolled upward. The *spetznaz* assassin was dead.

Stuart got up and saw the bullet holes in the wall. Turning, he made out where Mikhail's shot had drilled a small hole in the plaster—at about the level of Stuart's heart, had he been standing.

He set his pistol's safety, sat on the bed and looked down at the dead Russian. His hands were trembling, but he felt no remorse. Nervous reaction; it would pass. Still, he was left with a corpse to explain, while Brakov still had Diana. As an attorney, a member of the bar and an officer of the court, Stuart was acutely aware that he had an obligation to report the shooting—but he had to consider the consequences.

He went down to the bar and poured a double shot of scotch. He downed it with a water chaser and returned to the bedroom. Mikhail's wallet contained several brown-printed rubles and sixty-two American dollars. There was a plastic ID card with a photo of Mikhail, rank epaulets on both shoulders and a stern expression on his face. Stuart removed the dollars before pocketing the wallet.

He checked the clothing label and found that the suit had been purchased at Aux Trois Quartiers, a Paris department store near the opera. There was nothing else in the suit's pockets.

Stuart undid the shoulder holster and began undressing the body, shoes first. The liquor in his bloodstream made him feel better, limiting his revulsion at touching dead flesh. He worked quickly, before rigor set in, for the longer Mikhail's body remained unidentified, the better.

But sooner or later Brakov would realize that Mikhail was no longer a functioning agent, at which point replacements would be sent. Therefore, his house was a death trap.

He worked feverishly, stuffing Mikhail's shoes and clothing into a large trash bag and the revolver and shoulder holster into a smaller one. By now the entry wound blood was coagulating and the body beginning to stiffen. Stuart laid both arms at Mikhail's sides, stood up, and wiped the perspiration from his face.

If things worked out, he could dispose of the body after dark.

But if someone from the embassy came looking for Mikhail, that would make another problem.

Half an hour had passed.

Stuart went to the bathroom and rinsed his face and hands. He wanted another drink badly but couldn't afford to slow his thinking. He looked at the bearded face in the mirror and realized it looked strained and haggard. Well, why not? That god-damn letter, he thought as he left the bathroom, and decided to do something about it.

He retrieved Blake's letter from the floor and put it into a plain envelope, which he addressed to Special Agent Patrick O'Rourke, FBI Headquarters, Washington, D.C. He placed a stamp on the envelope and stuck it in his pocket. The time was now a few minutes before eleven—evening in Paris.

Where did all this leave Diana? In Brakov's power.

And from the decisive way Stuart had seen Brakov operate, he did not think the colonel would let her live, for in Brakov's mind he as good as had the letter. Alive she was a potential enemy; dead she could harm no one. Stuart gritted his teeth.

He glanced at the telephone again, as though invoking Diana's call. Forget it; better if all callers thought his line was busy.

As he took the receiver off its base, he noticed that his hand was trembling again. Steady boy, he told himself, get it together and face what you have to do: One, dispose of Mikhail's body. Two, leave Washington. Three, get back to Paris and find Diana, alive or dead. And four, make Brakov pay.

His lips were dry. He drank a large glass of cold water and went up to the bedroom, where he began fashioning a shroud for the *spetznaz* assassin.

CHAPTER 20

*D*uring the first part of the afternoon Stuart dragged Mikhail's sheet-wrapped body down to the garage and jammed it into the trunk of his car—no small trick, since it hadn't occurred to him to have the body stiffen with the knees drawn up.

He locked the trunk and went to the front of the house, where he peered through the curtains. Everything looked normal, so he poured himself a short drink. Then, with rags, soap, water, and cleansing powder, he eradicated Mikhail's blood from the bedroom.

Last year's painters, he remembered, had left a quantity of patching plaster in the basement, along with a can or two of surplus wall paint.

Carefully he plugged the bullet hole. While the compound was drying he checked the freezer and took out a bag of chicken à la king. Following instructions, he warmed it in the microwave oven. Before eating he checked again and decided his house wasn't being watched. Not yet, at least.

After eating he phoned the Brighams' house. When the Honduran maid answered, he asked for Mrs. Erskine. She came on the line almost at once. "Are you just in from Paris, Mr. Stuart?"

"That's right," he replied, "and I wondered if my sister and her husband are back from their cruise."

"Not for—let's see—another three days. The children will be so glad to see you again."

"I'd prefer you not tell them I called," he said, "because I'm going to have to leave almost immediately for California. But I'll be in touch when I'm back."

"What a shame—you're their favorite uncle, you know."

"Give them my love. Goodbye." He depressed the button, leaving the receiver off the hook.

He dipped a rag into the paint bucket and ran it over the dried patch, then returned the supplies. From a closet he removed a small suitcase and packed it with essentials. A seldom-used bank card, good for five hundred dollars a day, was in a bureau drawer, and as he pocketed the card he regretted not having cashed a check before the bank closed. Too late now.

He wondered how long his secretary would mind his office before looking for another job. Well, more was at stake than his law practice. Much more.

He had his diplomatic passport and Mikhail's sixty-two dollars, plus the American Express and Visa cards he hadn't taken to Paris. They were essential too.

Paris.

He dialed the overseas operator and asked for Paris information. The Paris operator provided the American Hospital number and Stuart placed the call.

He asked the switchboard operator for the room of Rolf Kingman. The operator said Mr. Kingman was no longer at the hospital.

"Then he's recovered?" Stuart asked.

"I have no information, sir," she replied, "none at all."

After hanging up, Stuart phoned the Department of State and asked for Kingman's office. When a secretary answered he said he was an old friend of Rolf's, that he was passing through Washington and wanted to ask Kingman to lunch.

He heard the secretary's abrupt intake of breath. "I'm afraid I have bad news for you, sir. Mr. Kingman died in Paris nearly two weeks ago."

"Oh, my God," Stuart exclaimed. "That's terrible."

"Yes, it is. Everyone misses him so. May I have your name? Mrs. Kingman would want to know you called."

"We never met, but thank you." He hung up and sat back in his chair. So the drug had been fatal. Why would the KGB destroy its own agent? Nothing was adding up.

He hoisted himself up from the chair, went back to the bedroom, and packed the Browning under his clothing. A customs inspection would find it, but he'd worry about that when the time came. Meanwhile, possessing it was good for morale.

Going downstairs to his garage, he placed the suitcase on the rear seat and the trash bags atop the sheeted corpse in the trunk. The trick, he cautioned himself, was not to get stopped for speeding or some other traffic violation and have his car searched for drugs.

Should he try to see Senator Chase, tell him the full story? But Chase was little more than an acquaintance. He might well call the law. The bleak fact was that there was no one he could turn to. From the moment he killed Mikhail he was on his own.

Toward four o'clock Stuart checked the street, then locked the house and opened the garage door. He backed out and soon was on Pennsylvania Avenue, driving past the White House toward the Capitol dome gleaming in the afternoon sun. Beyond the Treasury Department building he turned left and drove into the parking lot of Riggs Bank's main office. Using his card, he drew the maximum of cash from the machine. He posted the letter to O'Rourke at a nearby mailbox, then continued east on Pennsylvania across the Anacostia River to where it became Oxon Run Parkway, Maryland Route 4. As the parkway took him past Andrews Air Force Base, Stuart recalled the morning he had joined the delegation there for their VIP flight to Paris. That was three weeks ago, but to Stuart it seemed that months had passed.

Well, no going back to that moment, he told himself; he had the present and the future to deal with as best he could.

Just past the Marlboro Race Track Stuart turned south onto Route 416. So far he had watched the speedometer carefully, not wanting to be caught in a radar trap. Besides, he didn't need to reach his destination until dusk. He was familiar with the route, having driven it often to reach the Brighams' summer place at Plum Point, and he knew how fond rural police were of stopping city cars for infractions, whether real or fancied.

A beachside road led directly south to Plum Point, but at this preseason time of year, a D.C. plate would be remembered, so he continued south until he came to the Route 263 spur. From the turnoff it was only another seven miles to the Brighams' place; he hoped that the caretaker had already come and gone for the day.

The access road led through fenced dunes, the seagrass waving in the wind off Chesapeake Bay. Stuart drove as close to the boathouse as he could without losing traction in the sand, then left the car.

Kneeling at the flower border beside the kitchen steps, Stuart lifted the third rock and found the door key in a small plastic envelope. In the kitchen he drank a large glass of water and then poured himself a drink of Larry's Old Grouse. After that he took keys from the rack and headed for the boathouse. Larry's pleasure boat was a twenty-foot Chris-Craft rigged for water skiing, its engine housing dividing the front and rear cockpits.

Stuart got into the front cockpit and turned on the ignition. The engine caught, coughed, and died. He tried again, and this time the engine burbled smoothly. So far so good.

He turned off the engine and looked around the boathouse for heavy weights, finding three pyramidal ones tied to mooring buoys that had been stored inside for the winter. He cut the upper ends of each nylon mooring cord and lowered the three weights into the rear cockpit. Through the salt-stained window he watched the graying sky. The bay would be dark in another half hour.

Satisfied, Stuart left the boathouse and was walking up the sandy trail when he saw a jeep pull up beside his car. A man in a police uniform got out, one hand on his holstered revolver, and watched Stuart walk toward him.

"Evening," the officer said. "Mind telling me what you're doing here?" His words were polite, but the edge in his voice was unmistakable.

"Looking around," Stuart said. "I'm Mrs. Brigham's brother. She and Larry, her husband, asked me to come by and check on things."

"Things? Mind telling me what?"

"Oh, make sure the caretaker's doing what he'd paid to do. Check on the boat."

The officer nodded thoughtfully. "Mind showing me some ID?"

Stuart got out his passport and credit cards and handed them over.

"That your car?" the officer asked.

"Sure is."

"Registration?"

"Glove compartment." Stuart opened the car door and took out his D.C. registration card. The officer took it and, watching Stuart, activated his radio and called in the registration number.

The breeze cooled Stuart's face and neck, but his palms were wet with perspiration. "The family will appreciate knowing you came by—when they get back from their cruise," he told the cop.

"Cruise? Where to?"

"South America. On the *Queen Elizabeth II.*"

"That's something I'd like to do," the officer said, "someday. When they getting back?"

"Four or five days. I've been putting this off, decided I couldn't procrastinate any longer."

The radio crackled and the officer listened intently, muttered something, and hung the mike inside the jeep. "No outstanding warrants," he said, "so I guess you're okay." He returned Stuart's cards, then the passport. "With that beard you don't look too much like the passport photo."

"I'll probably shave it off in June or July," Stuart said, pocketing his ID. "It gets itchy in hot weather."

"Imagine so," the officer remarked, "but that don't seem to bother my kid. Just twenty and he won't shave it off—says it's part of his rock uniform." He settled behind the wheel. "Plays drums in a group around here. Well, kids do what they want to these days."

Stuart nodded amiably. The officer started the jeep and backed out alongside the house. Stuart gave him a parting wave and then walked slowly to the house.

In the kitchen he dried his hands on a towel and poured another shot of Grouse. As he sipped the drink he told himself he'd been unlucky to encounter the officer but lucky his trunk hadn't been searched. Still, there would be a record of his presence, if only in the officer's memory. But if Mikhail's corpse was never found, it wouldn't matter.

The large two-story house was built on four acres, isolated from road and neighbors by steep sand dunes, which was why Stuart had chosen it for this job: isolation and boat availability.

He forced himself to wait until darkness closed in before going back out to the car. Opening the trunk, he removed the two bags and stared down at the sheeted corpse. He left it in the closed trunk while he carried the bags to the boathouse. His ribs ached from the effort, and he rested a while before fetching the body and tumbling it into the stern cockpit. Working in darkness, he cut off the sheet and tied the weight cords tightly around Mikhail's ankles, belly, and neck. Then he stood up and took a deep breath. Gripping the knife, he plunged it into Mikhail's belly, making four deep stabs. The holes would vent decomposition gases, making the corpse less likely to float if the cords were somehow freed.

He found the bayside door switch, pressed it, and watched the heavy door begin to lift. A chilly breeze swept into the boathouse. Stuart got behind the wheel and started the engine, letting it warm up before easing the Chris-Craft from the boathouse into the open bay.

Waves slapped the bow, and spray wet the slanted windshield and spattered Stuart's forehead. When he increased engine revs, the boat responded. There were ten miles of open water between him and the far shore, and he had decided to jettison his cargo halfway. Twenty minutes should do it, he told himself, and settled back for the voyage. He was running without lights, not wanting to attract the Coast Guard's attention. Returning, he'd turn them on.

He freed Mikhail's holstered revolver from the bag and dropped it two miles offshore. He had no weight for the Russian's clothing, so he punctured the trash bag with his knife and trailed it alongside until water began seeping in, then let go.

He looked at his wristwatch dial; five minutes later he throttled back and set the clutch in neutral.

Almost at once the boat turned broadside to the waves, making it difficult for Stuart to climb over the engine housing to reach the rear cockpit. He could see oncoming waves by their moving phosphorescence and used the tilting of the gunwale to help him get the weighted corpse over the side.

It vanished with a splash. Stuart sat down on the cushioned seat and rested his face on his hands. The tension of the last hours had tightened his stomach into a hard ball. He felt like throwing up. After a while he sat upright and sucked in lungfuls of salt air. Finally steadied, after his gruesome task, he climbed back to the forward cockpit and turned on the running lights. Then he clutched the engine, throttled forward, and steered Larry's boat back to the boathouse.

Exhaustion hit him as he trudged up to the house, but at least this time no policeman waited. A real bonus, he thought, because

I'm ten times more tense now. He entered the dark kitchen, turned on the range light, and drank two glasses of water, following them with a short pull from Larry's bottle.

His hair was wet from spray, salt crusted his beard, and he felt contaminated by contact with the corpse, so he stripped and put his shirt and jockey shorts into the Maytag, added detergent, and went upstairs. He drew a hot tub in the Brighams' large bathroom, grateful that they hadn't cut off the electricity during the winter months. Stuart sank into the tub, soaked for a long time, shampooed his hair, and dried it with one of Pat's blowers. Towel wrapped around his body for warmth, Stuart went down to the laundry room and put his clothes into the dryer. Then he boiled a cup of water and added instant coffee, stirring in a little Martell cognac. He drank while his clothing dried.

Dressed again, he left the damp towel on the bathroom door, rinsed and dried his coffee cup, and turned off the range light. He locked the rear door, returned the key to its hiding place, and drove away.

At night there were fewer flights out of National Airport than from Baltimore International; besides, if Mikhail's associates were looking for him they would cover National. So he drove due north toward Baltimore and left his car in a parking garage not far from the federal courthouse.

Carrying his suitcase, he found a taxi, which took him to the airport. Scanning the departures board, he saw that a Continental flight was leaving for San Antonio in half an hour.

Stuart bought a coach ticket, checked his suitcase, and boarded. Eager as he was to get back to Paris, it would be foolhardy to fly there directly, under his true name.

He was headed south because he remembered that Texas border towns were almost effortless gateways out of the United States. Of equal importance was the border's notorious reputation for supplying false documents to aliens bent on entering the United States. Stuart had never before sought false documentation, but there was a first time for everything.

Stuart looked out at the airport lights and wondered if he would ever see them again. He was going up against a skilled, resourceful, and remorseless killer.

The plane lifted smoothly and steeply from the runway and gained altitude as it banked and turned south through the night.

CHAPTER 21

*A*fter checking in at an airport motel, Stuart requested an early wake-up call and went to bed. He slept restlessly. In the morning he rode the motel van to the airport. Even at that early hour the air was warm and gritty. In the coffee shop he ate a large breakfast, then drew another five hundred from the lobby banking machine.

After consulting the departure board, Stuart used his Visa card to buy a ticket to McAllen, Texas. After the short flight he took a van-bus six miles to the border and walked across the bridge to the Reynosa side. He avoided a suitcase inspection by showing his diplomatic passport; the official just waved him on.

As Stuart walked down from the border control building he was assailed by vendors of serapes, souvenirs, fruits, Chiclets, tacos, and soft drinks. Pushing through them he headed for a long row of waiting taxis, all painted yellow. In Spanglish the drivers offered to take him anywhere and everywhere—"girls, bars, anything you wan', señor." Stuart walked along the file until he spotted a cardboard sign propped on the dash of one taxi: ENGLISH SPOKEN.

Before getting in Stuart asked the driver, "You speak English?"

"*Sí*, señor. I mean yes, sir."

"That's better." Stuart smiled. "Can you use a little extra money?"

"Who can't?" The driver shrugged expressively. "I got a wife and two kids and hackin' don' do it. Where you wanna go?"

"Drive and I'll tell you."

"Which way?"

"Around town."

Stuart got in and sat back, suitcase on the floor beside him. The driver was about twenty-five, Stuart figured, with an incongruous Zapata mustache, dark-olive skin, and a smile that showed lime-white teeth. The driver made a U-turn and headed into downtown Reynosa. After a few blocks Stuart asked, "Suppose a man wanted a good set of papers. Where would he go?"

The driver's head half turned. "How good?"

"Perfect."

"Perfect costs much money, takes lotta time."

"Got no time," Stuart told him and handed over a ten-dollar bill—probably one of Mikhail's, he thought. And while the driver was tucking away the money, Stuart quietly opened his suitcase and got out the Browning. He slid it into his belt under his coat and looked out at the dusty, disorganized looking border city. The streets were narrow and potholed, lined with stands selling tacos, fruit juice and sliced fruit, *menudo*, and flavored ices. One and two-story buildings were a jumble of shops, grocery stores, cobblers, tire-repair garages, liquor stores, small bakeries, and meat markets. Many signs were in English as well as Spanish. They could have used zoning ordinances here, he told himself, but it's way too late now. The pistol felt good against his belly.

"So," the driver inquired, "how much you wanna spend?"

"Whatever it takes. Can you help, or not?"

"Sure I can help, mister."

Stuart loosened his tie and opened his collar. "You can start by turning on the air conditioning," he suggested.

"Don' work. Can' get parts here."

Stuart glanced around. They were less than a mile from the river, beyond which lay the land of spare parts and unlimited opportunity. "Are we heading for your contact?"

"That's right. Ten minutes."

Stuart fanned his face. Not yet noon and already the humid heat was overpowering. His armpits were sticky with sweat. They were heading south past junkyards, more taco stands, liquor stores, open-air eateries, and used-car lots. The potholed road needed repair; hell, Stuart thought, it needs total resurfacing. A sign pointed the route to Monterrey. Huge trucks swaying with their overloads overtook the straining taxi and rumbled by with blasts of thick diesel smoke, whose choking stench overwhelmed the curbside odors of frying and roasting meats.

Finally the driver turned off the main highway onto a rutted, ridged dirt road bordered on both sides by sagging fences. Skinny cattle grazed among shrubs and cactus. Ragged, dirty children played around one-room adobe huts. In the distance a buzzard circled in the hot updrafts, but around the jolting taxi the air was still. Stuart drew out his diplomatic passport and tucked it under the seat against the floor; he could think of no further use for it.

Ahead on the right stood a large rusted shed that looked like an abandoned garage or aircraft hangar. To one side of the closed sliding door an old man sat in the shade, wearing a large straw sombrero, tattered jeans, and pointed-toe boots, an empty Coke bottle on his lap. The old man sat forward as the taxi stopped. He and the driver exchanged inaudible words and a series of gestures before the old man got up, slid the door open just far enough to enter, and disappeared inside the shed. The driver came back to Stuart and leaned on the doorsill. "He has to check it out," he said, "see if it's okay."

"Why wouldn't it be?" Stuart asked. "There's money involved." With a shrug the driver turned away.

After a while the old man came out and waved, motioning them inside. "Seems okay," the driver said and opened Stuart's door.

Inside there was just enough light to make out the shapes of half a dozen late-model cars in various stages of dismantling. Stuart realized that he was in a chop shop, whatever other illegal activities went on. He followed the driver to a lighted office at the far end of the garage. One man was at a desk; two others in mechanics clothing stood against one wall. "They don' speak much English," the driver said.

"Looks like they don't make documents either."

"Not here—another place. This man"—he pointed at the desk—"is *jefe*—the chief. His name is Manuel."

Stuart nodded at him and turned to the driver. "Tell him what I want."

The driver spoke to Manuel, who was eyeing Stuart with noticeable care. He replied to the driver in several short sentences. Turning to Stuart the driver said, "He don' trus' you. Says you look like *narco*—DEA."

"Tell him if I was a drug agent I wouldn't need documents."

After the driver relayed that, Manuel spoke again and the driver said, "Or from the *migra*—U.S. Immigration."

Stuart shrugged. "Can't do business here, let's go."

Rising, Manuel spoke again and the driver's face paled.

"What is it?" Stuart asked.

"He wanna see your money."

"Ask him why. I'm not buying anything but documents, and this is the wrong place. I said let's go."

But the driver didn't move. Stuart saw Manuel begin reaching behind his back, but before the movement was completed Stuart had his Browning out. Covering them he stepped back and gestured with one hand at Manuel. "Turn around," he ordered. "Let's see what you were reaching for."

Slowly Manuel turned, hands at his sides. Stuart saw a Colt .45 stuck in his belt next to the spine. He reached across the desk and pulled out the gun, tossing it toward a corner. Manuel said, "Hey, don' do that, it's a good piece!"

"One of the best," Stuart said, "but what I'm holding is even better." He pointed the Browning at the two mechanics and they turned around, hands raised. No guns, but one had a long sheath knife on his belt. To Manuel, Stuart said, "There's been a misunderstanding. I came for papers, I didn't come to be robbed."

Manuel sighed, then shrugged. "Gotta be careful, man. When you got a good thing going you don' take chances."

"So?"

"I'll go with you, get what you want." He came from behind the desk and spoke sharply to the driver, who looked questioningly at Stuart.

"Let's go," Stuart said and covered Manuel until they were in the taxi, Manuel in the front seat next to the driver. When the taxi was bumping down the dirt road, Stuart leaned forward. "No more bullshit," he said in a hard voice. "If you're taking me to a trap, you're the first to die. Understand?"

Manuel turned his head. "Hey, man, I jus' wanna few bucks from a fool gringo, but you're okay."

"I'm better than okay," Stuart told him. "I'm in charge."

Manuel gave the driver directions and they headed for the eastern edge of the city, pulling up at the rear entrance to a large printing shop. A dozen or so weary-looking *campesinos* sat or lay under the shade of a large banyan tree some distance behind the shop. Stuart followed Manuel inside, hand in his pocket on the pistol grip.

Seven or eight presses were working, and Stuart saw an offset camera focused vertically on a plate being copied. The floor was littered with green cards resembling the INS originals that allowed aliens to live and work in the United States. Stuart followed Manuel along the presses to the office end of the printing shop. When the door of the small office closed behind them, the press noise lessened.

A man with ink-stained hands and overalls embraced Manuel, looked at Stuart, and gestured at a chair. In English Manuel said, "Paco, this man my fren'." He need papers. You fix 'im up, okay?"

The overalled man nodded and sat down behind the desk. "What kind papers?" he asked. "For U.S.A?"

"What kind you got?" Stuart asked.

"Passport?"

"A passport will be fine. Mexican, French, Canadian, U.S., German—I can use any of them."

"Where you gonna go?"

"Europe."

Paco reached back and opened one drawer of a file cabinet. From it he took a tray containing at least a dozen passports and shoved it toward Stuart. The assortment contained U.S., Honduran, Mexican, Guatemalan, Panamanian, and Costa Rican passports. Paco said, "What you like?"

"I don't speak Spanish, so it has to be U.S. or Panamanian."

Paco picked up the American passport. "Five hundred dollars."

"And Panama?"

"Panama? Two hundred."

Stuart examined the Panamanian passport. It had been used a good deal, but the date showed that it was still valid. "Looks good," he said. "I'll be right back."

He walked out of the shop to the taxi, retrieved his diplomatic passport, and returned to the office, where Paco and Manuel were drinking Corona beer out of chilled bottles. Stuart dropped the passport in front of Paco, whose eyes widened. "How much is this worth to you?" Stuart asked.

Manuel came over and stared down at it. "How much you wan'?

"A thousand dollars."

Paco shook his head. "Five hundred."

Stuart said, "I'll take eight hundred for it plus the Panamanian passport with a French visa."

Paco looked up at Manuel, who said, "It's a deal."

Paco added the new passport to his holdings and returned them to the drawer. He opened the Panamanian passport. "New photo, old name. Okay?"

The passport had been issued to one Jaime Gonzalez García, age thirty-eight. Close enough. Stuart nodded. "Okay. The eight hundred, now."

From a cash box Paco counted out eight hundred-dollar bills. Stuart picked them up and examined each one under the desk light. "If even one of these is queer," he said, "I'll come back and burn this place down. Understand?"

Manuel said, "Hell, man, it's good green. The best."

"Better be." Stuart followed Paco to a photo setup in a dark corner of the shop.

While Paco substituted Stuart's photo, Stuart accepted a Corona from the ice chest and drank with Manuel. "Still think I'm a drug agent? *Migra?*"

"I dunno—Paco's problem. I don' think you care about my cars."

"I don't." The smell of ink and benzine choked the air. "You own this place?"

"Most of it. I got many interests here."

"So you keep busy."

"Got to. Big expenses for protection."

"I can imagine," Stuart said. "But not too busy to rob a fool gringo looking for help."

Manuel grinned. "Hey, you looked easy. I didn' know you was carryin'."

Stuart smiled back and sipped more beer. After a while Paco came back and placed the passport before Stuart. The new photo had been smudged and somewhat aged. Paco turned to the French visa stamp. Issued by the French Consulate in Mexico City. A

Mexican Immigration stamp showed Reynosa entry on yesterday's date. "Looks good," Stuart said, and stood up.

Manuel said, "My percentage, man."

"Get it from Paco," he said. "And thanks for everything."

Hand curled around the pistol grip, Stuart left the shop and went out into the strong sunlight, which made him shade his eyes.

Paco came past him, envelopes in his hand, and delivered them to three men under the banyan tree. The taxi driver was still sitting behind the wheel, door open, radio blasting. When Stuart got in the driver asked, "Where you wanna go now?"

"Away from here." When they were a dozen blocks from the printing shop Stuart told the driver to take him to Reynosa's airport.

It was half an hour's drive south of the city. When Stuart got out he said, "How much you figure I owe you?"

"Twenty dollars okay?"

Stuart stroked his beard. "You took me to a bad place," he mused, "where they could have robbed me, or worse. Still, it worked out." He took out a wad of dollars. "I gave you ten, take another ten and be happy." He handed the driver a ten-dollar bill. *Adios.*"

"Adios, gringo," the driver sneered, gunned the taxi, and screeched away. Stuart carried his bag into the building and found that an AeroMexico flight left for Mexico City in less than an hour.

He bought a ticket for cash and went into the lavatory, which smelled like a stable. Alone, he put the Browning into his suitcase, then went back to the airline counter and checked his bag.

In a small, noisy café in the building, Stuart ordered a ham-and-cheese sandwich on what proved to be a very hard roll, and a cold can of Modelo Light. No Mexican beer, only Budweiser, he was told. Stuart smiled as he noticed that the beer was bottled in Albany, Georgia.

The airport was not a busy one and only an occasional landing or takeoff intruded on his thoughts as he lunched. At about this time yesterday, he remembered, he was cleaning up the mess on his bedroom floor and repairing the wall. Now he was in another country with a phony passport that he hoped would get him into France and allow him the freedom of movement to find Diana.

He could wander Paris endlessly and never find her—alive or dead. But one man knew her fate, and that man was Colonel Ilya Brakov, the strutting little *scheissmeister* of the cruel shoes and fingers. Another who might know was Yuri Bendikov. True, Bendikov had left the Aeroflot plane at Washington two nights ago, but he was highly mobile and might be found wherever the arms control mandarins met.

His first problem in Paris was to establish a secure base.

As he drank a second Budweiser, an Aero Commander settled in at the far end of the runway. As its wheels touched down, there were spurts of smoke, and as the twin-engine plane continued rolling, prop blast hit the border and raised dust devils, which pirouetted upward for a time and then dissipated. Tumbleweeds rolled across the runway. When the waiter brought his check Stuart asked, "When does it rain around here?"

"Next month, señor, then for two, three months." He wiped his neck on the cuff of his uniform sleeve. "Very dry, huh?"

Stuart looked at the overhead fan, whose blades were not moving. "Does that thing work?"

"Not since I been here, señor." He made change for the five-dollar bill and left pesos on a tray.

"How long is that?"

"Maybe two years." He thanked Stuart for the tip and went to another table. Stuart walked over to the small souvenir counter and looked over the meager selection of leather billfolds. He bought one of the alligator hide impressed with the round Aztec calendar and fitted his dollars into it—less than two thousand in all, but in Paris he could get what he needed from Percy. Stuart was paying for a pair of sunglasses when his flight was called.

He joined a queue of a dozen passengers going through the metal-detector frame, showed his boarding pass, and walked in scorching sunlight toward the old DC-9 bound for Mexico City.

CHAPTER 22

*U*nder the afternoon sunlight the brown smog covering the bowl of Mexico City resembled a huge, poisonous mushroom. The plane came down through it, making the cabin suddenly dim. Over the airport hung a dull grayness; mist streaked Stuart's window.

Getting his suitcase took a long time—some sort of airport workers strike was underway. When he left the baggage carousel Stuart entered the long, marbled concourse and began scanning the international departures board. SAS was leaving for Stockholm, Finnair for Helsinki, Lufthansa for Frankfurt, JAL for Tokyo—and Air France for Paris.

The Air France ticket counter was about two blocks down the concourse. Seats were available. The cost was almost half of his precious dollars, but he couldn't use a credit card because of the discrepancy between the names on his cards and his new passport. The ticket agent gave a cursory glance at his visa-stamped passport, and marked the departure gate on his boarding pass. Stuart checked his bag and went to the Banamex exchange window, where he bought two hundred dollars' worth of francs—enough to get him into Paris and cover one night at a two-star hotel.

At a small bar in the waiting room Stuart bought a double Black Label with mineral water. The surrounding air was much cooler than Reynosa's, this airport being almost seven thousand feet above sea level. Inevitably Stuart's thoughts drifted to Diana— her complex personality, her unpredictability, the ambiguousness of her relations with her husband, Edward Beamish, and himself. There was depth to her, unquestionably, but had he explored the limit?

He realized that he was thinking of Diana as though she were alive, not buried in some hidden grave, and promised to continue thinking of her so. Otherwise his Paris mission would reduce to vengeance on Colonel Brakov. Not that vengeance was bad in itself, but Diana's rescue made his mission far more important.

He sipped his drink and drew satisfaction from contemplating Brakov's bewilderment over Mikhail's failure to check in. By now, Stuart mused, Brakov's—or Bendikov's—agents would have searched his house for the missing Mikhail and for himself. For a while Brakov might speculate that Mikhail had defected, but when no asylum announcement was made by State, he'd realize that Mikhail was AWOL. Inevitably he would consider the possibility of Mikhail's death. Stuart was confident that Brakov would not return to Moscow until he had something of substance to lay before his chiefs. So he would remain in Paris, directing the search and grasping for a palatable explanation of how things had gone wrong.

But why was Blake Selwyn's letter so important to the KGB? he wondered again. Why had they killed and kidnapped for it? What was its true significance now that Rolf Kingman was dead? Well, Stuart thought, let the FBI counterespionage experts figure it out; it's their field, not mine.

It seemed reasonable that Brakov might have at least a loose connection with the Soviet Embassy in Paris, though he might not appear on the formal diplomatic list. For instance, Stuart reasoned, Brakov could be attached to UNESCO or one of the other international organizations located in Paris, whose senior employees enjoyed diplomatic immunity.

During his years at State, Stuart had learned that Soviet intelligence officers abroad were of two categories: legals, who worked out of embassies and consulates, and illegals, who adopted background legends and passed as local citizens. Brakov could be one of the latter, of course, though Stuart felt that the colonel's military hubris would eliminate any menial cover.

Stuart's Air France flight was announced in Spanish, French, and English. He passed through the screening gate into the hooded passageway that connected with the plane, a wide-body French-built Airbus 340. Seated on the starboard side, Stuart heard the pilot announce the flight time to Paris as six hours and twenty-two minutes. The plane was only partly filled, so the attendants served hors d'oeuvres and drinks without the usual irritating delay.

Sipping scotch on the rocks, Stuart heard the captain announce in French that the flight course would take them over the Yucatan Peninsula, the city of Havana, and the Bahama Islands before the long Atlantic crossing. Paris weather was cool, visibility was good, and the captain anticipated on-time arrival at Charles De Gaulle Airport. A steward made the announcement in Spanish, after which another stewardess repeated it in English. After that they passed out newspapers. Dropped on the empty seat beside Stuart were copies of *Excelsior*, the *Mexico City News*, and *Le Monde*.

It had been a long time since Stuart had read a paper, so he went through the *News* with anticipation unrewarded, because the paper carried little that did not directly affect Mexico. Two-thirds of the stories dealt with Mexico's economic difficulties and the apparently insoluble problem of reducing the capital's pollution to safe breathing levels.

From a menu Stuart selected sole amandine with rissolée potatoes, *petit pois*, a small endive salad, and a half bottle of Chablis. Coffee would come with the dessert cart, the attendant told him and moved on.

Stuart opened *Le Monde* and began reading a Bonn-datelined report headed "West Germany Pandering to Neutralists." According to the correspondent, the German chancellor was pulling every trick out of his bag to force NATO to give up short-range nuclear weapons, most of which were deployed on West German territory. The West German thrust, the text continued, had everything to do with West German politics and nothing to do with the NATO strategy that for forty years had perpetuated peace in Europe. The chancellor was said to be frantically trying to bolster his reelection chances by appeasing his own country's neutralists and pacifists. The chancellor's moves, the correspondent wrote, fitted neatly into Soviet strategy by removing the traditional trip-wire deterrent against invasion from the East.

Far from agreeing to modernize eighty-eight Lance missiles in Germany, the Bundestag debate revolved around eliminating them entirely. And the United States, hesitant to appear to influence West German foreign policy, was not commenting on the issue. The correspondent listed Italy, Belgium, Spain, Norway, Greece, and Denmark as NATO members sympathetic to the West German chancellor's new neutralist policies. But what these countries failed to bear in mind, the correspondent remarked, was that if the United States was forced to withdraw its short-range nuclear missiles, its ground troops would also be withdrawn, leaving Europe to face the Russian Bear with whatever conventional manpower it could muster.

Stuart laid the paper aside and recalled his morning walk with General Winkowski. Stuart realized that in addition to delicate arms-reduction negotiations with the USSR, the United States was also faced with stiffening the backbones of its NATO allies. Those negotiations, just as much as direct talks with the Soviet Union, had to be kept secret if there were to be any chance of succeeding and keeping Europe united and strong.

But if Blake Selwyn was right, Kingman's death eliminated the chance from now on that U.S. plans and positions would be revealed. The stakes were immense, he mused, for if Europe were absorbed into the Soviet empire, the day would come that would find America an armed fortress defending itself on its own territory—something that had not happened since the War of 1812.

Stuart opened the Paris paper again, this time to take in the political cartoon accompanying the Bonn story. Against a background of Kremlin walls and onion domes, two figures danced ecstatically. Music was coming from a large Red Army band and a four-piece German oom-pa band, its obese players in Tyrolean costume. One dancer was labeled Gorbachev, the other Rudolf Henschel, West Germany's foreign minister. The caption: "And when the music stops . . . ?"

Good question, Stuart thought and pulled down the seat-back tray for his meal.

The eastern horizon was beginning to lighten as the big Airbus came in for a landing at De Gaulle Airport. Stuart had slept during most of the flight, but ever since the cabin lights went on he'd concentrated on preventing French customs from detecting his pistol. He considered three alternatives: he could extract the weapon when he claimed his suitcase and conceal it on his person; he could declare it and have the Browning confiscated, with consequent possibility of arrest and an interrogation that would expose his fraudulent passport; or he could position himself among the last of the passengers and hope that between the late hour and inspector fatigue, his suitcase would pass through unopened.

Even as Stuart submitted the Panamanian passport to the immigration official, he hadn't decided. The forged visa satisfied the official and Stuart regained the passport before proceeding to the baggage carousel. As he stood waiting for his suitcase to appear, he looked around at the inspection area and realized that none of the customs stations were manned. Tacked across the front of two center stations was a red-and-black flag, the unforgettable symbol of a labor strike. Beyond the stations, taped beside an exit door was a placard informing arriving passengers that the customs personnel were striking for higher pay and shorter hours. Welcome to France. A wave of relief passed over Stuart. He picked his suitcase off the carousel and walked unchallenged into the lobby.

He rode the Air France bus to the Porte-Maillot AeroGare, took an escalator to street level, and got into a taxi, asking for a small hotel within a few blocks of the Étoile–Wagram, Ternes. One star would do, two-stars would be even better.

It was dawn now; the sky was gray and not yet streaked with blue. As the taxi took him around the Étoile, Stuart responded to the throat-tightening view of the Arc de Triomphe and the eternal flame beneath its towering arches. The taxi turned onto Avenue de Wagram and slowed as it neared the Place des Ternes. The driver made a U-turn and pulled up in front of a hotel whose sign read HÔTEL DE MÈTRE. At one side of the entrance doorway a glazed white plaque announced that the hotel was of the two-star category. The driver asked if he should inquire within.

"By all means," Stuart said in French, "and you may say that I am disposed to utilize the habitation for—let us say—six nights."

The driver left the meter running while he was inside, returned after a few moments, and lifted out Stuart's suitcase. Stuart paid the metered fare and tipped the driver generously.

The clerk had a registration form ready, and he took Stuart's passport while Stuart completed the form and signed it as Jaime Gonzalez García, imitating the original holder's illegible scrawl. Indicating a small café and bar adjoining the lobby, he informed Stuart that *petit déjeuner* was served there after 7:30; he could call for *café complet* in his room. As the clerk picked up Stuart's suitcase he noticed the Air France flight label around the grip and said, "If you just flew in you must be tired, m'sieu."

"I am," Stuart agreed, and as they went up the staircase to the second floor Stuart asked how long the airport strike had been underway.

"It began last week, m'sieu. A scandal of the sort one does not wish foreign visitors to be aware of. But"—he gave a Gallic shrug—"it is a strike here one day, there another. Truly the economic history of France."

After unlocking the door and opening the window, which gave out on an air shaft, the clerk said, "Hot water twenty-four hours a day. Bottled Evian is on the wash stand. I wish you a pleasant day, m'sieu."

Stuart tipped him and said he appreciated his assistance.

He locked the door, pulled down the bed covers, and began unpacking while the tub filled. He soaked for half an hour and then got between cool sheets. When he woke it was nearly ten. He dressed, breakfasted on scrambled eggs, hot croissants, and coffee, and went to the phone cabinet to place a call to Percy.

CHAPTER 23

They met at Fouquet's Café. Percy arrived first, because his office was just across the Champs Élysées, in the building that housed the Mercedes-Benz showroom. Stuart spotted his classmate at a table set back from the sidewalk, nervously toying with a *fine café*.

Recognizing Stuart despite his beard, Percy got up and hugged him warmly. "My God!" he exclaimed, "I thought you were either dead or forever lost!"

Then the waiter came over, Stuart ordered a *fine café*, and the two old friends sat studying each other. Finally Stuart got to the point. "I need your help, Percy, but before I tell you why, did anyone named Diana Selwyn contact you a few days ago?"

"No. At least not to my knowledge—and my secretary is very efficient."

"Then we'll put it down that she didn't." His drink arrived; Stuart sipped the cognac before adding it to the small coffee cup. "Diana is a client," he explained, "because her late husband, Blake—a diplomat—retained me for some rather odd business. At the time I didn't think much of it, but Blake died or was killed the next day, and ever since then I've been more or less on the run. If she's still alive, Diana is in danger because of me. And I'm in danger because of what her husband entrusted to my care." He couldn't restrain a short, bitter laugh.

"What can I do, Alan? How can I help you? You know me—anything, anything at all," Percy offered effusively.

"I thought you'd say that—counted on it. Now, before I get into the story—and it's a long one—I'm going to need a safe place to stay, a base where I can sleep, eat, and use a telephone. Second, I'll need money. And a car."

Percy nodded thoughtfully. "A place to stay . . . Alan, I told you about my *petite-amie*, didn't I? Melisse from the Lido?" He gestured across the Champs at the famous nightclub.

"The one Blanche made you give up?"

"Exactly. Well, I'd leased a small apartment for her over on Rue Balzac. It's vacant now, and is at your complete disposal. Rather nicely furnished if I do say so—fridge, TV, all the amenities."

Stuart smiled. "Mirrors on the bedroom ceiling?"

Percy blushed. "Not quite, old friend. But I confess I miss her enormously. In fact, we occasionally met right here after the Lido's last show and we'd walk through the night, as lovers do, over to the apartment, just three blocks away." He got out his billfold and extracted a key. "It's yours."

Thanking him, Stuart took it. "More than the beard I have a new identity." He slid the passport across to Percy, who stared in astonishment at the name and photograph.

"So I'm Señor Gonzalez," Stuart said, "and that's the name I'll use when I phone you."

"My God, this is all so mysterious! I always figured you worked for the CIA."

"Wrong, but if I had, I might have been better prepared for some of what's happened to me. Anyway"—Stuart sipped from his cup and set it down—"it began with Blake Selwyn's visit late one Friday afternoon."

At that hour there were empty tables around them, so Stuart was able to tell his story without being overheard. Percy interrupted with occasional questions to clarify points, shaking his head from time to time.

When Stuart was done, Percy commented, "This Brakov—if that's even his name—sounds like Khrushchev."

"Percy, if Triangle had staged *Kremlin Nights*, Brakov would have been perfect for Nikita. That's all I've got to go on—unless your brother-in-law Julien can get help from the DST, the Défense et Surveillance du Territoire." The judge might be able to apply the resources of France's internal security service, which, among other duties, was charged with surveillance of foreign embassies.

"I'll ask him today, without giving details." He drained his demitasse. "As you say, Diana Selwyn may well be dead, and because you obviously care for her, I'm sorry. But we'll find out, and soon. Now, you sent Blake's letter to the FBI. Was that wise, Alan?"

"I'm not sure," he admitted, "but it's moot now. Frankly, I wanted to get rid of the damn thing. If Kingman wasn't a Soviet agent, the letter can't hurt him, because he's dead. If he was, the letter gives the FBI something to work on. I had a body to get rid of, and everything else was secondary."

"I can imagine. Myself, I'd have been paralyzed with indecision. I do admire you. *Alors*, how much money do you need?"

"Twenty or thirty thousand francs will hold me for a while. I didn't bring checks, so how about an IOU?"

"Totally unnecessary. In fact, don't even think about repayment." He looked at his watch. "Let's do this: go to the apartment and I'll introduce you to the concierge, Madam Juvenal. I'll tell her you're a Chilean vineyard owner whose property I'm planning to buy. She's a widow with a son, unfortunately, retarded, who does maintenance around the building, so she's there most of the time."

"Nosy?"

He shook his head. "Quite discreet. I'd been in the habit of tipping her well to make sure Melisse had no problems. It's time I tipped her again. Now, you mentioned a car."

"Something inconspicuous, Percy. Fiat or small Renault. Use your judgment."

"For surveillance, *hein*? I'll lease it for a month if that's long enough."

"I hope I won't need it for more than a few days."

"Why?"

"Because Brakov won't stay in Paris much longer."

"If he's still here."

Stuart nodded. "It would help if I could find that prison house, but I was blindfolded."

"Brakov seems to have thought of everything," Percy remarked, "except for your getting the drop on Mikhail. But suppose you found the farmhouse? What would you do?"

"Search for a grave."

Percy looked away. "Let's hope it doesn't come to that, Alan."

Customers were beginning to fill the nearby tables. Stuart said, "Let's go, we've got things to do."

They left Fouquet's and dodged across the Champs-Élyséees through heavy traffic, ignoring the crosswalk and a gendarme's exasperated whistling. Gaining the other side, they stood for a moment watching a phalanx of leather-clad punkers with garishly dyed hair elbow their way through oncoming strollers. "That's the New Paris," Percy remarked. "Before it was the whores."

"I remember," Stuart replied. "The ugly ones trolling for business."

They began walking toward the Rue Balzac. The day was warm, the sun indistinct behind a haze of smog. Stuart glanced around, looking for the Eiffel Tower; the top was barely visible through smog. They passed a section of airline offices and at Rue Balzac they turned right and walked toward Avenue Friedland, passing a bakery, a butcher shop that sold horsemeat, and a vegetable store before reaching the four-story apartment building.

The exterior was gray stone and similar to adjacent ones in the block except for an incised marble plaque that memorialized the execution of a Resistance fighter in 1944. Percy opened the street door and they entered a well-kept courtyard. On the right was the office and living quarters of the concierge, who came out to greet them.

Madame Juvenal was a short, rotund woman in her sixties with grayish-white hair and thick spectacles. She invited them into her office and listened intently while Percy explained who his guest was and that he'd be occupying the apartment indefinitely.

As she slipped a fifty-france note from Percy into her apron, she offered, "Any service, large or small, your guest has only to let me know. *Merci mille fois*, M'sieu le Comte," she added, with a slight bow.

They went up to the third-floor apartment, and Percy showed Stuart around, pointing out the liquor cabinet and other details. He stopped at the bedroom door and gazed in nostalgically. "What memories, Alan! I can't get her out of my mind."

"But there'll be others."

"Oh, without a doubt. But Melisse—ah, she was something special."

Stuart went into the ample bathroom and noticed a large heart drawn with lipstick on the mirror. Across it was written: *"Je t'aime, mon amour,"* and the initial *M*.

Percy grabbed a wad of toilet paper and began to erase the message. "Better get rid of this," he said sadly,"—along with other memories." When the mirror was clean he said, "The place is yours, Alan. I'll come back with money, then the car."

"I don't know how to thank you," Stuart admitted emotionally.

"Leave thanks until your job is done." Percy hugged Stuart again, kissed him on both cheeks in the Gallic fashion, and was off.

The refrigerator was empty, the kitchen shelves bare, so Stuart went out and bought bread, milk, meat, and a supply of canned goods. After stocking the kitchen he returned to his hotel, packed his suitcase, and paid his bill.

The clerk—not the one who had checked him in—asked, "The room was not satisfactory, m'sieu?"

"On the contrary, entirely satisfactory, but urgent business takes me to Lyon."

"Then I will call you a taxi."

Back in the apartment Stuart unpacked his suitcase. Hanging up his suit and shirts, he noticed the faint scent of perfume—a last trace of Melisse. He used the telephone directory to locate an arms store and found that the nearest one was within walking distance, on the Rue de Lisbonne.

He answered a knock on his door, and the concierge handed Stuart a thick envelope. "From M'sieu le Comte," she said and withdrew.

There were thirty thousand francs in the envelope. He'd noticed the airport rate of about six francs to the dollar, so this was the equivalent of five thousand dollars. Removing two thousand francs, Stuart cached the envelope under a sofa cushion, then walked to Rue de Lisbonne and bought a nylon shoulder holster for his Browning. Noticing a small, clean-looking restaurant named Chez Edouard, nearby, Stuart ordered a filet mignon *à pointe* with fried potatoes and *haricots verts*. Simple fare, but well prepared and satisfying. He drank the house red, then a demitasse, and walked back to his new lodgings to wait for Percy's next contact.

Before stretching out on the bed Stuart adjusted the shoulder holster and inserted the pistol. The fit was snug, as he wanted, and the gun was inconspicuous under his coat. Taking off his coat and holster, he lay down to watch the midday TV news. The third segment showed a riot in West Berlin. The commentator said that a coalition of Greens, skinheads, and supporters of Passage, the peace organization, tried to force their way into East Berlin but were prevented by West Berlin police using water trucks and tear gas. The film cut to Edward Beamish seated in a West Berlin studio. To a reporter's question Beamish replied that much as he deplored violence in any form—Passage being dedicated to peaceful relations—he could understand the long pent-up desires of East and West Germans for reunification. "The Wall was an evil thing," Beamish pronounced, " and is today less a barrier than the symbol of an ugly past. Yet this historic city remains hostage to the doomsday weapons my country and NATO have placed all over West Germany. To free Berlin from its isolation, to enable all Germans to decide the future of their country, these horrific weapons must be removed. All across Europe the political situation is changing dramatically. We can alter the course of history if we take the first step. And I have faith that men of good will in the Kremlin will reciprocate without delay."

Maybe, Stuart thought, as he turned off the set, but it's a hell of a risk to take. Lying back, he stared at the ceiling, wondering why he hadn't thought of Beamish earlier. Beamish should know whether Diana was alive—or if she was dead, what had happened to her.

The phone directory was an old one, so Stuart dialed information and wrote the number of the new Passage office. He identified himself as an *International Tribune* reporter and inquired of the switchboard operator when Ambassador Beamish would be returning to Paris. Switched to the press office, he gave his name as Chauncey Merkins and was told that Beamish was expected back within the next few days. "I want to interview him," Stuart said. "I'll call tomorrow to set it up."

"I don't see your name on the *Tribune* masthead," the press officer said. "You must be new."

"Very new, so I want this interview to be a good one."

He hung up and answered a knock on his door. Percy came in looking flushed with success. "Got a Fiat for you, and you can park it in the *porte cochère*." He handed over rental documents and the keys and sat down. "Everything okay?"

"Fine. Did you reach the judge?"

"I did. Julien was very reluctant to bring in the DST, but I managed to persuade him by saying it was a matter of life or death." He looked at Stuart. "It is, after all."

"When will he have something?"

"Not for two or three days, I'm afraid—but you're comfortable here, Alan, aren't you? Rest up and take it easy."

"I plan to, although it's hard to relax when Diana's fate is in question. Was there anything else?"

"Ah—well, to tell the truth there was." He cleared his throat. "The judge made me swear on our family honor that you're not CIA—was I right to make that undertaking?"

"You were," Stuart replied with a trace of irritation, "but why was that important?"

Percy hesitated before replying. "Well, the CIA is notorious for revealing everything to any congressional dogsbody who asks. Then it's all over the press. You know that, Alan, and I can't blame Julien for being careful."

Stuart sighed. "Trouble is, he's right—I don't blame him either. The information I want is for, let's say, personal use only."

"I know, I know." Percy seemed relieved that Stuart hadn't taken offense. "Anything else?"

"Tell me where the Soviet Embassy is."

"They have a rather grand place—new since the war—that abuts the Bois de Boulogne. It's two long blocks down from the Porte Dauphine, next to the running tracks used by the University of Paris. I used to jog there while I was at the Law Faculté. Specifically, the comrades' embassy faces the Boulevard Lannes. Can't miss it, if that's where you're going."

"Thought I'd check it out—maybe I'll spot Brakov."

Percy stood up. "And if you do?"

Stuart' smile was grim. "Give him a chance to apologize."

Percy coughed. "Before you kill him."

Stuart shrugged.

"That's fair, considering all he's done to you—and Diana." Percy's hand gripped Stuart's arm. "In college you were quiet, Alan, kept to yourself, never got involved in anything upsetting. Now—well, you've changed."

"Circumstances change a man," he said quietly.

"I understand, believe me I do. And I wouldn't want you looking for *me*. Not with what you've got on your mind."

"It's something I have to do."

"I know, but be careful, will you? That's all I ask. Just be very damn careful."

"I have an edge," Stuart pointed out. "Brakov doesn't know if I'm alive or dead. He thinks I'm afraid and passive, so I don't think it would ever occur to him that I'd come back to find him."

"Stay alive, *cher ami*." Percy hugged Stuart once again and left.

At six o'clock Stuart drove down the Boulevard Lannes, past the Soviet Embassy. Set against the green background of the Bois, the embassy occupied one of the best residential locations in Paris. Facing a broad boulevard, the four-story château-style building far more resembled a mansion of the aristocracy than the workplace it was. And on three sides it was surrounded by the open athletic fields of the university, keeping the embassy free of neighbors. Leave it to the proletarians to set themselves up in magnificent style, Stuart thought.

Seeing no one entering or leaving the embassy gate, he continued as far as the Place de Colombie and turned a hard left onto Avenue Victor Hugo, then left again, back to Boulevard Lannes. After passing the embassy again he pulled in and angled his car so that while keeping the embassy gate in view, he appeared to be viewing late-afternoon runners, on the adjacent track.

A dark-uniformed *gendarme* strolled back and forth before the gate, walkie-talkie ready in the event of an unruly anti-Soviet demonstration. But there was no sign of a rumble today, Stuart reflected. The big *bagarre* was going on beside the Berlin Wall, and for the wrong reasons. Well, he couldn't solve the world's problems.

Theorizing that embassy personnel might be watching his car, Stuart got out and squatted by the nearest track, applauding as a dozen sweaty, straining runners went by. He stayed there for a quarter of an hour, glancing occasionally at the embassy gate, and was getting back behind the Fiat's wheel when he saw a black Renault drive up and wait while the gate opened. Through the gathering dust Stuart couldn't make out their faces, but the driver was a tall man, his passenger much shorter. Something about them seemed familiar, but as Stuart squinted the Renault pulled ahead, and all he could see was the car's trunk. The license plate was an ordinary Paris tag, not the diplomatic plate he'd expected. The two people could be French visitors or embassy service personnel. Neither was Colonel Brakov. As he drove back to his borrowed quarters Stuart told himself he shouldn't expect to find Brakov immediately. The exercise had been worthwhile in any case.

He made dinner for himself, drank from a bottle of Bordeaux, and watched television until he was sleepy enough for bed.

After breakfast Stuart went to a sporting goods store and bought a warm-up suit, a running outfit, and a tote bag. Noticing a knife display, he selected a six-inch double-edged blade.

The morning was warm, with enough sunlight to justify his dark glasses as he jogged around the track by the embassy. His muscles ached, and if he got nothing more from the morning's surveillance he would at least have resumed exercising. Remembering pacing around his farmhouse cell, anger flooded his mind. His breathing was short, and thirst rose in his throat, so he slowed to a walk and finished the circuit. As he drank at a water fountain, the embassy gate opened and the same black Renault came out. It turned north, away from Stuart, but he was able to identify Sergei at the wheel. The dumpy woman beside him was the Mongolian guard.

Pulling on his sweatshirt, Stuart quickly got into the Fiat and followed at a distance. Sergei drove around Porte Maillot and onto Route 13 past Les Sablons and through Courbevoie, where the countryside began to open up. The route's direction was generally northwest away from metropolitan Paris; Stuart suspected that the couple was heading for the KGB farmhouse.

A village traffic light held Stuart back, and as he drove on, the Renault was no longer in sight. Doubling back, he caught sight of the car on a side street in front of a grocery store.

From a block away, Stuart waited until Sergei and the woman left the store carrying bags. Three kilometers out of the village the Renault turned off the highway onto an access road that led to the farmhouse he had glimpsed by moonlight. By day it appeared to be just another country building, nothing sinister about it, but Stuart knew better. He drove past, watching the Renault enter a machinery shed, and when he could no longer see the building he turned around and drove back toward Paris.

It seemed unlikely that Brakov would stay there, since even Sergei and the woman appeared to be staying at the embassy, so he appraised the farmhouse as an interrogation and holding center.

From the apartment he phoned Percy, only to learn that no information had come from the judge. "Just be patient, Alan," Percy counseled in lawyerlike fashion. "If there's anything to produce, Julien will produce it."

Stuart told Percy where he'd located the farmhouse and said he intended to enter it by night. Percy volunteered to go along and help, but Stuart wouldn't let his friend take such a risk. "You're far more valuable where I can reach you if I need to. Anyway, it's really a one-man job."

"With care, Alan, with great prudence and care. As soon as I hear from Julien I'll call you."

For the rest of the day Stuart stayed in the apartment, but the phone remained silent. He made dinner for himself and slept until midnight. Then he dressed in dark clothing, armed himself, and drove out of Paris.

CHAPTER 24

After parking the Fiat in a grove half a mile from the farmhouse, Stuart pulled his dark warm-up suit over his clothing and a ski mask over his head and face. He had on ankle-high running shoes, the pistol in a right-hand pocket, and the knife's slender sheath threaded to his belt. Where he had stopped to top off the Fiat's gas tank he'd bought a small flashlight whose narrow beam was sufficient for his purposes.

The ragged edge of the new moon gave off little light. Stuart set off along the edge of a wheat field on a course that would approach the farmhouse from the rear. At that distance no lights showed, but shades might conceal them. Or was Diana in the cellar? Was she alive or dead? He would know soon enough.

The earth underfoot was soft, and soon the canvas uppers of his shoes were wet. Clouds blotted out the moon; the air was cool and still. In the distance he heard the barking of a dog, answered still more distantly, which made Stuart wonder if the farmhouse was guarded by attack dogs. It was a possibility he hadn't considered, because he'd neither seen nor heard guard dogs during his captivity. Besides, a well-trained attack dog wouldn't bark at the moon or echo a distant call.

Even though he'd seen no evidence of any during his imprisonment, he knew he should be alert to electronic sensors. Soviet technicians could install them without having to hire local electricians and arouse suspicion.

He walked the last hundred yards skirting the wheat field, and where it gave out into uncultivated land with a scattering of stark fruit trees Stuart rested, leaning back against a tree trunk. The dark farmhouse was probably empty, he told himself, but army training reminded him that he had to approach it as though it were occupied by armed enemies.

He cursed the lingering rib pains and wondered when he would be whole again, his muscles well toned, his body returned to good condition. Not for a while, boy, he told himself, not for a long while, and only after working at it.

A car was coming down the highway. He waited for it to turn, but it continued on until all he could see was its diminishing taillights. His breathing was normal again. His wristwatch dial showed 1:37. Might as well push on, get it over with.

Keeping to the orchard for cover, Stuart followed the border until he was well behind the machinery shed at the rear of the house. The shed concealed him from the house and he covered the distance rapidly, coming around the side of the shed to look into the stall where Sergei had parked the Renault. Empty.

For a few minutes he scanned the ground between shed and house for trip wires. His flashlight beam would find them but he had resolved not to use it until he was inside. He waited, listening, then went quickly to the rear entrance of the house. Putting his ear to the door pane, he listened again. Still no sound.

He tried the doorknob. Locked. Getting out his knife, he began cutting dried glazing putty from around the glass pane. It pried off in short strips, and when the frame was clear he pried out the glass with his knife point. He set the pane down carefully, reached in, and unlocked the door.

Hinges creaked as he opened it—the sound like primal screaming in his ears—and in that moment he heard a growl and the scrape of claws on flooring and saw the flash of fangs.

The dog's impact flung Stuart against the door jamb, jaws closed on his neck, still protected by the upturned collar of his warm-up jacket. The dog's weight forced him down. Snarling, the dog tore at his throat. Stunned by the unexpected attack, Stuart forgot the knife in his hand for a moment, but then he plunged it into the dog's belly and ripped the blade toward the heart. The dog's jaws left Stuart's throat and began snapping and tearing at its belly. Stuart used the flashlight to see the dog whirling around and pulling at its intestines, claws slipping on the bloody floor. Stuart drove the knife blade just behind the head into the spinal cord. Instantly the howling ceased, the dog—a Doberman—dropped in its own blood. Its head lifted once, the hind legs scrabbled, and it lay still.

Gasping, Stuart felt his neck and found fang punctures and some oozing blood. He tied a handkerchief around his throat and rinsed the bloody knife at the sink, then slid it back into its sheath. In its place he held the pistol, safety off. If anyone was sleeping in the house, the dog's yelping would have wakened them.

Flashlight off, he waited beside an inner door for the sound of footsteps or voices. When his heavy breathing slowed he turned on the flashlight and left the kitchen.

The top floor held a bath and two bedrooms, beds made. On the first floor he found the big room that had been his prison. The table and chair brought for Diana were still there, the bed was where he remembered it. He went into the next room—a storeroom with a VCR and shelves of videotapes—then entered the room where Sergei had been whipped. The T-shaped pole was there, lash lying on a chair, but otherwise the room was empty. Apparently Sergei's rehabilitation had been successful.

Stuart found the cellar door locked and kicked it in. He used a wall switch to light the rough stairway down which he had been dragged by Brakov's gorillas. The cell he'd been thrown into was empty. The adjoining one, Diana's, was also, but her wrist and ankle cords were lying where he had untied them not quite a week ago. He played the flashlight beam around the rest of the cellar floor, but the packed earth was gratifyingly level and undisturbed.

Back in the kitchen he drank deeply from the faucet. The fluid intake steadied him. He glanced down at the dead Doberman. It was a fine beast, well trained, and he had killed it only in self-preservation.

A cabinet in the small living room contained plum brandy and vodka. He drank the vodka straight and replaced the bottle. Sergei and the woman would wonder why the house had been broken into, since nothing would have been taken. But aside from the VCR and the videocassettes there was nothing of value. Let them conclude that a burglar had entered, killed the Doberman, and left badly bitten.

Stuart considered burning the place to the ground, but he knew that the Soviets would simply set up elsewhere. As it was, he knew where Sergei and the woman were likely to go, and that was much better than trying to locate them elsewhere.

During the long afternoon he had considered capturing Sergei and the woman, forcing them to reveal where Brakov was and what had happened to Diana. But the only way to prevent their alerting Brakov would have been to kill them both, an act so cold-blooded that he knew himself incapable of carrying it out. Neither had harmed him.

His neck and throat ached, his ribs pained from the dog's impact. He needed to cleanse the wounds and get some sleep. Stepping around the Doberman, Stuart left the house and headed across the field. Before getting into the Fiat he pulled off his ski mask and warm-up suit and removed his weapons.

As he drove back to Paris he reflected on how little he had learned at the farmhouse: Diana wasn't there—although she could be buried in a grave in the fields or the orchard—and Brakov wasn't sleeping at the farmhouse.

Turning into the *porte cochère*, Stuart felt that he was running out of time. The colonel would soon go back to Moscow or be recalled to explain his failure. Perhaps tomorrow would bring information from the judge. Wearily he trudged up the third-floor apartment. As he turned the key in the lock he heard the telephone ring.

"*Mon Dieu*," Percy snapped irritably, "I've been calling since one o'clock. That was three—more than three hours ago."

Stuart's grip tightened on the handset. "Meanwhile, you've—"

"Yes, my in-law called, and we met on a park bench. He said—and I believe him—that the information you want is better conveyed orally, directly from the source. His friends in that organization pulled in some special merchandise. It's perishable, *mon ami*, it may not last the night. You get my meaning?"

"I do. Tired out of my skull but ready. What's the plan?"

"I have to make a call. Go down to the street and stand in front of the doorway. A car will pick you up."

"When?"

"Fifteen, twenty minutes."

"Describe the car?"

"Hell, man, at this hour damn few cars will pull over just because you're standing there. Just get in." He groaned. "I don't understand these things, Alan, so for God's sake forget this call and any reference to my upstanding in-law."

"Understood. You didn't call, I didn't go anywhere."

Percy's voice was calmer as he went on, "I hope this turns out to be what you want. And if you feel like it, we could have a drink around five. The Crillon?"

"Uh-uh. My tribe frequents the place. Make it Fouquet's."

"Call if you can't make it." Percy broke the connection.

Stuart glanced at his watch. He went into the bathroom and checked his neck and throat. There were six tooth indentations; two showed broken flesh. The fangs hadn't really penetrated because of the warm-up suit and the fact that the dog's jaws had loosened when he fell. But another few seconds. . . .

He turned on the hot water tap and squeezed the small

wounds to cleanse them with fresh blood. Then he applied a hot towel, followed by ice cubes.

Ten minutes gone. He blotted away the wetness and buttoned his shirt collar to cover the wound. Then he got into his warm-up suit and went down to the street.

In eight minutes a black four-door Citroën turned the corner, and angled over to the curb in front of the apartment doorway. A man in the rear seat opened the curbside door and whistled. Stuart got in.

The car pulled away from the curb and the man—whose face Stuart couldn't see in the darkness—said, "There is no need to exchange names, m'sieu. I take you on trust as you must take me. By way of background, my service has been running an informant—a double agent with access to the Soviet underground. I'll call him Vadour. Until recently his production was satisfactory, though becoming marginal. However, we determined that he had begun supplying his Soviet contacts with more and better information than he was providing us.

"We were preparing to summon Vadour to a meeting to clarify matters, when a request arrived—through channels, of course—for information on a Soviet citizen by the name of Colonel Ilya Brakov. Now, that name is not unknown to us—it is one cover name of a skilled Soviet agent whose true name is Boris Ivanovitch Kazantsev. Through Vadour, among others, we have kept track of Kazantsev's comings and goings over the years. We regard him as a transient agent of the First Chief Directorate, used for sensitive assignments particularly in Western Europe. Kazantsev may be in Vienna one week, Stockholm the next, Oslo . . . and Paris. Now, m'sieu, this Vadour is a *mouton*, something of a dullard, but his memory is not to be deprecated. Yesterday afternoon he was—shall I say—taken into custody for interrogation. After he'd agreed that he had been less than forthright in his dealings with my service, the question of Kazantsev was put to him.

"At that point the *mouton* stopped bleating. Special incentives were applied, and in due course he agreed to continue our discussion, but by that time his health had deteriorated alarmingly. Not knowing what inquiries you wished to make of Vadour, m'sieu, we had no alternative but to maintain his vitality until you could question him in person."

"I appreciate that," Stuart said dryly. "A death-bed confession carries special probative value." He looked out of the window as the car eased around Rond Point and headed out Avenue Matignon. There was very little traffic at that late—or early—hour, only milk wagons, delivery trucks, and a few passenger cars on the streets. Honest folk still slept. The fatigue he had felt just before Percy's call was now overcome by adrenalin.

His escort was a stocky man in his late forties or early fifties, with a bristly mustache, and bent nose, and facial pocks that could have been made by shotgun pellets. The man wore a hat pulled well down on his forehead and a lightweight black raincoat. His hands were muscular, fingers short and thick, and he looked as though he could drop a steer with one neck punch.

When the radio crackled, the man lifted the microphone and responded. Replacing the mike he said, "I was afraid our man might not last, but"—he shrugged—"he sustains himself nobly."

"Commendable," Stuart remarked. "I have only a few questions for him."

The man's professional demeanor impressed Stuart, and he wondered what "special incentives" had been applied.

In another five minutes the car drove down into a parking area beneath an office building. As they got out, Stuart's escort requested, "I will ask that you forget the address of this building, m'sieu."

"It doesn't exist," Stuart replied and followed the man to an elevator door that he opened with an odd round key. At the sixth floor the man unlocked the door of a corner suite, locking the door behind them when they reached the reception room. An inner door opened into a dental office, containing the usual array of high-intensity lights and drill equipment. A green oxygen tank stood just inside the lighted area. Beyond it Stuart saw three men wearing black masks, two seated, the third standing. "Commissaire," he said respectfully.

The dental chair was slanted back. Strapped into it was a man, a sheet covering his body. His eyes were open above the plastic oxygen mask. The commissaire walked over to him. "Vadour, you will answer further questions fully and exactly."

The man's eyes blinked and Stuart stepped forward.

CHAPTER 25

M'sieu Vadour," Stuart began, "it is established that you are acquainted with a Russian intelligence officer who calls himself Colonel Brakov, but whose true name is Boris Kazantsev. On occasions when Kazantsev is in Paris, where is he to be found?"

The swollen, discolored lips moved. Stuart noticed a fringe of blood at the top of the sheet under Vadour's chin. The pain from the drills must have been excruciating, Stuart thought.

Through the oxygen mask Vadour's voice was muffled as he spoke. "I followed . . . him . . . to a building . . . on the Quai de Valmy . . . Tenth *Arrondissement* . . . facing the Canal de Saint Martin."

"Number?" the commissioner said curtly. "Be precise."

"It . . . was months ago . . . I don't . . . remember."

The commissioner reached over and pulled off the oxygen mask. Vadour gasped and his body arched as his lungs strained for breath. Presently he lay back and nodded. The mask was replaced and after a few moments the double agent went on. "Number one nine seven. Fourth floor . . . the door name is Ponthieu."

"He lives alone?" Stuart asked.

"I . . . believe so." His breathing was normal again.

Stuart said, "To make sure we're talking about the same man, what does Kazantsev look like?"

The swollen tongue licked his cracked lips. "Short . . . heavy . . . small eyes." He breathed deeply and the mask blurred with condensation. "Khrushchev . . . he resembles . . . Khrushchev."

The commissioner turned to Stuart. "You heard? Quai de Valmy one ninety seven. Not far from the Gare de l'Est. Stalingrad district, filled with malcontents, saboteurs, and thieves. Right, Vadour?"

"True . . . what you say is . . . true."

"Does Kazantsev go to the Soviet Embassy?" Stuart asked. He waited while Vadour mustered strength.

In a weak voice Vadour said, "I think . . . not."

"He doesn't travel as a diplomat?"

"Not . . . to . . . my . . . knowledge."

"Bodyguards?"

"I . . . never saw . . . any."

"Does Kazantsev carry a weapon?"

"Per- haps . . . concealed . . . but I never saw . . . one." His breathing became labored. One of the masked men increased the oxygen flow and felt Vadour's carotid.

Stuart said, "Where else does Kazantsev stay in Paris?"

"No . . . place I . . . know of," Vadour gasped.

The man at the oxygen control motioned Stuart aside. "If there is anything else . . . he has little time, m'sieu."

Stuart shook his head and turned to the commissioner, who said, "We finished with him before you arrived."

Vadour's body began trembling. His neck arched back until Stuart could see the whites of his eyes. He was dying.

Stuart said, "I have no more questions, Commissaire. Thank you."

"We are always glad to cooperate with the police judiciare," the commissioner said, "against the enemies of France." He nodded at his men and motioned Stuart from the office. "You are satisfied?"

"If the address is correct. Commissaire, may I ask why your men wear masks?"

"To inspire confidence in the subject. If he were able to see their faces he would know that he was going to die. Simple, no?"

Stuart nodded. He went over to the reception desk and took a pencil and paper. As he began drawing a map he explained, "I was held by Kazantsev at a farmhouse that contains video-surveillance equipment and basement cells. The woman I'm looking for was held there as well. Kazantsev may already have killed her." He sketched the orchard and wheat field around the farmhouse. "A man called Sergei and a woman who looks Mongolian attend the place. Both of them come and go from the Soviet Embassy." He finished the map and handed it to the commissioner, who studied it gravely.

"We have heard of such an installation but never its location," he said presently. "Thank you, m'sieu. Be assured we will look into it."

One of the masked men came out and spoke to his chief.

"Gone," he said.

"You know what to do," The man nodded and went back into the dental office.

The commissioner turned back to Stuart. "It is late and we both need sleep. May I have you returned to your apartment?"

"I'd appreciate it, there being few taxis at this hour." As they left the office Stuart asked, "What happens to the body?"

"A cadaver for the School of Medicine," he said indifferently. "Even in death Vadour will be useful to France."

As they got into the elevator the commissioner stated, "You understand that this episode never took place. To avoid committing anything to paper, it was necessary that you talk with Vadour."

"I understand," Stuart agreed. "Entrusting a secret to paper is the same as giving it away."

They walked to the Citroën, whose driver sat smoking behind the wheel. As Stuart opened the rear door, the commissioner said, "I hope you will find the lady alive and in good condition."

"So do I. Thank you, Commissaire."

"Because Kazantsev lacks diplomatic immunity, I leave him to you."

Stuart got into the car. The driver backed the car around, and as they drove from the garage Stuart saw the commissioner walking slowly back to the elevator. The case of Vadour was disposed of, Stuart thought. Next case . . .

He slept until late afternoon, heated a can of mushroom soup, and ate it with a ham sandwich. Then he left the apartment to meet Percy at Fouquet's.

His friend was drinking cognac with water and as Stuart sat down, Percy managed a strained smile. "Everything okay?"

"Thanks to you—and Julien."

"You got what you needed?"

"I think so." Stuart asked the waiter for cognac and water.

"Any news of Diana Selwyn?"

He shook his head. "That will come from Brakov—whose true name is Kazantsev. I gave the DST something useful in return."

"May I tell Julien there was reciprocity?"

"Please do." He took the cognac from the waiter and sipped slowly. "The DST is very efficient."

"They have to be. For years they were infiltrated by Communist elements. Worse, the DST was corrupted by orders from successive presidents to spy on opposition figures. Giscard changed that, and now the organization is professional again. Unfortunately, their main effort is directed at suppressing terrorists, leaving the Soviets a relatively open field." He sipped the cognac, then the water. "According to Julien."

"Tell him also that everything was conducted in complete anonymity. There is no paper record."

"That will relieve my brother-in-law. Now, what are your plans, Alan?"

"How about dinner with me?"

"Excellent. I'll go home, have a drink with Blanche, and meet you wherever you say."

"I've always liked Quasimodo's pepper steak."

"By Notre Dame? I'll make reservations for eight."

After Percy left, Stuart bought a paper from a newsboy and scanned it. Rudolf Henschel was in Moscow to discuss German reunification, informed sources reported. In Washington the Senate Foreign Relations Committee was conducting hearings on the confirmation of General John Winkowski as chief of the Arms Control and Disarmament Agency. Several senators opposed him as a hard-liner, calling Winkowski the wrong man at the wrong time. Confirmation was in doubt.

Stuart folded the paper and laid it on Percy's empty chair. A succession of attractive *poules*—hookers—came by, offering to let Stuart buy them a drink, but he declined pleasantly.

He drank a second cognac slowly as dusk became darkness. The sidewalk and boulevard were brilliantly lighted. People strolled up and down the Champs. Office lights went out, and night fell over Paris.

Stuart reached the restaurant early—Quasimodo was just across the footbridge from Notre Dame's cloisters—and selected a red Bordeaux, Chateau Latour 1959 Premier Cru, giving the wine time to breathe. Albert, the maître and owner, seemed to remember Stuart's face from previous visits—at least he said he did—and thanked him for adding M. le Comte to his clientele. "A notable family," he said with a slight bow, and asked if he might be permitted to recommend braised shrimp and a light bouillon before the entree. Stuart accepted the recommendation and ordered a Black Label on the rocks.

His friend arrived looking slightly flustered, saying that his wife suspected him of dining with a new *petite-amie* and was only slightly mollified when Percy maintained that his dinner companion was a Washington attorney he was considering retaining. "So," Percy concluded, "marriage amounts to a series of pluses and minuses. In exchange for a reliable bed companion, one surrenders one's freedom."

"Or is supposed to," Stuart said archly.

"Hey, no morality lectures from you after all you've been doing."

"There is a difference," Stuart pointed out, "between free choice and necessity. Now, relax and enjoy our dinner."

Percy sipped an aperitif before the bouillon arrived and they talked of college days and friends. Their pepper steak came in a large iron skillet, Albert preparing the savory sauce over an alcohol flame, adding a touch of flaming cognac just before serving.

After dinner they ordered cheese with their *fine café*, and before leaving, Percy said, "So you're going after Brakov now." The subject had not been referred to during dinner.

"That's why I returned to Paris," Stuart said soberly. "I have to hope he's still here and can give me Diana. Even though his name is Boris Kazantsev I think of him as Brakov, indelibly."

"Could he be looking for you in Washington?"

"Unlikely," Stuart replied. "If he asked Moscow's permission to travel there he'd have to give a good reason, and the true reason is that his operation came apart. Besides, if his men can't find me or Mikhail, there's little chance that Brakov could. So I figure he's either here or back in Moscow."

"Well, if I can help . . ."

"You've done enough already—too much. The rest is up to me."

"You'll call, won't you? Stay in touch?"

Stuart promised, and they parted. The time was 10:15, a good hour to reconnoiter Brakov's hiding place. He took a cab from the stand in front of Notre Dame.

The driver took him past the Hôtel de Ville and out the Rue du Temple as far as the Place de la Republique, then proceeded along Magenta to the Gare de l'Est, where Stuart got out and paid the driver. From there it was a block to the Quai de Valmy, a dreary industrial street bounded by a smelly, refuse-choked canal. Checking street numbers, Stuart turned north and found 197 in the block before the Place de Stalingrad. Every other doorway seemed to be a grimy, working-class bistro that gave off loud, discordant music and the rancid smell of old beer. Drunks lolled along the curb, others stumbled against one building, ricocheted to the next, and made their way down the street. Tattered, superannuated *poules* gathered under lightoliers, ready for pocket picking or alley sex. Not quite the area Stuart would have chosen, and for that very reason it was ideal cover for the KGB officer.

The doorway to 197 was open. There was no concierge, probably never had been. In the dark hallway a man and woman embraced clumsily. Alley sex? The hall was more secluded than an alley. Stuart heard a burst of harsh laughter as he took the uneven stairway upward.

Fourth floor, the dying Vadour had said. Door name: Ponthieu. The cooking smells of turnips, cabbage, and beets assailed Stuart's nostrils. Not that any of the building's denizens were cooking, he thought; the smells were as permanent as the scarred, stained plaster walls.

As he started up the third flight of stairs, Stuart pulled the Browning from its holster and shoved it into his side pocket. He climbed slowly and carefully, putting his weight on the risers to keep the ancient steps from creaking and announcing his coming. The air grew mustier, heavy with the smell of mold. At the near end of the hall the window was broken and rainwater pooled on the dirty floor. He stepped around it, walked quietly to the first door, listened. A television squawked, voices argued. Stuart used his flashlight to read the scrawled name: Girodet.

Next door. Name: Paulliac, B. It had to be the last one— unless Vadour, dying, had cheated his torturers.

But, no, the *mouton* had craved his oxygen too desperately. The name on a smudged card was Ponthieu.

Stuart smiled and scanned the door joins for inside lighting. Dark. "Ponthieu" was sleeping or away. Stuart pressed his ear to the door panel, but the only sounds came from other apartments and the street below. His flashlight revealed two locks. One was an old keyhole that could be defeated with a bent coathanger wire, but its bolt was not even shot. The other, newer, was manufactured by Scribe. He wiped the grime from its face and read the code number: 47J32F. Memorizing the number, Stuart dirtied the lock with grime from the floor, listening a few moments longer, and went out the way he had come.

At the Gare de l'Est Stuart consulted the telephone directory's commercial section and found several locksmiths offering twenty-four-hour service. The first two shops did not answer. The third responded and Stuart asked if the locksmith had Scribe blanks and key codes. "Yes, m'sieu," the sleepy voice replied. "Lost your key, eh?"

"I did, but fortunately I made a note of its number. Your place is on Boulevard Picpus—which end?"

"Toward the Place de la Nation, a block from the Métro."

"I'll be there shortly."

He took the yellow Métro line and five stops later emerged on the Place and found Boulevard Picpus. Helpfully the locksmith had turned on the light over his door. He let Stuart into narrow shop with worktables on either side. Their scarred wooden surfaces were cluttered with tools, drills, and grinders. The man himself was stooped, old, and unshaven, his hands embedded with grime. His face was pinched and lined, his lips seemed bloodless, and he coughed thickly from time to time.

After Stuart wrote down the key code, the locksmith consulted a dirty, dog-eared booklet and selected a brass blank from a panel labeled Scribe. Using protective glasses the locksmith cut the blank, wire-brushed it and polished it smooth. Handing it to Stuart he said, "Sixty francs, please."

Stuart whistled as he got out the money. The locksmith said, "After all, m'sieu, you have disturbed my rest. This is an accommodation for you, saving you from breaking down your door, is it not?"

Stuart smiled at his logic, handed over seventy francs, and pocketed the shiny key. "A considerable accommodation," he agreed and bade the locksmith good night.

Stuart rode the Métro back, walked casually along the Quai de Valmy—which had grown even noisier in his absence—and turned in at Brakov's building forty-seven minutes after he had left. Even so, the interval provided ample time for Brakov to have returned and retired for the night. The hour, Stuart noted, was 12:18.

A drunk was snoring on the hallway floor as Stuart started up the stairs. There was less TV noise and family chatter but the air was still fetid. Reaching the fourth floor, Stuart got out his flashlight and tiptoed to Brakov's door. No light showed through the joins, so he played his light around the door edges, looking for possible traps—a piece of paper, a bit of string. Nothing was visible, so if Brakov had taken the precaution of trapping his door, it had to be from inside.

For a long time Stuart listened, ear against the panel, but as far as he could tell the apartment was unoccupied. He wet the new key with saliva before sliding it slowly into the keyhole. Browning in his right hand, he turned the key with his left and felt the bolt begin to move. His mouth dry, he dropped to a squat and pushed the door open.

The room was dark. Stuart waited a few moments before rising, then locked the door softly behind him. He shined his flashlight around the room and saw better-looking furniture than he'd expected, a dark TV set, and an open kitchen doorway. There were dishes and pans in the sink. Water dripped from the faucet. He moved further into the apartment, toward what was probably a bedroom, and saw the door was ajar.

Was Brakov in bed? Was he asleep, or alerted by sounds of entry? Standing beside the wall, Stuart toed the door open, shined the light on the bed, and covered it with his pistol.

Empty. Covers pulled back and rumpled. He peered into the

small bathroom and saw a razor and a stick of shaving soap on the wash basin. No curtain for the shower stall. Its tiles were stained with rust and mold crawled down the sides.

Entering the kitchen he saw a pan on the stove. The grease smelled fresh. The refrigerator contained an open liter of milk, potatoes, turnips, and a piece of meat that was wrapped and moist. Atop the refrigerator was a nearly empty bottle of vodka and two unopened bottles of red wine. The meat had been bought within the last twenty-four hours, most likely that morning.

In the bedroom closet he came across the brown suit Brakov had worn at the farmhouse—the first solid evidence that Brakov was using the apartment. Stuart felt deep relief. This was the payoff.

Dirty laundry was heaped on the closet floor. Stuart probed it for weapons and found a suitcase underneath. The suitcase was partly packed—or partly empty—holding clean shirts, socks, shoes, and a gray suit. In reprisal for the fate of his lamb chops, Stuart urinated on the contents, wetting them thoroughly. He closed the suitcase and piled it with Brakov's soiled laundry, then he left the bedroom.

In the front room he arranged a chair in a far corner facing the door, made himself comfortable in it, and placed the Browning on his lap, the flashlight beside it. The time was 12:32.

Adrenalin flooded his veins. He was eager for the door to open on Brakov's ugly face. Without willing it, he began thinking of Diana.

CHAPTER 26

Off in the distance church bells tolled. As though in answer, the harsh baying of a police Klaxon penetrated the night. Four stories below, street voices argued, feet scrabbled . . . there were drunken shouts, running feet, a hoarse cry . . .

Was Brakov out meeting an agent? Bedded down with a whore? At the embassy communicating with Moscow and Washington? In the intelligence business, Stuart knew, night was as good as day. Like the nocturnal locksmith, Brakov and his colleagues toiled around the clock. In Moscow it was dawn; in Washington, evening.

He could hear a train chugging into the yards of the Gare de l'Est, the warning bleat of its horn a lonely sound that made Stuart feel even more isolated from the rest of humanity.

His eyelids were heavy. He opened them with a start, wondering how long he'd dozed. Must stay alert, he told himself. Can't let Brakov catch you off guard.

Then he thought of something he should have done before. He pointed the flashlight beam at the ceiling and spotted a fixture with a single bulb. Dragging a chair under it, he unscrewed the bulb partway, then he got down and tested the switch beside the doorway. The room remained dark.

Minutes advanced as slowly as a glacier. Stuart fought sleep by sitting forward, then getting up and walking around. But each time he returned to the chair he dozed off, wakened by his chin hitting his collar bone. He stretched and yawned. Two fifteen. His body ached for sleep.

Finally, just before three, he heard heavy footsteps. A key grated into the lock and the bolt slid open. Stuart was fully alert as the door opened inward.

He saw the man's bulk before the door closed, heard the light switch click back and forth, then an exclamation, "*Gavno!*"

Stuart shined his light on the man's face and sighted his pistol. "Hands up," he snapped, "you're covered."

Slowly Brakov's arms raised, pig eyes squinting in the light. His features showed shock and disbelief as he growled, "*Stuart!*"

"Yes, your former prisoner. Lie face down, you miserable piece of shit. Do it! Now!"

Slowly Brakov sank to his knees and lay face down. Stuart's foot probed his back for a weapon, felt nothing. "Roll over," he ordered. "Open your coat—slowly."

Like a thick log Brakov's body turned over. One hand, then the other laid open his coat. No shoulder holster, no pistol in the coat pockets. Brakov's face was flushed. "So—you killed Mikhail."

"With this," Stuart said, and shined the light on his Browning. "Before he could follow your orders, you bloody bastard."

Brakov's tongue licked his thick lips. "Now you've come back to kill me."

"You got it," Stuart answered coldly, "but I might be in a mood to trade. What did you do with Mrs. Selwyn?"

Brakov grunted. "Let her go, of course."

"Where is she?"

He managed a shrug. "I don't know. After you left with Mikhail she was returned to her hotel."

"You're lying, Brakov—I should say Boris. Yes, we'll use

Boris from now on, Comrade Kazantsev." When his eyes widened, Stuart said, "If you're wondering about the letter, it's with the FBI, so forget it."

"You fool!"

"I was a fool to keep it so long. How many killings? Selwyn, Scott, Kingman, the embassy driver—and me, if Mikhail had been a little faster."

"The embassy driver's death was accidental."

"Vehicular homicide," Stuart pointed out, "is murder. You ordered them all, Boris. But why Kingman?"

Kazantsev's lips drew into a sneer. "You're very clever, Stuart. I made the mistake of underestimating you, but—"

"So did Mikhail. Now, let's go back to Mrs. Selwyn. Her body's not in the farmhouse. Did you bury her in the field? The orchard?"

"So you found the house—again I congratulate you. But I had no reason to kill her—she'd served her purpose, hadn't she? She left the house alive and unharmed."

"Liar!" He kicked Kazantsev's thigh viciously. "*Where is she?*"

"With Beamish," Kazantsev groaned.

Stuart bent over, loosened Kazantsev's belt, and pulled it free. He made a sliding loop through the buckle and said, "Turn over."

Slowly the heavy body rolled over, face down. Stuart slipped the noose over the Russian's head and quickly tightened it around his throat, holding one foot on Kazantsev's spine for leverage. The Russian was choking, cawing for breath, his feet and hands pounding the floor. Stuart loosened the leather noose. "As you once said, Boris, no more bullshit. This is your last chance to come clean." He tightened the noose again and saw Kazantsev's hands reach back to grab the belt. Stuart pulled harder in a deadly tug-of-war, then gave the throat just enough slack for air. "Talk," he ordered, "or I'll kill you now."

"You'll kill me anyway," Kazantsev gasped. Suddenly his back arched and he rolled over, unbalancing Stuart. Kazantsev kicked Stuart's leg and jerked down on the belt. Stuart fell forward, the flashlight leaving his hand. Kazantsev's arms were around him now, squeezing, crushing. The man was immensely strong, his body weight overpowering as he rolled atop Stuart and fought for the pistol. Stuart dropped the Browning and got both hands around Kazantsev's throat, thumbs in his windpipe. Then he drew back one arm and pistoned his fist into the Russian's chin. The head snapped back and for a moment the powerful arms relaxed. Stuart started drawing the knife from its sheath but couldn't move it because of the Russian's flailing arm. Nor could he claw Kazantsev's face. In desperation he wedged a leg between the Russian's thighs and slammed his knee into his crotch.

With a howl Kazantsev released Stuart and both staggered to their feet. Doubled over, Kazantsev butted Stuart backward, falling on top of him and impaling his thorax on Stuart's knife.

The Russian's mouth opened, his eyes moved wildly, and he rolled aside, grasping for the knife. Stuart went for his fallen pistol as Kazantsev jerked out the knife and lurched at Stuart, slashing blindly, blood spurting from his mouth. Before Stuart could level the pistol Kazantsev toppled forward, the knife still in his hand. Stuart picked up the flashlight and played it over the Russian's body. It shuddered and lay still, bulk like a walrus.

Shaking from exertion, pain, and fear, Stuart took the vodka bottle from the refrigerator and swallowed a mouthful. He wiped off his prints and replaced the bottle, then mounted the armchair and, still trembling, twisted the light bulb into place. The bulb flared and Stuart looked down at Kazantsev's body. He hadn't killed the Russian, but he was responsible for his death.

As he got down from the chair Stuart noticed blood on his coat, so he went to the bathroom and cleansed it with cold water. Kneeling beside the corpse, he extracted Kazantsev's billfold and put it into his pocket. The longer it took police to identify the body, the better.

The vodka was relaxing him as the adrenalin dissipated. He sat in the chair and looked around, then fixed his gaze on the dead man. He was a fighter, Stuart thought, give him that. Even dying he never gave up. But how much truth had Kazantsev spoken? It was hard to think of Diana working with Russian agents, but in the labyrinth Stuart had unwittingly entered, almost anything seemed possible.

From Kazantsev's billfold he got out some francs, crumpled them, and tucked them under the body. Maybe a whore, male or female, or some thief from the street, had fought M. Ponthieu and stolen his billfold. How much time would the Paris police spend looking for the killer? Not much, not in a district where drunken violence was as common as garbage on the streets.

His breathing had slowed, body tremors stopped. His leg hurt from Kazantsev's kick, and so did his ribs, compressed by the powerful arms. He wondered if they were broken again.

He shoved the pistol into his shoulder holster and looked around the room a final time. What he could see of Kazantsev's face was fixed in a rictus, the open eye dulled by death. Stuart turned off the ceiling light, polished his prints off the switch and door lock, and closed the door quietly, hearing the spring bolt click into place. The building was still as he went down the dark staircase.

At 3:40 most of the bistros were closed but a few were still open, catering to dedicated drinkers and unattached whores. He walked along the quai and over to the Métro station.

Alone, Stuart dropped Kazantsev's billfold into a trash can. After ten minutes a red-line train pulled in. Stuart had the car to himself as he rode to the Étoile. He surfaced near the Arc de Triomphe and walked slowly to his apartment, where he soaked in hot bathwater until he felt better. After drying off, Stuart drank half a glass of Percy's cognac and got into bed. He was too tired to deal with anything but the need for rest, but before sleep sucked him down into its dark void he realized that tomorrow would begin the search for Diana.

CHAPTER 27

Stuart got up around noon and walked stiffly to the kitchen for coffee and a croissant. Body aches reminded him of the fight, and he realized that although the KGB would not necessarily link Kazantsev's death to Alan Stuart, its search for Mikhail and Stuart would continue. He had no idea how many of Kazantsev's agents had seen him after the car wreck and at the farmhouse, but Yuri Bendikov knew what he looked like, so it was essential to stay clear of him.

Diana was with Beamish, Kazantsev had gasped. Truth or misdirection? Beamish could be located through the Passage press office. Had Diana accompanied him to West Berlin, gone to Ibiza, or stayed in a Paris hotel?

While soaking in another hot bath Stuart gently probed his ribs and decided that none had been rebroken in the struggle. His leg contusion from Kazantsev's kick was an ugly-looking mass of yellow and purple, and he massaged it carefully. He dried, dressed in clean clothing, and was making a second cup of coffee when the telephone rang. He heard Percy complaining, "You didn't call. I've been worried."

"I was out last night—late."

"I see. Any . . . luck?"

"I found the man I was looking for and he's no longer an obstacle. It's the lady I need to find."

"Then she's alive."

"That's what the man said."

"Sounds as if you're making progress. Also, I wanted you to know that Blanche is dragging me out to Rambouillet today. I'm to look over the house with her before we move in, but I'll be back in Paris this evening if you need me."

"I hope I won't," Stuart said, "but it was good of you to call."

"Listen—your concerns are my concerns. And while I've got you, my in-law is relieved that everything went so well. The papers won't carry the story, but at dawn a certain farmhouse was raided and two persons taken into custody. They could give no satisfactory account of themselves so they're being held for serious questioning."

"Has their embassy intervened?"

"Not yet, and I doubt it'll happen. Julien thinks they'll be deported as undesirable aliens."

"Black marks on their records." Stuart smiled. The day's first satisfaction.

"How about lunch tomorrow?"

"Not sure where I'll be, but I'll call your office if I can make it."

Stuart settled by the telephone and called the Passage press office, again giving his name as Chauncey Merkins. The press officer said Ambassador Beamish would be in later in the day and gave the tentative time of five o'clock for the interview. Stuart thanked him and said he would call later to confirm.

Because Diana had been staying at the Hilton, Stuart phoned. As expected he was told that she was no longer a guest. His next call was to the Soviet Embassy. He inquired if M. Bendikov had returned from Washington and learned that the second secretary was expected in Paris the following day.

While his mind was absorbing these details, Stuart realized he had overlooked an obvious source. Telephoning the Selwyn residence in Washington, he gave the maid his real name, reminded her that he was Mrs. Selwyn's lawyer, and asked to speak with her. The maid told him Mrs. Selwyn was traveling in Europe. Stuart asked how long it had been since she had heard from Mrs. Selwyn.

"It was last week, sir, but you can come whenever you like if you need to work in the office."

"I really need to speak with her," Stuart pressed. "Any idea where I can locate her, or when she'll be back?"

"No, sir, but I'll leave a message saying you called."

Stuart thanked her and hung up. As of last week Diana had been alive and traveling in Europe. So Kazantsev had told the truth on at least one crucial point. He telephoned the Crillon, the George V, and several other first-class hotels asking for Diana, but all responses were negative.

Still, she was alive. Why hadn't she tried to contact him, find out if he'd survived the Washington trip? He could understand her terror at being kidnapped, but that was behind her and she'd gone back to Beamish.

Inductive reason told him she'd played him for a fool. Her continuing liaison with Beamish and her apparently cordial attitude toward Bendikov could not easily be ignored. Nor could her lack of concern over his fate. Stuart thought of her with anger and resentment, but even as he did so he wondered what she could have done to find him. It was he, after all, who'd gone underground, used false identities to cover his tracks. Knowing nothing of that, how could she have reached him?

Well, he thought, I'll confront her, demand answers, and if I'm not satisfied I'll go back to Washington and reassemble the scattered shards of my life without her.

Never before, he admitted, had he felt toward any woman as he felt toward Diana Selwyn. More than her physical beauty was involved, much more. There was her lively intelligence, her bearing, her breeding, the similarity in things they liked . . . her uninhibited passion when they made love . . . One final try, and if he lost her that would be the end of it. But he would have tried.

At two o'clock he took his laundry to a *blanchisserie* down the street for pickup in two days. He bought an afternoon paper and read it back in the apartment. A Washington story said that General Winkowski's confirmation hearings had ended and a committee vote would be taken shortly, with confirmation in doubt. Senators Prideman and Vane had announced that they would vote against confirmation.

"Those pricks!" Stuart said aloud. Neither deserved to shine the general's shoes, much less blackball him. No wonder capable men were increasingly reluctant to serve the government, when strutting midgets could abuse them in public forums and get away with it. That was a phenomenon the founding fathers had never anticipated.

He phoned the Passage office and was told that Beamish had agreed to the five o'clock appointment. At four Stuart drove to Passage headquarters on Boulevard Haussmann, parked across the street from the building, and settled down to wait.

At half past four a cream-colored Mercedes stretch limo pulled up at the building and Edward Beamish got out. The other passengers stayed in the back seat, and as the Mercedes pulled away Stuart recognized Diana Selwyn.

He was half prepared to see her alive, but it still shook him, and he delayed starting the Fiat. He needed to get control of himself. Making a U-turn, Stuart followed the limousine to the Étoile and up Avenue Carnot, where the driver continued beyond Rue Pierre Demours.

The Mercedes pulled up in front of a handsome apartment building with an ornate façade. The driver got out and carried Diana's luggage into the entrance, then opened the door for her.

She was wearing an attractive organdie print, gloves, and an azure hat with matching bag. Her high-heeled shoes shaped her legs to advantage, and Stuart watched with churning emotions until she disappeared. He found a parking place farther down the block and walked back to the apartment building. He punched the return button to bring the elevator down from the third floor, got into it, and rode up, throat tight, heart pounding.

Stuart rang the bell. He heard footfalls nearing, then stop at the other side of the door. "Who is it?" Diana's voice called.

"*Des fleurs pour madame*," he replied.

The door opened and Diana gasped. "*Alan!*"

He stepped inside and closed the door. "Surprised to see me?"

"Well, of course I am. I had no idea where you were—God, I've been worried!" She stepped toward him and placed her arms around his neck, but Stuart pushed them away roughly.

"Worried about what? That I didn't give Blake's letter to Brakov? His name is Kazantsev, Boris Kazantsev of the First Chief Directorate. Or did you know?"

"Know?" She stepped back, confusion clouding her features. "Why should I know anything about him?"

Looking beyond her, Stuart could see the interior of the apartment. It was large, light, and to his surprise furnished with modern pieces whose bright steel frames were hung with soft leather in hues of beige and light chocolate. Cocktail and end tables were of glass and stainless steel, the thick carpeting café au lait. There were free-form ceramic lamps and Picasso and Renoir prints on the walls, and he recognized work by Cézanne and Klee.

All this he glimpsed in the moment before replying to Diana's question. He breathed deeply, spoke in a hard voice. "You've always known more than you admitted, a hell of a lot more." He locked the door behind him. "Going through that cell act to make me cooperate with Brakov. 'Give him anything he wants,' you pleaded, so I laid my life on the line to protect you. My *life*, Diana, and you didn't give a damn whether I survived. No, you went off with Beamish; too bad about old Alan, right? I'd saved your skin and that was all that mattered."

"How can you say that?"

"Because you made no effort to find out what happened in Washington."

Standing close to her, Stuart sensed the aura that had attracted him from the first. He could almost feel the remembrance of warmth of her naked skin against his; he desired her and it kept him from striking her. God, his emotions had never been more confused. Her face was flushed, he had an impulse to reach out and touch it, crush her lips with his. Her face tightened. "I didn't have to, Alan. Listen to me. I knew you were alive, I didn't know where you were, how to reach you." She breathed deeply. "Because of what we've felt for each other I believed you'd come to me. Waited for your return."

"How could you possibly know I was alive unless Brakov told you. It *was* Brakov, wasn't it?"

"No." She shook her head, turned away.

"Who then?"

"I—I can't tell you."

His laugh was short, bitter. "More lies, Diana. Lie after lie, and I've been the simpleton believing you. But if you're afraid to tell the truth because of Brakov, don't let that hold you back. You see, I killed him."

"You—killed him?" Her hand covering her mouth, she stepped back from him.

"Yes, *darling*, I'm no longer the simple Georgetown lawyer handling old ladies' estates. To stay alive I've become a man on the run, a killer from necessity, handy with knife and gun."

"And you've decided I'm responsible. Alan, you couldn't be more wrong. I started once to tell you about Beamish but the time wasn't right and—"

"Well, it's right now. C'mon, lady, let's hear the tale." He paused, hands clenching and unclenching. "That can wait. We'll go back to your unconcern about my life."

"No, no, that's wrong, too. That night, after you left for the airport, I was worried sick. You've got to believe me." Her face was anguished.

"Why should I? You didn't go to Percy's place, never even called him." Anger choked his throat. "You let me think you were dead so I came back to find Brakov—Kazantsev—and drag the truth from him. Last night he came close to killing me. Alive he was smart, skilled, and strong as a bull—but I killed him."

Face pale, she whispered, "And now you've come to kill me. Alan, if I was what you think I am I'd deserve it, but your reasons are all wrong. I'm *glad* Brakov is dead, glad you got away from his man in Washington. And what destroys me is the way everything's worked out to make you hate me. I—I never intended that."

"What did you intend?" He sat down in an upholstered chair, looked up at her face. "I'm waiting for explanations. Make them good, baby, as persuasive as you can."

She came to him, reached for his hand, but he drew it away. She breathed deeply, sighed, and began. "For more than two years I've been working for the FBI."

He laughed shortly. "Jesus, can't you come up with anything better than that? You're versatile, I concede that, but the idea of you working for the FBI is too ludicrous to—" He broke off and his voice hardened. "Okay, prove it."

"She doesn't have to," came a voice from the doorway, and Stuart shot up to see a man emerge from an inner room, the neatly dressed man from the bank parking lot. "I'll do it for her." He walked toward them.

"Who the hell are you?" Stuart demanded.

"Special Agent Arneson." He tossed a credential holder at Stuart, who opened it and compared the photo with the man's face. "These things can be forged," he commented, handing back the ID.

"True. But you can phone the embassy legal attaché for confirmation, Mr. Stuart. You're a friend of Pat O'Rourke and recently sent him a highly interesting communication."

"That's who told me you were alive, Alan," Diana explained.

He stared in bewilderment at the two of them. Suddenly all his reasoning was reversed, after all he'd gone through.

Agent Arneson continued, "This apartment is rented by the FBI in connection with the ongoing case against Yuri Bendikov and his agent, Edward Beamish."

Diana said, "I think we could all use a drink." She left the room and Arneson sat down facing Stuart. "You've gone through a great deal," he said, "but until now there wasn't any secure way of letting you know what was behind it all. You and the *spetznaz* guy calling himself Mikhail were trailed from Dulles to your place. We saw the two of you go into the bank and return to your house. After that Mikhail was never seen again. You drove away and the tail car lost you in downtown traffic." He paused. "The assumption was that you'd killed Mikhail and disposed of his body. Where the hell is it?"

"I should face a manslaughter charge? Bullshit, Arneson. No one will ever know."

He held up his hands. "Hey, we're happy you offed the bastard. I won't press you."

"Suppose only Mikhail had left the house—with Selwyn's letter?"

"He'd have been picked up on a pretext, searched, and the letter copied, allowed to go his way."

"Nice," Stuart said, disgusted. "And where was the FBI when Mikhail tried to shoot me?"

Arneson shrugged. "A risk we couldn't cover," he admitted. "But some of us thought you'd be smart enough to protect yourself." He smiled.

Diana appeared with two bottles on a tray, glasses, and ice. "Bourbon for me," Arneson said. "Like always."

"And scotch for you, Alan, I know." She made three highballs and sat down beside Arneson, who went on, "Because the Soviets couldn't figure out your role, Mr. Stuart, it was essential to keep them puzzled by letting you react as any innocent person would." He drank from his glass. "So you finished off Kazantsev last night? Congratulations."

"Apparently I've been doing all your killing for you."

"Well, you wouldn't expect the FBI to go around liquidating Soviet citizens. It's not in our charter."

Stuart looked at Diana. "Hear that? What a damn fool I've been, since the moment Blake came into my office."

"If you'd leveled with me, and given me Blake's letter," she said tightly, "a great deal of this needn't have taken place."

He turned to Arneson. "Why was that letter so important? Especially after Rolf Kingman was killed?"

"First," explained Arneson, "you have to understand some things about Blake Selwyn. He wasn't the career-oriented patriot you and a lot of others considered him to be. He was recruited years ago back in Prague—by the KGB."

"You *know* that?"

"A Czech defector told us first. And Blake's first wife tended to confirm the report—after their divorce, of course."

"What do you mean, 'tended to confirm'?"

"Ah, the legal mind. I should have said she voiced her suspicions of Blake to the FBI." He sighed. "We almost certainly would have discounted her allegations but for the fact that the Czech defector had already fingered Blake."

"But Blake stayed in the department, got steady promotions . . ."

"Surely you understand that evidence was needed to prosecute, or even to dismiss him from State. Besides, as Selwyn moved from country to country his contacts were monitored. Unwittingly he exposed two Soviet spy rings abroad. Then he was reassigned to the department and things got complicated. That's when we approached Mrs. Selwyn." He nodded at Diana.

"I'd formed my own suspicions," she said quietly. "In both Vienna and Geneva I'd seen Blake rendezvous with a man I didn't know. Then one night in our house, after we'd gone to bed, I heard Blake go down to his office. In wifely innocence I tiptoed down to see if he'd like a hot chocolate, brandy, or something to help him sleep. Instead I saw him using a tiny camera to photograph pages labeled top secret. I was horrified—my husband was a traitor.

There was no other possible explanation." She looked away. "From that moment on I felt that Blake's treachery annulled our marriage. I considered leaving him, of course, but I was afraid he'd realize what I'd found out and have me killed—or kill me himself. For days I went around like a zombie—until an FBI agent spoke to me and asked for my help."

Arneson put down his glass. "A counter espionage specialist persuaded Mrs. Selwyn to stay in place and report on her husband's contacts and after-hours activities. It was hard and distasteful for Mrs. Selwyn, I know, but with her information we were able to identify her husband's control as Yuri Bendikov, although they seldom had face-to-face meetings except at diplomatic gatherings where everyone mingled.

"Surveillance of Bendikov revealed a parallel operation involving former ambassador Beamish and the formation of Passage. Initially there was a feeling in the bureau that Beamish was a public-spirited, internationally minded citizen looking for something in the foreign affairs area to replace the position and prestige he'd enjoyed at State. Inside the beltway, as you may have noticed, Mr. Stuart, a lot of ex-congressmen and former government officials stay around looking for something to do. Some connect, most don't. So—"

"Wasn't Beamish watched? Wasn't his phone tapped?"

Arneson grimaced. "Some very painful court cases have imposed rigid strictures on what the bureau can do vis-à-vis a U.S. citizen when there's no warrant. And there wasn't enough on Beamish to authorize physical and technical surveillance. These days you practically have to find a suspect with a smoking gun before you've got the 'probable cause' a judge will accept." He shook his head. "Maddening. So we asked Mrs. Selwyn to develop a low-key relationship with Beamish. Beamish went for it, but he was very, very careful never to reveal anything beyond a social relationship with Bendikov based on a mutual interest in disarmament. Still, Mrs. Selwyn was able to report their travel plans, which enabled us to have them covered abroad."

"I hated spying," Diana said. "I still do."

Her words flooded Stuart with relief. Arneson's explanations were demolishing the edifice he'd constructed with logic and inductive reasoning, enabling Stuart to see Diana as he'd wanted to see her. As rage and resentment flowed from him he felt hollow. Deceived, yes, but for reasons he could understand, and his mind welcomed and embraced the new truth. He heard Arneson saying, "When Selwyn was in Geneva or Vienna with disarmament delegations we had no way of preventing him from passing information orally to his KGB contacts. But at State we arranged that his access to really important documents was gradually restricted. A month before Blake approached you, Mr. Stuart, Assistant Secretary Kingman refused to let Blake read a report on Soviet negotiating positions acquired from technical intelligence—"

"Then Kingman knew about Blake?"

"He was Blake's superior. We went to him quietly, told him our suspicions, and Kingman agreed to cooperate, but he was nervous about it, unsure if he was doing right by a fellow departmental officer. To Kingman it was an ethical problem, but to his credit he kept the faith."

"And got himself killed," Stuart snapped. "Jesus, you guys stay in the background pulling strings while someone else takes the risks. I was expendable too."

"Come to that, we're all expendable." Arneson drank deeply from his glass and eyed Stuart. "Only so much we can do, friend. Only so much we're *allowed* to do. Also, the director let us know that the White House didn't want a new spy scandal involving State and the Russians as long as there was a chance of concluding an arms control agreement." He sighed. "General Winkowski bucked the administration—he wanted the scandal to blow sky high. To his credit, he never leaked a word, but the White House isn't actually supporting his confirmation—hands-off policy. And without tough support from the Administration, including State, it looks as though the general isn't going to make it."

"Talk about treachery." Stuart grunted and drank more scotch.

"Call it what you like," Arneson said diffidently. "It's how things get done inside the beltway. You were with State; surely you came to realize that the merit of an issue doesn't guarantee it's going to fly."

Stuart shrugged and looked at Diana. Like a chameleon she seemed to change according to her surroundings, the people she was with.

"Meanwhile," Arneson continued, "Mrs. Selwyn hinted to Beamish that she preferred his foreign policy to that of the United States. We dangled her in front of the opposition to see what would happen. Well, they liked the bait and they bit. It wasn't long before Bendikov himself pitched her."

Diana elaborated. "At a Soviet Embassy party he took me aside and said he had the impression our interests had much in common. He suggested that I serve the cause of international peace by letting him know what Blake and Beamish were up to. He wasn't crude—no offer of payment—just waved the peace banner. Two days later I said I'd be willing to assist him."

"So Bendikov figured he had a very sweet deal," Arneson remarked. "Blake Selwyn was an agent and Beamish at least a solid sympathizer. Now he has an informant reporting on both of them. Of course, he didn't know that Mrs. Selwyn knew her husband was his agent, nor did he clue Blake in to his wife's involvement."

Stuart said, "So Bendikov's approach coming after Diana's hints to Beamish established a conspiracy between Beamish and Bendikov."

"Sure, just what we wanted. But try proving it in court."

Stuart nodded. "Point taken. Now let's get to Blake's letter. Why did he write it?"

"To protect himself," Arneson said. "As I told you, Blake was being excluded from significant State decisions and information. He must have sensed the isolation, gotten worried, and come up with a scheme to vindicate himself. The letter was his insurance policy. Plus there was a chance that it would discredit Rolf Kingman and bring him down. Looking at Blake's letter objectively, it was a brilliant ploy. I doubt I'd have come up with anything so Machiavellian."

"I agree the guy was brilliant," Stuart said, "but there's one point you missed: Blake didn't give me the letter directly. He left it with Harvey Scott to forward in the event of his death."

"Maybe so, maybe no. Fact is, you don't actually know what instructions Blake gave Harvey Scott."

"I know what Scott wrote me, and what Scott said over the phone." He paused to reflect. "But I concede that Scott might have told me something entirely different had we met in Springfield. Unfortunately—"

"—Scott was disposed of before you and he could talk things over. What we know is that Blake prepared the letter well before he came to see you, Mr. Stuart, and entrusted it to his family lawyer to hold pending further instructions."

"Why did he do that?"

"You and Blake weren't close friends; he couldn't be sure you'd swallow his tale and be willing to represent him. I think he created an enticing drama by hiring you in advance to investigate the circumstances of his death. He was right in thinking you'd agree to his proposal but wrong in thinking he wasn't in personal danger. So he didn't come on too strong with his story of vague suspicions. Mainly he wanted you to believe him and be available. You'd receive the letter from Scott if and when he was interviewed by State security or the FBI. Then you'd testify to the best of your knowledge and belief that Blake didn't want to make charges against Kingman he couldn't substantiate—which would give Blake the moral high ground."

"But he was killed because of the letter." Stuart turned to Diana. "Wasn't he?"

"I assume so," she said.

"What we've worked out," Arneson picked up, "is a scenario in which Blake tells Bendikov that even though he may be under suspicion, he is safe because of a letter left with a lawyer he could trust."

"And *that* got him killed?"

"You have to understand the Soviet mind, Mr. Stuart. An atmosphere of conspiracy and suspicion permeates every KGB move. How was Bendikov to know that the letter contained only what Blake said it did? For all Bendikov knew, the letter was Blake's confession of his long Soviet involvement, naming names—including his own. Bendikov must have weighed the possibilities and come down on the side of his own personal safety, rendering Blake expendable. After all, his production had dropped off, which indicated that Blake was already under suspicion. He probably felt Blake would spill everything if threatened with disgrace. So he liquidated a fading agent who'd become a threat to himself and his controller."

Stuart said, "That's your theory."

"Got a better one?"

When Stuart was silent, Arneson took a long pull from his glass and set it down. "Bringing us," he said, "to the Beamish-Bendikov combination."

Stuart looked at Diana. "Which you fellows can handle on your own."

Arneson leaned forward. "On the contrary, Mr. Stuart. Beamish has to be caught red-handed with Bendikov. We need proof against them both, and you and Mrs. Selwyn can help us obtain it."

CHAPTER 28

Stuart stared at the FBI agent. "You're crazy!" he exploded. "I've had enough of this. How about you, Diana?"

For a while she said nothing. Finally she slipped from her glass and turned to the FBI agent "We've come this far, Alan. At least we ought to hear what he has in mind."

Stuart got to his feet. "Hell with it," he snapped. "My life's been torn apart and I've been jerked around like a puppet. Now I'm asked to volunteer for a mission so illegal even the FBI won't touch it? No thanks."

Arneson smiled briefly. "Oh, my office can make all the support arrangements. But as far as being present on the scene when they're compromised, we can't do it. Now, as to what's illegal, Mr. Stuart, you've killed two men by your own admission, one in Washington, one here in Paris. Where would you prefer to be booked?"

Stuart glared at him. "Blackmail? Screw you, Arneson, You haven't got a body. You've got nothing."

Arneson relaxed in his chair. "Circumstantial evidence is enough. Let's suppose you're acquitted of killing Mikhail. How will that affect your law practice? Your way of life? And if you remember the Code Napoleon, you'd have to prove yourself innocent of killing Kazantsev. You'd spend a lot of time in unsanitary French prisons while working out a defense. And in the event you were freed, the publicity would force the KGB to settle the score. Sit down, Mr. Stuart, hear me out, and then make your decision."

Stuart sat down numbly. Diana spoke up. "I know you don't care for Edward Beamish, Alan, and actually, I loathe the man. He gives me the creeps, and the way he plans to disarm our country scares the hell out of me. It should scare you too. Defeating him—and Bendikov—is worth a little more effort, don't you think?"

He swallowed. "You and Beamish are lovers."

"Oh, he's hinted, made passes, but appearing with me in public is enough of an ego trip for Edward, far more satisfying than sex—which I've denied him."

Arneson said, "Tomorrow night Passage is hosting a large reception in the Crillon ballroom for leading European members and French government officials. The president has been invited to attend. The Soviets will be there in force, including Yuri Bendikov, who's making a special trip from Washington to be on hand."

"I knew he was returning tomorrow," Stuart said. "but I didn't know why."

Arneson commented admiringly, "You do very well on your own, have all along. What I have in mind is arranging a Bendikov-Beamish meeting here." He glanced around the room. "This place is miked like you wouldn't believe, every room, plus video cameras—all the latest technology."

"Go on."

"Mrs. Selwyn has agreed to attend the reception with Beamish, so he'll pick her up here. I hadn't figured out how to draw Bendikov, but your unexpected appearance on our doorstep, as it were, solves that."

"Bait, eh?"

Arneson nodded. "Haven't quite decided how best to use you, but it'll come to me."

"I'm sure you'll let me know," Stuart said dryly. "You're a fount of inspiration." He gazed at Diana, whose face was composed. She's been at this a lot longer than I have, he realized, and Arneson's idea—if it works—is her final payoff. "Suppose I go through with it. No more harassment or sly proposals?"

"You'll be clean. Forget about us, we forget about you." He leaned forward. "Okay?"

Stuart looked over at Diana. "What's your decision?"

"It's what I've been working toward for so long—so, yes, I want it finished. Alan, don't you? Then there'll be no more of—what we've both gone through. Is anything more important?"

"Nothing," he agreed, "not if it's over with once and for all."

"I want a different kind of life, Alan." Her eyes beseeched him.

"God knows I do, too. Enough is enough." He faced Arneson. "Okay. I'll go along with it."

"Good." Arneson leaned forward and patted Stuart's knee. "Need that." He sat back and tented his fingers. "Diana, let me table an idea and you punch holes in it, okay? Bendikov will arrive tomorrow. Get in touch with him. Say you've heard from Alan Stuart, who's brought Blake's letter to Paris. Tell him you're working on Stuart to get the letter, but you're afraid, you need backup—"

"Why would I be afraid of Alan?"

"Because he's hinted at having killed at least one KGB agent and he's jealous of Beamish. Okay? Bendikov should be so eager to get his hands on that letter that he won't question your state of mind. He'll come over to collect it." He turned to Stuart. "You'll be passed out in the bedroom. Diana will tell Bendikov that the letter's hidden someplace but that you'll get it for her when you're sober."

He looked sideways at Diana. "Give Bendikov a drink and keep him here until Beamish shows. Then go into the bedroom to check on Stuart. That gives Bendikov a chance to talk privately with Beamish, controller to agent. It'll be on film, of course, and we have to hope that incriminating words are passed—enough to build a case. If money changes hands that would be even better." He paused. "Much better."

Stuart agreed, "Suppose Bendikov decides to kill me in reprisal for Mikhail?"

"He'll want to," Arneson replied coolly, "but here it would compromise his agent—Diana. By the way, where'd you off Kazantsev? In his Quai de Valmy pad?"

Stuart stared at him in astonishment. "You knew about the place?"

"Sure."

"I went to a lot of trouble to locate it, when you—"

"You weren't cooperating with us then, Mr. Stuart. In fact, for a time we weren't sure what your motives were."

"Why the hell not?"

"For one thing, you were Blake's confidant of choice. Then you played very cagey with Mrs. Selwyn about any documents Blake might have entrusted to you. Also, you and Blake knew each other at State, so it was possible—just possible, mind you—that you shared a covert Soviet connection."

"Jesus, with you guys everyone's guilty—"

"Until proven innocent, you were going to say? Well, in the espionage game that's pretty much true. It's called positive vetting, and it's what the British cousins ignored, allowing the Cambridge Ring to operate with impunity for decades."

"I don't like your game," Stuart declared. "I prefer to trust people."

Arneson shrugged. "You trusted Blake Selwyn. Look where it got you."

Stuart felt his face flush. "I'd rather not be reminded, okay? So, Diana and I are in the bedroom, and if all goes well, Beamish and Bendikov compromise themselves. Then what? The Seventh Cavalry storms in?"

"Not quite. My script would have Diana leave with them for

the Passage reception. You go back to wherever you're staying—where is that, by the way?"

Stuart grunted. "I don't want the place miked or phone tapped."

"Suit yourself. Anyway, when this place is clear, the surveillance tapes are collected. If the evidence is there, we move against both men."

"Bendikov has diplomatic immunity," Stuart pointed out, "in case you forgot."

"Even so, he can be exposed and discredited. Same goes for Beamish. Once its head is shown as a Soviet agent, how long can Passage last as an organization? And if Beamish is so unwise as to return to U.S. jurisdiction, he'll be subject to prosecution for espionage. Whichever way it goes, Beamish is finished. Bendikov too."

"So the real goal is destroying Passage," Stuart said thoughtfully.

"You have a problem with that? Passage may not have started out as a Soviet front, but it fast became one."

"My sister's an ardent supporter," Stuart said, "despite spousal advice. Idealism dies hard, and I won't want Pat to know I had a hand in exposing her favorite peace organization."

Diana promised, "She won't hear it from me, Alan."

"Right," Arneson said spiritedly. "Mum's the word—and of course, bureau involvement could never surface."

Stuart smiled. "Well, well. That would give me a little something over you, wouldn't it?"

For a moment Arneson looked crestfallen. "Just don't push it," he said in a hard voice. "The best operations are those the public never hears about. This one qualifies." He drained the last of his bourbon. "Sometime tomorrow, before noon, say, we'll meet and go over the plan, work out any wrinkles." He stood up. "Glad you showed up, Mr. Stuart. Be in touch."

"One final question," Stuart interjected. "With all the changes in Central Europe, the new freedom to travel East and West, won't Passage just become an anachronism?"

"If cross-border travel was Beamish's only goal, sure. But the other—the most important—part of his agenda is unilateral nuclear disarmament. I don't care if the Berlin Wall vanishes like Carthage, those Soviet missile silos won't just disappear, or their mobile missile carriers. It's not in the Soviet nature to suddenly turn peaceable, turn swords into plowshares. Beamish and his cohorts would like the world to think so and he frames that pitch very attractively. So he's a threat, Mr. Stuart, a menace to Western security as long as he's alive."

Arneson left then, and after locking the door behind him Diana turned to Stuart. "Well, " she said tightly, "alone, at last. I want to know what you're thinking."

"Thinking? Realizing how gullible I've been. How you let me lurch around in the dark, when you could have explained things from the start."

"I couldn't," she pleaded, coming toward him. "I was under orders, Alan, and it never occurred to me that you'd get in harm's way."

"But you thought I might be one of Blake's collaborators," he persisted.

"At first it seemed possible, but afterward I never doubted you."

"After what?"

"After we made love. After I saw you with Prudy and Greg. I knew you loved your family too much to ever do anything against our country—their country. The one they'll grow up and live in."

"That's not positive vetting."

"Female intuition," she explained softly. "My intuition, Alan. But I have to say you're not an easy man to be around. You've got so god-damn much male pride that any little thing affronts you."

"Yeah? Take a look at yourself; more masks than a novelty shop. Which is the real Diana? Who am I talking to today?"

"The one who fell in love with you," she said quietly. "Couldn't help myself—it just happened. And I hated deceiving you."

"Does that include our scene in the cell? How did that come about? You weren't working for Kazantsev?"

She looked away. "Bendikov asked me to help Kazantsev get Blake's letter. I couldn't refuse without damaging my cover. Besides, I was helping to free you, to get you out of France. I knew the FBI would follow you and Mikhail, so I had no idea they'd let you be endangered."

"Well, they did," he said sourly. "Bastards, especially the guy who just left. Screw principle, he's a politician."

"He's also intelligent and dedicated. More scotch?"

"No, just some ice."

Coming back from the kitchen she said, "I'm hungry. Breakfast in West Berlin and I don't like German cooking. I avoided the Lufthansa snack—sausage and rolls—so suppose I make us an omelet?"

"Fine." His resistance was gone.

"Chives? Onions? Cheese?"

"Cheese is fine. Or we could go out for a bite."

"I don't think we ought to be seen together until after tomorrow night, do you?"

"You're right." His tongue felt thick, his words blurred. Good scotch, but he'd had a little too much of it. Besides, he was emotionally exhausted. Forcing himself out of the chair, he stretched out on the sofa, felt his eyes close without willing it, heard Diana call, "It won't take long."

"Wha- what won't take long?"

"The omelet, dear. Relax and I'll take care of things."

When he opened his eyes he saw Diana seated in a chair reading by a table lamp. The windows were dark. He sat up groggily. "How long did I sleep?"

"Oh, about two hours." She folded the book and stood up. She had changed into a delicate peach peignoir. "I went out to buy a few things for dinner—if you'd like to join me."

"I would."

"Coffee?"

"Please. And two aspirin."

She brought back the coffee and aspirin, and as she came toward him Stuart noticed how the flimsy material flowed and clung to her body. After washing down the aspirin with the coffee he said, "I feel like a castaway."

She smiled. "Occasionally I wondered what you'd look like in a beard. Now I know. Are you going to keep it?"

"Depends."

"On what?"

"Whether you like it."

She breathed deeply. "That's the nicest thing you've said since coming here. But if I have a choice, I say it goes. In a few days, of course." She sat next to him and took his hand. "I've missed you terribly, Alan. One thing that kept me going was thinking that if anything happened to you, I could take revenge on Bendikov. I would have, too. But it's much better having you here. How do you feel now?"

"Groggy, hung over. That's powerful scotch you serve."

"You went after it like a thirsty camel."

"I was disturbed—all my carefully reasoned conclusions were flying apart—and I made the mistake of drinking while Arneson talked." He looked at her. "Quite a talker, isn't he? I thought he'd never shut up. I suppose the omelet is history, as they say."

"It was quite good, too, but it's dinnertime now, and I have French chops whenever you're hungry."

"That's now." He struggled to his feet. "After a wake-up shower."

"Fresh towels in the bathroom, courtesy of the FBI."

He looked around. "I didn't realize the bureau boys lived so well."

"Usually they don't. This is my stage setting."

He took her hand. "I hope those bastards realize how privileged they are to have you doing their dirty work."

"They take it in stride," she said. "Can you accept it?"

"I can't accept anything that endangers you. Thinking Kazantsev had harmed you gave me the strength I needed to finish him off. Otherwise I'd have kept him alive long enough to force some truth from him." He drew her against him, circled her body with his arms. Her face tilted and their lips met in a kiss that lengthened and deepened. His hands touched her breasts tentatively at first, then molded them possessively as her nipples became erect. "I've wanted your touch, dearest, wanted *you*," she murmured throatily. "Always praying you'd return." Her loins pressed against his. "So we could be together again."

"I've wanted the same," he confessed, "when I was half crazy with worry over you." He kissed her forehead tenderly. "Now that I understand, we both have things—deceits, deceptions—to discard. No obstacles between us. Darling, I can't lose you again."

"And you won't," she promised. "Now take care of your hangover while I make dinner."

His hand caressed her bottom, circled her thigh and rested between her loins. For a moment her body relaxed, her eyes closed, then she moved gently away. "Later," she said quietly, "let's not hurry things. I want our reunion—this night to be perfect in every way."

"So do I." He kissed her hands and let her go.

The cold shower made him gasp. His head felt as though it was going to explode, but he stayed in the shower until thoroughly chilled, then dried off and dressed.

She had set places for two on the dining table. Two candles in silver holders cast a warm glow over the place settings. Stuart uncorked a bottle of Beaujolais while Diana brought in their food: frilled lamb chops, asparagus with hollandaise sauce, and a small tomato-and-lettuce salad. He helped her to her seat and poured the wine.

"I love shopping in Paris," she said. "Everything is always so fresh and there's such a variety, it's hard to choose." She lifted her glass and touched his. "Toast?"

"Why not? To success."

She drank. "And after that?"

"See what happens, play it as it goes."

"That's awfully indefinite, isn't it? Always the careful lawyer."

"Life is indefinite," he replied soberly, "and fragile. That's a lesson I learned the hard way." He cut into a juicy chop.

"Feel like talking about it? I know bits and pieces and I can imagine other things, but I really want you to tell me."

"From my side of the street?" He smiled faintly. "To stay alive I had to do things I'd never done before, never even considered. I learned how to dispose of a corpse, get phony travel documents, surveil subjects, and kill an attack dog." He swallowed the rare meat and sipped some wine, reluctant to say more."

"From the beginning, Alan, even though it'll make me feel even worse than I do."

"In that case," he offered, "we'll go back to that long-ago Friday afternoon when Blake came into my office and told me a heavy tale." Once into the story, he found it coming out with surprising ease, as though he were purging himself of something undesirable.

Talking slowed his eating, but now he wanted Diana to hear it all, from his side: flight, fear, pain, danger . . . the skills he'd had to learn without preparation, the desperate struggle with Kazantsev, how he'd always been searching for her . . .

When he'd finished and sat back, she declared, "It's incredible, and I admire you so much for accomplishing it on your own. Alone."

"Far from it," he admitted. "Percy—my friend you avoided—got me money, lodging, information, even a car. I'll owe him for the rest of my life."

"Will I ever meet him?"

"Perhaps," he said. "He knows about you, but right now he doesn't think too highly of you."

"But you wouldn't have believed me without Arneson."

"No," he admitted, "I wouldn't have." He sat forward. "I've never lied to you, Diana, not about anything important. About Blake's letter, yes, but only because I didn't want to involve you."

"But you believed what Blake said about Kingman."

"I believed almost everything Blake confided in me. Why not? Hell, I was his lawyer, and people aren't supposed to lie to their lawyers." He looked at her face, softened by the candlelight. "Something you might keep in mind."

"Point made," she said slowly. "So I have to wonder if you'll ever believe me again. Fully."

"Let's get Arneson off our backs. After that we'll talk about trust. My definition and yours."

They had coffee on the balcony, looking out at the lights of Paris, some muted by haze, the Eiffel Tower's peak diamond-sharp against the black night. "It's a lovely city," she mused. "I've been thinking of living here."

"When I was at the Sorbonne I knew I'd come back to Paris, always be drawn here. But I never thought I'd return looking for a woman and be ready to kill to find her."

Her fingers threaded in his. "Can we put that behind us and start over—for tonight?"

"We can." he said and kissed her full on the lips.

Her body pressed against his and she whispered, "Even when you despised me I couldn't stop loving you."

"It's a weakness we share." He took her arm and led her into the bedroom.

They made love with a feverish intensity he hadn't experienced since their first night together—even then. Lost was found, treasure reclaimed, sensual secrets exposed in an ecstasy Stuart felt was almost sacred.

They slept arm in arm until daylight flooded the room and they heard the telephone ringing . . . ringing . . . ringing.

Naked, Diana got up to answer it.

CHAPTER 29

*A*fter a continental breakfast—defined by Stuart as coffee and a hot roll in bed with honey—he did the dishes while Diana made more coffee in the ancient percolator. Drying his hands on the dishtowel Stuart asked, "How do you feel about Arneson knowing I spent the night here?"

"We're of age and this is Paris." She kissed his cheek. "Let him think what he wants." She carried cups and saucers to the coffee table and added a bottle of Hine cognac. Stuart poured some into an empty cup and sipped. "I'm not generally a morning drinker," he said, "but this could help me tolerate Our Leader. Fortunately, he won't be here long."

"You really don't like him, do you? Because he stood by when you needed help?"

"The chemistry don't mix, as they say." He finished the cognac and smacked his lips.

The doorbell rang, a key slid into the lock, and Arneson came in, wearing a natty two-piece gray suit, white shirt, dark tie, and gray felt hat. "Morning, folks," he said cheerfully. "Work out your problems, did you?"

"We worked *on* them," Stuart corrected. "So what's on your mind this morning?"

With practiced skill, Arneson skimmed his hat onto a corner chair. "Seldom miss," he said and sat on the sofa. Diana filled their coffee cups and sat down facing the FBI man. Stuart pulled up a chair beside her.

"I got to thinking," Arneson began, "that to make sure Bendikov gets here at the right time, Mrs. Selwyn ought to call him this afternoon, tell him she's working on something very important to him, and ask where will he be at half past seven."

Stuart nodded. "Good idea."

"I like it," Diana said. "No details, but playing coy, hinting at a big surprise to come."

Stuart said, "I thought the idea was to let him know I was going to surrender the letter to Diana."

"Too risky," Arneson pronounced. "After thinking it over I realized Bendikov might well rush over prematurely and ruin everything." He glanced at the Hine bottle, shook his head, and took his coffee black. "Also, Diana, you might phone Beamish and confirm that he'll be here at eight. Would that be in character?"

"I think so. It's an important night for Edward, so he'll be conscious of timing." She picked up her cup, sipped, and made a face. "This *is* fresh coffee, I swear it is—it's the percolator that's old."

"Need to make audio-video checks?" Stuart asked.

"Did that yesterday," Arneson answered him, "before Mrs. Selwyn arrived. Ten by ten." He nodded in satisfaction. "Don't worry about the technical side; concentrate on your parts." He looked at Stuart. "No gunplay, right? If you're carrying, leave it at your place."

"No problems," Stuart said. "I've got blisters from waving guns around. I leave that to you duly constituted authorities."

Arneson smiled. "I laid out my plan for the legal attaché and asked him to poke holes in it." He sipped from his cup. "He couldn't."

"Conscientious," Stuart said, "or do you report to him?"

"In Paris I do—more of a courtesy than anything. He has the DST liaison, in case we ever need the locals."

Stuart thought of his night with the commissioner. Which masked DST man was the dentist, he wondered, the one who knew which nerves in Vadour's mouth to work on. "But you don't figure you'll need local backup tonight."

"This is strictly U.S.A." He got up. "Thanks for the coffee. Questions?"

"I can reach you at the usual number?" Diana asked.

"From noon on. After six I'll be in the LP." He smiled at Stuart and explained, "Listening post, where everything feeds in."

"And where might that be?" Stuart asked.

"Ha-ha. Gotta keep some secrets, don't we?"

"I suppose so," Stuart murmured. "Which reminds me of Blake's letter, for which I laid my life on the line. The letter's worthless, isn't it?"

"Smoke," Arneson concurred, and left the apartment.

Alone with Diana, Stuart admitted, "He has a way of reducing everything, making me feel ridiculous." He shook his head. "I wonder if Big Brother was listening last night."

"Arneson told me the system was not operating unless I was notified otherwise."

Stuart finished his coffee and began walking around the room, peering closely at wallpaper, corners, ceiling fixtures. After a slow circuit he commented, "Whatever's installed is well concealed—but I've heard they only need a pinhole for certain bugs."

"Beamish and Bendikov trust me," Diana said firmly. "They won't be looking for mikes or anything else. Now, how shall we spend our day?"

"I've got a couple of things to take care of at my apartment," he told her. "—laundry and such." He looked at his watch. "I should be back by two. You bought dinner, I'll buy lunch. Any suggestions?"

"A pair of tournedos, baking potatoes . . . spring peas?"

"What Paris needs more than pollution control is a good Jewish deli."

"Ah—you remember that fabulous feed from Joe's."

"Unforgettable." He slipped on his coat and kissed her.

"Don't be late," she whispered.

"Don't start without me." He unlocked the service door and went down the back staircase to the open courtyard. A rear carriage exit gave out onto the parallel street, saving his having to leave by Avenue Carnot.

Stuart went around the block and got into his Fiat, which was unmolested except for a pink ticket under the wiper blade. Parking at that location was strictly forbidden, according to the checked violation, and the owner was to report to the Commissariat of Circulation at . . . Stuart crumpled the ticket and dropped it in the gutter. Littering, no doubt, was an additional offense.

Back at his apartment he left his car in the *porte cochère.* Then he collected his laundry from the *blanchisserie* and paid for his suit's dry cleaning.

Percy was out of his office, according to the secretary, so Stuart left a message from Señor Gonzalez saying all was well. He changed his clothing and packed, putting everything into the his suitcase, except the Browning pistol. He ejected the magazine and counted the cartridges. Six left; bullets one and two were several thousand miles away. He put the pistol into his suitcase and carried it down to the car, locking it in the trunk. Then he walked down to the market and bought food for lunch.

A taxi took him over to Diana's, where he returned via the same courtyard and service stairs. Diana hurried into the kitchen to unlock the door. She kissed him, took his shopping bag, and began emptying it. "I reached Bendikov," she said. "He's all eager and mystified, and he promised to be here before eight. I laid it on pretty thick, but not unbelievably so."

"You think he'll come?"

"He's meticulous about meetings."

"And Beamish?"

"I have to call again later."

"Scotch, cognac, or wine?"

"A little wine, I think, if you're pouring."

He made himself a mild scotch, and while the potatoes were baking Diana shelled peas, set water to boil, and poured wine over the tournedos for marinating. "Now we can relax and enjoy our drinks," she announced.

He kissed her and said in a low voice, "I doubt this kitchen is bugged, but I don't want to be overheard. After lunch—"

Her finger stopped his lips. "Yes. After lunch. Siesta time, right? Togetherness?"

"If it includes making love."

"Sweetheart, I've been thinking about it all morning. Last night was so—exciting that I'm . . . God, you turn me on!" She licked her lips lustfully. "What a lover!"

He nuzzled her breasts. "You're fantastic," he murmured, "who could want for anything more? And where'd you learn it all?"

"Naughty books we passed around the dorm."

"Likely story," he grinned, "but I'll accept it provisionally. Now, if I can set aside the promise of things to come—and it's hard—after siesta I want you to pack whatever you want to keep. Pack everything but what you're wearing to the reception tonight. Make sure you leave nothing behind that could possibly identify you."

"Why, Alan?"

"Because once the thing goes down, we're moving out."

"You're worried about the outcome?"

"I always worry—it's habitual."

"Including fingerprints?"

"Especially fingerprints." He drew her more closely against him. "You know Arneson. I don't, but I read him as a man who won't take blame if something should go wrong. Instead of having us to point at, I'd prefer he do his own explaining."

"Well, he should—it's his operation, not ours."

"How clearly you read me." He smiled, and kissed her again.

Lying beside her, Stuart took her hand between his. "In addition to all your other talents you're a marvelous cook."

"*Femme de cuisine*," she said. "Before I met Blake I spent a summer here taking part of the Cordon Bleu course. I still remember some of it."

"What else did you do that summer?"

"Confessional? Met a Danish boy, fell in love, fell out of love . . . Paris is no place to be alone."

"How right you are. Twenty-four hours ago it looked gray and unattractive. Today the sun's out, flowers are blooming, acacias litter the walks with their hairy seeds. I didn't see those things yesterday, because I wasn't with you."

She kissed his forehead. "When you want to you can be wonderfully romantic. Is that because you've had your will of me?"

"Partly. But I thought it was mutual. Or were you pretending?"

"Bastard! I couldn't fake a climax if I tried. You're an iron man, know it? Even when I'm limp as a rag I can't stop coming. There. That's the truth and you better believe it. Now, shall I start packing?"

"No hurry." He drew her into his arms again.

At five Stuart left the apartment with Diana's two bags, one filled with nonessentials, the other with things she couldn't spare, including her passport. A taxi took him back to his apartment, where he locked her travel bag beside his own in the Fiat's trunk. There wasn't enough room for her second bag, so he took it up to the apartment and placed it in an empty closet. He phoned Percy again, and recounted, "I found the lady and everything's working out!"

"Delighted, Alan, I really am! Will I get to meet her?"

"Eventually," he said, "if things go well. Now I can leave Paris. I wanted you to know."

"When are you going?"

"Tonight." Unless Bendikov decides to kill me, he thought.

"May I ask where you're going?"

"At this point I don't know, but I'll try to tell you where I leave the car."

"Unimportant. Uh—are you still in danger?"

"Afraid so—but I'll disentangle in time." Thanking Percy for all he'd done, he replaced the receiver and lay down on the bed, going over everything in his mind, searching for anything he might have forgotten. Percy's query was a good one: where were they going to go? Ibiza, maybe, if Diana thought it a good refuge. Her father's place in Jamacia? Not good—anyone looking for Diana would eventually check it out. Where, then?

He was tired of running and hiding. He needed to stop and collect his thoughts. Tranquillity for a month was his personal prescription, but for now he'd settle for a week.

Why not the south of France? It was early in the season, true, but a small Fiat with Paris plates wouldn't attract attention. Since they both spoke French, they wouldn't be immediately noticeable as tourists. Marseilles was grungy, Stuart remembered, Monaco a little too posh. How about Nice? There was a good flow of people through Nice. Yes, he'd ask Diana how she felt about holing up in Nice.

From there they could fly to Barcelona or Madrid, even Lisbon. He remembered the big casino and hotel across the Tagus mouth at Estoril. His parents had taken him there as a child, pointing out the remnants of refugee royalty as they strolled and dined. So long ago . . . in the end, you were left only with memories. His were mixed, and he wanted the opportunity to improve on them.

And what of Diana? He wondered what those two years spying on her husband had been like. It had taken guile and courage to do it, and he realized she was far more formidable than he'd ever given her credit for. And if that weren't enough, she had insinuated herself into Beamish's circle, then let herself be recruited by the KGB. What a woman!

He understood that her dissembling in prison had both gotten him out of France and gained her points with Bendikov. Through her, Arneson must have learned where Stuart was being held—why hadn't he done something? Stuart gritted his teeth.

Arneson, he imagined, saw himself as a chess master moving pieces around a huge board, only the pieces were flesh-and-blood humans. His was the professional detachment of an executioner who pulls a remote switch. I hate taking his orders, Stuart told himself, but I hate Beamish and Bendikov even more.

He got up and drank a little Martell. He was okay, hands not trembling, just the old dull pains here and there. He just hoped Arneson would resist the impulse to crash the party.

Suppose Beamish and Bendikov kept their mouths shut, as wise agents should—what then? Draw the curtain and reopen another night? Not with me in the wings, Stuart decided, or Diana either. We're not trying out in New Haven. However it turns out we'll be long gone by dawn. Let Arneson write a new script with new players.

Well, he was thinking too much about the FBI man, and now it was after six. Stuart locked the apartment door behind him and went down into the *porte cochère*, now dim in the fading light.

Stuart got out his Browning, put it inside his coat pocket, and locked the trunk back up. Then he drove through thickening traffic over to the street behind Avenue Carnot, parking as close to the apartment building's service entrance as he could. He checked the gas gauge.

After locking the car door he glanced around for stake-out surveillors, saw none, and looked up at the rear of the buildings. Apartment lights were on all the way to the mansard roof. Diana should be dressing. He touched the Browning in his pocket and wondered what the night would bring.

He walked around the perimeter of the big open courtyard and stopped just inside the main entrance, where the archway hid him from the street. From its darkness he peered, invisible, at Avenue Carnot.

A few yards down from the entrance, parked on the other side, was a car. Black, local. Oncoming headlights swept the interior, showing a man and a woman in the front seat. They might have been lovebirds but for a third person, a man sitting behind them.

Watchers. From Bendikov, vetting the area before their boss arrived? Or Arneson's helpers, in position before the opposition came?

Cold flashed down his spine as he considered the excellent probability that, whoever they were, they were waiting for *him*.

Stuart retreated into shadows, crossed the courtyard, and took the inner staircase.

CHAPTER 30

As before, Stuart entered through the service door and kissed Diana's cheek. "You're gorgeous—don't want to smudge your makeup."

"I'm almost ready. Shouldn't we do something about you?"

He decided against showing her the surveillance car. It was enough that he knew. She followed him into the living room, where he commented, "Too much light."

"What about the cameras?"

"They'll spot an ant on the rug." He turned down the dimmer. "That's better."

He went to the liquor cabinet and took the bourbon bottle into the bathroom, where he rinsed his mouth with it and made a face. Diana said, "But you don't like bourbon."

"That's why I'm wasting it." He spat the mouthful into the basin, dribbled more whiskey on his palm, and patted it around his throat. "If I'm to be a convincing drunk, I have to smell like one."

"Master of detail," she said admiringly, following him to the bedroom.

Stuart placed the open bottle on the night table, lay back on the covers, and moved around until he could see most of the living room through the partly open door. "Leave it like that," he instructed, "so I can see the scene unfold." He snored loudly.

Diana smothered a laugh. "That's horribly convincing, but *please*, not when we're together."

"Promise. Now come closer and sniff."

"Phew," she said, leaning over. "Please don't pass out—I'm counting on you."

"*A votre service*, Madame."

"So gallant, even when soused."

"That's me—and Dad warned against drinking. Why didn't I follow his advice?"

"Because you're *you*, that's why. An intractable case."

"Alas. Lights off, now."

"Just a bit more makeup and I'm ready for act one, scene one."

"I love you," he called softly as she went out.

She stopped, looked back. "Really? Well, I love you, too."

Eyes closed, he could hear her at the bathroom mirror, the snap of makeup containers, the clicking of her heels. In her evening gown she reminded him of a girl from Sarah Lawrence who used to train down to Princeton Junction on weekends during his sophomore year. Her hair was reddish-gold, nose upturned, eyes light blue, skin the color and texture of rich cream.

He remembered waiting for her to climb down from the B & O car, slim legs first, then the J. Press coat trimmed with fox fur that nearly matched her hair. Just before Christmas she had come wearing a silver marten stole that caught and held the snowflakes as they walked to his car. Her name was Emily Goodland from Beverly Farms. She was beautiful and intelligent and they had been deeply in love, and just before the holidays she had come to his bed a virgin. His throat tightened at the memory.

That was the last time he saw her, because her father flew Emily and her mother, brother and sister south in his Cessna for Palm Beach holidays. Investigators said the plane had run out of gas and crashed in a Georgia pine forest. Not Goodland, he'd thought at the time, woodland.

She had been his first true love, though he was only nineteen at the time. He still remembered Emily.

Diana's voice interrupted his reverie. "Coming on to eight, Alan."

As his mind wrenched back to the present his body began to tense. Slipping the pistol from his pocket, he shoved it under the pillow by his head. He thumbed off the safety and waited, sprawled slackly on the bed, eyes nearly closed, the bourbon searing his nostrils. Bendikov should have come by now, he thought. Had his watchers warned him away?

A one-note silver chime cut the silence like a saber slash. His body stiffened, then relaxed again. He heard Diana's soft footfalls on the thick carpeting. He could see her open the door and Beamish step in. But where the hell was the Russian?

"Edward," she said in a pleased voice, "you're right on time, and I love it!"

"You look ravishing," the former ambassador commented. "Ready to go?"

"I'll just be a few minutes," she said. "Yuri Bendikov said he needed a few moments with me before the reception, but he's a bit late. Mind waiting?"

"Not at all, my dear." He patted her hand, nuzzled her forehead. "But Yuri's usually so punctual.

Hope the mikes got that, Stuart thought.

"We'll have a drink," Diana offered. "Scotch for both of us?"

"Please, let me." He passed the dark bedroom door, satin lapels gleaming, and Stuart could hear the delicate clinking of crystal and ice.

Diana must have failed to convince Bendikov. Arneson's scenario wasn't playing right.

The doorbell rang.

"Must be Yuri," she called.

Stuart heard her open the door and greet Bendikov. "What is the promised surprise?" he asked eagerly.

She said something in a voice too low for Stuart to hear, then Beamish called, "Hello, Yuri. Hoping I'd see you."

"Well, Edward, this *is* a surprise." Coming into view beside Diana, Bendikov turned to her blankly. As she took his arm and drew him toward the bedroom door, Beamish offered, "I'll make myself scarce." He moved away toward a chair.

"Just a few moments," Diana said winningly and pulled Bendikov. "The surprise is this: Alan Stuart found me—I don't know how. And—"

"*Stuart!*"

"Very much alive," she went on, "and this morning he said he'd brought Blake's letter from Washington."

"*Wonderful!* Where is it?"

She sighed. "He said he'd bring it this evening, but when he got here he was half drunk and said he'd forgotten it. I made him promise to bring it tomorrow, so I'm sure I'll have it then. Don't feel bad; I wanted to surprise you, and I will, even if I have to bring it from him."

Bendikov shook his head disappointedly. "How did he find you, Diana?"

"He muttered something about spotting me in Edward's car, but I really don't know. Then, damn him, he sat here drinking, telling me wild stories about running and hiding, until I got him into the bedroom.

Bendikov glanced quickly at the doorway. "He's *here*?"

Stuart closed his eyes and began breathing deeply just before Diana switched on the ceiling light. "Look at the pig," she said disgustedly. "Sleeping it off."

They came into the bedroom together, and Stuart could hear the Russian sniff the air a foot from his face. "He's drunk," Bendikov agreed. "I'd like to liquidate him now—but I *must* have that letter."

"I know," she said sympathetically. "I'll take off his shoes. Why don't you keep Edward company, have a quick drink before we all leave?"

"Very well." Bendikov left the bedroom and Stuart felt Diana begin unlacing a shoe. He overheard the two men talking in low voices. "Give them time," he whispered, and emitted a loud snore. Opening his eyes a fraction, he saw Bendikov pass a sealed envelope to Beamish, who put it quickly away in his dinner jacket. "That's it," he whispered.

"Thank God," she whispered. Brushing back her hair, she glanced out at the two men, who'd moved apart. When she turned off the bedroom light Stuart could open his eyes fully.

Beamish said, "It's incredible that that oaf came here, Diana. Can't we get rid of him?"

"I don't know where Alan's staying," she confessed, "and since he's doing me a little favor, I have to let him sober up."

"Disgusting," Beamish snorted. "Well, we'd better be going. Don't want to be any later."

"I'll just fix my hair. Be right with you." Diana closed the bathroom door.

As Beamish and Bendikov walked toward the entrance they put their heads together for a few moments. Beamish nodded and picked up his chesterfield from a chair. Bendikov, still in his coat, looked back at the bedroom, and his expression made clear his desire to strangle Stuart while his victim was defenseless.

If the cameras and tapes were operating, the FBI should have what it needed, Stuart figured.

The toilet flushed and Beamish pulled on his topcoat. To Bendikov he said, "We'd better arrive separately, for appearance's sake." Bendikov said something inaudible and glanced back longingly at the bedroom again.

Diana was still in the bathroom when the main door opened and a shocked Stuart saw Arneson come in, dressed as before, gray hat tipped up jauntily. "Evening, gents," he said, kicked the door shut, pulled out a silenced pistol, and shot Bendikov with two soft *plops*. Before the Russian's body hit the floor Arneson turned on Beamish and shot him twice. Screaming, Beamish clutched his chest. With a third shot Beamish collapsed backward and lay still.

"You can come out now, folks," Arneson called. "It's all over, and a good job, too."

Stuart crossed quickly to the door and stood beside the jamb, out of sight. When the bathroom door opened, he heard Diana scream.

Arneson walked toward her. "I'm sorry, Diana I really am, but there was no other way. I thought about it a long time." His eyes glittered.

"You *killed* them!"

"I did and I'm not sorry. Scum, both of them."

"But the tapes—you're on the tapes."

He shook his head slowly. "I deceived you. No tapes, no mikes, nothing but this." He raised his pistol as if to sight on Diana when Stuart shot him in the belly. The heavy, 9-mm impact pushed him back and doubled him over. His pistol fired into the floor and Arneson yelled, "Damn you, Stuart, come out where I can see you!" On his knees he fired at the bedroom door. The slug slammed the door inward and Stuart stepped out, pistol in hand.

"That's seven rounds," he said calmly.

Arneson was sitting on the floor now, left hand holding his belly. He lifted the pistol again, even though the slide was locked back, breech empty.

"You fool," Stuart barked "you could have done it the right way, by the rules."

"Rules?" A sickly grin parted his lips. "No rules, Stuart, didn't you learn?" He began to moan, and blood trickled from his mouth.

From somewhere behind them Diana shrilled, "We've got to call an ambulance. If you won't, I will."

"Forget it," Stuart said, "he's dying." As he walked past Arneson he heard his head strike the carpet. Kneeling beside Bendikov, he frisked him and found a small-caliber revolver in an ankle case.

Stuart walked back to Arneson and fired Bendikov's revolver

at the FBI agent's heart. The body arched and lay still, and urine darkened his crotch. Diana was weeping in loud racking sobs.

"Get hold of yourself," Stuart snapped, "and put on your coat." He wiped his prints from the revolver and clasped Bendikov's fingers around it, then nudged the grip a few inches away. Standing, he set the Browning's safety and slid it into his coat pocket. He moved over to the late ex-ambassador and pulled Bendikov's envelope from the jacket pocket. Tearing open the envelope he saw that it was thick with thousand-franc notes. Enough to pay the Crillon, he thought as he pocketed the envelope.

He walked past Diana into the bathroom, snatched two towels, and tossed her one. "Do the bathroom," he ordered, "wherever you touched." He wiped bedroom doorknobs, the bedstead, and the bourbon bottle before carrying it to the cabinet. "Bring your makeup bag," he called.

Red-eyed, she emerged from the bathroom and stood looking at Stuart, a blue leather makeup case in one hand. "What do we do now?" she asked unsteadily. "I can't believe what happened." She took a step toward Areneson's body, then looked away. "He told you no guns—why did you bring a gun?" A little girl's voice, tremulous, uncertain.

"Because he told me not to. And because I couldn't find pinholes for any mikes."

"Then you . . . knew?"

"I suspected. He was just too god-damn good, too confident of everything, never a doubt. This was his personal operation and we were the fall guys." He took her arm and pulled her into the kitchen. "Any prints here?"

"No," she said more calmly, "I went over everything this afternoon." Her body moved against his—for support, Stuart knew. "I've never seen killing before," she said in a remote voice, "and suddenly there are three dead men." She clutched his arm. "What do we do now?"

He grasped her arm, firmly and looked her straight in the eyes. "We run."

CHAPTER 31

*H*e drove south on Autoroute A1, past Roissy–De Gaulle airport, and two hours later gassed up at Auxerre. For the first hour Diana said nothing, still in shock from the shootings and the realization that they would have been next.

Before leaving the gas station Stuart had opened his suitcase, retrieved the Martell bottle, and packed his pistol. He took a swig of cognac, wiped the rim of the bottle, and made Diana down two swallows.

By now she was dry-eyed and the cognac warmed her. "I've got other clothing," she said in a dull voice. "When can I change?"

"Down the line," he replied. Steering back onto the highway, he told her about the watchers in front of her building. "Maybe they'll clean up for us," he said, "or else Beamish's chauffeur will get the concierge to let him in. So we have to make miles before daylight."

"I behaved like an idiot, Alan."

"You behaved like the average well-brought-up American woman that you are," he said gently. "No reproach from me."

"But you were prepared. Down the back way and out to the car, packed and ready to go. What foresight!"

"Something I've lacked these past weeks, but I was resolved to be prepared this time." He glanced at her smudged cheek. "Learned that in Scouts."

"Not at Bragg?"

"There too." Oncoming headlights flashed past. The road was terrific, quite a contrast to Reynosa's potholed excuses for roads. The dash clock showed eleven. "See if you can get a Paris station for late-breaking news," he suggested. He smiled at the newscasters' cliché, one he'd always loathed. Diana turned on the radio and searched the dial. Local stations only and few of them.

"It's early," he speculated. "We'll hear results tomorrow."

A few miles later he noticed that her eyes were closed. The car's motion edged her body into the corner. He was glad that she was sleeping. He stifled a yawn himself.

Toward Macon, in wine country, he saw the gas needle edge onto low. At two o'clock no gas station was open, so he drove on to the edge of the city and parked beside a small, attractive-looking inn. Four cars with local plates told Stuart that Le Roi George was a lovers' rendezvous; he went inside and asked the clerk for a room.

"All night?" the clerk asked, pushing the register at him.

Ignoring the sign-in sheet, Stuart passed him fifty francs. "All night," he replied, "and breakfast too."

The register slid aside.

"Need help with your bags, m'sieu?"

"I'll manage." He carried them to a second-floor room before returning to wake Diana.

They showered together, dried each other's bodies, and slipped between the cool sheets. They lay side by side, touching, but neither suggested making love. Death was still too close.

After a while Diana said dully, "I knew Arneson for nearly two years, worked with him all that time. I never thought he was crazy as he must have been."

"In a way. Stressed out, frustrated. A kind of combat fatigue. Cops get it, you know; it's not uncommon when the bad guys so often seem to win."

"So he . . ."—she faltered—"found his own solution."

Stuart nodded. "What you have to keep telling yourself is that we weren't responsible, not for any of it. If he hadn't killed them tonight he'd have found another way, another time." He stroked her hair gently. "He used the word 'expendable,' remember? Well, that's what we were to him. Expendable. And at the end, he was expendable too." Stuart looked away. "Strange, but I feel sorry for him. A good man gone wrong."

"A burned-out case," she murmured.

"To borrow a phrase, yes—that puts it nicely. So he was in a self-destruct mode, whatever happened. Now, I have an idea that's also a suggestion. Let's tell ourselves we saw the scene on television. The movie's over and we need sleep. Okay?"

"I'll try," she agreed doubtfully. "I'll try very hard."

They lay back then, her head on his outstretched arm, and when he woke later, her cheek was on his shoulder. He stroked her hair, kissed it, remembering how Emily used to sleep that way at the Biltmore in New York.

Well, he thought, the Biltmore's gone, along with a lot of other things from my youth, but I have a good woman now. I fought to find her and killed to save her, and that's sort of staking out a claim.

If one day he told her, he didn't think Diana would mind Emily. He felt her body, both cool and warm, kissed her hair again, and drifted off to sleep.

In the morning they had breakfast in the room. Last night he'd hardly noticed it, but now with sunlight filtering through lacy curtains he saw the candy-striped wallpaper, the heavy old oak furniture polished so that it glinted in the light; the worn but clean carpeting, the gleaming brass door handles and the dust-free dresser. The bathroom fixtures were spotless, towels a dazzling white, and no mold streaks on the shower curtain. Best of all, Stuart thought, there was neither TV nor radio. The owners of this assignation inn would know that their guests supplied their own entertainments and diversions.

Pulling aside a curtain, he looked down at the parking lot and saw that the Fiat was the only car remaining. That explained the fast room service, he remarked to Diana, who agreed. "And now that I'm sane again, I should do my share of the driving."

"Something the matter with this feather bed?"

"Not a thing in the world, precious, but I hear more than chariots hurrying near."

"Umm. Got a French driving license?"

"No."

"Neither do I." They laughed together. It was fine, Stuart thought, to be young, in love, and on the road in France.

They followed the Saône down into Lyon, enjoying the fresh greenery along the riversides, then the Rhône through the rolling countryside of the Ardèche, so much in contrast to the Paris they had fled. At Donzère they lunched at a country inn, *pot-au-feu*, fresh, crusty bread, and a house wine, full-bodied and delicious. "Maybe I'll become a travel writer, if this is what travel's all about," said Diana, leaning back in satisfaction.

"It is. Both of us have probably flown over this part of France a dozen times, but the roadside view is worth the effort."

"Speaking of travel," she wondered, "are we ever going back to the States?"

"When the heat's off, as mobsters say. God knows what's pending against me."

"Then I'll go first, take soundings."

At Avignon they stopped for aperitifs at a café, where Stuart bought a late edition of *Le Monde* brought in by rail. He scanned it as they relaxed, found nothing concerning the Avenue Carnot massacre—as it was bound to be tagged—and drove on down to Arles, where they took on gas again.

Marseilles was old, big, sprawling, noisy, bustling, and dirty. Its narrow cobbled streets made a labyrinth for Stuart to penetrate after he mistakenly left the highway and entered the port city by a lesser road. Sea-smells helped him steer toward the waterfront, where freighters loaded, honked mournful horns, and slid out to sea. He pulled up at the stone seawall. so they could look out at the grim old fortress, the Chateau d'If. "That's it."

"That's what? Or should I ask what's 'it'?"

"Where the Count of Monte Cristo was born, escaping a watery grave."

"Oh, Lord, I'd forgotten. But I haven't read that marvelous story since I was twelve."

"Read it again," he recommended, "so it'll come easier when you read to the children."

"Oh." She gazed at him. "Whose children?"

"Ours, I hope." He took her hand. "Would you mind?"

"I'd mind if we weren't married—and you haven't even proposed."

He laughed. "I thought that was implicit. We're sexually compatible—"

"—God, yes!"

"—and we get along well." He kissed her hand. "Besides, your biological clock is running down."

"That's absolutely the *worst* proposal I've ever heard." Her finger traced the smile on his lips. "Suppose I were pregnant now—would you trade me in on a younger unpregnant model?"

"Hmmm. Only if she were livelier in bed than you are—and I don't think that's possible."

"Oh, you pig! You absolute, chauvinist pig," she said in pretended pique. "Typical male dedicated to the pleasure principle. How gross, sweetheart—but I love you despite it."

"No one's perfect," he sighed, "though you come pretty close.

And now that we've tramped thought that briar patch, will you marry me? Is that conventional enough?"

"It's what my father asked my mother, and my answer is the same as hers: Yes, my love. What took you so long?"

"It was a rough road," he said as he kissed her. "A dark road of duplicity and danger. A road we won't travel again."

"Never," she vowed, and held him so tightly he could feel the pounding of her heart.

After a while he said he was thinking of leaving the Fiat in Marseilles and buying another car. "With Bendikov's money," he explained. "I counted it. Eighty thousand francs."

"Agreed," she said, "but in my name." So they paid cash for a four-year-old Renault with good rubber and brakes. Stuart phoned Percy and told him the name of the garage where the rented Fiat could be reclaimed, and learned that the police were looking for a bearded foreigner in connection with three deaths at an exclusive apartment on Avenue Carnot. "*Three* deaths, Alan? Are you that good a shot?"

"The American agent killed two. I shot him to save our lives."

"'Our'—so she's with you, *hein?*"

"In tow," Stuart said, "and I'll repay your loan when I can."

"Don't worry about it. Just be happy, okay?"

"I'll try."

They took the coastal highway around through Toulon, Hyères, Saint Tropez, and on to Cannes. "I've been thinking of Nice ever since Paris," he said, "but Cannes is just as good."

"Lousy beach, honey."

"Too cold to bathe, anyway. But we can sun." So they registered as husband and wife at the Mer Bleu, a small hotel set back from the Mediterranean and Stuart felt as though they really were married. Close and comfortable together, no arguments, no looking back on past mistakes or misunderstandings.

The first thing he did was to shave. When Diana saw his smooth face she sighed, "Now, *that*'s my man. Just look at my chin, all chapped from your bristles."

In Cannes the season was transitional between spring and summer. There was sunshine, and flowers along the walks, but stiff winds lashed in from the sea, scudding spindrift across the beach, raging surf over the offshore rocks. That kept Diana and Stuart from the promenades, whose fashionable old hotels were operating with off-season staffs that still managed to provide good service and excellent food. Except for permanent residents there were few visitors in Cannes when they arrived. Two busloads of Japanese tourists came one morning, took photographs until lunchtime, and vanished into a one-star seafood restaurant. After an hour guides loudly whistled their charges into the buses, which drove off trailing windblown gusts of diesel smoke.

Their hotel room was small, but its corner location provided a wedge-shaped view of the Mediterranean. It held a few pieces of provincial furniture, a feather bed, and a noisy steam radiator, their only source of heat. At night, of course, it was turned off by the management, but at least they could sleep without disturbance.

Being with the woman he loved, sensing no immediate danger to either of them, had a lulling effect on Stuart. For a week they scanned the Paris papers before learning that the police were now declaring the Carnot case solved. A deranged American had shot M. Beamish and a Russian diplomat named Bendikov and been killed by the latter. No motive for the slayings was given beyond mental illness, and with the consent of the American and Russian authorities the case was officially closed.

Diana gave a whoop of glee and crushed Stuart in her arms. "I'm going to get a flight home tomorrow," she announced, "and I'll call you if it's safe to come."

"How will you know?"

"Hire a discreet lawyer."

"I'm discreet."

"I mean one not too discreet to be frank with his client—me."

He thought it over. "Suppose it's *not* safe?"

"Then I'll come back, and we'll never go home again."

"All right," he said. "Call my sister, will you, and tell her I'm okay? Just that, no more."

"Of course. Alan, you really want to go back, don't you?"

"I wasn't cut out to be either a fugitive or an expatriate. Besides, I have a living to earn. By now my clients must have given up on me and I'll have to find others. I have a house. I think about it, worry about it. And I think about the future—our future, darling."

"So do I. I wasn't meant to be a gypsy, either. And our children are entitled to roots, solid ones like ours. I'll have all that in mind when I make my rounds."

He hugged and kissed her, thinking of the time ahead when he would be without her. Then he said, "There's an FBI agent I want you to contact. His name is Pat O'Rourke. He came with our delegation to Paris and knew a few things about Blake. I think he'll talk with you, let you know how things stand from the bureau's point of view." He looked away. "I'm sure he knew nothing of Arneson and you. Hell, he may even think I'm dead. I don't have to tell you how to approach him or what to say, honey. Just find out what he knows."

"I'll see him first." She kissed him. "I love you and I'll miss you."

"I'll miss you more than you could imagine."

She started packing.

He drove Diana to the Nice airport for the Air France flight to Mexico City. "Stay there a day," he'd suggested, "to muddy the trail. Then fly to Toronto and go home from there. And when you phone me, call from a public phone—airports are good."

"The voice of experience."

"Don't knock it."

"Yes, love."

He watched her plane circle out over the Mediterranean and gain altitude as it banked southwest. When it entered the white clouds he walked back to the car. Once again a girl I loved is flying away from me, he thought. He prayed that this one would return.

For five days he read newspapers and paperbacks, ate, slept, and jogged along the flower-lined Promenade. The air was cold, the wind stripping sand from the beach and piling it against the bathhouses, but the sun was warm. He was unbearably lonely.

When her call came through, Stuart turned off the television set—he'd been watching the Masked Marvel—and gripped the receiver.

"Weather's fine here," she said cheerfully, "and I'm calling from home. Will you join me?"

"What's the hurry? The weather here is improving daily. Come back, honey. What have you got to lose?"

"My thought too," she said softly. "What have I got to lose?"

Diana replaced the telephone on the desk and sat back in what had been Blake's chair, the hum of Connecticut Avenue traffic an undertone to her thoughts. Looking around the study she saw that all of Blake's books were gone. Movers had taken away most of the downstairs furnishings; tomorrow the bedrooms and the rest of the house would be cleared out and taken to the estate-sale house that had already paid her sixty-seven thousand dollars for the contents. The check lay on the desk for deposit to her account in Bern.

The emptiness of the house depressed her. Its sale was arranged, and when she left tomorrow she wanted to take no memories of it along, for she was never coming back.

She looked at the desk clock: 3:15. The men would be coming soon, and now she was prepared. Men, she thought, with more than a little deprecation. The men who had been closest to her had been unfortunate: Blake had been too weak to earn even her respect, much less her love; Alan was so strong and resourceful that she had come to fear him. Both had been drawn to her by love or lust—was there a difference? She ran one hand idly through her hair, grateful that there would be just enough time tomorrow for a new styling at Jean Paul's.

Her gaze traveled to the fireplace where Alan had noticed the charred papers. He had an investigator's instincts, she'd learned— how else could he have found Kazantsev? And killed him, she reflected, after managing to outthink and kill Mikhail. A formidable man, Alan Stuart.

So unlike Blake. Diana recalled their late-night drive through the dark countryside, Blake's puzzlement over her suggestion. She had reached over and turned off the ignition; the Chrysler had slowed at the edge of the road.

She had smiled then and lifted her lips for his kiss. So feminine of Blake always to close his eyes when they kissed. But his eyes opened when he felt the prick of the needle, staring at her in disbelief, moving back as she slid away and opened the door. She remembered his breath rattling in his throat as his body went rigid, then slack. She had moved him gently to rest on the steering wheel before she left his car. Her own was hidden in a nearby coppice.

His letter, she thought—Blake's infamous, searched-for letter. She remembered her cold, desperate fear that Blake had betrayed her. Instead he had tried to save himself, but she had learned that only after it was too late. And he had died a gentleman, protecting her to the end, because he loved her with a fool's blind adoration.

Beamish had desired her, too. Poor Edward, a pompous bumbler in need of constant guidance, though useful as a figurehead. Bendikov had quarreled with her over Blake and Edward, about many things, but Yuri was an obstacle no more. Arneson, the burned-out psychotic, had taken care of them both. She'd diagnosed his madness early on and had played up to him, letting him think he was directing her when in fact she was controlling him.

Well, that chapter in her life was almost ended. She was ready for a new assignment, one involving more authority—and risk. She had never turned from danger. It, not power, was her aphrodisiac.

The doorbell interrupted her thoughts. She left the library to open the door.

Two men followed her into the library and stood silently, respectfully, as Diana took her seat behind the desk. One man had light brown hair, the other's was dark and close-cut; both were well dressed, shoes polished, and Diana inwardly approved. They were specialists of skill and reputation; the brown-haired one had terminated Kingman in Paris.

"He goes by the name of Gonzalez," she told them, "and is staying in Cannes at the Mer Bleu Hotel. Room seven."

The darker-haired man nodded. "Room seven, Mer Bleu Hotel. And your instructions, comrade?"

She looked at them calmly. "Kill him."